Our Scorched Hearts

TENNILLE MARIE

This book has some tough topics. Please note the trigger warnings before reading this book – miscarriage, war scenes, suicide, cancer.

Although many of the lovely places portrayed in this novel are very real, the novel itself and the characters, organizations, and events portrayed are completely made-up and fictional. The author let her imagination run wild and if someone or something in this story seems real, then that is just a testament of how wild her imagination has run.

Our Scorched Hearts

Published by: Purple Iris Printing, LLC

P.O. Box 861

Benton, Louisiana 71006

ISBN   978-1-962329-05-7 (hardback)

ISBN   978-1-962329-06-4 (trade paperback)

ISBN   978-1-962329-04-0 (ebook)

To all the veterans and nurses who served in the Vietnam War.
We can never repay you for your service.

Prologue

S he stared down at the metal framed hospital bed. Her eyes burned from lack of sleep. She wanted to cry, she wanted to scream, but she stood there silently. Her life would never be the same. Her family's lives would never be the same. This war took and strangely it gave. Unfocused, dead eyes stared up at her, and in them, she saw the reflection of her dreams disintegrate into nothingness. *He's gone*. The weight of that thought sent her to her knees.

Part 1

TO THE WAR WE GO...

Chapter 1

Ruthie, September 1967

Ruthie tried not to fidget. She folded her hands together and forced them to stay on her lap, but the urge to bite her nails grew with each beat of her heart. The woman sitting across from her, behind the metal desk, stared down at Ruthie's résumé. She'd pulled her gray hair back into a bun so tight, the skin at her temples strained. The dress uniform she wore had been bleached perfectly white until it almost glowed, and black cat-eye glasses sat on the tip of her nose. She looked up from the paper, gave Ruthie a glare, and returned to reading. Ruthie adjusted in her seat. The pastel yellow dress she and Hazel had picked out for the interview began to cling to her back.

"I see you graduated from Westark in May."

It wasn't a question. It was a statement. Ruthie nodded even though the woman never looked at her. "Yes ma'am." Although her stomach twisted in knots, thoughts of that happy day flooded through her. She'd graduated top of her class with an associate degree in nursing. The first one in her family to ever go to college.

"I'm so proud of you, peanut," Daddy had said while he hugged her around the neck. She tried to let the memories of his love and support flow through her now, but Mrs. Battle Axe sniffed the air like she'd found something ridiculous on Ruthie's résumé, and the happy memory faded as quickly as it came.

"So, I see you're not married."

Ruthie wondered if she meant it to be a jab. Most people never intended it to be that way, but it always was. *How is a beautiful twenty-year-old like you still without a husband? Maybe you're just too picky. My husband's cousin's son is single, maybe ya'll could go out on a date?* And why did it matter if she was married or not? She would make a wonderful nurse! The best! Ruthie's jaw clenched and her hands moved to the arms of the chair. She gripped them so hard, her knuckles turned white. *Hold it together. You can do this.*

"Is that a problem?" she asked, trying to keep the snippiness from her words.

Mrs. Battle Axe's eyes flitted up to look at her. "It's not a problem for me. As long as you're not looking to find a husband here."

Ruthie narrowed her eyes. "I can assure you I'm not."

"Also," she said as she picked up a pencil and pointed the end in Ruthie's direction, "we have a moral standard, so when you're not working, even though it's your own time, we expect a certain kind of woman to work here. Do you understand what I mean?"

It took sheer willpower not to roll her eyes, but Ruthie understood.

"Yes ma'am. I promise I will work hard and do a good job," she said.

Mrs. Battle Axe laid down the pencil. "Well in that case, you're hired. We could use all the help we can get. But I'm still not sure why you'd want to work here in Waldron. This hospital is so small. I'd think an unmarried girl like yourself with such good grades would have wanted to move to Fort Smith or Little Rock. Some place bigger where there's more fish in the sea."

Ruthie gritted her teeth. She had the job, and she didn't want to lose it as soon as she got it. "My family is here. My dad and sister, Hazel, and her husband." She purposely didn't mention that she'd always dreamed of leaving but was too chicken-livered to do so.

"Oh, I heard Hazel is finally pregnant."

Ruthie blinked. Word spread quick in these parts. Hazel was only about twenty-two weeks along, and as far as she knew, they hadn't told many people. She and Joel had started trying for a baby right after their wedding day. No one ever tells you the equation young love plus marriage doesn't always equal a baby. Hazel had taken it hard. But now things were starting to turn around.

"Yes, she is. They are very excited."

Mrs. Battle Axe shook her head, "I'm sure they are. They've been married for quite a while."

"Just four years," Ruthie inserted.

Mrs. Battle Axe tsked. "Well, at least now they can start becoming a real family."

Weren't they already a real family? Ruthie shook the thought from her head. "Yes, they are very happy." She felt like a puppet on a string. Say the right thing. Hold your head the right way. Get the job. Keep the job.

Mrs. Battle Axe, or Joan Battalou, stood up from her seat and held out her hand. *I have to stop calling her Mrs. Battle Axe*, Ruthie told herself. Ruthie took her hand and gave it a firm shake.

"Welcome to Waldron Memorial Hospital. Now, let's go see Ms. Krissy Maxwell. She'll set you up on the rotation and get you all lined out."

Krissy Maxwell sat at the long reception desk. A huge metal filing cabinet sat behind it along the wall. Beside the metal cabinet hung a picture of boats on a calm sea. The sunrise in the distance made the water around the boats an orange-red color, which almost matched the color of Krissy's hair. Her white nurse's cap sat lopsided on her head.

"So, this must be the new victim," Krissy said, a sprinkling of freckles scattered across her nose seemed to dance with her giggles.

Mrs. Battalou gave Krissy a hard stare. "Ms. Maxwell, this is Ruthie McKay. She's our new hire. Please set her up on the rotation. And give her the list of etiquette rules as well. I'd also like you to give her a tour and introduce her to the other nurses."

Krissy nodded, but before she could respond, she abruptly stood up from behind the desk. Her smile turned serious. "Hello Dr. Sullivan."

Mrs. Battalou twisted around. "Oh, Doctor. So sorry I didn't see you there. Do you need anything?"

"I'd like a cup of coffee," he said in a gruff voice. Ruthie noticed that he didn't look much older than Mrs. Battalou. Streaks of gray made little lines through his dark hair just above his ears, and his frown made the wrinkles around his mouth more pronounced.

"Yes sir, right away." Mrs. Battalou turned to Krissy. "Ms. Maxwell, please get Dr. Sullivan a cup of coffee, and while you're at it, show Ms. McKay where the coffee machine is. She'll be needing it soon enough."

"I'll be in my office," Dr. Sullivan said as he walked off.

Ruthie looked at Krissy, who gave her a quick shrug. "Follow me. I'll show you around."

As they walked down the hallway, Krissy pointed out all the important areas she felt Ruthie needed to know while Ruthie peppered her with questions.

"Are all the doctors here like Dr. Sullivan?"

Krissy rolled her eyes. "You mean pleasant to work with? Yeah, they're all like that. They're the kings, and we are the paupers ready to do their bidding. Dr. Sullivan is the worst. But after him there's really only Dr. Rimmer and Dr. Ashley."

"Oh, I know Dr. Rimmer," Ruthie said, remembering the doctor that had cared for her and Hazel their whole lives. He'd also treated her father after he was accidentally shot in the woods weeks before Hazel's wedding. The secret of that night made Ruthie shiver. Even though Daddy had told everyone it had been a random hunting accident, everyone in town suspected otherwise. If they ever discovered that Joel had been the shooter and her family had lied about it, there'd be trouble for sure. No one would care that it had been an actual accident.

Krissy opened a door and motioned for Ruthie to follow her inside a dark room. She flicked on the light. The florescent lights sputtered and buzzed as they came to life. "Yeah, Dr. Rimmer is my favorite. But he'll be retiring soon. This year I think."

Ruthie's heart fell. She hoped she'd get a chance to work with him some before he left.

Krissy held out her hands. "Now this room here is the dungeon."

Ruthie looked around. The room had a Maytag washer and dryer, brooms, mops, buckets, a closet full of linens and towels, and more cleaning spray and disinfectant than Ruthie had ever seen. Krissy walked by a baby blue machine. She laid her hand on top of it.

"This is our bedpan washer. You just throw them in there, and in two to three minutes, they come out all nice and hot and ready to use."

Ruthie nodded as Krissy showed her how to start the machine and how much disinfectant and cleaning liquid to put in.

"Do you mind me asking, why did you call this place the dungeon? The lights are so bright."

Krissy giggled. "It's what all us nurses call it. It's because if you're in here and Mrs. Battalou catches you, she'll put you to work washing or scrubbing something, even if it has nothing to do with your patients, and then there's no escaping. It never fails. My advice to you is if you gotta come in here, grab what you need, and get out quick."

Ruthie nodded, making a mental note, *get out quick*.

"I always fantasized about being trapped in here during a power outage with Elvis, but then he went and got married," Krissy said, looking dreamy eyed toward the ceiling.

Ruthie laughed. "You fantasized about being stuck in a dark room with Elvis and a bedpan machine?"

Krissy shrugged. Then suddenly, the door of the dungeon flew open and crashed against the wall with a loud bang. Krissy and Ruthie screamed.

"What are you all yelling about? Come help me!" Mrs. Battalou said, her cat-eye glasses crooked on her tomato red face. "Mrs. Anderson got out of her hospital bed again and fell. Good grief, that woman has to weigh at least four hundred pounds."

"But I haven't gotten Dr. Sullivan his coffee yet!" Krissy exclaimed.

Mrs. Battalou blew out a rush of air. "The king will just have to wait."

Ruthie suppressed a giggle.

Krissy looked at her. "I guess you're starting today?"

Ruthie couldn't help but smile. This was real. What she had always wanted. She was a nurse.

Chapter 2

HAZEL

Hazel shivered. A cool crisp wind blew up her skirt as she bent over to retrieve the sack of groceries from the passenger seat of her old Pontiac Tempest. The day had started out beautifully, but by afternoon, the sky outside the huge, plate glass windows of the Piggly Wiggly had turned a dark gray. It had stayed that way the whole afternoon, as if the sun had just given up and called in sick for the rest of the day.

Hazel hefted the grocery bag onto her hip. *I wish I could have called in sick.* Today marked twenty-two weeks of her being pregnant, and this was the strangest day by far. After all this time, she was finally starting to show some. A small bulge barely noticeable had begun to peek out from beyond the folds of her dress. Still, she couldn't put her finger on why she felt so strange. She didn't feel nauseous. She didn't hurt. She just didn't feel right. Try telling that to a doctor. *Sir, I just don't feel right.* She chuckled to herself and shook her head. That would get her nowhere. As she walked to the duplex that had been her and Joel's home since they were first married, she noticed a Tupperware container on the stoop. She couldn't help but smile when she read the note on top of it.

"Sandra made chicken and dumplings. Enjoy! Your mail is underneath the container. Have a wonderful night." It was signed, "Milton."

Oh, how she loved her neighbors.

Hazel got the door unlocked and stepped over the container. She hurried to the kitchen and set the grocery bag on the pale, yellow laminate countertop before going back to retrieve her and Joel's dinner. Joel would be over the moon. Sandra's chicken and dumplings was his favorite dish.

Hazel bent down to pick up the container, but before her hands could even touch it, a sharp pain shot through her lower back to her abdomen. She gasped and grabbed the doorframe. She sucked in a deep breath, but the pain had gone just as quickly as it had come. *What was that?* Her heart raced, and she tried to will it to slow down. *I'm fine,* she told herself. *Whatever it was is gone now.* But whatever it was had frightened her. A gust of wind from the open door blew the end of her skirt up and she shuddered. *I've got to get inside. This cold air is going to make me sick.* She bent over, slowly keeping tabs on any aches and pains she felt, but there was nothing. *I'm fine. Everything is okay.* She scooped up the container and the day's mail, which consisted of a few envelopes and the newspaper. When she stood upright, she took inventory of her pain, but there was nothing, and her stress evaporated. She laid a hand on her stomach.

"You better behave in there," she scolded.

She walked to the kitchen and laid the mail and the Tupperware on the counter beside the brown paper grocery bag. As she reached inside the bag to remove the half gallon container of chocolate ice cream she'd bought, her eyes wandered to the back of the folded newspaper. A small name printed near the top made her freeze. She fumbled for the paper, spreading it out to read the obituary section. The paper crinkled in her grasp. The room around her began to spin. Hazel reached to grasp the kitchen counter and squeezed to hold herself upright. She couldn't catch her breath. As she read, her mind reeled.

> Sinclair – On Friday, September 8, 1967, Ms. Irene Sinclair passed away, aged 78 years, beloved mother of Mrs. Elizabeth Sinclair McKay Holland and

grandmother of Olivia Holland of Mansfield and of Hazel and Ruthie McKay of Waldron. Remains at the parlors of Waston-Bluefred & Co. Funeral scheduled for Saturday at 2 pm at Mansfield First Baptist Church.

Her heart pounded in her head. How long had it been since she'd last spoken to her grandmother? A week, two weeks? Hazel blinked. She couldn't remember. They hardly ever saw her since she'd moved into the nursing home in Mansfield. Still, the last time Hazel had spoken to her grandmother, she'd sounded strong, not sick or weak. But she'd died and no one had even told her or Ruthie. Probably no one in Waldron even knew until this article came out. Hazel squeezed her eyes shut. Her grandmother was gone. Hazel thought about how after her and Joel's wedding, her grandmother had come to their duplex. In her hands, she held a huge, beautiful patchwork quilt. When Hazel opened the door, her grandmother had pushed it into her hands.

"I know I don't deserve your forgiveness." Her grandmother's voice had trembled when she spoke. "I was wrong for lying to you and your sister and not telling ya'll the truth about your mama. I should have told you she was living in Mansfield and not California." She laid a small, wrinkled hand on the quilt. "But I made this for you and Joel. And I wanted you to have it. My daughter is selfish. But you and Ruthie have grown up to be beautiful, kind young women. And I know your daddy is proud of you, because I sure am."

Hazel's hand went to her mouth. How could her grandmother be gone? She needed to call Ruthie, and she needed to call her now. She'd have to call the hospital. Ruthie worked in the evening. She hurried to the rotary telephone that hung on the wall next to the Frigidaire. Her finger only spun the dial once before a sharp pain sent her doubling over. She held her stomach and a warm red liquid ran down her legs. Hazel felt like her chest had caved in on itself. Her vision blurred as tears began to stream down her face. All this time, she'd secretly feared this would happen. After all those years of trying to get pregnant, she'd known it was too good to be true.

She'd known all along that her dream of becoming a mother would never happen. Today, she lost her grandmother, and now she'd lose her baby too.

Chapter 3

JOEL

After work, Joel went straight to Judy's Drive-in to pick up a triple chocolate fudge milkshake. He wanted to surprise Hazel with it. He shivered as he walked back to his truck, holding the cool Styrofoam cup. The cold wind blew straight through his canvas work coat. It chilled him all the way to his insides. His boots sloshed through the muck left from yesterday's rain. The muddy mess had been tracked onto the floorboards and splashed onto the undercarriages of all the vehicles Joel had worked on, leaving him dirtier than usual. Still, the cool wet weather had done nothing to dissipate Hazel's intense craving for chocolate, especially chocolate milkshakes. The more chocolate, the better.

He flipped on the radio and turned through the static until he found a channel he liked. He drummed his fingers on the steering wheel and hummed to "Working in the Coal Mine" by Lee Dorsey. His fingernails were embedded with grease and dry mud still stuck to some of his fingers no matter how hard he'd tried to clean them.

As the song ended, the radio announcer cut in. "Hello Waldron, can you believe it? It's been over four years since President Kennedy was assassinated, and it still seems surreal. I feel like I've been living in a daze, no offense President Johnson. For all you out there still living in a fog like I am, here's "Play a Sad Song" by Bobby Williams. We'll never forget you, Mr. President."

Joel quickly reached down and turned off the radio. He couldn't handle it today. Not with the war. Every time he listened to the radio or the news, there was never anything good to hear. But had it really been four years since President Kennedy's assassination? Already? Where did the time go? President Kennedy's death shocked the world and him too, and shortly after that, President Johnson started sending American troops to Vietnam. If it wasn't for the business classes, he'd started taking at night again in Fort Smith, he'd probably already have been drafted. But for now, he had a student deferment. The thought made him feel guilty. All those men being shipped overseas to fight in a war, and he's working on cars, sitting in a dumb classroom, and able to kiss his wife at night. Thinking of Hazel made his guilt disintegrate. She needed him. It had taken so long for her to get pregnant that he'd begun to think it wasn't meant for them to have children. A sadness he couldn't explain had settled on them over the years because of it. And now, he could hardly believe it. Joy radiated through his chest every time he thought about a little hand gripping his finger.

He remembered sitting with Hazel in Dr. Rimmer's office, impatiently waiting to hear the results of her pregnancy test. His hands had been so sweaty no matter how many times he'd wiped them on his work pants. He remembered the incessant hum of the fan as it oscillated in place, making the papers on Dr. Rimmer's desk rustle. They'd waited two weeks to get the results of Hazel's pregnancy test, and every day they waited, his stomach roiled. Hazel said she didn't need a doctor to tell her what she already knew, but Joel needed to hear the confirmation.

When Dr. Rimmer finally looked up from the papers, Joel's heart jackhammered in his chest. Dr. Rimmer gave them a wide toothy smile that reached his kind eyes. "I'm happy to announce you are going to be parents," he said.

Hazel had sat there silently.

Joel frowned. He'd heard the words, but they wouldn't penetrate into his thick skull. He'd asked, "What does that mean? Is she pregnant?"

Dr. Rimmer laughed at that. "Yes, of course, son, you're going to be a father."

A father. When he first heard those words, a love so strong grew inside of him. He hadn't even met this child, and he would already give his life for him or her.

After the appointment, he and Hazel had started immediately working on the serious project of selecting a name for their unborn child. "What about Anita for a girl?" Joel had asked on their way home from the doctor's office.

Hazel sat close by his side in the truck. Their fingers interlocked.

"No way, I knew a girl named Anita. She was awful. What about Allen for a boy?"

Joel shook his head. "Not Allen."

"Why not Allen?" Hazel asked.

Joel had shrugged. "I don't know. I don't like it."

"Well, that's not a good reason."

He turned and gave Hazel a quick peck on the side of the head. "It's good enough for me."

Hazel chuckled, "Fine, not Allen."

They still hadn't decided on a name, and they were what, at twenty-two weeks now. They'd have to decide on something, but they had a little while longer, and he enjoyed their funny little skirmishes each night as they tried out new names.

He felt dazed with joy when he pulled into the parking spot in front of their duplex. He noticed Hazel's car parked in its place, but the Lewises' car was gone. *Maybe they're at church*, he thought. He carefully got out of the truck, trying not to squeeze the milkshake's Styrofoam cup.

At the door, Joel jingled his keys looking for the right one. He stopped when he heard the telephone inside ringing. He held up the key ring as he tried to maneuver the keys in his fingers while keeping hold of the slick Styrofoam. The telephone continued to ring. The shrill sound came through the thin door. *Why wasn't Hazel answering the phone?* With that thought, the keys slipped from his fingers and landed with a plop on the stoop. "Dumb, dumb," he muttered. He bent down with a groan. He grabbed the correct key off the stoop and unlocked the door, pushing it open with his shoulder. "Hazel?" he called.

The loud ring of the rotary telephone blared from the kitchen. He turned to shut the front door, but his work pants hung on a loose nail protruding from the doorway. He sighed when he heard the slow ripping of cloth as he pulled his leg free from the nail. Hazel's angry face passed through his mind. How many rips and buttons had she fixed since they'd been married? He was pretty sure he couldn't count that high. The telephone's incessant ring made him want to claw it off the wall. He rushed to the kitchen and snatched the receiver off the telephone. It shook and jingled on the wall. He held the receiver to his ear. "Hello? Hello?" he panted. "Hello?" Nothing. He only heard the long, buzzing tone of the deadline.

He muttered under his breath and hung up the telephone. He spun around in the kitchen. *Where's Hazel? Was tonight something?* He couldn't remember her telling him that she'd be out. He noticed the brown paper sack, Tupperware container, and mail sitting on the kitchen countertop. In two strides he was there. He sat the chocolate milkshake down and reached into the grocery bag. He pulled out a container of chocolate ice cream. The soft carton collapsed in his hand and melted chocolate ice cream leaked out the sides. "Shoot," he yelled, tossing it into the sink. He flipped on the water and rinsed his hands of the sticky mess. He grabbed a dish towel to wipe off the counter. He couldn't understand it. Why would Hazel not put the ice cream in the icebox?

He picked up the mail from the counter and flipped through the envelopes. *Bills, of course.* "Hazel?" He called again, but there was no response. His insides twisted as a sense of dread fell over him. This wasn't like Hazel at all. He sat the mail down. "Hazel!" he yelled and rushed through the duplex. He spun around in the living room, but nothing looked out of place. Like a madman, he ran to their bedroom. Nothing. The bed had been made. Folded clothes sat on top of the patchwork quilt Hazel's grandmother had given them. He wanted to scream. He rushed to their small bathroom and threw the door open.

18

The sight inside the bathroom made bile rise in the back of his throat. A white towel stained pink and red lay near the toilet. His mind became a foggy blur as he stood there taking in the scene. The ring of the telephone sliced through the silence, startling him. He took off through the duplex. He grabbed his keys off the kitchen counter, leaving the telephone ringing. He slammed the front door shut and leaped into his truck. He knew where she'd gone. His tires squealed and slid as he pulled out onto the road. He accelerated. He had to get to Waldron Memorial Hospital. His whole body shook with fear. Blood rushed through his head. *I can't lose her. Oh God, I can't lose her*, he repeated over and over to himself.

He pulled into the emergency entrance and threw the truck into park. It jerked back and forth, and he felt a wave of dizziness pass through him. He opened the door and ran to the back of the truck and vomited. He had to get a hold of himself. He wiped his mouth with the back of his hand and ran through the hospital doors, pushing the memories away of the last time they were all here with Mr. McKay. He ran to the nurse's desk. Her head darted up from the files she'd been looking through, a startled expression on her face, "Can I...."

"Where's Hazel Davenport?" he hollered, interrupting her.

"Joel."

His head whipped around; Ruthie stood in the hallway. She wore a white nursing dress and cap. She gave him a grave look. Her eyes were watery. *I'm too late.*

"Hazel?" The only word he could say.

"She's fine," Ruthie said.

His stomach clenched, "The baby?"

Ruthie's eyes darted to the floor. She gave a small shake of her head, and his heart plummeted. She looked up, tears ran down her face. She took his hand, gripping it tight. "Sandra and Milton found her and rushed her to the hospital, but there was nothing that could be done. She's going to need you now."

Joel nodded. A huge lump formed in his throat, and he tried to swallow it down. Their baby was gone. The dreams of a tiny hand holding his finger made his eyes blur with tears. He wiped them away. He had to be strong for Hazel now. He let Ruthie lead him down the hallway to a hospital door.

His body felt numb, like it wasn't his own. They stopped at a door that sat ajar. A streak of light made a long line across the gray hospital floor. His stomach tightened when he heard Hazel's sobs coming from inside the room. He pushed all his fear and sadness to the side and went in. He went straight to her and wrapped his arms around her. Her face pressed into his chest, and he felt her tears wet his shirt.

"The baby's gone. Gone," she said between sobs.

He caressed her hair. "I know, I'm so sorry."

A deep sinking feeling came over him, but he pushed it away. He could not fall apart. Still, he couldn't stop the huge drops that fell from his eyes and landed in Hazel's hair. He didn't know how long they held each other and cried, but his body wouldn't let her go.

"Hazel," he said, moving so he could see her tear-streaked face. "I love you. We are going to get through this together."

She pressed the side of her head back into his chest. "I had so many plans and," her voice broke, "dreams..."

She didn't have to finish. He knew what her dreams had been. To be a mother, to hold their baby in her arms, to watch him or her grow. He ran his hand down her back. "I know, sweetie."

"The baby was a little girl. She was so tiny." Hazel began to sob.

He squeezed her closer. He'd almost lost it then. A daughter he could never hold. He swallowed. His throat felt thick. "Hazel, we'll get through this." And even though he didn't know how, he knew those were the words she needed to hear.

Chapter 4

HAZEL, SEPTEMBER 16, 1967

Hazel sat on the sofa in the duplex, clutching her arms around her middle. The thin material of her black dress did nothing to protect her from the chill in the air. It seeped through the walls of the small duplex. Her eyes ping ponged from Joel to Ruthie then back to Joel again. They stood in front of her, arguing like she wasn't even there, like she couldn't hear them.

"She shouldn't be going," Joel said.

"But she wants to go. Still, it might be too much for her because *she* will probably be there." Ruthie emphasized the word she, as if their mother, who abandoned them, had no name.

"She can't handle it," Joel claimed.

Maybe he's right. Maybe I can't handle it.

"I think she can handle it, but should she?" Ruthie countered. "No one even called to tell us grandmother died or about the funeral."

"She needs to rest."

Ruthie nodded her head, "I agree, she needs to rest."

Joel crossed his arms, "So we agree? No funeral?"

Ruthie crossed her arms to match his position. "I think so. No funeral."

They both looked over at Hazel—their proclamation final. Hazel rolled her eyes. Since she'd lost the baby on Wednesday, they'd not left her alone for one second. While she appreciated what they were trying to do, she desperately needed time alone. She needed to wallow in her grief, to let the darkness of her sorrow swallow her for even just a moment. She couldn't fully cry. If she shed one tear, they were on her, hovering around her, asking if she was alright.

They'd had a funeral for the baby, Madelyn Ray, on Friday morning. That was the name she and Joel had chosen for their baby girl. The funeral wasn't a huge ordeal, like she knew her grandmother's would be. They didn't even have a real service. She'd stood at her baby's graveside at Duncan Cemetery. Everyone she loved gathered around her. Her father said a prayer. She'd cried silent tears while Joel wrapped his arm around her shoulder. She leaned on him and he on her. After the prayer, they all took a handful of dirt and tossed it into the small hole where the tiniest of boxes laid. Joel had purchased the plot the day after they'd lost her. She'd only weighed one pound. Too tiny for her lungs to take breaths on their own. As the dirt fell, they all said their good-byes to the baby no one got to meet.

It had crushed her, and honestly, she wasn't sure she'd ever be able to be herself again. Her heart felt like it was stuck in that tiny grave with Madelyn. *My little baby, my sweet little girl.* She had no idea if she could really handle seeing her mother again. The woman who didn't want the daughters she had, when Hazel would give her life to have the one she'd lost. But her grandmother was family, and she had to go. Family honored the life of those they loved no matter what. Hazel swallowed the lump in her throat. She would honor her grandmother today even if it made her uncomfortable to see her mother, even if it ripped away another piece of her heart.

Am I strong enough for this? She doubted it, but that did nothing to change the fact that she would not be missing her grandmother's funeral today.

"I'm going," she said flatly. She didn't meet Joel or Ruthie's eyes but picked a blank spot on the wall in front of her to stare at. "I will go. Neither of you are the boss of me. I will honor my grandmother's life today because it's the right thing to do."

Chapter 5

RUTHIE

Numerous flower arrangements sat around her grandmother's dark mahogany casket at the front of the country church. Their sweet smell made Ruthie's stomach roil. Even though the cool air prickled her skin, her dress clung to her damp body. She shifted in the pew. Hazel gave her a side-eyed glance. *How was she even sitting still?* It was all Ruthie could do not to get up out of her seat, walk to the pew across from her, and slug her mother in the face. Her mother sat beside her fancy husband and the little girl Ruthie and Hazel had only seen once. She thought about how years ago on Hazel's wedding day, she and Hazel had spied on her mother and her new family. The little girl had to be about fourteen now. She was all wavy blonde hair and big doe eyes. *She's just a child*, Ruthie told herself, and none of this was her fault. So instead of blaming the little girl, who looked so much like herself, she thought about putting her fist into her mother's nose as the preacher droned on and on about the wonderful life of her grandmother.

Even though Hazel had forgiven their grandmother for all her secrets and lying, Ruthie could never fully let it go. Every time Hazel had gone to visit their grandmother in the nursing home, Ruthie would make up some excuse not to go. As far as she was concerned, their father, Hazel, and Joel were all the family she needed. A memory of the graveside service they'd had for Madelyn Ray popped into her head and the anger she felt dissipated some. She remembered the cold dirt in her hand. The little pieces of jagged rock that felt dry in her palm. She remembered releasing it over the too small hole where Madelyn's casket lay. *Hazel should be home*, she thought. *She shouldn't be here. It's too much.* She desperately wished Joel had come with them. He'd been ready, dressed in nice pants and a tie. But right before they'd walked out the door, the telephone had rung. Mr. Hal Sutherland, Joel's boss, had called asking if he'd go into work. Apparently, a stomach bug had run rampant in the Sutherland house and he and Mrs. Anne, his wife, were very ill.

"I'm so sorry," Joel had apologized. He hugged Hazel before he left for work. "There's no way Mr. Hal can get the shop opened, and there's lots of people coming to pick up vehicles today. If I don't get there and get them what they want, they may tear down the shop's walls."

Hazel had understood, of course. But Ruthie had thought, *let them tear down the walls. Being with Hazel was more important.* Still, Ruthie wasn't young and dumb anymore. She knew bills were a real thing and every month, they demanded to be paid. With Joel's classes and now Hazel's hospital bill, Joel needed his job.

She reached over and took Hazel's hand in hers. It felt cold and small. She gave it a squeeze. *Had Hazel's hand always felt this fragile?*

"Let us pray," the pastor said, holding his hands in the air.

Instead of bowing her head, Ruthie looked side to side. She twisted in the pew to get a good look at the back of the church. She had to find a fast escape route out of here. The last thing she wanted, and Hazel needed, was to talk to their mother. She spied a door in the front on the left side but worried it might lead to Sunday school classrooms or a fellowship hall or something like that. The only clear exit she could see was the door at the back, far away from where they sat now. Her stomach clenched. It would be difficult to get there quickly. Hazel moved slowly still—not fully healed. Before Ruthie knew it, the pastor said, "Amen. Now please remain seated. We will start in the back and work our way up to the front."

Geez Louise! Ruthie wanted to kick herself. She'd forgotten about the flippin' receiving line. There's no way they could escape, not with everyone in the whole sanctuary making their way up to the front to gawk at her grandmother. They'd shake her mother's hand. They'd shake her and Hazel's hands too. They'd whisper things like, "sorry for your loss, she was a good woman," before exiting the church. Then they'd exit out the door in the back, leaving her and Hazel, their mother, and her new family in the church—alone, together! The bile rose in the back of her throat. The receiving line was meant to be a way for everyone to extend love to the family members who'd lost a loved one. It also gave the family a few minutes to say their good-byes in private before heading to the graveside for the final part of the service. But Ruthie didn't want privacy. She wanted to get Hazel out of this situation.

A woman with a huge beehive leaned over to hug her. The strong smell of the woman's floral perfume and hairspray filled her nose, making her headache worse than it already was. She needed to think. She couldn't concentrate on rescuing herself and Hazel with all these hugs, handshakes, and platitudes, and before she could think of a viable plan to excise herself and Hazel from this predicament, the last row behind them rose to their feet and began to shuffle toward the casket. Ruthie's heart leapt in her chest as the last of the people in the sanctuary made their way to the casket. Chills ran down her arms even though sweat made her dress cling to her back.

Then as she feared, it was just her, Hazel, their mother, and her mother's new family left in the church sanctuary. At first, no one moved from their pew. The weighted silence hung in the air like smoke from a brush fire. Ruthie thought about just grabbing Hazel's arm and jerking her out the door in the back, but she looked over at Hazel. Hazel stared at their grandmother's casket, their grandmother's profile barely visible over the wooden side. She looked like she was sleeping peacefully. Ruthie wondered if she had any idea how much turmoil her dying had caused.

Hazel stirred beside her, and Ruthie grabbed hold of her arm.

"What are you doing?" Ruthie whispered, but Hazel didn't respond. She began to stand. Ruthie tried to pull her back down without making a scene. Hazel's eyes locked with hers. She pried Ruthie's fingers off her arm.

"I'm going to speak to her."

"No, you are not," Ruthie ordered, but she couldn't stop her.

Hazel walked over to the pew beside them. Ruthie scurried to catch up with her. If she couldn't stop her, she'd sure try to protect her from whatever this woman might do.

When their mother saw them, her eyes widened, and she stood. She held out her arms as if to hug them but must have thought better of it because she folded them across her middle.

Hazel nodded, "Mother."

Even Ruthie could hear the venom in that word. The man sitting beside their mother rose and looped an arm around her shoulder as if to protect her. Ruthie wanted to laugh. Her mother's new husband looked thin, almost like a toothpick, but Ruthie noticed he had kind eyes. The little girl hopped off the pew, her golden curls bounced up and down. She clung to her father's arm.

"Hazel, Ruthie," their mother looked at them. Her eyes began to shimmer in the light. "It's... it's so good to see you." Ruthie thought she could hear a faint waver in her voice. Their mother looked as perfect as ever. Her hair pulled back in a bun, not one hair out of place. The pleated skirt of her dark dress hung below her knees.

"It was a lovely service," Hazel said, ignoring her comment.

Their mother lowered her eyes, "Yes, yes it was."

Hazel touched Ruthie's arm. "Well, we better be going. We aren't going to make it to the graveside."

Ruthie's chest, that had felt so tight, loosened somewhat. They were going home. She could almost breathe again. They turned to leave, but before they could even take two steps, their mother spoke to them.

"It was so good to see you girls."

At their mother's words, Hazel froze, and her body went rigid.

"Let's just go," Ruthie whispered.

Hazel shook her head and instead turned to face their mother—head on. Everything felt so strange. Usually Ruthie was the carefree, throw it to the wind, say what you want type of girl, but here in the sanctuary with their dead grandmother a few feet away, she'd lost all words, and Hazel had gained them.

With raised chin, Hazel said, "I can't say the same for you." She swallowed. "Seeing you ripped my heart out all over again."

Hazel turned back to the door. She grabbed Ruthie's hand and gave it a good squeeze. Together, they walked away from their mother, out the sanctuary door, and into the sunlight.

Chapter 6

HAZEL, FEBRUARY 1968

"Hazel, isn't your shift over?" Louanne said. A small, bright pink bubble matching the color of her lipstick popped out of the center of her puckered lips. She sucked it back into her mouth and smacked.

Hazel blinked her eyes. *Is Louanne's hair teased higher than normal today?* Louanne's fuzzy cream sweater accentuated her huge curves. Hazel glanced down at her plaid dress. She'd lost weight. She didn't mean to, but she hadn't been hungry lately or really at all anymore. Now, all her clothes seemed to swallow her. In a daze, Hazel looked up at the round clock hanging on the back wall of the Piggly Wiggly. It was six. Her shift had ended thirty minutes ago. She shook her head. She couldn't get it together. She barely had enough energy to get out of bed and come to work. Her days felt like an endless string of nothingness.

"Let me just clean up and..."

"I've got it," Louanne said. She moved around Hazel, practically pushing her away from the cash register. "You get home. You know Mr. Crutchfield won't pay you for working past your shift."

Hazel narrowed her eyes as understanding finally set in. An attractive blonde-haired gentleman in khaki pants and a collared shirt pushed a cart full of beer and steaks toward Hazel's cash register. *Of course*, she shook her head. Louanne never eagerly helped her unless it benefited herself in some way. If Hazel had the energy, she might be annoyed, but really, she could care less about Louanne and all her romantic conquests.

Hazel began to make her way to the employees' area in the back of the store where she kept her purse and coat. She straightened items on the shelves as she went. The employee area was a large open space with cement floors and flickering florescent lights. The place gave Hazel the creeps. She shivered. The air in the back always felt a few degrees cooler than the rest of the store because of the huge icebox that sat near the wall, constantly humming. On the opposite side of the room, boxes with new canned goods were stacked along the wall beside Mr. Crutchfield's small office. They would have to shelve those tomorrow. Hazel sighed.

The door of Mr. Crutchfield's office hung open. He sat at his desk, leaning back in his chair. His hands rested behind his head. The news blared from his radio. On the radio, men discussed the war. They argued about the new death toll numbers, and the failure of the Tet Offense where thousands and thousands of young men perished. They were furious that after such a failure, the government would choose to increase the number of American soldiers being sent to Vietnam. It sounded to Hazel they all agreed that the draft was a bad thing. The whole conversation set her teeth on edge and made her stomach turn. She knew in her heart if it wasn't for the few classes Joel took at Westark and his student status, he'd probably have been drafted already. Maybe he would have been one of the ones killed during the Tet Offense. She shivered. She wished talk of the war didn't permeate every part of her days, but she couldn't get away from it. From the radio to the television, or even Mr. Crutchfield's customers that came into the store, the war was everywhere, and it affected everyone in some way.

She reached for her locker door. The metal lockers looked as if they'd came straight from a high school locker room. Most of the doors hung at different angles and never quite closed right. Her locker door squeaked and protested when she pulled on it until it finally popped open. She grabbed her coat and looped the thin strap of her purse around her shoulder.

"Hazel? Are you still here?" Mr. Crutchfield called from his office.

"Yes sir."

"Don't forget your paycheck." He ripped a check from the book on his desk and waved it in the air. "It's past five-thirty. You know I'm not paying you for more than your time."

"Yes sir, I'm sorry. I got distracted."

She entered his office. The smell of stale cigar smoke and strong after-shave made her crinkle her nose. The light above them reflected a white spot on his bald head. Hazel tried not to stare as he handed her the check. "As long as we're on the same page. No pay for the extra time," he said.

She nodded and took the check from his hand. She couldn't help it, but her eyes flitted to the amount written on the line. Such a small amount. "Yes, we are on the same page, sir."

"Good, good," he said, turning up the radio and leaning back in his chair.

"This year has already started out bloody and we are only in February. What do you think that means for the rest of the year?" the radio announcer asked one of his guests.

Hazel hurried from the office, not wanting to stay a minute longer.

꧁꧂

As the sun began to set, the sky transformed into brilliant smears of purple and red. A chilly wind blew Hazel's hair and nipped at her nose as she exited the store. Joel would be so angry with her if he knew she'd walked to work this morning. The temperature in the morning had started around thirty-seven degrees, but it had risen to fifty-two by the afternoon. If it wasn't for the wind, it might have been bearable. Still, she didn't mind the cold. Feeling the cold wind sting her skin was the most she had felt all day, and she needed to feel something. She needed the fresh air to expand her lungs and stretch them out. She loved her job, but she hated being cooped up in the store all day. The walk from Piggly Wiggly to the duplex was only about a mile long. Well... it would have been a mile long if she hadn't chosen to start taking a new route after last week.

Her heart clenched. She couldn't believe she would rather walk a fourth of a mile more than run into her best friend, Alice, again. But the pain in her chest at the memory of running into Alice and her husband, David, last week made her double over. Hazel placed her hands on her knees and willed herself to calm down as she sucked in the cool air. It burned in her chest, but she couldn't stop the flood of memories. That afternoon had been abnormally warm and sunny.

"Hazel!" Alice had waved to her. "Oh, my good gracious, how I've missed you." She'd wrapped her arms around Hazel's neck. "We've got to get together. I'm going absolutely mad being stuck at home with the baby."

Even over Alice's shoulder, Hazel could not take her eyes off the light green stroller David pushed up beside them. Her eyes were drawn to it like a moth to a flame. A gurgle and whine came from inside the stroller and Alice released Hazel. She reached inside the stroller. "Sweet girl, did you lose your baby doll again." Alice searched around inside the stroller until she found the doll. She laid it near her daughter and shook her head. "She's always slinging that doll around somewhere. I don't know how many times we've had to get up in the middle of the night to find it."

"How old is she now?" Hazel asked, unable to think of anything else to say.

"Fourteen months," David said. The huge smile across his face as he looked at Alice and then at his daughter radiated all the happiness he had to be feeling.

It was David's smile that tore her heart from her chest. She thought of Joel and how he would never be able to smile like that at his own child. She thought about Madelyn Ray every day. *Would she have had a special baby doll?* She'd be about six months old. The thought made Hazel's whole body hurt and she had to get away. She turned to Alice. "Oh, my goodness, I've got to go. I forgot to take a pot roast out of the oven. I'll see you soon, okay?"

"But didn't you just get off work?" Alice asked, with eyebrows raised.

"Sorry, I've got to run," Hazel said over her shoulder as she rushed away as fast as her legs would carry her.

31

"Hazel, are you okay?" Alice called to her.

But Hazel never turned around. Since that day, Alice had tried to call her several times. The rotary telephone, hanging on the kitchen wall, would ring, but Hazel wouldn't answer it. She'd gotten close a couple times, but always stopped herself. She'd stare at it ringing. The vibrations passing through the kitchen wall. She had no idea what other calls she'd missed, but she didn't care. After she didn't answer, Alice took to calling Ruthie.

"She just wants to talk to you," Ruthie told her. "She wants to apologize."

"There's nothing to apologize about. She should be proud of her baby," Hazel said. Still, she couldn't stop the jealousy she felt from sprouting in the pit of her stomach and working its way to her heart. It made her feel guilty and angry. She had no idea why, but she felt angry at Alice. So, until Hazel could muddle through her mess of feelings, she'd just avoid her.

As Hazel neared the duplexes, a child's laugh shook her from her thoughts. Her shoulders slumped forward when she saw Sandra sitting outside on the stoop of the duplex while six-year-old Mikey played outside in the yard. He pushed a yellow dump truck around with his hand. Sandra leaned forward on the stoop, trying to pick up a rock for the dump truck, but she couldn't reach it, her pregnant belly hindered her progress. Hazel sighed. Even in her own home, she couldn't avoid children or pregnant women.

"Good evening," Sandra said, glancing up. She held a hand over her eyes to shade them from the setting sun.

When Mikey saw Hazel, he leapt up off the ground and ran to her, locking his arms around her legs. She teetered and held her arms out to steady herself.

"Auntie Hazel!" he cried and squeezed her legs so tight, his face scrunched.

She bent down to hug him. "How was school today?"

"Fun! I went fast down a slide."

Hazel chuckled, "Well that does sound like a fun day."

"Mikey, you let go of Auntie Hazel's legs. You're gonna make her fall. Come gather your toys. We need to get inside, so you can eat your dinner and get a bath."

Mikey looked up at Hazel with his big chocolate eyes. In a conspiratorial whisper, he said, "I don't like baths."

Hazel couldn't help but smile. "Me either," she lied.

Sandra began to stand from the stoop. Hazel rushed over and held out an arm to help her. Sandra took her arm and grunted as she pulled herself upright. "I'm getting bigger every day," she shook her head. "Not sure I'm going to be able to handle two. But I guess I better get used to the idea."

"It's going to be fine," Hazel said. "I'm always here to help."

Sandra reached out and touched her arm. "How are you doing? You look like you've lost weight."

Hazel wanted to tell her everything. How she couldn't sleep at night even though she felt exhausted. How seeing her pregnant and Alice with a healthy baby girl made Hazel's chest feel hollow inside. How she lost track of time and didn't have the energy to care about anything. But she couldn't voice these things. She couldn't talk about it, or her friends and family would suffocate her with even more attention when all she really wanted was to be left alone. Hazel tried to brighten her smile. "Oh, me, I'm fine. Don't worry. I've not lost any weight at all. It's this dress. It's a size too big."

Sandra narrowed her eyes. Hazel could see she wanted to press, but to Hazel's relief, she didn't.

"Well alright, but I wanted to let you know, I used the key Joel gave me and put some fried pork chops and greens in your icebox. Just warm them on the stove and you've got dinner."

"Oh, my goodness, thank you!" Hazel said, feeling a small weight lift off her chest. Now she didn't have to work up the energy to make dinner. Her kind friend had done all the work for her.

"It's nothing."

"Mama, I'm hungry."

They both looked down. Mikey stood near them. The knees of his jeans were stained with dirt and grass.

"You're a mess, child. Go grab your toys. You're going to need a bath before dinner."

"Awww Mama, but I'm hungry."

"The faster you clean up, the faster you'll get some food."

Inside the duplex, Hazel didn't even bother to turn on the lights. She collapsed on the sofa and stared at the blank television screen. The light from outside began to fade and the living room grew darker. When the doorknob jiggled, she bolted straight up. She had no idea how long she'd been sitting in the dark or even when the sky outside had turned black. She tried to use her fingers to untangle her hair. Ruthie and Joel came inside, laughing.

"Hazel!" Ruthie said, still giggling. Ruthie flipped on the living room light and plopped down on the sofa beside her.

Hazel rocked from her added weight. The light burnt Hazel's eyes, and she squinted, trying to appear like she had been doing more than just sitting and staring into the dark void. Joel bent down and gave her a light peck on the lips. "How was class?" she asked him.

"Boring like usual," he chuckled. "That drive to Fort Smith is starting to get to me."

"Yeah, we pulled in at the same time. His eyes looked like he was half asleep." Ruthie picked up a small square decorative pillow from the sofa and held it against her middle. "My day was anything but boring. That Dr. Sullivan... Whoa! He can go ape at the drop of a hat. Yelling and carrying on. And we just have to nod our heads and say, 'yes sir,' when Mrs. Battalou knows a ton more than he does. But she can't correct him because he's the doctor."

"That's terrible," Hazel said, trying to sympathize.

Joel walked toward the kitchen.

"Sandra left us some food in the icebox." She started to push up from the sofa. "I'll warm it for you."

He turned and held out a hand to stop her. "No, you sit. I got it. Visit."

Hazel couldn't help but smile. She turned back to Ruthie.

Ruthie grabbed her arm. "Oh, I forgot to tell you! I put in an IV today, and I did it perfectly!"

Hazel thought about Ruthie pushing a needle into someone's skin to find a vein. She remembered when Ruthie had been in nursing school and how she and the other students had to practice their sticks on each other. She shivered. She could never do anything like that. "That's great," she said, trying not to clench her teeth.

"How was your day?" Ruthie asked.

"The same old thing. So, where's Dad tonight?" Hazel asked. She didn't want to talk about her day, or anything related to her. It would be too tempting to let her feelings out, and she couldn't do that. She couldn't give Ruthie and Joel anything to worry about. They were busy and she didn't want to add worrying about her to their list.

"He said he was going to Ms. Faye's after work. They were going to meet Mr. and Mrs. Sutherland for dinner."

The smell of warming pork chops drifted into the living room.

Ruthie's stomach growled. "I'm famished. I didn't really get to eat lunch today."

Hazel waved a hand. "You go eat. I'm not hungry."

Ruthie leapt off the sofa. She grabbed Hazel's hand and pulled her up. "You gotta eat. I prescribe it."

Hazel rolled her eyes. "You're not a doctor."

At the table, Hazel used her fork to push the greens around in a circle on her plate. What she really wanted to do did not involve sitting at the table and trying to be social, it involved crawling under her grandmother's homemade quilt and sleeping. Still, even with her dulled senses, she could tell something wasn't quite right. Joel and Ruthie were acting suspicious. Their chatter had quieted—too much. The silence between them felt heavy and charged. And how could she not notice them stealing looks at each other between bites of food. *What conspiratorial secret are they keeping from me? Why won't they just spit it out,* she wondered. Each furtive glance had begun to irritate her until she couldn't handle it anymore. When Joel again looked at Ruthie then back down at his plate, she'd had enough. She sat her fork down on the table hard. It made a loud thump, causing Ruthie to jump.

"Okay, what's going on?"

Joel and Ruthie shot a big-eyed stare at her, and then at each other. Ruthie made a face at Joel, and he gave a quick shake of his head.

"Well," Joel started. "Ruthie has something she wants to ask you."

Ruthie glowered at him.

"Fine, I'll say it," Ruthie said. She laid her fork down and took a sip of water from her frosted glass. She turned in her chair to face Hazel.

"You know I love you, but..."

Hazel's body stiffened. "But?"

"I know it's been hard for you."

Hazel wanted to laugh. She had no idea, but she kept her face straight as Ruthie continued.

"But Hazel, you can't spend your life just working and moping around, sitting in a dark house. It's not good for you. You need to get out, back into the world. I think you need to feel a part of something again."

Hazel's jaw clenched. She looked at Joel, who had become focused on cutting his pork chop into very small pieces. He refused to look up from his plate and make eye contact with her.

Ruthie kept going. "I want you to come with me. We can both join the Scott County Women's Coalition. We can do it together!"

"What? Why?" Hazel said, too exhausted to feel angry.

"Alice and Margarette Ann are already members. So, we'd get to visit with them. They only meet once a week on Tuesday nights."

Hazel shook her head, "I don't know."

Ruthie ran from the kitchen. She came back, holding her purse. She dug inside and pulled out a pamphlet. She pushed it toward Hazel, who frowned and took it. Pictures of women from the past wearing red dresses and a string of pearls covered the pages of the thick pamphlet. It talked about how the coalition served the community, assisted the homeless, and helped with better education. Hazel closed it and handed it back to Ruthie.

"Plus," Ruthie continued her persuasion attempt. "They have been very helpful in sending care packages and letters to the soldiers in the war. And Margarette Ann said they are looking for other ways to pitch in too. What better way for us to help than to join the coalition?"

When Hazel didn't answer, Ruthie looked down at her plate. She took a bite of pork chop. The prongs of her fork scraped against the plate.

"You don't work on Tuesday night," Joel interjected.

Hazel's eyes met his. He coughed and looked back down at his plate. He shoveled a huge fork full of greens into his mouth.

Hazel sucked in a breath. *This is ridiculous.* She stared down at the partially eaten dinner on her plate. *I don't spend all day moping around.* She

36

at least thought she'd hidden it better. She looked at Joel then at Ruthie, both were concentrating very hard on their plates. Maybe she did need to get out. To force herself to do something other than sitting on the sofa in the dark. She already felt her body protest at the idea, but she'd have to push those feelings aside. She needed to do it. She felt like she died with Madelyn Ray, but she hadn't. She was still breathing, every painful breath. She knew she needed to do this, not just for her family, but for herself too.

"Do they serve snacks during these meetings? Cookies or something?"

Ruthie's head shot up and a smile spread across her face. She nodded yes.

Out of the corner of Hazel's eye, she saw Joel's mouth move into a half grin.

She sighed, "Fine then, I'll come with you."

Chapter 7

RUTHIE, APRIL 1968

Gregory Hemings fumbled to undo the top button of Ruthie's white nursing uniform in the backseat of his 1966 Ford Mustang. Ruthie pushed his hand away, making her nursing hat slide sideways on her head. Ruthie squeezed her eyes closed. Greg kissed her neck, his hot breath and wet mouth working its way up from the base of her neck to her ear. She tried to be in the moment, but all she really wanted to do was straighten her hat. Her back pressed hard against the metal side of the car. It sent a sharp pain through her, and she winced. She'd been on her feet all day and her back ached. She placed her hands on his shoulders, and lightly pushed.

"Hey, my back. I'm going to be left with a bruise."

"Oh sorry," he mumbled. He scooted a fraction over on the seat, but it didn't help.

She sighed.

"Don't forget to get your popcorn and sodas," the cartoon popcorn kernel sang from the huge movie screen.

They hadn't even made it past the commercials. Ruthie's head dropped to the side against the vehicle's glass window. The coolness made her shiver. She rolled her eyes. Greg's sloppy kisses on her neck had started to grate on her nerves. She tried again to weakly push him away, but when she raised her head, he took her earlobe into his mouth. His wet lips and the sucking noises were driving her crazy, and not in a good way. His warm breath tickled her neck. He groaned.

"Greg, Greg," she said, patting his back. "Let's slow down."

She laid her hands on his chest and pushed, but he either didn't hear her or didn't care to slow down. She reached up and grabbed the skin on the underside of his arm and pinched. Hard. He flinched and reared back to rub his arm.

"Ouch! What was that for?"

Ruthie moved to sit up against the seat. Immediately her back felt better. She straightened her hat and pushed strands of her wavy blonde hair back behind her ears.

"I need a breather," she said.

Greg hmphed and crossed his arms like a petulant child. "You always need a breather."

Ruthie made herself flash him one of her best smiles, even though she wanted to slug him in the face. She leaned in to lightly kiss his cheek. "That's because you're always raring to go on full speed."

Greg chuckled, "That's how I run. My heels are always on fire."

Ruthie moved closer to him, looped her arm around his, and leaned her head on his shoulder. She watched the opening credits to *Beach Red*. She hated they were watching a war movie when every day the war filled the news. She didn't know how Greg could stand it, but he'd insisted they come see it.

"I forgot to tell you. Hazel and I joined the Women's Coalition. I think she's really enjoying it. It's nice to see her smile again. And we're really doing some good, I think. We're starting to gather things our soldiers need in Vietnam so we can ship it to them."

"What kinds of things?" Greg asked without looking at her. His eyes plastered to the movie screen.

"You know, things like soap, canned soup, razors, small sewing kits, just things they may need. We are even writing personal letters to go in the packages to hopefully give them some encouragement."

"Of course ya'll are," Greg huffed and shook his head.

Ruthie leaned up, "What? You don't think it's a good cause?"

"It's a waste."

Ruthie tensed and her body began to grow hotter. "What do you mean?"

Greg snorted as he turned to look at her. "Are you serious? I mean look at Ronnie Hartley. He was a great football player and could have gone to college on a scholarship. And become, who knows what, famous or something. He was the best football player this town ever saw, and he's off fighting a war."

"But that was his dream. He wanted to join the Army like his daddy and grandpa."

"Exactly, a waste!"

Ruthie wasn't sure how that proved anything. Her pulse began to race. The thought of Ronnie sent a sharp pain in her chest. What she wouldn't give to have him here beside her instead of dumb Greg. But that dream would never come true because Ronnie had left right after graduation to join the Army and serve this country. He'd followed his dream, and thanks to Ronnie's encouragement, she'd followed hers too. She'd gotten his address from Joel and had written to him not long after he left. She'd thanked him for the kind words he'd whispered that night at prom, which now felt like ages ago, while they swayed to the music. The thought of him holding her close made her heart ache. She remembered the crush she had on him back in the day. Good grief, how her heart would thump when he walked by! Now, they were friends, or pen pals of sorts. Their friendship would be nothing more than that, but the thought of him still put a smile on her face and made her want to kick Greg for thinking Ronnie was dense for following his dream. "Ronnie's choice to join the Army was not a waste. It was an honorable thing to do," she said, sticking up for her friend.

Greg chortled. "Honorable until he dies."

Ruthie gasped, "Don't say that!"

"But that's not the worst," Greg continued. "People like Ronnie throw their lives away on their own accord. Those poor saps being drafted. Now there's the rub. They don't even get a choice. Someone else makes the decision to throw their lives away for them. It's either go to Nam or go to jail."

Ruthie frowned. *He wasn't exactly wrong on that point.* She hated that men were having their choice stripped away from them and being sent away from their families and homes. "Aren't you worried?" she asked. "About becoming one of those poor saps being drafted?"

Greg laughed, "Nah, I'll never be drafted, and I'm sure the heck not volunteering."

Ruthie let go of his arm and moved to look at his face.

"How can you be so sure?"

His head lolled over to look at her. She could see why so many girls wanted to go out with him. He had a strong movie star chin and dark wavy hair slicked back over his ears. His ice blue eyes were piercing in the flickering movie light.

"My dad's doctor friend wrote me a fake letter sayin' I had a physical infirmity. I think he said I had bad eyesight or something. I'm practically blind," he laughed. He closed his eyes and put his hands out, acting like he couldn't see while trying to grope her.

She slapped his hands away. "Stop that!"

He opened his eyes and at least had the decency to look sheepish. He shrugged, "I'm just playin'."

The rage in her began to boil as he stuck out his lip and pouted. "Come on now, give this poor blind man a kiss."

He leaned in to kiss her and she shoved him away.

"I'm done playing," she said and grabbed the front passenger seat. She pulled herself through the opening, back to the front of the vehicle. She plopped down into the passenger seat. She folded her arms across her chest. Anger seethed through her.

"Hey, what's going on?" Greg asked as he leaned up between the seats to look at her. "You never want to watch the movie. Was it something I said?"

She couldn't put a pin on what exactly had made her so angry. Was it the talk of Ronnie dying? Was it the war or Greg avoiding the draft with a lie? She didn't want Greg to be drafted. Shoot, she didn't want anyone to be drafted. Still, paying a doctor to lie to avoid it had to be morally wrong. She looked at Greg, her face flushed hot. "Well, I want to watch the movie tonight, Greg. I really want to watch it tonight."

❧❧❧❧❧ ❦❦❦❦❦

G reg dropped Ruthie off in the parking lot of the duplex. He peeled out without saying good-bye. Dirt flung from his tires as they spun. Ruthie raised her chin. *Good riddance*, she thought, looking at the millions of stars peppering the dark sky. It surprised her to see the flickering lights of televisions on in every duplex. *What in the world is happening?* Even Sandra and Milton's lights were on. *Good grief!* It was way past Mikey's bedtime! And shouldn't Sandra be getting rest? She was due any day now. Ruthie started toward the duplex she shared with her father but spun around, deciding to swing by Hazel's first.

Hazel's door was cracked open, and Ruthie quickly realized Hazel and Joel weren't there. She shut the door and knocked on Sandra and Milton's door. Hazel opened the door, her eyes rimmed red and watery. Ruthie opened her mouth to ask what was going on, but Hazel put a finger to her lips, took her arm, and dragged her inside.

Joel sat on Milton and Sandra's floor, holding a half-asleep Mikey in his arms. Milton and Sandra sat on their sofa, holding hands, staring at the television. Their faces streaked with tears. An anchorman spoke about something, but Ruthie couldn't quite understand.

"It can't be true," Sandra said, before starting to sob.

Milton wrapped an arm around her and pulled her closer to his side. "He's gone, my love. He's gone."

Ruthie sank to the floor near Joel. She needed to be close to the television to hear. *Who was gone? Had someone died in the war?*

What Ruthie heard took her breath away. Martin Luther King, Jr. had been assassinated. The violence had been on their home soil this time and not across an ocean, thousands of miles away.

42

The anchorman's face seemed to grow longer the more he talked about the details of the incident. "The loss of Reverand King is a national tragedy," the anchorman said, his voice solemn.

"Everything is going to change," Sandra whispered.

Milton shook his head. "No, there's enough people out there to keep his legacy alive. We'll keep his legacy alive."

Still, Ruthie wondered, if someone would murder a peaceful man like Reverand King, was there any hope for any of them? She swallowed. "Can I go to church with you this Sunday?" she asked Milton.

He looked at her and gave her a weak smile. "Of course, you are more than welcome."

"I feel the need to pray."

Chapter 8

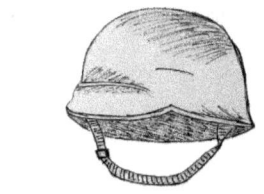

JOEL, MAY 1968

Dark blue clouds filled the sky, and the thick hot air clung to the ground like a heavy blanket. The abnormal warmth and damp ground created a fog so thick Joel could only see the road right in front of the truck. His headlight beams were unable to penetrate the dense foggy wall. It made everything outside appear eerie. Joel felt unsettled as he drove home from work. He had to work late again. He shook his head, and his stomach twisted when he thought of how many times this year he'd missed classes or skipped studying to work. He'd asked Mr. Hal to hire an extra pair of hands, but Mr. Hal said the war had made finding a good worker hard, and even though they were short-staffed, people still needed their vehicles. So Joel had to work. He and Hazel needed the money anyway for bills, so his schooling became less important. Thank goodness classes were over now for the summer. He'd taken his finals two weeks ago. He thought about how nervous he'd been to take the tests. He'd not had one minute to study, and it made it hard to think with his heart pounding between his ears. He just hoped he'd remembered enough to skate by with a low C in his Principles of Management class.

Joel's sweaty hair stuck to his skin. He wiped his arm across his forehead. Even in the shadows of the night, he could still see the black grease stains smeared across his hands and arms. He hated how his fingernails were perpetually caked with grease. His fingernail beds looked like black crescent moons, and he could never get them clean. He turned the steering wheel into the parking lot of the duplex. The tires sloshed through muddy potholes, making the truck bounce. He grabbed the white paper bag holding his dinner before it could fly off the passenger seat. Its paper darkened in spots from the grease. The smell of the hamburger and fries made his stomach growl. He'd made a run to Judy's Drive-in after work since Hazel had called to say she'd be late getting home tonight. Piggly Wiggly had gotten a truck full of fresh produce and the main stock boy went home sick with a stomach bug or something. Hazel told him she'd like to earn the extra money Mr. Crutchfield offered for the help and even though he didn't like her working late, he knew they could use the extra money.

He parked the truck and flipped off the headlights. The blackness enveloped him, and he wished he'd just told Hazel to come home. The small glow of the porch light near the Lewises' front door cast a faint light on the yard in front of their home. *They must have left it on for us,* Joel thought, and again he marveled at how lucky he and Hazel were for having such wonderful neighbors.

He grabbed the paper sack and jogged to the mailbox to get the day's mail. Inside the house, his stomach ached with hunger. He went straight to the kitchen. He debated for a second about doing the proper thing and using a plate, but when his stomach growled so loudly he thought for sure it would wake Milton and Sandra. Instead, he dropped the mail on the Formica table and plopped down in the wobbly chair. He quickly took the hamburger from the sack. His hands couldn't move fast enough for his stomach. His mouth watered as he unwrapped the grease-stained butcher paper around the burger and sunk his teeth into it. The taste of melted cheese and warm burger made his eyes roll back in delicious bliss. Grease ran from the thick burger patty onto his lips, and he wiped his face with the back of his hand before sticking a handful of fries in his mouth to chase the burger.

When his brain could finally process something other than hunger, he reached across the table and pulled the mail toward him. *I hate mail. It's either bad news, bills, or junk*, he thought. But mostly, he knew it would be bills from the hospital or for Madelyn Ray's tombstone, not to mention all the other bills they got just for living. Joel took another bite of burger, then wiped his greasy hands on his work pants. He slowly thumbed through the mail. Under the water bill, he saw a thick white envelope addressed to him from the community college. His heart began to race. *Boy, they sure got those grades out fast*, he thought. He wished he'd left the mail in the mailbox at least for another night. The burger in his stomach now felt like a large rock. He took a deep breath to steady himself and ripped the flap of the envelope open. *Surely I pulled out at least a C. I'd take a D if it meant I passed.* Joel's fingers shook as he removed the folded paper and opened it. All of his hopes of barely skating by vanished in a puff of smoke. There beside the line of Principles of Management was a big fat F. He stared at it. *How will I ever be able to tell Hazel and Mr. Hal?* He should have told them when he started having trouble keeping up. He should have just dropped the class and focused on paying the bills, but how could he. Mr. Hal had encouraged him to go to school. He wanted him to gain some business sense so Joel could run the garage one day after he retired. And Joel liked the idea of one day owning his own business.

Inside his head, he could hear Hazel's voice telling him everything would be okay. He could take the class again. Joel's shoulders slumped forward. No longer hungry, he pushed the remaining burger and fries away. Taking classes cost money and they barely had enough to scrap two pennies together. And here he'd gone and wasted their hard-earned money. *It's so unfair!* He dropped his balled fist on the table, making it rock. He knew he should have spent more time studying, but how could he when living life was so expensive. He had to work to pay the bills and once he got home, he'd been too doggone tired to study. He had no idea how many times he'd woken up on the sofa asleep with his textbook laying across his chest. He glanced at the report card again. He'd have to think of a way to break it to Hazel before she got home. He reached across the table and grabbed the burger, ripping off another big bite. It would be fine. He'd try again. Maybe ask Mr. Hal for a loan or something to pay for the class.

He flipped through the rest of the mail as he munched on the rest of the burger. He opened the thin pages of an advertisement paper from Piggly Wiggly showing this week's specials. He folded it and laid it to the side for Hazel to clip the coupons. Underneath the paper, a small, yellow-tinted envelope caught his eye. *What's this? Surely not something else from the school.* He picked it up. His name and address had been scribbled on the envelope in black messy ink. He looked at the sender's information. It came from an address he didn't recognize. Above the address were the words "Selective Service." The hamburger in his mouth turned to chalk and he choked the rest down. His blood froze inside him. *My student status is gone.* He'd failed his class and brought this on himself. He wanted to hide the letter. Never open it. If he never saw the contents, did the letter really exist? His hands shook and he laid the envelope down before rubbing them across his pant legs. He had to open it. He had no choice.

His fingers fumbled as he turned the envelope over and ripped the flap open. He tried to calm his rapid breathing before pulling out the thick paper inside, but he couldn't get himself under control. He removed the paper from the envelope and held it out. His eyes blurred and he couldn't read it. He blinked and a feeling of lightheadedness passed over him. *Be a man*, his pa's voice echoed deep within him. His pa. *What would he think about this? What advice would he give me?* Joel's pa had gone to war and come back a changed, hard man. Even though he'd tried to stop drinking the hooch, Joel couldn't keep up with the number of times he'd fell off the wagon. His pa's life had been a rollercoaster of regrets and violence. And a life like that was not something Joel ever wanted for himself or for Hazel.

Joel held the paper so the kitchen light hit it. The paper looked official. A seal with an eagle surrounded by stars and a banner reading "Selective Service System" marked the left-hand corner.

He read the caption, "The President of the United States, To Joel Aaron Davenport."

His heart sank and he doubled over. All his hope shattered in a million pieces. He'd hoped it had been misdelivered or it had been a mistake, but seeing his name in black print solidified it; this was no blunder on the part of the sender. This letter was meant for him.

How'd they get word from the school about his grade point average dropping so quickly to revoke his student status? He'd never know the answer to that, but his hand shook so violently, he had to lay the letter on the table to continue reading.

"Greetings," he read and almost laughed. What an absurd way to start a letter like this.

> You are hereby ordered for induction into the Armed Forces of the United States and are ordered to report to the Lobby of the U.S. Post Office on Main Street in Fort Smith, Arkansas on July 27, 1968, at 6:30 a.m. for forwarding to an Armed Forces Induction Station.

Joel couldn't make out the name of the person who scrawled their signature on the line under his orders, but a deep hate burned inside the pit of his stomach for them. Under the signature in small print were directions informing him of what to bring with him. Near the bottom he read, "Willful failure to report at the place and hour of the day named in this Order subjects the violator to fine and imprisonment."

The violator? He'd already heard talk at the garage of people running to Canada or burning their letters and getting jailed for it. *For how long,* he wondered. *Would it be worth it?* He shook his head; he wasn't going to do that. He didn't run. He dragged a hand down his face. He'd heard that many others had volunteered immediately after getting their letter, hoping to get a better placement, maybe giving them some kind of choice over the matter. He wasn't sure that would even help.

Since America had entered the war, every day the radio and television endlessly spoke about communism and how America couldn't let Vietnam fall into the evil communist's grasp. He'd heard the word communism since he'd been little. To Joel, it sounded like some scary folklore or fable.

He wasn't even sure what it was exactly, and now he'd be forced to fight against it. This invisible force. He sucked in a breath, if only he had some magic beans and a beanstalk. Or a magical spell like in one of Hazel's stories.

Hazel! The thought of her name made his mind blur. As if he'd summoned her from afar, the telephone let out a loud ring, rocking violently on the wall. Joel jolted in the chair and his heart caught in his throat. It had to be her calling to tell him she would be coming home soon. Panic set in and he shivered.

How am I going to tell Hazel?

Chapter 9

HAZEL, JULY 1968

Hazel lay in the dark, staring at her bedroom wall. Her whole body felt sore and ached from crying. She could feel the pressure of Joel's body touching her back. She listened to him breathing. She shuddered and clapped a hand around her mouth to hold back the sob wanting to escape. She'd have to say good-bye to him today. He'd be gone for ten weeks for basic training. After that, the Army would more than likely ship him off to war. She couldn't stand it. *How can they take my husband?*

She felt Joel move and the bed mattress rocked as he turned. He wrapped his arm around her waist and pulled her closer to him. He pushed his face through her hair and kissed the nape of her neck. She trembled.

"Shh, I know," he whispered.

She thought she'd only been shedding silent tears. He grabbed her shoulder and turned her to him. He propped himself on his elbow beside her. His face inches from hers. His warm breath hit her wet cheeks, making her shiver. He leaned down and gave her a light kiss. They stared at each other, neither saying a word. They'd talked so much over the last few months since he'd received his draft notice that there were no more words to say. He was going. He lowered down to press his lips hard against hers.

She groaned and enclosed her arms around his neck. The heat from his bare skin warmed her. She pulled his body closer. She wanted to remember all of this, his touch, his smell, the feel of his hands on her body.

Later, after they'd made love again, he held her in his arms. Even though she lay close to him, her body still felt cold. The deafening ring of the alarm clock startled her. *Is it three-thirty already?*

Joel rolled over and hit the clock hard. "I hate that thing," he said, leaning up in the bed.

She lay on her side and watched him. He rubbed his eyes with the heels of his hands, then stretched his arms above his head and yawned. Moonlight streaked across his face from the window. *He's so handsome with his strong jaw and stubbled chin.* She wanted to burn each line of his face into her memory.

"It's so early," he said. His mouth opened wide, and he let out another loud yawn.

Last night, he'd decided to leave two hours early to make sure he made it on time. He didn't want something to happen, and the government think he'd deserted. He leaned over and kissed her cheek.

"I'm going to get a hot shower. It may be the last one I get for a while."

She threw an arm over her face, covering her eyes. "Don't say that."

He pulled her arm down to force her to look at him. "I'm going to miss you terribly, but you are going to make it. You will have your dad and sister and Milton and Sandra. You won't be alone. And I'll write to you every chance I get. Who knows, maybe I'll get there, and they won't want me."

"I hope they think your incompetent and useless."

Joel chuckled, "We can only hope."

It was still dark when he gathered his bag to leave. Ruthie and their father had woken. They walked over from the duplex they shared and stood by Hazel. They all watched as Joel threw his bag in the bed of the truck, the one Mr. Hal had let him borrow all those years ago. Hazel crossed her arms around her body. A cool wind blew, making the new wind chimes Joel had bought her clink and tinkle in the breeze.

"Now when you hear the wind chimes play their music, remember to say a prayer for me," he'd said as he hung them between their door and the Lewises' door.

She shook her head. She'd never forget to pray for him.

As if the music had summoned them, the Lewises opened their door. They crept out and slowly closed it behind them.

"Mikey and baby Emanuel are still sleeping," Milton said.

"Mannie won't stay asleep long," Sandra said, deep dark circles had settled under her eyes. "I don't think he's slept more than two hours straight since we brought him home from the hospital. But we couldn't miss the good-byes."

The word, "good-bye," made Hazel shake. Ruthie laid a hand on her shoulder. Hazel blinked her eyes to keep from crying again, but they'd already begun to fill with tears.

Joel gave Milton and Sandra a hug. Then walked to where she stood with her father and Ruthie.

He shook her father's hand, but her father pulled him in for an embrace. "You be careful, son, you hear?"

"Yes, Mr. McKay, I will. Please take care of my Hazel," he said, looking at Hazel.

Her stomach clenched. *His Hazel.* She felt herself breaking down. She wanted to hold it together for him. She wanted him to think she was brave too. She'd heard basic training could be mentally and physically demanding. He needed to focus on what he had to do and not worry about her. But her resolve to tough it out was quickly slipping, and she felt her emotions on the verge of breaking apart again. She could already feel herself sinking into the same darkness that surrounded her after losing Madelyn Ray.

He bent down to hug Ruthie, who sniffed and wiped the streaks of tears running down her face. At the sight of Ruthie's tears, Hazel lost it. Joel made it to her in two steps and wrapped her in his arms. "I love you," he whispered.

Hazel tried to say it back, but she couldn't get out the words. Her throat closed shut and sobs rocked through her body. Joel tightened his arms around her.

"Shh, it's okay. I know," he whispered into her hair.

When he released her, it felt as if her heart would stop beating. He still stood before her, and she missed him already. Her body shook, and he ran his hands down her arms to steady her. He looked over at Ruthie.

"Don't forget your promise."

Hazel's head whipped toward Ruthie. *What promise?*

"I won't forget," Ruthie said, slugging him gently in the arm. "You take care of yourself."

He smiled, and his eyes drifted on each person there. Milton and Sandra, Arvel and Ruthie, then lastly to her. He bent down to give her one last quick kiss before turning and heading to his truck. Hazel felt like he took a piece of her heart with him.

They all stood outside in the dark and watched until his truck lights disappeared down the street in the distance.

Hazel wrapped her arms around her middle and shivered. "What was that about? What promise are you keeping?" she asked Ruthie.

Ruthie slipped an arm around her back and leaned her head on Hazel's shoulder. "I promised to get you out of the house. To not let you coop yourself up inside."

Hazel's breath hitched. *Oh, Joel*, she sighed. Of course, he'd try to care for her even when he was gone.

***

On Tuesday, work passed by in a blur. Hazel's mind and emotions twisted in a continuous cycle of worry and sadness. A few times, she'd had to excuse herself to go to the restroom to cry. Joel had been gone one whole week. She'd received a letter in the mail when he first arrived. It had been short and to the point. He was doing well, and he missed and loved her like crazy. When the clock at the back of the store's hands hit six, she bolted from the store for home. She'd held in most of her tears almost all day, and she needed privacy to let them pour from her eyes. But when she opened her door, the television blared up to meet her, and Ruthie came out of the kitchen.

Hazel must have looked surprised because Ruthie wiped her hands on her skirt and said, "Don't worry, I didn't break in. Sandra let me in. I just washed all your dishes, so now you don't have an excuse to miss tonight's meeting."

Hazel's stomach clenched. She needed to be alone. She couldn't handle people, not tonight. She shook her head. "I can't Ruthie. I'm really not feeling up to it tonight." The resolve and tears she'd been holding back began to flow down her cheeks. She wiped her face with her hands, and her fingers came back stained with black mascara.

Ruthie hurried to her and gave her a tight hug. She patted Hazel's back. "You can do it, and you will. I made Joel a promise not to let you sit and wallow by yourself." She pulled back to look at Hazel. "And geez Louise, most of these women understand exactly what you're feeling. Many of them already have husbands or sons fighting in the war. You're going. You need it."

First, Hazel wanted to scream at her. She didn't care about anyone else's husbands or sons. She was worried about Joel. Her Joel. Hazel's shoulders slumped forward. All her fight left her. It wasn't true, she did care about the other women's husbands and sons. She'd seen the women at the meetings as they shared letters they'd received in the mail from Vietnam, their enthusiasm palatable. She'd also seen the distant look they got in their eyes as they spoke about missing the men in their lives. She wondered if she had that same distant look now. She squeezed her eyes shut. Joel would want her to go, so she would go.

⁕⁕⁕

They left for the meeting early. The sun set the blue sky on fire, but Hazel's world felt gray and dim. Ruthie drove Hazel's car while Hazel sat in silence, staring out the window. She watched as they passed houses and yards with mothers calling their children in for dinner. Fathers parked their vehicles and got out after a long day of work. Anger began to seethe inside her heart. Apparently not everyone was forced to leave their families.

Once they made it to the library, Hazel and Ruthie entered through the side doors. Immediately, hands and arms surrounded Hazel.

"Oh, you poor dear," Alice said, squeezing Hazel so hard she couldn't breathe.

A pregnant Margarette Ann reached around her belly, that grew bigger every day and grabbed Hazel in a side hug. She'd only been married a year to the town's new pharmacist and already a baby was on the way. Tears poured down Margarette Ann's face and dripped on her shirt. "I-I can't even," she heaved in a breath, "imagine. I d-don't think I could handle it." She clamped her free hand over her mouth.

Ruthie shook her head, "Margarette Ann, why are you crying? It's not like Scott is going to be drafted. He has asthma and his glasses are as thick as the bottom of a Coke bottle. He isn't going anywhere."

Hazel couldn't help but smile at Ruthie's description of Scott. Alice finally released her hold on Hazel's neck and took Hazel's hands in hers, "Oh sweetie, you must feel just awful. What can I do for you?"

Hazel looked from Alice to Margarette Ann, to Ruthie, and she knew Ruthie and Joel had been right. She had people. Maybe she could do this—maybe she could be strong for Joel.

Chapter 10

RUTHIE, AUGUST 1968

Ruthie's frazzled nerves had her on edge. The bottom of her feet ached in her shoes and her nurse uniform clung to her back as she headed toward the dungeon. The curved metal bedpan she held needed to be dumped and washed in the bedpan machine. She and the other nurses had taken to calling the bedpan machine "Arnold" in honor of Krissy's pig-headed boyfriend that cheated on her. Ruthie felt like she'd not had one minute to herself all week. They'd had several emergencies at the hospital, so every day was run and go. After busy days like these, she'd given anything to go home to the duplex she shared with her dad and collapse on the sofa. He didn't care if she put her aching feet on the coffee table to watch television. But instead of relaxing, she felt the need to walk over to Hazel and Joel's duplex and spend time with Hazel. Although Hazel had told her on numerous occasions she didn't need a babysitter, Ruthie thought maybe she did. Plus, she had to keep her promise to Joel and get Hazel out of the house. So, no matter how busy or tired she was, Ruthie would drag her sister to the movies at the new indoor theater that had opened downtown or to Fort Smith for some window shopping.

Ruthie pushed the dungeon's door open. The smell of strong cleaning chemicals burned the inside of her nostrils and the harsh glare from the florescent lights made her squint. The washing machine and dryer rattled as they washed and dried hospital bedding. Ruthie hurried to rinse the bedpan before throwing it in Arnold. She wanted out of the dungeon and quick. If she got caught in here by one of the superior nurses, she'd be stuck in here for hours, cleaning and sterilizing things in the huge metal sink. She hated cleaning. Her hands were already rough and cracked from the last time she had to serve her penance in the dungeon.

Ruthie threw the bedpan in the machine and rushed to the door. Before she could open it, the door flew open, and Joan Battalou burst inside. She leaned over, panting.

"Oh Ruthie," she said, her chest heaving. "There's been another emergency."

Ruthie's heart began to pick up speed. "What happened?"

"Two car wrecks. They were speed racing or speed failing more like it. The idiots could have killed themselves. One driver ended up with a broken arm and leg and needs surgery. The other driver ended up with only a sprained ankle. Not from the wreck, mind you, but from tripping as he ran away from the wreck." Joan shook her head. "Can you wrap the ankle sprain? Krissy and Charlene are already assisting Dr. Sullivan with the other driver."

Ruthie pushed a loose blonde curl behind her ear. "Goodness, what flakes! Yes, of course, I can wrap the sprained ankle. What room?"

"Room two. Everything you need is already there. And when you're done, go clean room one. There's quite a mess in there from the other driver." Joan wiped her sweaty brow with her arm. "Boy, you'd think the scorching hot weather would keep everyone indoors, but not this year. Instead, it's driven everyone mad."

Ruthie had to agree. This month had hit an all-time record high for heat and emergencies.

She made her way to room two. The door stood open a crack and Ruthie heard murmuring and giggling coming from inside. She slinked closer to the entryway and leaned her head near the opening to listen. Her breath hitched when she recognized one of the voices.

"Yeah, I mean I wanted to go to Nam. You know, and fight with the boys. But I got bad eyes from an old football injury. And the doctors refused to let me go. I begged. Even fell on my knees. But it was no good. I even threatened their licenses, but, you know, in the end, I couldn't go."

"Oh Greg, you're so brave," a high sing-song voice said.

Ruthie's stomach twisted. Her emotions still raw from watching Hazel fall apart after Joel left in early July. Plus, the thought of Ronnie already there fighting and risking his life made her want to punch Greg in the nose. She squeezed her eyes closed. She couldn't punch a patient and that's exactly what Greg was, a patient. She took in three long breaths and pushed the air out through her nose. She had to get a hold of herself. When her heart rate had slowed somewhat and she felt composed, she grabbed the chart from the plastic pocket on the front of the door and entered room two.

She looked down at the chart, not ready to make eye contact yet. She flipped the pages over, half examining the information. Her heart pounded in her chest, but she willed herself to be calm.

"Good evening, I will be wrapping your ankle."

"Ruthie?"

The muscles in her back tightened. She lowered the chart. Greg sat on the hospital bed with his foot propped high on three white pillows. He wore a wrinkled collared shirt stained with dirt. His pants were torn at the knees, but his hair sat perfectly in place thanks to the hair grease. The woman beside him wore a pink tailored dress with a thin matching belt cinched around her small waist. Her brown bouffant hair rose inches from her face.

"Excuse me?" Ruthie tilted her head, feigning like she didn't recognize him.

"It's me, Greg." He pointed to himself with a dirty hand. He looked at the brunette beside him, whose face had contorted in confusion. "We went out a few times."

"Oh," the brunette said, her voice dropping an octave. Her face scrunched and she narrowed her eyes on Ruthie, sizing her up. The brunette puckered her bright red lips.

Ruthie stepped forward and returned Ms. Red Lip's stare. "Would you mind heading to the waiting room so I can begin?"

Her red lips turned down and her head whipped to look at Greg. She took one of his hands in hers. "But I want to stay here with my Greggy. He needs me."

Ruthie flipped through the chart. "Well, I guess you can stay since he's too scared to sit by himself for a simple ankle wrap."

Out of the corner of her eye, she saw Greg's body stiffen.

He coughed, "Please Diane, wait in the waiting room. I'll be fine." He lifted her hand and kissed the back of it lightly.

She puckered her bottom lip, letting it stick out far and full. "But?" she whined.

He kissed the back of her hand again, "I promise, it won't take long."

She gave Ruthie a death glare. "Fine. I'll go, but I won't be far."

Oh, good grief, now that's a threat if I ever heard one. Ruthie tried not to roll her eyes. She had to act professionally.

Diane turned sharply and stomped out the door, her pink kitten heels clicking on the hard floor.

Ruthie closed the door behind her and got to business. Silently, she pulled up his pant leg to look at Greg's ankle. His ankle looked like a huge swollen bulge. The skin had pulled taut and already started to turn purplish around the area. In the room, Mrs. Battalou had left rags with a bowl of warm soapy water, towels, and the wrapping material. Ruthie took the rag and wet it. She began to lightly rub the rag along his foot and leg to clean away the dirt and mud.

Greg cleared his throat, "So, how you been?"

"Good and you?" Ruthie continued to clean but did not look up.

He chuckled nervously. "Well, I'm great. Except for this, you know," he said and motioned to his ankle.

"Heard you were speed racing."

He scratched at a dry mud spot on his arm. "You heard that?"

She looked up to meet his eyes and he gave her a half grin.

She nodded and continued to wipe the dirt and grime from his leg and ankle. "Well, you do seem to be doing good. She's very pretty."

Greg pushed a hand through his gelled hair. It didn't move. "Oh Diane, yeah, she's um, fun," he said. His cheeks turned a light shade of pink.

"I see," Ruthie said, carefully patting his foot and ankle with a dry cloth.

She grabbed the bandage and began to wrap. She started at the ball of his foot below his toes. "I overheard you mention something about Vietnam as I was coming in."

He gave her a full toothy smile. "Yeah, you know, Diane was asking about it. I told her I'd have gone if it wasn't for my eyesight. It's bad, you know."

Ruthie nodded and continued to wrap. She wasn't sure if he remembered telling her about how his father had gotten a doctor friend to write a fake letter to keep him from being drafted. Maybe he'd forgotten all about it or maybe he'd repeated the lie so many times, he'd begun to believe it. She didn't look at him as she moved the bandage to make a figure eight pattern from his foot to ankle.

"Ouch, um, Ruthie that's a little tight."

She looked at him, blinking her eyes. "Is it?" she asked in a sweet voice.

His face grimaced, "Yeah, just a little."

She pulled the bandage tighter.

"Oh," he said, gritting his teeth.

"Sorry about that," she apologized, not feeling sorry at all. "But it needs to be tight to keep the ankle secure," she explained, wishing she could call Diane back in the room and pull the bandage hard enough that he'd confess all his lies. She shook her head. *What would be the point?*

Ruthie wrapped the bandage twice more around his lower leg, a few inches from his ankle and finished it by securing the bandage with a small fastener. She lightly patted his ankle.

"Ow," he flinched.

"All finished," she said, turning to walk out of the room.

"Thank—" he started to say, but she walked out the door without waiting for him to finish.

After work, Ruthie plopped into her car. The seat burned the skin on the back of her legs. She squirmed around until she found a place that didn't scald her so she could pull out of the parking lot. Although she hated the heat, she loved how the sun still shone brightly in the sky even though it was past seven. She drove, knowing she needed to head to Hazel's house, but she couldn't make herself turn the wheel of her car to head that way. Instead, she went to the elementary school to find her dad. He stayed there most days after he'd gotten his janitorial duties done and worked in the shed at the back of the school. The principal, Mr. Crowley, was one of her dad's old school buddies. He'd given her father permission to use the shed for his woodwork. Her dad still called all the carpentry he was doing a "hobby," but she wasn't so sure it qualified as a hobby anymore, not really. His handmade rocking chairs, tables, and canes had really taken off, and people from as far as Magnolia, Arkansas, came to purchase them. Sometimes the money he made from selling things from his so-called hobby made him more than being the janitor at the elementary school.

She turned the wheel, pulling onto the dirt road that ran to the back lot of the school. Small green holly bushes lined the road. A shot of red raced past her windshield, making her swerve. She stopped to catch her breath. She watched the cardinal land on a bush, pluck a leaf off with its beak, and fly away. Her heart sank. She remembered when she was little, running through the woods with Hazel. They'd search for birds, so they could document their findings in that old bird book their father had gifted to them. They'd pretend to search for their princes. Well, Hazel had found hers, but Ruthie wanted more than just a prince. She wanted adventure. She craved it. Had it really been that long ago that they played in the forest? Could she fly off one day like that cardinal? She doubted it. She shook her head, pushing the gas pedal to drive on.

When she drove past the school, she couldn't help but smile when she saw her dad sitting outside in front of the shed in one of two rocking chairs, sipping from a coffee mug.

"Isn't it too late to be drinking coffee?" she asked, getting out of the car. "Drinking coffee this late is bad for you." She opened her mouth to give him a proper scolding, but he held up his hand.

"Well, I'll be, Ruthie, it's good to see you too," he said with a sarcastic tone. He took another sip from his coffee mug. "It's water anyway. I didn't have anything else to use."

She chuckled and plopped down in the rocking chair beside his. She ran her hands down the armrests. The wood had been expertly smoothed. "This chair is nice."

"Thank you," he said, his grin broadening. "Just trying them out before a nice couple from Mountain View comes to pick them up tomorrow." He took a sip from the coffee cup. "I'm so glad to see you, but I wasn't expecting you. Don't you usually visit with Hazel after work?"

Ruthie bit the inside of her jaw. "Yeah, I do. And I'm heading there after this. I just wanted to come see my good ol' dad. Is anything wrong with that?"

He narrowed his eyes. "No, of course not. I'm always glad to see ya."

She felt shame burning her cheeks. She desperately needed to talk to someone about this crazy urge inside her constantly growing bigger. Seeing Greg today with that girl tipped her over the edge. She didn't even like Greg! Still, it was everything he represented. She loved Waldron and her family with all her heart, but she needed to feel free. She needed to get away, like that cardinal. Live a life somewhere other than here. A headache began to form, and she massaged her temples. Her thoughts were a muddled mess. Even though they were just thoughts, she felt guilty for even having them. The guilt scraped at the back of her mind all day and night. She thought she might be starting to go mad. She glanced over at her dad. *Would he hate me if I told him?* She rocked back and forth in the chair. The gravel crunched underneath the rocker. She wasn't sure how to even put her feelings into actual words. *Would it hurt him if he knew I want to leave here? I'm a horrible daughter.*

"Is there something else, peanut? Is it work?"

She smiled. He could always tell when something bothered her. She shook her head, "Work is just so..."

He chuckled, "Work?"

She laughed, "Yeah, it's a lot, but I love it. I feel like it's what I'm meant to do."

He took another sip from his cup and gave her a side-eyed look. "You know, you don't always have to go to Hazel's after work. You can have some fun on your own, do your own thing, or rest. She's strong too. Even though it doesn't seem like it sometimes. She is. And she doesn't need you babysitting her. Plus, she has me and her friends too."

Ruthie clenched her jaw. Hazel was part of her problem. Being free to have an adventure of her own meant breaking her promise to Joel. He'd asked her to do one thing—keep an eye on Hazel. A weight settled on Ruthie's chest. She looked over at her dad. She'd have to be careful around him and keep her emotions in check because he could read her mind. Or it seemed that way a lot of the times. *What if he sees everything bothering me? What if he's figured out what I want to do and tries to stop me?*

"I know she doesn't need a babysitter. I don't like her being alone, that's all. And I promised Joel."

"Is that all that's botherin' you? Is that everything?" he asked with one eyebrow raised.

She gave a curt nod, "Yep, that's everything. I think I'm just mostly tired."

"Hmm," her dad mused. "Want a drink?"

She involuntarily touched her throat. Keeping her secret desires in check was hard work, and she did feel parched. She coughed. "Yes, just a sip. That would be great. Thanks, Daddy."

He passed her the coffee mug.

She took the mug and took a deep sip. When the liquid hit her tongue, she gasped and spat out black coffee onto the rocks in front of her feet. "Hey, you lied! You said you were drinking water."

He leaned back in the rocking chair, a crooked smile spread across his face, and he folded his arms across his chest. "Well now, that makes us both liars. But I guess when you're ready to talk, you'll come tell me what's really bothering you."

Chapter 11

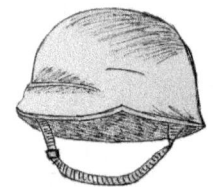

JOEL, SEPTEMBER 1968

It was September, but in his house, it was Thanksgiving. He'd been allowed to telephone home last week to tell Hazel the news. They were sending him to Vietnam. They'd give him one month to get his affairs in order and then he'd be shipped off to the war. Every time he heard the word "war," his stomach clenched. On the telephone, Hazel tried to sound light, but he could hear the strain in her voice.

"Then it's settled, we'll have a huge Thanksgiving dinner when you get home and then a couple weeks later, we'll celebrate Christmas. We'll put up the tree and decorations and everything. I'm not letting you miss anything," she'd said.

He didn't argue with her. In the back of his mind, a voice said, "Yeah, celebrate with your family, it'll probably be the last time you see them."

He'd tried to push those voices away, but no matter how hard he pushed, sometimes he couldn't stop them from sneaking through.

"I'll have Dad find your pa and let him know too."

Joel felt a lump form in the back of his throat. "Have you heard from him any?" Before he'd left for basic training, he'd traveled to his old house on the hill to tell his pa about being drafted. His pa had been back on the booze again, the air thick with the sour smell of alcohol. His pa had done so good for a while, not visiting any bars and staying away from the junk. The good times, though, were short lived, and it crushed Joel every time he back tracked.

"You're gonna die, boy, if you don't run. Run to Canada and take Hazel with you."

That had been his pa's advice. Advice he'd considered but didn't take.

"Yes, I saw him last week in the store. He looked, um, better."

Joel knew Hazel was being kind and trying not to worry him. She quickly changed the subject back to the celebrations.

After their telephone call, the next two weeks had felt like the longest he'd had since he'd arrived at basic. He wanted to get home. He needed to hold Hazel in his arms, but the days passed by at a snail's pace. Until finally he stood in front of his front door. A huge wooden turkey hung from a hook. It sat perfectly straight, so he knew Milton had hung it. He could hear excited murmuring and muffled words from behind the door. Even though the duffle bag on his back weighed a ton, his whole body felt light. He'd come home.

When he opened the door and walked inside, his eyes barely had time to register all the happy smiling faces before Hazel rushed to him, knocking him back out through the doorway. They stumbled down the cement stoop, but she didn't seem to mind. She wrapped her arms around his neck. Her face wet with tears. She dotted his face with kisses. His forehead, both cheeks, his nose, his chin, and finally his lips. His heavy duffle bag sent him off kilter and he dropped it. He needed both arms to embrace his wife. He kissed her lips hard, savoring the taste of them. It had been too long, and he pulled her closer to him.

At the front door, he heard someone clear their throat. Joel and Hazel stopped and turned to see Ruthie, leaning against the door frame with arms crossed in front of her. A sly smile spread across her lips.

"I mean, we can all go if you both need some time alone."

Hazel's cheeks flushed pink, and Joel laughed. He grabbed Hazel, leaned her back in a smooth dance move, and kissed her deep before lifting her back up. Her hair had gotten longer, and it swished in the air. He gave her lips another light peck, then grabbed the strap of his duffle bag and swung it over his shoulder. He took Hazel's hand in his, feeling the fragile softness. He looked into her dark, beautiful eyes and together they went inside.

Yips and squeals made the cramped duplex fill with noise like a stadium. He couldn't quite figure out how everyone was able to cram inside the small space. The smell of turkey and fixings made his stomach ache and his mouth water. He hadn't had good food in ages, and Tupperware containers covered the kitchen counter. Joel felt like a rubber ball being bounced from one smiling face to another. Each person hugged him, patted his back, or kissed his cheek.

"It's good to have you back, son," Mr. McKay said, clapping him on the shoulder.

"You look so thin. Hal, doesn't he look so thin. Are you hungry? I made your favorite peach cobbler," Mrs. Anne said. Her hair fixed into a high bun that sat frozen on top of her head. The stiff hair brushed across his cheek when she leaned in to hug him.

"Thank you, I can't wait to get a big helping of it."

A boy that wasn't so little anymore ran to him with arms wide open. Joel hefted him up in the air and swung him around in a circle. Mikey threw his head back and laughed.

"I can't believe it. It's like you've grown a foot since the last time I saw you," Joel said.

Mikey's bright smile beamed across his face. His head nodded vigorously. "I'm six now."

"Whoa! You'll be driving a car soon."

"Not too fast with that, mister," Sandra said, walking to them. She gave Joel a tight hug. "No first grader of mine is going to be driving a car."

"Awww, I could do it Ma," Mikey said.

Joel tickled him and he giggled. "Well, when you're old enough and your mom approves, I'll teach you. Deal?"

Mikey nodded, "Deal. I'm going to go get my new truck to show you. It's green."

"I'd love to see it," Joel said and set him down on the ground. He ran off through the crowd, dodging between legs toward the living room.

"Well, there's the Army man," Milton said, coming toward Joel. In his arms, he held a babbling baby.

Joel held out his finger. Emanuel tried to grab it and stick it in his mouth. "He's grown too, good grief. How long was I gone?"

Milton smiled, "Too long, man. We sure missed you around here."

Hazel came up beside Joel, her arm slipped around his waist. "He's such a sweet boy. He's already pulling up."

Joel looked at her. A momentary fear seized him, and he worried if the baby would bring back bad memories for Hazel of losing Madelyn Ray. *She can't go back to that dark place, not with me being gone and not able to help her,* he thought. But he quickly realized he didn't need to worry, and his fears dissipated into nothingness when he saw the happy glow on her face.

She leaned over and carefully kissed the baby's cheek. "Isn't Mannie so adorable?"

A calm passed over Joel, and he knew Hazel would be fine. With the crowd of people surrounding them, he knew she'd be cared for and loved while he fought in Vietnam. He couldn't take his eyes off of his wife, she looked beautiful, not skin and bones anymore. He bent down to kiss her. "Adorable," he agreed.

"It's great to have you back, man," Milton said.

"It's great to be back."

He and Hazel said hi to Alice and David. Their young daughter dressed in a frilly pink dress. Joel saw Margarette Ann. She looked like she might pop any second. He leaned over and whispered in Hazel's ear, "I thought she would have had the baby by now. She looked like she was ready to before I left."

Hazel giggled, "I'm not certain because they haven't said, but I think they might be having twins."

Joel gave a low whistle, "That'll be a blast."

Hazel hit him and laughed.

Joel watched as Scott made Margarette Ann sit down on the sofa and refused to let her get up. He made his way to the kitchen to get her a drink.

"Due this week," he told Joel, "And I still couldn't get her to stay home. She said only labor would keep her away."

Joel and Hazel thanked him for coming and followed him into the living room to say hi to Margarette Ann. Before Joel could say anything, Ruthie looped an arm around Joel's neck, putting him in a headlock that nearly knocked him over.

"It's good to have you back."

He stumbled then righted himself. "It's good to be back," he said, reaching up with his arm to ruffle the top of her blonde hair.

She laughed and let him go. "Hey, that's cheating! And I'm an adult now," she protested and patted her hair back down.

Margarette Ann chortled and put her hands on her stomach. "Please Ruthie, don't make me laugh. I'll give birth to these babies right here on this sofa."

Hazel looked at Joel, her eyes wide. "Twins!" she squealed.

❧❧❧❧❧ ❧❧❧❧❧

L ater that night, Joel laid on the bed patting his own bulging stomach. He felt a little miserable, and he'd probably be sick later, but still, he couldn't stop himself. Each bite tasted like the first time. The first time he'd had turkey, mashed potatoes, cornbread dressing, peach cobbler. He groaned.

He could hear the water running from the bathroom sink. Then the clink of Hazel tapping her toothbrush against it. He turned to his side and waited for her to come out. When she did, she paused in the doorway. A long dark shadow of her silhouette stretched across the bed. The shadow made it impossible for him to see her expression. She wore a light blue nightgown that hung loosely from two tiny straps on her shoulders. He could almost make out the outline of her body through the sheer material. Down deep, his body stirred. It had been too long, and he'd missed her badly. So badly, he could physically feel his heart hurting. She walked toward him. He leaned up and clasped her forearm in his hand. He pulled her down onto the bed beside him and wrapped her in his arms.

Her brown eyes were dark circles in the night. "Did you enjoy your Thanksgiving?" she whispered.

"I did," he said, pulling her body closer to his. He smelled her fresh floral scent and felt her warmth against his bare chest. "I missed you so much."

Her eyelashes fluttered, and she shook her head. "I missed you more than that."

"It's not possible," he said. He ran his hand over the smooth skin of her arm, and she shivered. He planted a light kiss on her chin and moved up to her right cheek near her lips. Her warm breath began to come out in pants. He kissed her left cheek at the corner of her mouth. She groaned when he acted as if he would kiss her lips but instead moved to the tip of her nose. He wanted to savor this moment, not rush it. He'd dreamed of this moment so many nights on that thin hard mattress in his bunk at basic training. When he couldn't stand it anymore, he pressed his lips hard against hers. Hazel arched her back, pushing her body tight against him. He let himself go and lost himself in a rhythm he was sure he'd forgotten.

The next morning, he woke up entwined in sheets and Hazel's legs. A chill spread over him and he saw their comforter on the floor. He moved so he could rest his head in the bend of his arm. Hazel stretched beside him; the soft skin of her back rubbed against his side. His heart fluttered. She yawned and flopped over, grabbing the sheet and pulling it around her.

"Brr, it's chilly in here."

A crease ran along her forehead from the pillow and her eyes were heavy from sleep. She looked beautiful. She smiled at him, but it quickly faded. Her eyes glistened.

"Please don't leave me again."

Joel's heart fell. He kissed her. A tear ran down her face to their lips. He tasted the saltiness. He leaned back, "I don't want to. You gotta know that."

Hazel nodded. He reached up and took her face in his hand. With his thumb, he wiped away her tears.

"It'll only be a year. Eighteen months at the most," he said, even though he knew it could be as long as two. "That's only five hundred and forty-seven days. What's five hundred and forty-seven days compared to a lifetime?"

Another tear escaped from the corner of her eye, and he stopped it with his thumb.

"Promise?" she asked, her voice heavy.

"I promise," he said, knowing it may be a promise he couldn't keep.

Chapter 12

HAZEL, OCTOBER 1968

H azel rose early and heated some water in the kettle on the stove. When the kettle whistled, she rushed to remove it from the heat and slowly poured the steaming liquid into the aluminum hourglass siphon cup that sat on the top of her coffee pot. The hot water drenched the fresh coffee beans she'd placed inside the paper filter. Below the cone, a magical substance began to drip into the pot. The smell of coffee energized her. She needed to have it together today. As she continued to pour, she looked around the kitchen. She'd hung Christmas decorations everywhere. Tinsel had even made it into the kitchen. It hung in draping arches around their few cabinets. She knew her house and the Lewises' house looked strange with Christmas decorations on the front doors while everyone else in town had pumpkins on their porches. But she wanted to make things special for Joel. The news had been filled with only grim reports from the war. The death count of the soldiers climbed higher every day, and Joel would be there soon. Surrounded by danger. *What if he never came back?* The thought passed through her mind so quickly, she shook, splashing some of the hot water onto the kitchen counter.

"That smells wonderful."

The sound of Joel's voice startled her, and she spun around, drenching the counter with more water.

"Whoa," he said and rushed to grab a dish towel. "I didn't mean to startle you."

Her cheeks blazed with heat. "Oh sorry, I was just thinkin'." She hurried to sit the kettle back down on the stove and watched as he cleaned up her mess. She prayed he couldn't read her mind or know what she'd been thinking.

"So, what do we have planned for today," he asked, wringing the wet towel into the sink.

She rushed him and wrapped her arms around his waist. He let out an oof before wrapping his arms around her.

She placed her chin on his chest and looked up at his face. "Well, this evening, everyone will be here to open presents. And Dad and Ms. Faye are bringing a ham."

He bent down and kissed her forehead. "By everyone, do you mean my pa too?"

She made herself smile. She didn't want to tell him what she had to do to get his pa to come. When she'd called his pa last week, she'd been surprised that he'd answered the telephone at all. She'd feared that she'd be forced to hike all the way up the hill to the old house to find him. The relief she'd felt about not having to trek out to the woods by herself was short-lived as the conversation did not go like she'd expected.

"Mr. Davenport?"

"Yeah, that's me."

"It's Hazel. Um, we're having a sort of Christmas party for Joel this Saturday. You know he's leaving on Sunday. I wanted to invite you. I know he'd love to see you before he left."

The silence that followed made the hairs on the back of Hazel's neck stand. She could practically hear him chewing it over in his mind.

"Christmas party?"

"Yes, he won't be here for Christmas, and I didn't want him to miss it."

He laughed, the sound deep and scratchy. Then without missing a beat, his voice went flat. "Is Hal Sutherland going to be there?"

Her head swarmed and she didn't know how to reply. She knew Joel's pa hated Mr. Hal, but neither she nor Joel had any idea about why. She'd suggested asking her dad about it, but Joel had said, "Why do we care? Whatever it is, it has nothing to do with us." And that ended the conversation. The problem forgotten—until now.

"I won't be coming if Hal's going to be there," Mr. Davenport had said, the words sounded like a threat.

Hazel's chest constricted, making it hard to breathe. She had to think fast. To say something, but nothing sensible came to mind. So, she lied. "Don't worry, Mr. Hal said he couldn't make it." The shame she'd felt at that moment made her nauseous. *What am I going to do? How can I keep Mr. Hal and Mrs. Anne from coming to the party?* She'd just seen Mrs. Anne in Piggly Wiggly, and she'd been so excited about the party. *This is terrible!*

"Good, then I'll be there. I can't believe my boy is going off to that godforsaken war."

He'd hung up without a good-bye. Hazel had stood there frozen with the receiver pressed against her ear, for how long, she didn't know.

"Hey, what's going on in that beautiful head of yours?" Joel asked, shaking her from her memories.

She blinked, "Oh nothing, just thinking about tonight."

"You didn't answer my question, is pa going to be here?"

She nodded, "Yes, yes sorry. He'll be here." She stood on her tiptoes and gave him a quick kiss on the lips before heading to the counter to finish the coffee. She carefully removed the hot siphon cup and placed it in the sink. She poured the hot brown liquid into the two mugs she'd set on the counter. She turned and handed him a mug. She so wanted tonight to be special, but her stomach twisted into knots. She'd spent days after her telephone conversation with Joel's pa fretting about what to do. She'd hardly slept a wink. Her fingernails were bitten down to the quick, and she still had no idea how to fix the situation. But there was no more time left, and she couldn't procrastinate anymore. She had to do something before whatever this thing was between his pa and Mr. Hal ruined the night. She took a sip from her mug. When the warm coffee hit her tongue, a thought popped into her head. *Holy cow!* She could kick herself for not thinking of it sooner. She'd call Mrs. Anne. She'd know what to do. She always knew what to do and who else better would know the history between Joel's pa and her own husband.

She watched as Joel took a sip from his own mug. She needed to get out of the house without him suspecting anything. "You got any plans this morning?" she asked, trying to keep her voice casual.

"Nah, not really."

Her heart sank as she casually took another sip of coffee.

"Well, you know what..."

Joel's words made her lift her head and her heart picked up its pace.

"There is actually something I'd like to do before I leave."

It took everything inside her not to pepper him with questions and rush him out the door. She breathed in and let it out slowly before responding, "Oh yeah, what's that?"

"I might run up to Ronnie's parents' house and visit them. I haven't seen them in a while, and I promised Ronnie I'd check up on them from time to time."

The tight muscles in Hazel's back loosened. "That's a wonderful idea." She smiled. *He'll be gone for hours. I'll be able to finally get this mess with his pa fixed.*

❦

When Hazel arrived at Billy's Coffee and More, Mrs. Anne sat in a booth already waiting for her. She'd been happy Mrs. Anne had suggested meeting for breakfast when Hazel had called her.

In front of Mrs. Anne sat a white mug with the word "Billy's" across it in red bubble letters. People filled almost every booth, eating breakfast and drinking coffee. Waitresses rushed around delivering orders. The air smelled of grease and bacon. Hazel's stomach growled when the cook yelled from the grill, "Order's up!" Hazel had no idea Billy's was such a popular Saturday breakfast spot, and it was a good thing Mrs. Anne had arrived early.

"Good morning," Mrs. Anne said, getting up to give her a hug.

Hazel returned the hug and smiled as she slid into the booth across from Mrs. Anne. "Thank you for coming."

"Of course! I am so excited about tonight. Christmas in October! What a wonderful idea. What do you need me to bring? I know your dad and Faye are bringing a ham."

Hazel's stomach roiled as a waitress zoomed to her. "What can I get ya to drink?" The waitress's dark ponytail swished as she bounced on her toes.

"Oh, well... I'll just have a glass of water." Hazel's heart jack-hammered inside her chest. She didn't need more coffee; she already had the jitters. *What have I gotten myself into?*

"Ya'll ready to order?" the waitress asked, holding out a small writing pad and pencil.

"Yes," Mrs. Anne said brightly. "I'll have the Billy's light with the one egg, an English muffin, bacon, and hashbrowns."

The waitress scribbled it down on her pad of paper. "How you want that egg cooked?"

"Scrambled."

The waitress turned to Hazel. "What about you?"

Hazel stared at the one-page laminated menu, her eyes not focusing. Mrs. Anne was excited about tonight. She bit the inside of her cheek. She looked to Mrs. Anne and then at the waitress, who stared at her, her toe tapping against the black and white tile linoleum. Hazel waved a hand in front of her face. "Wowzers, it's hot in here."

The waitress's eyebrows furrowed. Her pencil posed and ready to take down her order.

Hazel sucked in a breath. "Um, I'll just have the same."

The waitress snatched her menu from her hand. "Okay, I'll get those orders in now," she said over her shoulder.

Hazel glanced across the table. Mrs. Anne's forehead creased, and her mauve lips pinched. Before Hazel could open her mouth and let everything spill out, the waitress zoomed to them with Hazel's water.

Hazel's hands darted to the hard plastic cup. She grasped at it like it was her last lifeline. Her hands trembled as she lifted it to her lips to take a sip. The cool water rolled down her throat, but it did nothing to calm her nerves.

"Is everything alright, dear? You seem…" Mrs. Anne raised her eyebrows. "You seem off this morning."

Hazel took another sip of water to steel herself, but the water went down her throat the wrong way. She began to cough and cough. People in the other booths looked her way. Her face blazed under their stares. She sat the cup down and laid a hand on her chest to calm herself.

"Hazel, goodness, are you okay? Do I need to get some help?"

Hazel shook her head, "No, no. Please no, I'm fine."

But Hazel could clearly read the look on Mrs. Anne's face. Mrs. Anne did not think she was fine. *I have to do this. I need to just spit it out.* "Well actually, I need to talk to you about something. Not about the party tonight. Well, sort of about the party, but not really. Does that make sense?"

Mrs. Anne's eyebrows rose to her hairline. "Not really, sweetie." She frowned and took a sip of her coffee. "If it's something not good, I find it better just to say it quickly like pulling off a Band-Aid."

What good advice, Hazel thought. She took in a big breath and let the words rush out. "Joel's pa is going to be at the party tonight."

The coffee cup in Mrs. Anne's hand froze mid-air near her lips. Hazel searched Mrs. Anne's face for a sign of anything suggesting that Joel's pa being at the party would not be a problem, Hazel hoped she'd been making a mountain out of a mole hill, but she couldn't read Mrs. Anne's expression.

Mrs. Anne sat her cup back down without taking a sip. "Hmm, well I don't think we realized Thomas would be there."

Hazel wanted to take another sip of her water, but she resisted, too worried she'd choke again. She plowed on through her words not stopping to take a breath. "I know Mr. Davenport and Mr. Hal have some sort of—well, I guess, some sort of disagreement. But it seems that was long ago, and do you think they could put it behind them for tonight. Just for the party. For Joel?"

"Does Thomas know Hal and I will be there?"

Hazel's stomach twisted. "Well, no. I called to invite him, and he did ask if Mr. Hal would be there." She bit her lip. Her face heated under Mrs. Anne's gaze. She tried to swallow the excess saliva in her mouth, but it stuck in her throat. Hazel's words came out as a whisper, "I told him no."

Mrs. Anne tsked and shook her head.

Hazel's hand darted across the table to grasp Mrs. Anne's hand. She felt Mrs. Anne stiffen, but she didn't let go. "That's why I'm coming to you. Whatever happened is in the past. Don't you think they could get along just for one night? Joel leaves tomorrow." Even though she tried not to let it happen, tears pricked her eyes, and her throat constricted. "What if he never comes back?"

Mrs. Anne squeezed her hand. "He will come home, Hazel. Don't you worry one minute about that. He will come home to you." She gave Hazel's hand one final squeeze then slowly withdrew her hand. She turned her coffee mug, so the handle faced away from her. She didn't meet Hazel's eyes. "I think it's best if we don't go to the party tonight. I'll tell everyone I'm feeling under the weather."

Hazel's heart fell. "Please Mrs. Anne, can't everything be okay for one night? What happened? Surely it can't be that bad that y'all would miss saying good-bye?"

Hazel watched as Mrs. Anne picked up her purse and fished through it. She pulled out her wallet and placed a ten-dollar bill on the table. "This should cover our bill. Ask the waitress to wrap up my order and take it to Ruthie."

"Mrs. Anne?" Hazel's voice broke as she stared across the booth at this woman who'd been like a mother to her. The woman who'd showed her how to put on makeup, took her shopping in Fort Smith, talked girl talk with her. She'd never noticed before how frail Mrs. Anne looked; her skin so pale.

Mrs. Anne glanced up to meet Hazel's eyes. Her irises glistened with tears under the harsh restaurant lights. "Hazel, it's not my story to tell, but if you and Joel knew the truth of the matter, you wouldn't be sitting here with me right now. Thomas has every right to hate us. And one day when you and Joel find out, you will too." She rose from the booth, clinging to her purse, and left without another word.

Chapter 13

RUTHIE

"**R**epeat it again. I need to hear it again," Ruthie said.

Hazel slipped oven mitts onto her hands and opened the oven door. She pulled out a pan of sugar cookies cut into Christmas shapes. There were stars, stockings, wreaths, and snowmen. She laid the pan on the burners. Sweat glistened across Hazel's forehead and she used her forearm to push away a strand of dark hair stuck to her face. "I told you already," she sighed, "she said if we knew why Joel's pa hated them, we would hate them too." Hazel's mouth turned down and her arms hung at her sides. "Now could you please get a plate for the cookies," she said, her voice harsh.

Ruthie threw her hands up, "Okay, good grief, I'm just trying to help figure out what's going on."

"I don't think we can figure anything out. It's too strange. Help me get the rest of the food ready before everyone gets here." Hazel pointed a finger at her. "And not a word about what happened to Joel when he gets back from Ronnie's parents' house. I don't want him to start worrying. He's got enough on his plate, and I don't want to add some old feud between the men he cares about to it."

Ruthie chewed on her bottom lip. "Yeah, I think you're right with the not telling him part. I mean what could he do before tomorrow anyway."

Hazel nodded, "Now get the icing we made and start icing these cookies."

Ruthie saluted her, "Yes, Mrs. Bossy Pants."

Ruthie rushed to Hazel and Joel's front door to let in their first guests, her dad and Ms. Faye. "Oh goodness," she said, shocked to find perfectly wrapped presents in golden paper with red sparkling bows sitting on the cement stoop.

"Those gifts are wrapped beautifully. Who are they from?" Ms. Faye asked.

"Dunno," Ruthie said, reaching down to turn over the gift tag on the first one. She read, "To Joel. From Hal and Anne." The other two were marked for her and Hazel. She picked up the package marked for her.

Her dad scrunched his face, "I thought Hal was coming tonight. That's what he said yesterday at the coffee shop."

Ruthie's mind raced to remember what Hazel had said Mrs. Anne's excuse for not coming would be. She hated lying to her father, but as the words came out of her mouth, she didn't really see any other choice. "Um, well I think Mrs. Anne isn't feeling well."

Her dad raised one eyebrow.

Shoot! He always knows when I'm lying.

He shook his head but left it alone. "Alright," he said suspiciously but bent down to pick up the other two gifts, "I'll help you carry them inside."

U nder the circumstances, Ruthie thought the Christmas party in October was going wonderfully. No one spoke of the war or the election where Nixon was sure to become the next president. All through the night, her eyes were drawn to Hazel and Joel. Many times, she had to resist the urge to stare at them. They sat on the sofa, Hazel clutching Joel's arm. No matter where they had moved during the party, they were together, touching each other. A light kiss on the cheek, Joel's arms wrapped around Hazel's shoulder, her hand on his knee, or their hands tightly grasped. Ruthie's eyes stung and she blinked to keep tears from pouring out. Everyone wore a smile, but she knew inside, everyone's hearts were filled with a mixture of feelings ranging from rage to deep sadness. She could read Joel's pa the easiest. He wore a constant scowl, his arms folded across his chest. He only smiled once when Joel got up to remove a small gift from under the tree and hand it to him before sitting back down next to Hazel.

The tree looked beautiful. Sandra and Milton had brought Mikey and Mannie over before the party to help decorate it. Sandra danced around the room holding Mannie to her chest while she and Hazel covered the tree in strings of popped corn like when they were little. She loved sharing their tradition with Mikey. He'd giggle uncontrollably every time he snuck a piece of popcorn out of the Pyrex mixing bowl to eat instead of pushing it onto the large needle attached to the string.

"Go on, open it, Pa," Joel said, encouragingly pointing to the small package sitting on his pa's lap.

Joel's pa looked down at the shiny green paper with the gold bow and his eyes widened, like he'd forgotten about it. He ran a hand through his hair.

"I don't, well darn, you didn't need to get me anything," he said, stumbling over his words.

Joel's smile spread wide across his face. "I know. But I wanted to."

His pa nodded, and with speed, he tore the paper off the present. Ruthie wondered how long it had been since he'd received a Christmas present, then her thoughts bounced to last week when she'd seen his truck parked at the Bulldog Pub. She looked down at the gifts in front of her feet. Joel probably didn't know about that, and she wasn't going to be the one to tell him. Not today, not before he left.

When Joel's pa opened the gift, he pulled out a thick silver chain with a cross hanging on it. He held it up in the air and stared at it. The cross spun slowly on the chain.

"What do you think, Pa? It's for protection." Joel said, his smile wide.

"I can't take this," he said. The flatness in his voice made everyone in the room grow quiet. To Ruthie, the silence felt charged, like lightning could strike at any moment. The hairs on her arms stood.

"Of course you can, it's Christmas," Joel said. Although his voice sounded jovial, Ruthie could hear the strain underneath the words.

Joel's pa shook his head. "No." He stood and pushed the chain and cross toward Joel. "You take it."

"But Pa, I got it for you."

"You're the only one in this room who's gonna need protection." He threw up his hands, "I don't have any idea why everyone here is acting like it ain't true. All stupid smiles and dumb talk about nothing that matters. You're going to end up some number they flash across the television screen just like everyone else forced to go to that godforsaken country."

Ruthie's eyes flashed to Hazel. Her face had gone sallow and her eyes watery. Joel's face turned bright red. He opened his mouth to say something, but before he could get out any words, his pa thrust his hand out. "Don't bother," he said and dropped the chain on the ground near Joel's feet. "I'm leaving anyway."

He stormed out of the duplex, slamming the door behind him. The whole place seemed to rock with the force of it.

Joel bent over and scooped up the chain. He looped it around Hazel's neck before wrapping his arms around her. She pressed her face into his chest. Ruthie could feel her own heart cracking.

"Don't listen to him," Joel said as he squeezed Hazel closer to him. "I'm going to be fine. Don't you dare listen to him. You hear me?"

After that, the night grew more solemn. Mikey and Mannie's smiles were the only ones she saw as they opened their gifts and pulled out the new toys Hazel and Joel had gotten them. Mikey held his new red, View-Master Stereoscope Viewer to his eyes. Every time he'd pull the lever on the side down, he'd ooh and aah as the image swept to the side with a click and changed to something new.

Ruthie sat on the edge of the sofa next to Hazel. As she opened the gift from Hazel and Joel, she tried to force her mouth to smile. She wanted things to go back to how they felt before Joel's pa acted like a fool. She'd wanted one night of peace without thinking about the war for both of them, but they couldn't even get that thanks to him. Her blood started to boil, and she shook it off. She opened the small white box in her hands. Inside lay a new watch with a thin leather band. She had no idea how much it cost them.

"It's beautiful. I love it. Thank you both," she said, moving to give them a hug.

"I'm so glad you like it." Hazel smiled, her cheeks damp.

"Well, I wanted to get you one with Mickey Mouse on the face, but Hazel said no. She said you needed a professional looking watch," Joel said and rolled his eyes.

Ruthie chuckled, "It's perfect. Now open ya'll's presents."

Ruthie watched as Hazel slowly peeled away the wrapping paper from the gift Joel had gotten her. She'd gotten him stationery so he could write home whenever he got a chance. When Hazel had carefully tore the last piece of wrapping paper off, a leather-bound journal lay in her lap. She blinked and held it up.

"It's for your writing. It's been too long since you've sat down and wrote a story," Joel said, placing his hands on top of hers. "You used to write all the time. I know life has gotten in the way, but while I'm gone, I want you to write again. Then you can read me all your new stories when I get back."

She wrapped her arms around his neck. "Thank you. I love it."

Ruthie's throat constricted as she tried not to sob. *How are we ever going to make it without Joel here?*

Joel stood from the sofa and wiped his hands on his jeans, "Well, I think that's all the presents. Does anyone want something to drink?"

Ms. Faye stood, "I'll make us all some hot apple cider; you don't trouble yourself. But what about those gifts Arvel set by the door?"

"Oh!" Ruthie exclaimed. "I nearly forgot. Those are from Mr. Hal and Mrs. Anne." She jumped up and grabbed them. She handed one to Hazel and one to Joel, and she had one as well.

"I hate that they weren't here," Hazel sighed.

"Well open it up," her dad encouraged.

Ruthie and Joel sat back down on the sofa. Hazel crunched in the middle. With everyone's eyes on them, they tore through the gold paper at the same time.

Joel got his unwrapped and opened first. He pulled out a small sewing kit and a tin of cookies. He picked up a note written on thick white paper from inside the box and read it out loud. "The miles you march will be long. But remember, every hole can be repaired." He stared at it and after a beat, he said, "I'm sure I'll get lots of use from this. Hazel, could you thank them for me."

"Of course," she said as she continued unwrapping her gift.

Ruthie looked at Hazel and couldn't help but smile. She'd always been the slowest present opener, trying to preserve the beautiful paper and not tear it. Ruthie's gold paper laid in tatters at her feet. She opened the box and inside saw the beautiful cover of a book on traveling. She picked up the notecard and read it to herself.

"For your dreams and the many adventures we know you will have on your future journeys." Ruthie's face heated at least ten degrees, and her head spun at dizzying speeds. *How'd they figure out her secret? How did they know she wanted to leave Waldron?* She hurried and closed the lid of the box.

"What was it?" Sandra asked as she bounced Mannie on her knees.

"Yeah, what was it?" Milton echoed his wife.

Ruthie felt so hot, she was afraid the top of her head may catch on fire. "Oh, well," she stumbled. *I can't tell them.* Her eyes flashed to her dad then to Hazel. *They can't know. I'm just like mama and I want to leave my home too.* Shame burned in her chest. "It was nothing special. Just a book."

Her dad looked at her. "What kind of book?"

She tried to think of what to say, but before she could say anything, Hazel yipped and then plastered a hand across her mouth.

"Holy moly! What's wrong?" Ruthie said, relief flooding through her at the distraction.

While everyone's eyes were on Hazel, she shoved the gold paper inside the box to cover the book and wadded the note card into a ball before pushing it far beneath the wrapping paper.

Joel peered over Hazel's shoulder, "The box is empty."

Hazel shook her head, "No, there's this note card inside." She held it up.

"What does it say?" Ms. Faye asked.

Hazel sniffed, "It says, 'Don't worry about dinner or lunch, your food for the next two years is on us. Mr. Crutchfield has created a tab for you at the Piggly Wiggly.'"

Ms. Faye gasped. "Free groceries for the next two years! What a sweet blessing. That Hal and Anne are such kind souls."

Hazel nodded then turned to Joel. "Could you really be gone for two years?"

Ruthie saw something pass across Joel's face, but it was gone so fast, she wondered if Hazel had noticed it too.

"Nah, I'll be back before you know it," he said, giving Hazel a peck on the cheek.

Chapter 14

HAZEL, DECEMBER 25, 1968

Hazel lay in bed. No magic existed on this Christmas day—not without Joel. She'd give anything to go back to their October Christmas so she could see Joel's face again. She stared out into the darkness. A sliver of light from the bathroom's closed door stretched across the bottom of the bed. She could hear Ruthie rustling around in there, trying to be quiet. She appreciated that Ruthie had stayed with her for the last two months. It was nice to have company, but she knew Ruthie would eventually have to move back to the duplex she shared with their father. Hazel stretched her arms above her head. When she lowered them, her arm passed across Joel's empty side. The coldness sent a shiver through her body. She turned to her side, propping herself up with an arm. She rubbed the cool sheets where his body should be laying. The longing inside her heart felt so cavernous. It had taken everything inside of her not to fall into that same darkness she'd felt after losing Madelyn Ray.

To keep going, she'd worked extra shifts at Piggly Wiggly. She'd helped with fundraisers at the Scott County Women's Coalition. She'd visited Alice and played with her daughter. She'd babysat Mikey and Mannie so Sandra and Milton could go out. But even all her busyness couldn't take away the news reports or the death tally that continued to tick upward every day. The news showed scenes of protests spread throughout the country. Angry people with fists raised in the air. She'd seen people holding signs and chanting at the top of their lungs. Some of the signs said things like "END THE WAR," "BRING OUR BOYS HOME," or "WHY WAR? TRY PEACE." She'd liked those signs. But the messages on other signs sent chills down her spine. They called the soldiers "BABY KILLERS" and one even said, "MY SON DIED IN VIETNAM." So, Hazel hardly ever watched television anymore.

She'd received a few letters from Joel on the stationery she'd bought for him. The first letter said he'd made it safely to the Army base in Vietnam. She'd gotten a few other shorter ones telling her how much he missed her. Every time she opened the mailbox and saw a letter from him inside, her heart would race like it might explode out of her chest. Those letters were her only lifeline to him now, and she needed them like she needed air to breathe. Since she knew he'd probably feel the same way about receiving letters from her, she wrote to him almost every day. She hoped he received them all.

Ruthie tiptoed out of the bathroom. "Oh shoot! Did I wake you?"

Hazel yawned, "Nah, it's fine. I can't believe you gotta work today. On Christmas."

Ruthie sat on Joel's side of the bed, jostling Hazel like a boat rocking on turbulent waters. Ruthie bent over the bed to slip on her shoes. "Yeah, you know, the newer nurses get all the fun."

Hazel picked up a pillow and hit Ruthie on the back. Ruthie gasped then picked up Joel's pillow and hit her back.

"So, what do you have planned today, lazy bones? Since Piggly Wiggly is closed."

Hazel stretched again, her shoulders extending like they might pop out of their sockets. "I think I'm going to make some cookies for Mikey and Mannie since we've already given them our Christmas gifts when Joel was here. I still want to give them something on Christmas."

Ruthie sprung up from the bed, making Hazel bounce. "Well, that sounds wonderful. But you better save some cookies for me." She pointed her finger at Hazel and waved it.

Hazel smiled, "I will. Goodness gracious, you and your love of cookies."

Ruthie giggled. "You know it. See you tonight." She grabbed her purse that lay on the top of Hazel's dresser and looped the strap around her shoulder.

"Don't forget Christmas dinner tonight."

"Never," Ruthie said.

Hazel rolled her eyes and dropped back on the bed. Since Ruthie had been working at the hospital, she'd started to be repeatedly late for things like family dinners and coalition meetings. Her hospital schedule was unpredictable, she'd told Hazel. Sometimes she'd clock out and then an emergency would rush through the door with someone needing stitches or a cast. Still, Hazel knew Ruthie loved her job. Hazel shivered at the thought of all that excitement. She could do without it. Give her the boring Piggly Wiggly checkout line any day.

After Hazel showered and dressed, she got started on the cookies. As she folded the chocolate chips into the dough, she could hear vehicle doors closing. Her ears perked up. It sounded like multiple vehicles. She walked to the front window with the mixing bowl propped on her hip, the spoon in her hand. She moved the curtain back with her elbow to peer out the window. Outside several vehicles were pulling into the parking lot. There were so many that they blocked her car in and surrounded the mailboxes. The men and women exiting the vehicles were dressed in their Sunday best and heading to her duplex, well, to Sandra and Milton's half. Soft muted conversations began to pass through the paper-thin walls.

What in the world is going on? Are they having a Christmas party for their parishioners? But why at their duplex? She'd been over to Milton and Sandra's side of the duplex a million times, and she knew it was identical to hers, small and not the ideal place for a big Christmas party, especially when they had a church with plenty of room. She frowned. Sandra had told her they had no plans, and it would just be her, Milton, and the kids today. *Could she have forgotten?*

Hazel walked to the oven and began to drop rounded balls of dough on the cookie sheet. She bit her bottom lip. Selfishly, she'd been hoping for some time with the Lewises today, especially Sandra. She needed a friend to talk with to help get her mind off the overwhelming sadness that threatened to creep inside her each day. *Plans do change*. She sighed and lowered the oven door. She slid the cookie sheet inside. She looked at the clock that hung on the wall beside a picture of bright daisies in a vase, a wedding gift from Ms. Faye. Ten minutes and the cookies would be done. She looked around her house. Without Ruthie, it seemed so quiet. She could still hear the muttering and murmuring coming from the other duplex. She strained her ears, but she couldn't make out words except—*Do I hear crying? Could it be Mannie?* She wasn't sure. It didn't sound like a baby cry. She shook her head and wiped her hands on her apron. That settled it, she'd go over there and take a big plate of cookies with her. It wasn't being nosy if you brought a gift. Or at least, that's what Mrs. Anne always said.

❧❧❧❧❧ ❦❦❦❦❦

W hen the cookies had sufficiently cooled, Hazel placed them on her best plate. She walked the ten inches to Sandra and Milton's door. She found it ajar. She squinted her eyes, trying to peer inside the small crack. Most everyone inside stood and spoke in hushed tones. Their faces drawn and pinched. Hazel's heart quickened. *It looks more like a funeral than a Christmas celebration.* A sobbing sound came from somewhere inside. Her stomach twisted. *Something is wrong.*

She pushed the door open with her shoulder. A man and woman standing near the door glanced at her with long faces. The smell of freshly baked chocolate chip cookies filled the melancholy atmosphere. Mikey ran from the kitchen.

"Hazy, Hazy, you're here."

Hazel bent down so he could see the cookies on the plate. He looked at her with huge brown eyes.

"One for me?" he asked, pointing to himself.

Hazel smiled, "Of course, let's just ask your mama first. Make sure it's okay."

Mikey's face fell, and he looked down at the floor. An older woman with a navy wool hat placed a dark wrinkled hand on Hazel's shoulder.

"I don't think Sandra would mind, dear, if Mikey had one of your cookies. They smell delicious."

Hazel nodded. Mikey's head darted up and his nose twitched.

"Why don't you take two cookies," Hazel said bending down again so he could reach the plate.

His face brightened as he grabbed a cookie for each hand then ran off. Hazel stood back up. *What in the world is going on here?* She held the plate of cookies out so the older woman could take one.

"I hope it's okay to ask, but do you know what's happening? Are Sandra and Milton alright? Is everything okay with Mannie?" The questions poured from her like a busted faucet. Fear started to creep up her chest to her throat, choking her.

The older woman nibbled the cookie. "This is quite delicious."

Hazel held the edges of the plate tighter, fearing she may shake the poor woman to get answers. *What is going on? Is someone sick or dying?* Sadness hung in the air like cigarette smoke, suffocating everyone. Her breathing became shallow. "Please, please is something wrong? Is there anything I can do?"

The woman looked into Hazel's eyes. "Sandra and the boys are fine."

Hazel's heart dropped. "Milton? Oh, my heavens, no."

The older woman patted her arm. "No, no, it's not what you're thinking. Pastor Lewis is not sick or dyin'."

Hazel blinked and she furrowed her eyebrows.

The woman pursed her lips. "Well, he may be dyin' on the inside, but that's a different story."

Hazel's thoughts swarmed inside her head. She startled when she felt a tug on her skirt. She looked down to see Mikey. A little smear of chocolate ran across his cheek and small crumbs were scattered across his shirt. Hazel took her thumb and moved it in a light circle on his face to clean the mess.

"Mama said come see her."

"She did, sweetie?"

Mikey nodded, "She's in the bedroom."

"Okay, let me just set these cookies in the kitchen."

The kitchen was jam-packed with people. At the small kitchen table sat four women, one very pregnant. Their eyes were red rimmed and damp.

Hazel decided to set the cookies on the table near the pregnant woman. She thought she could probably use one. Hazel nodded at the women as she sat the plate down on the wobbly table. The pregnant woman's eyes lit up and she gave Hazel a slight smile and reached for a cookie on the plate.

Hazel rubbed her sweaty hands down her skirt. Mikey motioned for her to follow him. The sobbing sound grew louder with each step they took toward the bedroom. Sandra and Milton's duplex was laid out just like her and Joel's, except opposite. If her bedroom was located toward the left of the kitchen, the Lewises' was located toward the right. The closer she and Mikey walked toward the bedroom, the more her stomach twisted into knots.

The lights in the bedroom were dim and it was crowded. The smell of mixed perfume and aftershave hung heavy, making Hazel's nose twitch. Sandra sat on the edge of the bed holding Mannie, who slept peacefully in her arms. When her eyes met Hazel's, the edges of Sandra's mouth turned up, but her smile didn't reach her swollen red eyes.

"You should have told me you were here," she said and slowly rocked Mannie.

Sandra positioned Mannie on her shoulder. He'd grown so much; he filled Sandra's arms. With her free hand, Sandra took hold of Hazel's hand. "Come sit," she said, pulling Hazel down beside her.

Hazel's heart picked up pace as she whispered, "Sandra, what's going on here?"

Sandra's eyes grew watery, and she wiped her cheeks with a free hand. Mannie let out a whine.

"Oh, shhh, sweet baby," Sandra said, bouncing Mannie lightly.

Sandra's gaze went to the back of the room and Hazel followed it. The men standing around seemed to part and Hazel saw Milton. He sat in a chair near a worn wooden vanity. His body slumped over with his elbows on his knees. His head rested in his hands. Sandra leaned over slightly and picked up a piece of paper that lay on the bedside table. She handed the paper to Hazel.

The paper felt light and her hand trembled as she held it out to read. She stared at the neat, typed wording. For a minute, Hazel didn't understand the meaning of the words on the paper. The words blurred together. She blinked and read it again.

> Sir, The Draft Board has considered your appeal on the exemptions of ministry and conscientious objector. After full consideration, the Board respectfully declines your appeal. You are to report to Fort Smith, Arkansas on Friday, January 10, 1969, to begin training. This is the Draft Board's final decision. Failure to report as directed will subject you to a fine and imprisonment.

Hazel saw five signatures scrawled at the bottom in blue ink. Thoughts ran wild in her mind. She couldn't make sense of what she'd read. It couldn't be right. It had to be a mistake. Joel had failed a class, and they took him from her, but Milton served as the head pastor of a church. *How could they do this?* She looked at Mannie. He had children. Little boys who needed their father. It had to be a mistake.

"A man from the draft board delivered it today," Sandra said.

Hazel's throat went dry. "On Christmas day?"

"Yes," Sandra shook her head. "He laughed when he handed it to me." Sandra's face went hard.

"But he's a pastor, a minister." Hazel stammered, "H-how can they do this? He qualifies for an exemption."

Sandra sighed. "The draft board is located in Fort Smith. They don't know him, except for that he's a Black man. And there aren't any Black men on the draft board."

A man standing beside them in a navy suit with red tie said in a gruff voice, "I heard one of those board members is a grand wizard of the Ku Klux Klan."

Hazel's body began to shake. "But this ain't right!" she said louder than she meant too.

Mannie whined and stirred in Sandra's arms.

"Oh sorry!" Hazel whispered.

"Pastor Milton, you should refuse to go," said a man with wrinkles so deep they looked like large crevices. His white hair gathered around his ears. "I mean, President Nixon himself said he'd put a stop to the draft and bring us peace with his secret plan to end the war. Since he hasn't done his part, you shouldn't have to do yours."

Milton shook his head. With a voice thick with sadness, he said, "No, Brother Sims, I will follow the law whether I agree with it or not. If they sentenced Muhammad Ali to prison for five years and stripped him of his world title, what do you think they would do to me? Give me ten years? Twenty?"

Sandra's breath hitched and she patted Hazel's hand, "You can't go getting all depressed on me with Joel gone. You hear me? I'm going to need you too." She looked down at Mannie in her arms. "We all are."

Hazel's stomach clenched and she nodded.

"I'm going to need you too," Hazel said.

Sandra pulled Hazel into a hug—Mannie's warm body between them. She whispered in Hazel's ear. "We'll get through this together."

Hazel marveled at Sandra's strength, and she hoped some of it would rub off on her. But a fire in her chest burned. Sandra and Milton are good people. They wouldn't go down there and yell and curse, even though they had been done wrong. They'd choose to follow God no matter how people spit on them. This situation wasn't right, but what could they do? What could any of them do? A helpless, sinking feeling settled on Hazel. She leaned into Sandra and let her tears fall.

Chapter 15

RUTHIE, JANUARY 1969

R uthie unlocked the door to Hazel and Joel's little duplex. As she turned the key, she noticed her nails were gnawed down to the quick. She'd need to stop that bad habit before it got worse. But her insides had been twisted in knots for almost a month now. How could she tell Hazel what she'd done? Ruthie suspected her father already knew. He seemed to know everything. She wanted to tell them both on Christmas day. She'd imagined them sitting down to a nice Christmas dinner together. Then after they'd finished their pie, she'd spring the news on them. There'd be no way they could be furious with her after having pie. But things didn't go as planned because when she'd gotten home from work, Hazel had told her the news about Milton. Now Milton was gone, and Ruthie still hadn't confessed to her family what she'd done. She worried that Milton's situation would make her news seem like the world was ending, but to her it seemed like the opposite, a beginning. Even though guilt pulsed through her chest, she still couldn't help what her heart felt—excitement. But her time to procrastinate had ended, she had to tell them now.

Ruthie pushed the front door open. She called out as she laid her purse on the coffee table. "Hello Hazel?" Nothing. She frowned when she didn't see Hazel, not in the living room nor in the kitchen. Heat from the oven filled the small space and she could smell something cooking.

"Hazel," she called out again.

A rustling from the back caught her attention. She started to walk toward Hazel's bedroom, talking loudly so Hazel could hear her. "So, Margarette Ann said she thinks Dad and Ms. Faye are finally going to tie the knot. She heard from someone who heard from someone else that Ms. Faye was in Fort Smith looking for a conservative white dress in a wedding store."

She stopped when she went through the door. Hazel wasn't in the bedroom. Then she heard an unmistakable sound that she'd recognize even if she wasn't a nurse—retching. Ruthie rushed to the bathroom door. She tried to open it, but it was locked. She beat on it with a balled-up fist. "Hazel? Are you alright? Let me in, I can help."

She pressed her ear to the wood door. She heard it again, Hazel vomiting. She beat on the door harder. Her body instinctively went into emergency mode. "Hazel, you let me in this instant!"

The toilet flushed. She heard thumping and rustling, then water running in the sink. She ground her teeth.

When Hazel opened the bathroom door and saw Ruthie, she jolted. She clasped her chest. "Holy cow! What are you doing here?"

Ruthie sucked in a deep breath. "What are you talking about? I've been beating on this door for minutes now and calling you." Her anger dissipated some when she noticed how thin and ashen Hazel looked. Hazel wiped at the corner of her mouth with the back of her hand. She gave Ruthie a forced smile.

"I'm sorry. I've had a cold for a few days, and my face and ears are so stuffed up. I can't hear a thing. But I'm fine."

Ruthie narrowed her eyes at her sister. She didn't believe her for one hot second. But she laid the back of her hand across Hazel's forehead. "Hmm, no fever."

Hazel rolled her eyes. "I told you, I'm fine. It's just all this congestion."

"But you didn't sound fine," Ruthie said, motioning to the bathroom.

Hazel waved a hand in the air like it wasn't a big deal. "I think I just ate something today that didn't settle well, that's all. I don't want to miss the coalition meeting tonight. Everyone's sharing their letters. I can't wait to hear how their husbands and sons are doing."

Although letter night was Ruthie's favorite night too, she didn't think Hazel should be going. "I think maybe you should stay here tonight and get some rest. You've been doing so much lately. Working full time, helping Sandra with Mikey and Mannie."

"Pish posh," Hazel said, grabbing Ruthie's wrist to look at the watch she and Joel had gotten her. "We better hurry. We gotta leave in twenty minutes. I don't want to be late. You know how it fills up on letter night." A smile brightened Hazel's face. "And I got my own letter to share."

Ruthie internally rolled her eyes. Although she loved hearing that Joel was healthy and doing well, most of his letters to Hazel were mushy. There wasn't a lot about of details about Vietnam, the country or its people. Hazel didn't mind though. She'd read his love letters over and over until she fell asleep.

Hazel nudged past Ruthie. "Oh my, I almost forgot. I need to get our frozen dinners out of the oven."

As Hazel hurried out of the bedroom, Ruthie followed her. She knew something wasn't right. She felt it in her bones, but she couldn't put her finger on it. Hazel had no fever, so maybe it was true, and she'd just eaten something that didn't settle well.

When Ruthie sat down at the kitchen table, Hazel placed the warmed Swanson dinner in its foil tin on the plate in front of her and sat down. Hazel wasted no time digging into hers. Ruthie raised an eyebrow. *So much for being sick a moment ago.* A pea ran off Hazel's fork and she picked it up off the table, popping it into her mouth. She looked up at Ruthie, who hadn't even picked up her fork to start eating.

"It's meat loaf and peas. You don't like it?"

Ruthie picked up her fork and took a small bite. She watched as Hazel poked another big fork full of peas and meatloaf into her mouth.

"It's fine. Thank you for making it for me."

Hazel nodded and took another big bite before stopping. "Why are you staring at me?"

"Just a few minutes ago you were very sick."

Hazel tilted her head to the side. "Well, yeah, but I feel fine now and I'm starving. So hurry and eat or we'll be late."

❧❧❧❧❧ ❧❧❧❧❧

When they arrived at the library for the meeting, all the chairs in the small space were full except for a few in the back. Ruthie and Hazel slipped into them.

"We should have left earlier," Hazel complained.

Alice and Margarette Ann were seated closer to the front. They turned around and waved. Ruthie wished they could have saved them seats, but seat saving was against the rules per Nancy Graham now Livingston, the elected president of the coalition. *Who voted for her anyway?* Ruthie leaned over to Hazel and whispered, "They must have gotten here a whole hour early for those seats."

Hazel nodded and began speaking to the other woman sitting beside her. Ruthie recognized her immediately as George Piles's mother. Ruthie and George had graduated together. Hazel showed Mrs. Piles her letter from Joel while Mrs. Piles held a letter of her own. George's letter had pictures he'd taken of the landscape. George's mother handed them to Hazel, and she sat back so Ruthie could see them too. The landscape in the small square photographs looked stunning. Green mountains, thick trees, plants she'd never seen before. There was a picture of a huge body of water. She took the picture from Hazel's hands and turned it over. Written in blue ink on the back were the words "South China Sea." Ruthie felt the yearning again. She'd need to tell Hazel tonight what she'd done. Ruthie's legs practically twitched with the desire to splash in the water. She quickly handed the picture back to Hazel. She forced her eyes away from George's pictures and scanned the full room to get her mind off of what she had to tell Hazel and her dad tonight.

For some reason, the vibe in the air felt different, electric even. Ruthie looked around at the chattering women. There were a lot here tonight.

More than she'd ever seen, even for a letter night. Ruthie bent forward to eavesdrop on the conversation of two women seated in front of her.

"I can't believe they are really going to do this. Tonight! I almost fainted. Have you seen the protests lately? If we're not careful, people will be angry with us for even helping those soldiers over there. We shouldn't even be in this war anyway!"

"Oh, I agree, Geralyn. I will tell you one thing—I don't care if they draw my name out of that stupid hat Nancy has, I ain't going. That's for sure. Who elected Nancy president anyway!"

Geralyn huffed her agreement, "Not me, I tell you. Not me. But you don't have to worry. I heard its only for the younger ones who are childless. Those are the ones they'll ask to go."

Both women nodded their heads and clutched their purses tighter to their chests. Ruthie's stomach twisted. She'd missed something. Why wouldn't they help the soldiers at war? That was the whole stinkin' reason for the coalition! Who cared about the protests! But it sounded like something different was planned for tonight. Ruthie raised her hand to tap Geralyn's shoulder to ask, but before she could get her attention, Nancy Graham Livingston called the meeting to order.

"Good evening, ladies," she said loudly from behind the podium in the front of the room. "The Scott County Women's coalition is now called to order."

A mass of women in the middle seats continued to chatter, ignoring her. Channeling her head cheerleader days, Nancy clapped her hands together and in a much louder, clipped tone said again, "Good evening, ladies."

The sound of chatter stopped like it hit a bus and died. With everyone focused on her now, Nancy flashed the crowd a huge toothy grin. Big white teeth glowed between her signature red hot lips. Her short blonde hair cut had been curled until it poofed around her head.

"Good evening," some of the women chimed back.

Nancy clasped her hands together in front of her. "Well, I'm sure many of you are excited about tonight! It's letter night, ladies!"

Everyone cheered and clapped.

"But before we get started, we have a special guest speaker."

That's when Ruthie noticed her. The woman sat toward the side of the podium. She wore a light blue collared shirt with a matching skirt. Dark buttons ran up the shirt. In the center of the shirt's sleeves were red cross patches.

Nancy looked toward the guest and cleared her throat. "I am pleased as punch to welcome tonight Ms. Regina Newman from the American Red Cross. Please join me in welcoming her."

Many of the women looked at each other as if surprised to have a guest speaker. A few women began to clap, and others joined in, but it sounded more hesitant to Ruthie and not the enthusiastic kind you'd expect for a special speaker.

Ruthie heard Geralyn lean over to the woman beside her and whisper, "Here we go."

What in the Jiminy Crickets is going on?

Ms. Newman stood up and walked to the podium. She wasted no time. She reintroduced herself and began a lengthy description about the American Red Cross and what it did, especially to help the men fighting in Vietnam. Everything she said sounded amazing to Ruthie. The Red Cross was really doing something, not sitting around chatting and reading letters every Tuesday night like this group. She couldn't understand what Geralyn's issue was with Ms. Newman. She thought the work the Red Cross did sounded vital and important. Yes, the coalition had helped many families whose husbands and sons had gone to war, but that seemed small potatoes now that she knew what the American Red Cross was doing.

"So that brings me to why I came here tonight," Ms. Newman said, pausing to make sure everyone looked at her.

Geralyn moved closer to the other woman and whispered, "Oh boy."

Ms. Newman gripped the podium. "We are in serious need of more volunteers."

A hushed chatter spread across the room.

"You can play a vital role in this war. We need women willing to go overseas and women willing to be on the front line at home. We need Donut Dollies, hospital workers, teachers to help with training and educating Vietnamese women and children. There are also clerical opportunities. The assistance we provide to our fighting men is indispensable. They need you. Please consider volunteering—whether it be here or there. You could make a real difference in this war. Thank you for your time."

Nancy returned to the podium and put a hand on Ms. Newman's shoulder. "Isn't it wonderful what the American Red Cross is doing?"

Everyone nodded and applauded as Ms. Newman returned to her seat.

"Now I know that many of us have little ones like me," Nancy said, laying her manicured hand over her heart. "And we could never fly way over there to assist our fighting men. Even though we'd love to, we have babies to take care of here."

Many of the women in the audience nodded. Their heads bobbing on their necks.

"But," she paused and looked around the room. "There are many of you here tonight that haven't been lucky enough to find a husband or you haven't been blessed with children yet."

Ruthie glanced at Hazel. Hazel's mouth hung open as if Nancy had physically slapped her. Ruthie felt it too. It was like Nancy had singled her and Hazel out because of their unlucky ability to land a man or have a child. She gritted her teeth. *How dare she? The audacity! The arrogance!*

Murmuring spread through the room as Nancy reached down and fiddled with something behind the podium. She pulled out a round clear fishbowl filled with what looked like folded slips of white paper.

Nancy continued, "That's why I and the other coalition leaders have decided if none of you are willing to volunteer to help the cause, then we will encourage you."

"What?" Ruthie said too loudly, causing Geralyn and the other woman to turn and glare at her. Ruthie's face flamed, but it wasn't embarrassment she felt. It was outrage. "They are going to make women volunteer! How can they do that?" she whispered.

"Shh, I can't hear," Hazel said.

Nancy held up her hands. The murmuring grew across the room. "Please ladies, listen, inside this bowl are names of coalition members that are between the ages of eighteen and twenty-seven, who are either not married or have no children."

Ruthie looked toward Ms. Newman. Her face had gone completely pale. She shook her head side to side. Ruthie knew right then and there that this stupid idea was all Nancy. *Of course it was!*

"Now I'm going to draw out five names. And those names are the women we expect to volunteer. Yes, yes, you can volunteer locally, but we expect something more from the women drawn. We expect you to seriously consider volunteering by going to Vietnam. We want to increase our female presence now don't we ladies. And just think you will be representing us—the Scott County Women's Coalition! What better way to serve your country? And who knows, you single gals might just land you a husband while you're there." She gave the audience a wink.

Ms. Newman rushed to the podium. "Ms. Livingston, I'm not sure you quite understand. We want women who actually want to volunteer. Not ones who are forced by some um…" she looked at the fishbowl sitting on the podium. "Well, some very strange lottery system."

Nancy shook her head. "Oh, don't be silly now, we're not forcing them… We are just actively encouraging them."

"Well, it feels pretty forced to me," said a woman from the middle row of seats. Many of the women around her nodded and mumbled their agreement.

"We shouldn't even be in this war!" a woman yelled from the back. "Have you seen the picket lines in front of the army recruiting building in Little Rock?"

That sent the others murmuring.

"Yeah, they've got signs that say stop the war and the war is evil."

Nancy's usually pretty face contorted and began to turn a shade of red that nearly matched her lipstick. She pressed her lips tight in a straight line. The next time she spoke, her usual singsong voice was flat. "We are not forcing anyone," she annunciated each word. "And until our wonderful President decides to end our involvement in the war, the Scott County Women's Coalition will do everything it can to support our men."

Ruthie's shoulders slumped forward. Well, she did agree with Nancy there. No matter what people thought about the war, the men fighting there, like Joel and Milton, deserved to be supported and not forgotten.

Nancy held up a hand. "Now, I will draw five names from the bowl. The coalition will strongly encourage these five women to volunteer in some way because it will look good for our community. But we are in no way forcing them to do so. They may decline if they so choose." She looked up toward the ceiling before her gaze settled back on the audience. "Of course, it would be a shame to decline such an honor. Especially since that's why we are all here in the first place. Isn't that right, ladies?"

No one responded.

Ruthie pushed her back against the chair. Encourage them to volunteer. It felt more like humiliating them until they volunteer. Ms. Newman walked to her chair, picked up her coat, and headed for the exit. Nancy either didn't even notice that she left or didn't care. Ruthie looked at Hazel. Her hands were gripped in tight fists on her lap. She wanted to grab Hazel's arm and get out of here before Nancy started to draw the names of her victims. She moved to whisper that they should leave, but a chill ran down her spine when she heard Nancy call out the first name.

"Hazel McKay. Congratulations Hazel! You're the first name chosen to volunteer." Nancy placed a hand over her eyes and scanned the audience like looking out over a vast sea. "Hazel, where are you? Maybe you can be stationed wherever Joel is located."

Ruthie's blood boiled until it almost tipped over. Nancy wasn't so naive. She knew things didn't work like that. *The nerve of her!* Hazel started to slowly lift a trembling hand and Ruthie wanted to knock it down. Better yet, she wanted to storm the podium and knock Nancy down. *How dare she!* But before she knew what she was doing, she leaped up from her seat. Her chair rocked from her momentum.

"I volunteer to take Hazel's place. I've already joined the Army Nurse Corps. I leave in two weeks."

The applause that rose from the women shocked Ruthie. She'd been so ready for taunts and criticism like she'd received from Mrs. Battalou. When she'd told Mrs. Battalou that she joined the Army Nurse Corps and would be leaving, Mrs. Battalou told her that she'd ruined her life and her nursing career. But the acceptance and encouragement from these women, women who had brothers and husbands and sons fighting in the war, made a warm spot bloom in her chest. Still, Ruthie strained to keep her eyes only on Nancy at the front. She couldn't bear to look at Hazel. Not right now.

Nancy clapped her hands to hush the crowd with pressed flat lips. If Ruthie didn't know any better, she might have thought Nancy was jealous. "Well, isn't that just wonderful," she said without enthusiasm. "Thank you for volunteering."

Ruthie gave Nancy a mock salute then plopped down in her chair. Her damp shirt touched her skin, making her shudder.

"Now let's have another volunteer," Nancy said, putting her hand back in the fishbowl.

Ruthie rested her hand to her forehead. She felt like she had a fever. Hazel grabbed her arm and pulled it hard toward her. Her nails dug into Ruthie's skin.

"What are you doing? Better yet, what have you done?"

"I'm taking your place." Ruthie beamed a smile at her and hoped this situation would keep Hazel from being too angry.

"I wasn't going! I was going to gracefully turn them down later," Hazel whispered. "Why didn't you tell me you joined the Army Nurse Corps? Does dad know? He's going to kill you!"

Ruthie watched as Hazel's eyes began to fill with tears. "First Joel, then Milton, and now you. But they had no choice, and you did. Why do you have to leave me too?"

Ruthie wrapped her arms around Hazel. She felt a sob stick in the back of her throat. "Maybe I'm more like mama than I want to admit." She sniffed. "And there's no way you could have gracefully turned down Nancy. That's classic. She'd have humiliated you at every meeting. In front of everyone. She'd make you feel like an outcast, and you'd quit. And you don't need to quit."

Hazel shrugged. "I could handle her." She grabbed Ruthie's hand and squeezed. "But you are not like our mama. I knew you wouldn't stay in Waldron forever. You want adventure. I love that about you. But two weeks! I need more time with you before you leave."

As Ruthie looked into Hazel's eyes, everything seemed to snap into place and a sense of dread and sadness filled her. She squeezed Hazel's hand back. "I was so excited to go, but now I wish I had never signed up." If only she could rewind time and undo the moment she chose to write her name down on that list. "You don't need this extra stress and worry."

"What are you talking about?" Hazel asked, her eyebrows furrowing. "I can handle things too. I can be strong just like you and Joel."

Ruthie shook her head, "I know you can. That's not what I mean. Hazel, don't you know... You're pregnant."

Hazel's mouth flew open. "I am most certainly not," she whispered too loudly.

Geralyn and the women seated beside her both turned in their seats and glowered at them. Ruthie glared back before leaning closer to Hazel and whispered. "Yes, you are. You despise peas and this evening you couldn't get enough of them. You were sick and then you were starving. I may not be a doctor, but I know a pregnant woman when I see one. It just took me a while to realize it."

Hazel's face turned white, and her hands went to her belly. "Holy cow!" She looked at Ruthie with huge eyes. "What am I going to do?"

Ruthie chuckled, "Have a baby, that's what you're going do." Ruthie's heart fell. She'd miss every bit of it.

Part 2

THERE'S NO GETTING AWAY FROM THE WAR.

Chapter 16

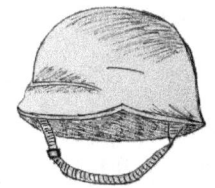

JOEL, FEBRUARY 1969

J oel sat down with his back against the bumpy hard sandbags piled five feet high in front of the hootch he shared with the twenty other men of the 101st Airborne Division. The bottom of the hootch was made of long wood boards and the upper half was screens. The aluminum roof rattled at night when the wind blew and sounded like baseballs hitting it when it rained. The hootch had been elevated about a foot off the ground to keep out the mud during the rainy season, but that was a waste because the red clay mud got in anyway. Tracked in from boots or sloshed in when the door was opened. Inside the hootch, small cots lined both sides of the walls, separated only by metal cabinets used to house their uniforms and shoes. He sure missed sharing a room with only Hazel. Being in a room of loud, obnoxious men took its toll sometimes. But at night, everyone felt so doggone tired, all the roughhousing ended. Any snores from the sleeping men were covered by the nighttime sounds of the Phu Bai Combat Base. But most of the guys called their new home Camp Hochmuth in honor of a commanding general who had died in the war. Joel wondered if, when he got home, he'd be able to sleep without the constant *whoosh* of helicopters coming and going or the constant roar of vehicle engine motors.

He could hardly believe he'd been in Vietnam for nearly five months. The almost twenty-hour flight and the bumpy ride in the back of an M54 military truck to get here was nothing more than a blur now. The first day he arrived, when the M54 drove through the rows and rows of concertina wire, his heart pounded in his chest. None of the men sitting in the back of the truck with him had said a word. Their vacant eyes drifted from side to side, taking in their new surroundings. He'd wondered how many of them would make it back home in one piece. Once he'd been drafted and made the decision not to run to Canada, he'd written to Ronnie to see what he should do. He'd heard about a five-month long Non-Commissioned Officer training course where he could come out with a sergeant ranking. He'd never told Hazel about it. He didn't want to get her hopes up, but he thought the course may keep him out of the jungle a little longer. Ronnie had written back immediately with the words "DO NOT DO IT!" written in caps and underlined in dark pencil several times. He'd told Joel that everyone called the NCOs "Shake-n-Bake" sergeants, and no one liked or respected them. So Joel took his private ranking and became a man at the bottom of the barrel like most everyone else.

He moved and adjusted away from the edge of a sandbag poking his back. His first night at Camp Hochmuth had been one of the worst. The mortars that night had been especially brutal, like the Viet Cong had decided to welcome him to the war. He remembered the first time he'd heard the shoosh of the rockets flying through the air. It had comically reminded him of when he shot off fireworks during the Fourth of July, but it was nothing like the Fourth of July. When the ground shook around his feet from the explosions, adrenaline shot through his system like electricity. He'd rushed to the nearest bunker to hunker down, forgetting to even put on his helmet. He'd been reprimanded for that later. Now, when the VC or NVA sent out rockets, electricity still buzzed through his system, but he knew how to handle it and what to do.

After arrival, he barely had time to trade his American money for funny money before the work started. He learned quickly that at Camp Hochmuth, his mechanical skills were of high value. Since he'd been here, he'd repaired M151 and M54 trucks, M170 field ambulances, and he'd even started to learn how to do basic repairs on the behemoth tanks and helicopters. His favorite by far to work on were the Snakes, or the Bell AH-1G Cobra helicopters. Where the Hueys were all round in front, the Cobra was pointed, sleeker, and better for attacks. Plus, he felt it was his duty as a "Screaming Eagle" to help keep the Cobras in tip-top shape. Because without them racing ahead and laying down enough cover fire to clear any landing zones, he and the other Eagles were nothing but dead ducks.

The warmth from the sun seeped through his army-issued green T-shirt, and the muscles in his back began to relax. He looked at the bright blue sky lined with tiny puffs of clouds. In Arkansas, they'd be bundled up in coats and scarves with frozen red fingers and noses. He thanked God that the terrible rainy season had passed for now. He'd never been so wet in all his life. The mess from all the mud sloshing under boots and tires. The constant feeling of dampness. He and the others had hung wire lines across their hootch to hang their wet clothes, but they never fully dried. Many men ended up in the base's hospital with severe colds and sinus infections. Joel sucked in a breath of fresh air and enjoyed the sun on his face. A light breeze blew, and he closed his eyes. Still, what he wouldn't give to be back in Arkansas with Hazel instead of here with trucks kicking up red, oil-soaked dust and the constant hum of the airstrips and motor pool. He held the letter he'd received today from Hazel tight against his chest. Every time he got a letter from her, he felt like the luckiest man alive. So many men got no correspondence from home, and he felt blessed to get letters on a regular basis.

His heart ached for her. On perfect days like this, he wished she were with him to experience the beauty of this country. And it was beautiful, with the rolling hills to the west and small hamlets and rice lands to the north and east—all that green. It took his breath away. He'd watched the farmers work their farmland with water buffalo as if the war wasn't surrounding them. Since he'd been here, he'd gotten to spend a lot of time in that green doing defensive positions around Camp Hochmuth. When it was his platoon's turn, they'd spend a few weeks out there writing letters, sleeping on a waterproof poncho liner, or playing cards during the day, but at night, they moved silently, ambush style. He'd heard one of the lieutenants say that their directive was to keep the VC from the surrounding villages where they'd get supplies, water, and recruits. On all his platoon's trips outside the wire, they'd never seen anything though. Never had one reason to fire their M16 rifles. Joel figured the VC knew they were there and avoided them. After his platoon's weeks in the green were over, they'd hump it back to Camp Hochmuth in the same dirty, sweaty fatigues they'd left in, exhausted and ready for a hot meal.

"You gonna read that letter or hug it all day?"

Joel smiled and opened one eye. "Shut up, Sutton."

Chad Sutton stretched his arms high above a head full of red straggly hair. He'd decided against cutting it again until the commander ordered him too. Light and dark freckles speckled his face and moved as he stretched his mouth into a huge yawn.

Chad dropped to the ground next to Joel, propping his body up with an elbow. "So you gonna read it or what?"

Joel leaned up. He and Chad had arrived at the Phu Bai Combat Base together. Chad slept in a bunk right next to Joel's. During their time together, Joel had learned that Chad was from Oklahoma, and he rode bulls for fun. During the rainy season, Chad complained about his knees and blamed it on an old bull riding injury. He looked over at Chad, who was staring at him with one reddish blonde eyebrow raised. Joel smiled. "Don't rush me now," Joel teased. "I'm savoring it."

Chad leaned over and swatted Joel on the leg. Joel laughed and started to tear off the end of the envelope, making sure not to rip the precious letter inside.

"Hey guys, what's up?"

Joel watched as Warren Pendleton sat down beside them. Pen had arrived at the same time as he and Chad, but he never seemed to fit in. What Joel had learned about Pen over the months was Pen's father had forced him to join the Army. Something about family tradition, and Pen would be a disgrace if he didn't. During the first night of mortar attacks, Pen had cried, and many of the men, especially stupid Harvey Davis, wouldn't let him forget about it. Joel knew Davis too well. He'd had the privilege of meeting him at basic training in Fort Smith. The guy didn't know when to stop. But it was more than just being obnoxious, he could be downright mean. In Joel's mind, Harvey Davis was trouble with a capital "T."

Chad sat up and crisscrossed his legs underneath him. "Oh, Davenport over here is sissifying the mail. Come on, just read the letter so I can live vicariously through you. You know my folks never send me anything. The only letters I get is when they give me those silly "any soldier" letters. Do you know how hard it is to write back to elementary school children and tell them only good things? And not scare the jeepers out of them? The only way I get to hear about what's really going on in the normal world is when you read your letters. Plus, I'm really starting to dig all that mushy stuff." Chad winked and elbowed Pen in the side.

Pen pushed him off and took out a letter from the front pocket of his green shirt. "My girl wrote me too."

Chad's eyebrows shot up and he turned all his attention on Pen. "Well, come on. Y'all are killing me. What did your girl say, Pen?"

They watched as Pen opened the letter. He carefully unfolded the creases. He held it up. The writing only filled half the page. Joel watched as Pen's eyes moved side to side, quickly scanning the words.

The lines of Pen's mouth turned down. "Well... she misses me."

Chad slugged him in the arm. "Now, that's good, ain't it."

Pen scratched his face. "Maybe. But she says she's not sure how much longer she can do this, you know, wait for me. She wishes we'd have gotten married before I left."

Chad cleared his throat. "You should write her back. And tell her how amazing the wedding will be when you get home. You know absence makes the heart grow farther."

Pen's eyes widened.

Joel coughed, "Fonder. He meant fonder."

"Yeah, fonder, that's what I said."

Pen shook his head, "Yeah, I guess." He looked at Joel, "What does your letter say?"

Joel hurried to pull the letter from the envelope and opened it. He wanted to hurry and change the subject from Pen's shaky relationship. When he looked at the paper, his breath caught in his chest. He recognized that beautiful scrawl with its curly loops and hearts instead of dots over all the i's. He could feel Chad and Pen's eyes on him. He began to read the words to himself first, making sure there was nothing he felt uncomfortable sharing. Within a few words, the world surrounding him dropped away into blackness. He heard nothing, not the whirl of the choppers as they came in, not the rumble of truck engines. All he heard was the sound of Hazel's voice in his ears, as if she were sitting right beside him, reading the words of her letter to him. His heart began to thud against his chest.

"Hey, you okay man?" Chad asked. "It's not one of them 'Dear John' letters, is it?"

Pen looked down at the letter in his hand and shuddered.

Joel shook his head. He couldn't speak. His throat felt thick with emotion.

Chad looked at Pen. "This don't look good."

"No," Joel spit out. "It's good." He sucked in a breath. "Hazel's pregnant."

Chad reared back and roared out a cowboy whoop. He reached over and slapped Joel on the back. The slap echoed loudly and stung.

"Congratulations, man!"

Joel's insides felt like Jell-O. The elation he felt mixed with terror. He was going to be a father. But what if things went wrong again. *What if she loses this baby too?* He wouldn't be there. He couldn't comfort her or try and keep her from falling back into that bleak darkness again. Fear began to rise in his chest. Hazel would be alone. He shook his head. *No!* Ruthie and Mr. McKay were there. Alice and Sandra too.

He'd gotten a letter from Hazel last week telling him the news about Milton. It had infuriated him, but what could he do? Nothing. Just like now. Hazel was a million miles away with his child growing in her womb and there was nothing he could do to help her. Every fiber of his being needed to be with her right now.

A boot kicked red dust up from the ground into Pen's face, pulling Joel from his fears and thoughts.

"What are you, numb nuts doing?

Pen rubbed the dust from his eyes. "Hey, watch it, Davis!" he screeched.

"Watch yourself. Lieutenant Roberts is looking for you."

Pen scrambled up off the ground. "What? Where?"

Harvey Davis pointed to the wooden hut used as the latrines. The screened walls only partially concealed the people using the makeshift toilets.

"The latrines?" Chad asked. "What's going on?"

Davis folded his arms across his chest. A smug smile spread across his lips. "Well, cowboy Raggedy Ann, it seems that one of the honey pots is full and needs to be shoveled out and burned. Ever smell a burning honey pot? That stench will stick on you for weeks."

Pen's face fell.

"What's that got to do with Pen?" Joel asked.

"Well, Pendal-ding-dong here," Davis said, using his thumb to point toward Pen, "was late to his patrol shift this morning. So he gets the honor of shoveling the crap." Davis looked toward Pen. "And I made sure to leave something nice and juicy for you."

Pen's face contorted and he turned paler than normal, but he said nothing. Joel leaped to his feet and Chad stood up with him.

Davis held out a finger, "Stay out of this, hickory dickory. I don't want any trouble with you."

The heat rose in Joel's face, and it felt like his body was on fire. Harvey Davis gave everyone nicknames. Joel's nickname had evolved since basic training from country hick, to just hick, then to hickory dickory doc, to Joel's least favorite, hickory dickory. Joel folded his letter along the creases and put it gently in his T-shirt's breast pocket. With his chest raised, he walked up close to Davis, putting himself in his space. Davis didn't back away. He took a step closer toward Joel. They eyed each other, noses inches apart. Joel could see Davis's chest rise and fall, the unshaven black stubble dotting his face. Joel's jaw tightened. Months of harassment had accumulated to this, and Joel felt his limit had been reached. His body trembled with anticipation at what he wanted to do with his fists.

"Hey, hey guys! Let's not do this," Chad said, moving to their sides with hands held out. "We don't need any trouble. Neither one of you wants to deal with the consequences if you settle this here, right now."

"Yeah, I'll go see Lieutenant Roberts. No big deal, guys. Leave it alone," Pen pleaded.

Joel didn't budge, not an inch. He stared into Davis's unblinking light green eyes. Joel gritted his teeth until his jaw ached and clenched his hands into fists. His nails dug into his palms. *It would be so easy. So easy to smash my fist into his stupid face.* He wanted to feel the bones crack and his teeth break. His chest rose and he sucked in air. Air he didn't want to share with Davis.

Joel felt a hand on his shoulder. Chad said, "Come on, man, don't let him ruin today. Don't spoil the news. You're going to be a father. Don't spend today in the hot box."

Davis blinked and took a step back. He dusted off his shirt, breaking eye contact with Joel and popping the tension between them like a balloon. Joel wanted that tension back. He wanted to escalate it, but it was gone. Davis took another step back and looked at Joel.

"I guess congratulations are in order."

"Yeah, yeah," Chad said, nodding his head and moving his body between Joel and Davis.

"So I guess we'll finish our conversation on another day," Davis said and gave Joel a mocking salute.

"Definitely," Joel sneered.

Davis began to walk away but turned and paused. "Be careful hick, I heard our platoon is gearing up for a huge air assault. Soon it'll be our turn to see some action." He whistled low. "Lots of snipers out there ready to snipe soon-to-be fathers." He laughed. "Oh, and don't forget the bouncing betties hidden in that jungle. Accidentally step on one of those and you'll blow your legs right off. Hate for that baby to end up fatherless."

Joel's body flinched and tightened. Chad's strong hands blocked his path to Davis. Joel tried to jerk away, but Chad pushed hard against his chest, keeping him away from Davis.

Davis gave him a wink and turned, jogging to the huge metal building used as the chow hall.

"It's not worth it," Chad said, still pushing Joel back.

When Davis was out of sight, Chad dropped his arms.

"I don't know, it might have been worth it, just to slug his ugly mug," Joel said, trying to calm himself.

Pen stood beside Joel and stared toward the chow hall. "Do you think he's right? About the air assault?"

Joel shrugged, "We've been here a lot longer than others. So maybe."

Chad spit on the ground, "Well, I'm ready."

Joel wasn't sure if he was ready. Chad didn't have a future child on the way. Joel had responsibilities. People who needed him. *Could I really shoot someone?* He thought of Mr. McKay lying on the ground, bleeding from a gunshot wound to the leg that he'd caused. But it'd been a mistake. Thinking of the past sent a shudder through his body. Joel knew he would and could shoot if it meant keeping himself alive to come home to Hazel and their baby.

"I guess I better head off. Gotta report to Lieutenant Roberts and get my chewing for being late." Pen walked slowly with slumped shoulders in the direction of a wooden beamed building where the commanders stayed during the day.

Joel looked at Chad, and Chad rolled his eyes. It was as if he could read Joel's mind.

"Seriously, Davenport?"

"Come on, let's help him. You know he needs it."

Together they jogged to the supply shed where shovels, tools, and a hodgepodge of other barrack necessities were stored. Joel grabbed a shovel and threw it to Chad. He caught it and slung it over his shoulder. Joel grabbed two more shovels and flung them over his shoulders, letting them balance on his shoulder blades.

"Just think, after this we'll be able to go home and start our own crap removal services."

Chad laughed, "You're full of it, man. Completely full of it."

Chapter 17

RUTHIE

Ruthie stood beside Hazel, staring at the old house in the middle of the forest. She had forgotten how much of a pain getting out here was, and how isolated and away from everything they had lived when they were children. A frigid breeze blew her blonde hair to the side, sending a chill down her spine. She wondered about basic training and how difficult it would be. Ruthie pushed cold fists into her jacket pockets. Since her father had sold the house, it had been newly painted, the warped boards on the porch replaced, and the old light fixtures repaired. The place didn't seem the same. The doctor who owned it now had done a good job on the repairs. But it didn't feel like her home anymore because of course it wasn't. "Doesn't look the same, does it?" she asked.

Hazel shuddered. "Goodness it's cold today."

Ruthie frowned, "You shouldn't be out here. It's too cold."

"Oh stop," Hazel huffed. "I'm perfectly fine. Some days I still miss this place, you know. But at least the owner said we could come whenever we wanted to our old tree—the magical spot." Hazel nudged Ruthie with her elbow.

"Oh, good grief, we were so strange."

Hazel fake gasped. "Strange! You zip it! Spending time with you under that tree and reading you the stories I'd written are some of my fondest childhood memories."

Ruthie gave her sister a hip bump. "Mine too."

Hazel dug inside her purse and pulled out a notebook Ruthie recognized.

"Hey, is that the journal Joel gave to you?"

A small grin spread across Hazel's face. Her cheeks pinkened and she nodded. "I wrote a story for ol' times' sake. I'll read it to you under our tree."

Ruthie's heart exploded with joy. "You wrote a story for me? But it's so cold."

"I can handle a few minutes longer if you can," Hazel said, smiling so brightly it made Ruthie's insides warm.

Ruthie grabbed Hazel's hand and gently pulled her to the forest.

※ ※ ※ ※

Ruthie sat on a low hanging tree branch. Hazel laid down a blanket she'd brought and sat on it with her back pressed against the thick tree trunk. Ruthie noticed how the branches seemed lower now than they did when she was smaller. Today, she and Hazel had to get on their hands and knees to get to the trunk without hitting their heads. The sunlight peaked through the few brown leaves left, leaving diamond shapes across Hazel's face. As Hazel's soft and sweet voice mixed with the songs of the birds, Ruthie closed her eyes, and she felt her chest loosen for the first time since she'd joined the Army Nurse Corps. She'd drive to Houston, Texas, this afternoon to start basic training. Then maybe after that, she'd ride her first airplane to a world across the ocean—Vietnam. The wind ran its cold fingers down her neck and Ruthie shivered. She tried to focus on Hazel's story filled with kind giants, fuzzy rabbits, and magical fairies. It truly was a beautiful story, but no matter how she tried to concentrate on it, her mind would wonder about the unknown and unexpected. Most days she felt selfish for wanting this adventure. How could she leave Hazel, especially at a time like this with her new niece or nephew on the way? But Hazel had done nothing but encourage her, and so far, her pregnancy seemed to be going well. Guilt scrapped at Ruthie with its sharp nails, but she could never go back. She'd signed the paper to join. What was done was done.

"The end," Hazel said and rubbed her small baby bump. "I hope I'll be able to take this little one out here one day."

Ruthie's hand found a brown leaf still clinging to the branch. She plucked it off and twisted the stem in her fingers. "You should. The baby would love it out here."

They sat in silence, letting the sounds of the forest soothe them.

Ruthie glanced down at Hazel. "You know, Joel's right. You really do have a talent. You should write stories and sell them."

Hazel snorted and shook her head. "Don't be silly. No one would buy a story about a magical tree giant or fairies that protect the forest."

Ruthie tore the dry leaf into bits and flicked the pieces at Hazel.

"Hey!" Hazel laughed, dusting off the brown flakes.

Ruthie giggled, "You have no idea how creative you are and how wonderful your stories are. Of course, people would buy them. Can you imagine parents reading your stories to their children before bed? You are way more than just a Piggly Wiggly cashier."

Hazel rubbed at her eyes with the back of her hand. "I'm going to miss you," Hazel said, her voice thick. "I'm so sorry. I know I said I wouldn't cry."

Ruthie jumped off the branch. She pulled Hazel up and wrapped her arms around her in a tight hug. "I'm going to miss you too, every day."

After Ruthie and Hazel had shed a few more tears, they walked back to the old house and got into Hazel's car. Hazel drove them back to the duplex so Ruthie could grab her bags and say good-bye to their father. She couldn't believe the time had passed so quickly.

Emotion swelled inside Ruthie's chest when Hazel pulled into the parking spot in front of the duplexes. Everyone stood outside—her father,

Sandra and the boys, Margarette Ann and her family, Alice and her family, Mr. Hal and Mrs. Anne, and Ms. Faye. Everyone waved when they pulled in and parked. Mikey held balloons. She remembered Mrs. Battalou's discouraging statements about joining the Army Nurse Corps. To her, Ruthie's life was ruined. But here, the people she cared most about supported her. Even though her father wasn't happy about her decision. When she'd told him about it after the Women's Coalition meeting last week, he'd said, "I don't like what you've done, peanut. But I'll be behind you every step of the way."

Hazel laughed, "Ruthie silent. That's a first."

Ruthie leaned over and gave Hazel's arm a soft pinch. "I can't believe you did this."

"It wasn't just me. We all wanted to tell you good-bye." Hazel put the car in park and turned toward Ruthie. "Look, I know you've felt guilty for leaving, but see, I've got so many people. There's no need to worry about me." She sniffed, "And I want you to know that I am so incredibly proud of you. Volunteering to serve as a nurse. It's so brave."

Ruthie had to look away when she saw the tears begin to spill out of the corners of Hazel's eyes. She dabbed at the corners of her own eyes. "I thought we were done crying."

"Not yet we're not!" Hazel said, pulling her in for another tight hug.

Chapter 18

HAZEL

Hazel pushed herself away from the toilet. Her knees ached and a sharp pain pricked her back just above her left hip bone. Sweat rolled down her back, dampening her dress. With a shaky hand, she reached up and flushed the toilet. Surely the constant nauseousness would end. She touched her stomach. A tiny kick on her right side calmed her nerves. *Well, at least someone else isn't happy with all this vomiting either.* Hazel couldn't remember being so nauseous with her last pregnancy. She stood and wiped her mouth with her arm before heading to the little mirror over her bathroom sink to see what shape she was in. She sighed. Her face looked clown-like, blotchy and smeared. Dark circles rounded her eyes, and not one hint of the lipstick she'd applied earlier existed. One black streak of mascara stretched from her lower left eye across the side of her face, as if someone had used a marker to draw on her skin. *Jeez, there's no way I'm going to make it on time. Not today. Mr. Crutchfield will kill me.*

She hurried and splashed water on her face before reapplying her make-up. She rushed out of the bathroom and grabbed her purse and keys that lay on the little table. She glanced at the sofa. The memory of Ruthie sleeping on her sofa after Joel had left for Vietnam made her eyes sting. Oh, how she missed them. She sucked in a breath that caught between her ribs. She couldn't lose it right now. If she started crying, she'd have to reapply her makeup for a third time.

Outside, Hazel took in a long deep breath, letting the crisp morning air fill her lungs. Dirty, left-over snow settled in the corners of the stoops near her and Sandra's front doors.

"Good morning."

The words made Hazel practically come out of her skin. She laid a hand over her racing heart. "Whoa! I didn't see you there."

Sandra sat on the small concrete stoop outside her door. Her fingers laced around a mug that sat on her knees. Steam wafted from the top, and Hazel breathed in the smell of fresh roasted coffee. Her favorite smell, the one she used to crave every morning, made bile rise in the back of her throat. She crinkled her nose and scrunched her face. *What is this child doing to me?*

Sandra's eyes grew wide. "Oh shoot, I'm sorry. I forget that your favorite thing in the world now makes you sick," she said and tossed the coffee out on the ground.

Hazel chuckled, "Don't get rid of your coffee because of me! It's perfectly fine. One day I'll love coffee again, or at least that's what I tell myself anyway."

Sandra gave her a half smile that didn't quite touch her eyes. For the first time, she saw Sandra's eyes were red rimmed and swollen.

"What are you doing outside? It's freezing. Are you okay?" Hazel asked.

Sandra shook her head. Tears glistened across her lashes as she squeezed her eyes closed. "I couldn't sleep. Not without him there. Mikey crawls into bed with me now and again. That helps some, but..." she sniffed. "I just miss him, you know?"

"Yeah, I know."

Sadness hung on Sandra like a coat three sizes too big. Hazel wondered if people could see it on her as well. She wondered if all the women left behind gave off invisible signals of misery, worry, and loneliness. Hazel longed to lower herself to the stoop beside Sandra and mope with her for the rest of the day. But she didn't have time, she couldn't be late. Hazel looked into

Sandra's sad dark eyes and folded. She collapsed down on the stoop beside her and looped an arm around Sandra's shoulder. Sandra relaxed into her.

They sat like that—in silence—for a few moments, listening to the car engines as they passed, the tires crunching over pavement and snow. Hazel felt a twist in her heart. She missed the forest sounds that surrounded her old house in the woods. She thought about the days she and Ruthie spent under their magical tree. She wrote her best stories there. Since Ruthie left, she'd started writing again in the notebook Joel had bought for her, especially at night when she couldn't sleep, when all the worries and fears she pushed away during the day invaded her mind. She'd spend countless nighttime hours filling the pages with talking animals, found romance, and courageous heroes until she couldn't keep her eyes open.

"Hey, don't you got work today?" Sandra asked.

Hazel jolted. "Oh shoot!" she said, leaping up from the stoop. She bent over and kissed the top of Sandra's head.

Sandra chuckled and waved her off. "See you tonight? For dinner?"

"Of course," Hazel said. She turned and waggled a finger at Sandra. "Now don't you let those sweet babies drive you crazy today. I'll play with them when I get home."

Sandra smiled and rolled her eyes, "Yes, Mrs. Bossy Pants."

Hazel hoped Mr. Crutchfield wouldn't kill her for being late, or even worse, fire her. Luckily when she arrived, she found him still in the back storage room counting inventory. She hurried to put on one of the new aprons he'd given her and Louanne last week, then hurried to the front of the store. As she passed Mr. Crutchfield's office, she noticed the door hung open, and he'd left his radio on. Her ears perked up. She paused in front of the door to listen.

"Women, we must stand up. This war must end. Join the Women Strike for Peace next month as we march against the war. Take a stand," a woman proclaimed.

Hazel hurried out, not caring to hear the rest. Protests against the war were everywhere now. It felt like everyone was constantly angry. Angry at the government, angry with their leaders, and angry with the men fighting in the war, men like Joel and Milton. She swallowed hard. She thought of Joel. *I've got to tell him about Ruthie.* He'd received her letter about the baby already. Joy filled her when she thought about the letter she'd received from him in return. His words were filled with excitement, "We're going to be parents," "I can't believe I'm going to be a father," "I wish I was with you," "I miss you with my whole heart." Every letter from him took her on an emotional Tilt-A-Whirl. She laughed, she cried, she missed him terribly. She knew though, if she told him that Ruthie was at basic training, learning drills for emergency rooms and how to fire a gun, he'd be filled to the brim with worry for her. She didn't need him to worry about anything other than getting home safely. She teetered the fence daily on whether to tell him or not.

Hazel reached behind her to undo her apron strings. She'd tied them too tight and needed them looser before she suffocated. She walked to the front as she tied her apron again. Louanne stood by her cash register, admiring her red polished fingernails. She fanned her fingers out so Hazel could see them.

"What you think?"

Hazel moved behind the other register. "Pretty," she said, hardly looking while she straightened the space around her. She hated it when Louanne beat her to work. Not only had she beat her here, but she looked beautiful today. Hazel felt like a queasy, sweaty mess.

"You were late," Louanne said flatly. She drummed her long red nails on the counter. "He asked where you were."

"Oh?" Hazel's heart dropped. A cold sweat broke out over her skin, dotting it with goose bumps. She needed this job. She'd worked hard, so much harder than Louanne, but it felt like many times, the work she did went unnoticed. Mr. Crutchfield despised tardiness most of all. Hazel tore at her thumb nail while Louanne held up her perfect nails and inspected them.

"Don't worry!" she waved her hand. "I covered for ya. Told him you were in the restroom. You know with the pregnancy and all. But good thing you made it when you did," Louanne winked, her lashes thick and full.

Hazel laid a hand on her chest. The thumping of her heartbeat began to slow. "Thank you," she whispered. "You don't know how much—"

Louanne held her hand up, stopping her from finishing. Her voice lowered an octave, "Look, I've got a date tonight. And seeing as I covered for

121

you," she began to drum her red fingernails on the counter again. The *tick tap, tick tap* drove Hazel mad. "I told Mr. Crutchfield you'd volunteered to close up for me tonight."

A blaze of heat passed across Hazel's face and her blood began to boil. Of course, Louanne had taken advantage of Hazel's mistake. A tidal wave of memories of all the things she'd done to help Louanne came rushing through her head. All the times she'd covered for her, cleaned up Louanne's areas, eaten late lunches so Louanne could go on lunch dates, or handled annoying tasks Louanne couldn't possibly take the time to learn. Hazel wanted to rip Louanne's teased hair right out of her head.

"But... a date?" Hazel stammered, finding it hard not to scream. "On a weekday?"

"Um yeah," Louanne said, flipping her hair back. "I'm not lucky like you. I ain't got a man yet." She pulled at the brown apron that stretched across her ample chest. "I hate these things. I'm never gonna get a man wearing this paper sack. Oh!" She held up a finger like she remembered something. "Since you usually do the opening morning routine around here, I just left it for you. I was afraid to try. Didn't want to mess anything up, you know." She flashed Hazel a huge white smile.

A flash of red passed before Hazel's eyes. Her head spun and she gripped the counter. She needed to calm down for the baby. She took deep breaths, and without saying anything to Louanne, she left the area to go straighten the produce section. She picked up an over ripe cantaloupe to dispose of it. Small fruit flies dodged at the ripe juices leaking from a tiny crack on the side. She thought about throwing it at Louanne's head, but she dropped it in the trash with a thud before she did anything she'd regret. She wished Joel was here so she could tell him another Louanne story.

"I feel bad for any man that marries her," he'd said one night when they were cuddled on the sofa. "It's like she should come with some warning or something. Be prepared to lose all your money and live in misery your whole life. If that's what you're looking for, we've got the girl for you."

Hazel chuckled at the memory.

The setting sun sent rays of intense white light shooting through Piggly Wiggly's glass door. Hazel squinted as she turned the sign to close. She flipped the deadbolt, hearing the loud click as the lock set in place. The sides of her feet rubbed against the edges of her shoes. Mr. Crutchfield had left for the day at a little past four for an appointment, and Louanne had snuck out shortly after him. Hazel didn't mind though. She liked working alone.

Hazel grabbed a broom and began to sweep the floor. She paused and placed a hand on the lower part of her back. She stretched, feeling the tight muscles elongate and throb. After she'd swept, she walked to the back to return the broom to the closet near Mr. Crutchfield's office. As she began to retrieve the mop and bucket, the phone in Mr. Crutchfield's office began to ring. Hazel wondered if she should answer it. The door stood wide open. *What if a customer needs something?* She rushed to the telephone as fast as her swollen feet would let her.

Once she made it to his desk, the ringing stopped. Hazel's head lolled back, and she collapsed into Mr. Crutchfield's rolling chair. She'd never felt so tired in all her life. Exhaustion felt like a new skin she'd stepped into. It hung on her, dragging her down. She folded her arms on the desk and laid her head on them. A short nap wouldn't hurt. She could still make it to dinner with Sandra later tonight. The telephone rang again, making her practically leap out of the seat. She watched its white boxy body shake with the tone. *Answer it dummy!* She grabbed the receiver, hearing the featherlight chime as she picked it up and held it to her ear.

"H-h-hello? Piggly Wiggly," her voice wavered.

"Hazel?"

"Yes, who's this?"

"Oh, thank goodness, I tried your house. My, you sure work late. I'm sorry! This is Krissy Maxwell. I worked with Ruthie at the hospital. I think you need to head this way. Right now, actually."

"What? What's wrong?" Hazel's first thought went to her father in the hospital bed those many years ago. Not knowing if he'd survive. She shivered as her brain ping ponged to Sandra and the boys. *What if one of them is hurt?* Her throat tightened, but before she could ask who was at the hospital, Krissy explained more.

"It's Joel's pa. He's been in a terrible accident."

Hazel's skin prickled with goosebumps. Krissy's voice lowered to a whisper. "He's not expected to make it through the night. Can you get here quick?"

Hazel didn't know, but it didn't matter. "Yes, yes of course! I'll be there."

Chapter 19

HAZEL

Hazel's hands were sweaty on the steering wheel. Her back stretched tight like a rubber band. She realized she really knew nothing about Joel's pa. She knew about his past. He'd been an evil man and a horrible father. The hurt and pain he caused Joel still had Joel on occasion waking up in terror in the middle of the night. She laid a hand across her chest; she needed to slow her breathing.

Joel's pa had changed though, for the most part. He'd been willing to take the blame when Joel accidentally shot her father. A fire burned in the pit of her stomach at the memory. *It was his fault to begin with.* She shoved the anger down. He's in a hospital bed, dying. She needed to forget his past wrongs and do the right thing for Joel. He was still family anyway.

Joel had tried over the years since her father's accident to have some kind of relationship with his pa. She'd never said anything to Joel, but she never wanted his pa to be a part of their lives. Still, she knew when Joel looked at his pa, he saw all the blood family he had left on this earth. Her eyes blurred. She'd have to tell Joel about this somehow. She knew Joel probably already felt mountains of guilt and pain for being gone, and now he'd miss out on the last few minutes of his pa's life. Resolve settled on her. She'd be the one to hold his pa's hand then, since Joel couldn't.

Krissy stood at the door, waiting for her. Even though Hazel had only met her a handful of times, she grabbed Hazel in a tight hug. In her ear, she whispered, "Hurry, we need to get to his room quick. I'm not sure why, but Officer McConnell is in there."

Hazel gasped, "What? Why?"

Krissy pulled Hazel closer and lowered her voice, "He said he wanted to see if he was lucid enough to answer questions about the wreck, but he had other questions he wanted to ask too."

A cold sweat broke out over Hazel's body. Years ago, Joel had shot her father months before their wedding. Even though it had been an accident, they'd been afraid no one would believe it. Joel had an undeserved stigma attached to him because of his pa. Her dad came up with the idea to say it had been a hunting accident with some random hunter he'd never seen before. They'd all stuck to the lie just like her father directed. They'd kept the secret for so long, it had started to feel like the truth. Then one day none of it mattered anymore because everyone had forgotten and moved on, everyone except Officer McConnell.

"Take me there, and let's hurry."

Krissy led the way down the hallway. Hazel beat down the memories of being rushed through the hospital on a gurney when she'd begun to miscarry her daughter. She had to keep ahold of herself. She didn't have time to get emotional. Krissy stepped in front of a closed door and reached for the doorknob, but before she could touch it, it opened. Officer McConnell stepped out, holding his hat in his hands. His eyes widened for a split second when he saw them. Something almost akin to shame passed across his face, but it left in an instant.

"Hazel," he said, nodding his head.

Hazel gave him her best wintery smile.

"I'm sorry for what's happened. I know Joel would rather be here with his pa than over there in Nam."

When he said Joel's name, Hazel's blood ran cold. She wouldn't let him see her fear. She lifted her chin and set her jaw. "Yes, it's going to be very difficult for him to hear what's happened."

She held his gaze until he looked away. He gripped his hat tighter. "Well, I'll be moseying along now so you can have some time with Thomas. Too bad he won't be recovering like your father did."

Hazel felt like he'd slapped her face. She swallowed, feeling it stick in the back of her throat. When Officer McConnell started to walk away, Hazel felt her heart finally start to beat again. But after a few paces, he turned back toward her.

"When Joel gets back, you tell him I need to see him. Okay?"

Hazel's body froze and she couldn't move. Krissy wrapped her arm around Hazel. "Have a good night, Officer," she said, her tone hard.

McConnell pursed his lips like he wanted to say something more but thought better of it and left without another word.

❦❦

Mr. Davenport's room smelled overpoweringly of bleach. Hazel took shallow breaths. Joel's pa laid flat on his back. His eyes were swollen and bruised. Red stained bandages were wrapped around the top of his head. His hands rested at his sides, and his skin looked gray. A glass IV bottle dripped liquid into a tube which ran to bandages on his arm. If it wasn't for the slight rise and fall of his chest, Hazel would have thought he was already gone. Krissy laid her hand on Hazel's shoulder.

"I need to check on the other patients, but I'll be back later to look in on you."

Hazel nodded and moved a plastic chair close to Mr. Davenport's bed. She heard the door click closed behind her as she sat down. She wasn't sure what to do. *Do I take his hand? Talk to him?* She didn't know him very well. What do you say to your husband's father, the man who made most of his life hell? She laid her hand on the bed, feeling the coolness of the bedsheet. She slid her fingers over to his and laid them on top of the back of his hand.

His eyelashes flickered and his eyes opened, slits of white and color between the dark bruises. "Sarah? Is that you?"

Hazel cleared her throat, "No, Mr. Davenport. It's me. Hazel. Joel's wife."

127

A tear pooled in the corner of his eye and ran down his cheek. "I'm sorry, Hazel." He turned his hand so he could take hers completely in a weak grasp. "Thank-you-for-coming."

His words seemed to slur together, and she wondered if it was from the pain medication or his head injury.

"I'm glad you are here. I miss Joel." His words dropped off.

Hazel's eyes blurred and she blinked. "I miss him too. So much."

He gripped her hand a little tighter. "Don't worry, I told that officer it was an accident. I told him he didn't mean to do it."

Hazel sucked in a ragged breath. "Who didn't mean what?" she asked, feeling a coldness run down her spine.

His head lolled to the side to look at her with unfocused eyes. "Joel. He didn't mean it. You know that right?"

Hazel's stomach twisted. She nodded, "I know. It was an accident."

"He loves you."

Hazel bit her bottom lip to keep a sob from escaping.

He breathed in, and it sounded like cans rattling on the road. He winced, squeezing his eyes closed tight. When he looked at her again, she could see whatever light was there had started to fade. The skin on the hand she held grew colder, and his grip began to loosen.

"When I'm gone, tell Joel to talk to his family. He needs them."

Hazel tilted her head. "Mr. Davenport, Joel doesn't have any family left. Just you."

He sucked in another raspy breath. "Yes, his family. He needs them. His family. Make them see him. Make them do right by him. It's been too long. They did him so wrong."

Then he closed his eyes and never spoke again. Four hours later, he'd past on, leaving Hazel in a blur. Did Joel have more family? But who? She decided to keep Mr. Davenport's ramblings to herself and not mention them to Joel. Even though her head spun in circles, she took solace in knowing Mr. Davenport's last words were filled with concern for his son.

Chapter 20

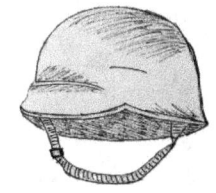

JOEL, MARCH 1969

Joel had expected to be marching in the jungle by now or be flown and dropped in some strange location during an air assault. But two weeks had passed, and still Harvey Davis's prediction had yet to come true. Joel felt thankful to be standing in the mess hall holding a metal tray, waiting to be served powdered eggs and floppy bacon instead of having to eat those terrible C-rations. They'd just got back from a week's patrol around the base, and Joel was famished. He held the metal tray against his side with one arm while trying to scratch a mosquito bite on his shoulder with the other. It didn't matter how much of the chemical-smelling, skin-burning bug juice Joel sprayed on—those things still got him. They didn't look like the small mosquitoes from Arkansas. These here looked more like skinny birds out to get your blood.

Outside, he could hear "Proud Mary" blaring from a radio as some of the guys took a break to play volleyball using a makeshift net they'd made from mosquito netting. Chad rushed in the mess hall and grabbed a metal tray. He shoved Joel from behind. Joel lurched forward, laughing.

"Good grief, man, what's got into you."

Chad's T-shirt clung to his chest. Blotches of sweat darkened the material. "We won! I slammed it hard in Davis's face. You should have seen it."

Pen ran up and jumped on Chad's back, giving the top of Chad's head a noogie. "Yeah, it was great! Davis's face turned bright red. I thought it was going to explode."

Joel laughed. "I wish I could have seen it. But I've gotta hurry. I got an M48 Patton to work on."

Chad and Pen bowed in mock honor.

"Whoa, it must be his first tank to work on," Chad jested while elbowing Pen.

"Nah, but I feel like a kid in a candy store every time I get my hands on the engine of one of those things."

Chad and Pen laughed. "Square," Chad joked.

Joel shook his head. "Takes one to know one. Hey! I heard Bob Hope may be coming this way."

Pen grabbed a metal tray. "I sure hope he brings all his dancers with him."

Chad gave a low whistle. "Oh yeah, I could use some of that."

Joel rolled his eyes and held his tray out. A worker dressed in sweaty whites rubbed his brow with his forearm before shoveling eggs onto Joel's tray.

"Hot one today?" Joel said, trying to make conversation, but the worker just nodded. It was crazy to think about how at home the weather would be brisk and cool, while here, the humidity could almost smother a person. It reminded him of the hot summers in Mr. Hal's garage with no air conditioning, just oscillating fans. He took his tray and sat down at the cafeteria table. Chad and Pen sat across from him.

"I heard they're showing a movie tonight. They got the reel for *Cool Hand Luke*. I never got to see it." Chad said, pushing a fork of eggs into his mouth.

Pen tore at a piece of bacon. "Yeah, I could watch that."

Joel agreed to meet them at the tent near the O club after his shift ended. Because the enlisted men weren't allowed in the officers' club, they'd erected their own area for fun and relaxation. Occasionally, when they got their hands on a movie reel, they'd hang a sheet at the back of the tent to project it on. It reminded Joel of the drive-in movie theater he and Hazel would go to in Waldron. He sighed. So many things reminded him of home lately.

"Davenport! Davenport!"

Joel whipped around. Danny Barnes, his platoon's medic, ran to him. "Lieutenant Roberts is looking for you man."

Joel sprung to his feet. "What? Why?"

Danny shook his head. "It's some kind of emergency. He's at tactical."

Joel looked at Chad's and Pen's wide eyes. He swallowed, feeling it stick in the back of his throat. He couldn't take in a full breath, like the wind had been kicked out of him. *Hazel. Something's happened to her and the baby.* His whole body went cold.

"I don't know what you're waiting for, but you better get moving," Chad said, knocking him from his stupor.

He scrambled out of the table and hit the door hard. He didn't stop running until he reached the large Quonset hut where Phu Bai Combat Base's tactical operations center was located. He rushed inside. The cool air made him shiver. Lieutenant Roberts and a few other officers stood talking in hushed tones. Joel gritted his teeth and marched straight toward them.

Lieutenant Roberts saw him. "Good, Davenport. This way."

Joel paused and saluted.

"No time for that. Come on, boy."

Joel followed Roberts further inside the hut to a table where several square boxes with knobs were positioned. A weird long microphone sat in front of them. On top of one of the boxes sat a rotary telephone.

"Sit," Roberts motioned to the chairs in front of the crazy looking set up. Joel sat, and Roberts picked up the receiver. "Now this here is MARS, or Military Auxiliary Radio System. Your wife, Hazel, is already on the other end."

The blood rushed loudly inside Joel's head and his heart pounded between his ears. Something had happened to Hazel.

Roberts shoved the receiver toward him. Joel flinched back not wanting to take it. It was better if he didn't know.

"Take it, son. Now when you speak lean in towards the microphone. Once you've finished a sentence and want her to speak, you have to say the word 'over.' That lets the operator know to patch it to the other person so you can hear her reply. Got it?"

Joel couldn't breathe. In a daze, he took the receiver Roberts held in front of his face.

"Just say 'over' when you're done talking. It's easy, boy. Got it, solider?"

Joel nodded his head.

"Make the most of this time. You only have five minutes. Who knows when you'll get another chance like this." Roberts patted Joel's shoulder before walking off and leaving him alone.

Joel's hand felt slick on the receiver, and it trembled when he held it to his ear. He leaned in.

"Hello. Hello." But he heard no reply. Blood rushed to his face when he remembered the directions Lieutenant Roberts had just told him moments ago. He leaned forward and tried again. "Hello Hazel, over."

"Joel! Joel it's you. I miss you so much. Over."

Hearing her voice sent Joel's head spinning. At that moment, his whole body ached from the home sickness he felt. "I miss you too. More than you'll ever know." He swallowed hard and forced himself to ask the question he wanted to know more than anything. "Are you alright? Over." What would he do if her answer was no? He had no idea. He'd swim across the ocean to get back to her or go crazy.

When he heard her voice say, "I'm good. The baby and I are doing good. Over." He thought his heart would leap out of his skin. He could breathe again. He ran a hand down his face to compose himself. He didn't want to cry. Not here, in front of Roberts and the other officers, but the relief loosened every muscle in his body, and he felt light. "It's so good to hear your voice. I love you so much. Over."

"I love you too. They say we only have a few minutes, and I have to tell you something. I didn't want to send it in a letter. It... it wouldn't be right. So, I scheduled a call because I wanted you to hear it from me."

The line went silent. Joel sat up; afraid the patch had been broken. But then he heard her soft sobs from across the ocean. He wanted to comfort her, but she wouldn't hear him until she gave him the line. Hazel had to say the word over so the operator would give him a chance to speak.

"I-I need to tell you that your pa. Your pa passed away a few weeks ago. He got in a wreck. Hit a tree. There was nothing the doctors could do."

She started to cry harder, and he wanted to scream at the operator. *Just patch me through!*

"I'm so sorry, Joel. I held his hand until he was gone. He wasn't alone. Over."

With the line patched back to him, Joel found his voice wouldn't work. He opened his mouth to speak, but nothing came out. What Hazel had said finally hit him like a sack of bricks. His pa was dead. If it wasn't for Hazel and her family, he'd be totally alone. He had no parents anymore. No uncles or aunts. No grandparents. It was just him now. He closed his eyes tight. He couldn't put his thoughts into words, so he said, "Over," to give the line back to Hazel.

"I'm so sorry, Joel. The funeral was simple but nice. My dad, Ms. Faye, Sandra and the boys, they were all there. I made sure his plot is near our family. Over."

Joel sniffed. "I wish I could have been there." Even though his pa had been horrible to him almost all his life, he meant it. He wished he could have been there to pay his final respects. Before he came to Nam, he and his pa had developed some sort of relationship. Though tenuous at best, it still was something. "I'm sure it was very nice. That was so kind of you to place him near your family. You didn't mention Ruthie being at the funeral. Did she have to work? Over."

Across miles of air and water, Joel heard Hazel gasp. "Um, well, yes. She did have to work. Actually, that's another thing I've been meaning to tell you. But hear me out... I didn't want you to worry. I still have so many people here. Sandra's a huge help. And Daddy too. Well, you know Daddy's always here. So like I said. Ruthie was working, except she's not at the hospital here anymore. She's at Fort Sam in Houston. She joined the Army Nursing Corps. She'll be done soon with basic and possibly heading to Vietnam as a nurse. See she volunteered. Oh goodness me. Our five minutes is almost up. I love you so much. Over."

From behind his shoulder, he heard Roberts say, "Tell her you love her, it's time to go."

Joel's head spun in different directions. Ruthie joined the army as a nurse! She wasn't there with Hazel. But what about her promise to him to care for her? His body stiffened when Roberts started to walk toward him.

He leaned forward. There were a million things he still needed to say, but he settled on the ones that mattered the most. "I love you so much, Hazel. I think about you every day. I will worry about you. I will always worry about you. Please write to me. Good-bye, my love."

Then with a small click, the line to Hazel's voice disappeared, and he had no idea if he would ever get to hear her voice again.

Chapter 21

RUTHIE

Ruthie laid her army-issued duffle bag on her small bed. She packed it with the few things she'd brought with her to basic training. She couldn't believe her time at basic had ended. The six weeks seemed to fly by. She remembered her nerves firing on all cylinders when she first arrived and they issued her her very own olive drab uniform consisting of a belted dress, fitted jacket, and how could she forget, the nurse's cap. She wondered if anyone ever really wore them in Nam. She'd also been given fatigues, which she liked better because they were more practical.

She couldn't believe how much she enjoyed the training. The first week had been completely bonkers. Having to learn basic military courtesies like how to properly salute indoors and outdoors. She did very much enjoy learning how to read a map, but her least favorite thing, the thing she could have done without, was the marching. Every day they marched with someone spewing commands at them. They marched in their uniforms, in their uniforms wearing helmets and ponchos, in their uniforms wearing basic heels—that by far had to be the worst thing she'd ever done. The lower part of her back always ached after marching in heels. Still, after the first week, the classes she took and things she learned only further piqued her interest. She'd learned how to deal with mass casualties, how to secure and wear a gas mask, and how to care for basic battle injuries. Although she'd already known how to run an IV line and splint limbs, she'd learned other things, like using machines to suck chest wounds and how to carry a litter with a man on it without toppling over or breaking her back.

Her teachers all told her she had some of the highest marks in the class, and if she wanted, she could probably request a military hospital in the United States. She'd overheard some of the other nurses talking. They wanted to be stationed in a U.S. hospital, but that wasn't what she signed up for. She'd signed up to go to Nam, and now, that's where she knew she was heading. It seemed surreal. She'd have enough time to go home, have a short visit with her dad and Hazel, and repack for the long trip.

When she spoke to her dad to tell him, to her relief, he never asked her how she felt about going to Vietnam, if she was scared or not. She felt a mixture of terror and exhilaration which she'd never be able to put into tangible words.

"Hey doll, what you doin'?" Patty Callahan said, making her voice drop a few octaves to sound manly. Patty plopped down on the bed across from Ruthie's. Patty had been her roommate the whole six weeks, and her fast friend. Her duffle had been packed since the morning.

"Just packing, sweet tart," Ruthie said, giving her a wink.

On their first night together as roomies, Patty and Ruthie had gotten into a deep conversation about all the nicknames men had called them in their lifetime. They'd chosen the ones that irritated them the most and immediately started calling each other by those names.

"Groovy, just groovy, doll," Patty chuckled. She threw herself back on her bed. "Are you as ready as I am to get home?"

Ruthie had never been away from home this long. She desperately need-ed to see her father and sister. But it scared her to go home because then she'd have to turn around and leave again, and this time for a year. Three hundred and sixty-five days away from home. She thought about Ronnie,

136

Joel, and Milton, if they could do it, then she could too. She pulled the strings to close the top of her duffle. "I'm as ready as I'll ever be."

"You sure you don't mind giving me a ride?" Patty asked. Patty lived in Shreveport, Louisiana, and although it was a tad out the way, Ruthie felt grateful not to be all alone on a good portion of the ride.

"We've been through this, firecracker. It's on the way." Ruthie shrugged. "Well, it's north of here and that's all that matters."

Patty laughed. "Fine. Okay." She narrowed her eyes. "Firecracker. Did you just make that up?"

Ruthie slung her bag over her shoulder. "I sure did."

"Well, let's get a going then Second Lieutenant McKay."

"You know it, Second Lieutenant Callahan."

They saluted each other in the exact way they had been taught before lapsing into a fit of giggles.

Before Ruthie knew it, she and Patty were heading home. She turned up the radio and let "*Light My Fire*" by The Doors blare with the windows down. The cool wind rustled their hair while Ruthie and Patty sang at the top of their lungs. They were free. For just a brief moment in time, they were free to be themselves before being shipped off to a new world thousands of miles away. A place where they'd be required to take a daily dosage of malaria pills to keep from contracting a disease that could give them raging high fevers mixed with the worst chills and drenching sweats—a real peach of a time, or so their instructors had told them. What in the world had she been thinking when she signed up for this?

Chapter 22

HAZEL

Hazel stood there as Ruthie and Sandra sat at her small kitchen table, staring at her—speechless. She felt perplexed and troubled. Still, having her sister with her, even for a short time, made the whirling mess inside her heart settle somewhat. She laid a hand on her stomach, which had grown. She'd borrowed the dress she wore now from Sandra because her clothes didn't fit anymore. Well, at least Mikey and Mannie were having fun. They paid no mind to the women sitting at the table still gawking at her. Mikey continued to build wooden blocks high in the air, and Mannie crawled around them giggling. The story she'd just relayed didn't bother them at all.

"I'm sorry. This is really hard to believe," Ruthie said.

Sandra nodded her head, eyes wide.

Hazel looked at her sister. She'd be heading to Vietnam soon. Every time she thought about her sister going to war, her insides twisted into tight knots. Ruthie had already requested items for her future care packages. She'd said one of the training nurses, the one who had actually been to Vietnam, had told them certain items would be hard to come by there, like lotion, makeup, feminine products, and perfume. Hazel didn't tell Ruthie, but they'd recently run a sale at the Channing Drugstore, and she'd already gotten her three tubs of Oil of Olay to send.

"Okay, why don't you tell us again. This time very slowly. I need to absorb all the facts," Sandra said.

Ruthie rubbed the side of her face. "Yeah, I need to hear it again too. I'm having a hard time processing this. It's...it's just so wild."

Hazel slumped down in a chair across from them, resting her hands on her stomach. She closed her eyes and tried to remember everything that happened—every single detail.

Her shift had ended, and she'd gone to the back to hang her apron in her metal locker and grab her purse. She'd looped her purse strap around her shoulder. She pushed the metal door closed. She could even remember the hinge squawking until it shut with a pop.

When she turned around, it was as if Mr. Crutchfield had appeared out of nowhere. He stood so close to her. She'd jumped back.

"Oh!" she'd gasped, laying a hand on her belly. She hadn't heard him come up behind her.

Hazel remembered how his lips were pulled into a tight line. His eyebrows knitted together, making deep wrinkles in the center where they practically met. His arms folded in front of his chest. Her heart had pounded inside her chest. What had she done wrong? Her mind raced through everything that happened in the store that day. Did she give out the wrong change? Say something a customer took as rude? Before she could say anything, Mr. Crutchfield pointed to her belly and in a gruff voice said, "I'm sure you're gonna want time off for that?" His finger moved closer to her belly.

Hazel had to force herself not to wrap her arms around her stomach to protect her baby. She wasn't sure how to reply. She stammered, "Um, yes sir, I mean at least for the delivery."

"Are you expecting to be paid for the time you are off?"

Hazel felt the muscles in her chest tighten. Her mind blurred. She'd never thought about it. She'd been too caught up in surviving day to day without Joel and worrying about Ruthie. Sandra had mentioned something about working and the baby last week, but she'd only been half listening. *What was it Sandra had said?* Hazel racked her brain to remember, then it came to her. Sandra had asked if Mr. Crutchfield would keep her on after the baby came. At that moment, a cold chill broke out over Hazel's body. She needed this job, and because she was pregnant, Mr. Crutchfield could fire her. Sandra had told her lots of employers do that because they don't care the time off you need is to have a baby. They'll just hire someone who doesn't need time off.

Is that what he wants? To tell me I'm being fired. Her eyes blurred and she blinked quickly. She wouldn't cry in front of him.

When she didn't answer straight away, he asked, "Your husband's gone to war, isn't he?"

She tried to swallow the lump forming in the back of her throat, but it stuck there. She couldn't speak, fearing more than words would leave her mouth, so she nodded.

Mr. Crutchfield's eyebrows sunk even lower. The scowl he wore affected his entire face. She almost wilted under the hard stare of his eyes. He opened his mouth then shut it. He exhaled loudly.

"You can have six weeks. Paid leave."

Hazel repeated the words in her head. *Six weeks. Paid leave. What's happening?* He didn't have to pay her anything while she was off with the baby. He didn't even have to keep her. He could fire her right now if he wanted.

Sandra interjected, interrupting Hazel's story and her train of thought. "That really is unheard of," Sandra said.

Ruthie laughed. "Yeah, and all this time I thought Mr. Crutchfield was a cranky old toot. And look... what a blessing."

Hazel nodded. "Yes, huge blessing. Now can I finish?"

Sandra and Ruthie looked at each other and giggled.

"Go on, go on," Ruthie said, rolling her eyes, but her smile brightened her whole face. And again, Hazel's heart ached to have to let her go.

Hazel leaned back in the chair. "Okay, so I asked, 'Excuse me, sir, what did you say?'"

But Mr. Crutchfield had just ignored her question and waggled his wrinkled finger in front of her face. He'd said, "I'll have to hire someone to fill in for you while you're gone. And just know, if they end up being a better worker than you, I'll be forced to replace you. Understand?"

Her head spun and she'd nodded even though she didn't understand. Her mind reeled around in circles. Was this good or bad? *What would I do if after six weeks, I have no job to come back to? Who would even take care of the baby while I work?* She'd felt the world starting to close in around her. She needed Joel. But she'd forced herself to say, "Yes sir, I understand."

"Good," his response curt.

Just then a slow wide smile spread across his face, revealing a chipped front tooth. *Have I ever seen him smile,* she wondered.

"Just so you know, there's never going to be a better worker than you, Hazel."

A lightness rose in her heart. He'd save her job for her. Before he could turn to go, she reached out her hand and touched his arm.

"Thank you, Mr. Crutchfield. Thank you so much," her words were thick.

He shook his head. "Mrs. Crutchfield would kill me if I ever got rid of you," he chuckled. "She loves you girls. And Ruthie volunteering to be a nurse. She is just amazed at how wonderful you girls turned out, even without a mother and all."

Hazel's breath had hitched from his words. Mr. and Mrs. Crutchfield had lived in Waldron their whole lives and knew everyone's business. Maybe, just maybe, they'd know about Joel's.

"Do you care if I ask you something?" In all the years Hazel had worked at Piggly Wiggly, she'd never really spoken to Mr. Crutchfield. He'd given orders and she'd followed his directives, and that had been the extent of their relationship.

He'd shrugged, "I can only tell you what I know. What ya got?"

Her nerves almost got the best of her, and she nearly lost her resolve to ask, but she set her jaw and plunged on through. "Did Joel's pa have any family around here?"

Mr. Crutchfield tilted his head and rubbed his chin. "I was sure sorry to hear about Thomas and the wreck and all. But nah, Thomas Davenport didn't have any family here. I don't even think he had any siblings."

Hazel's heart fell and her shoulders drooped. She'd hoped there had been some substance to Joel's pa's ramblings before he died. But there wasn't.

Just the incoherent words of a dying man. "Oh, well, I didn't think so. Thank you," she said and adjusted her purse strap.

"But you know, now that I think about it..."

Hazel's head had shot up to look at him, and she couldn't take a breath.

He met her eyes. "I graduated with Sarah, Joel's mama. Thomas only moved here to be with her. She's the one who really called Waldron her home. She lived here with her brother and mother." His eyes brightened, "Oh that Ms. Angel, what a fine woman."

Hazel almost choked on her shock. "Ms. Angel?"

"Yes, Sarah's mama. She made the best chocolate pie. It had the highest calf slobbers I'd ever seen. All that tall white méringue. Don't you tell Mrs. Crutchfield, but I still dream at night about that pie."

Hazel's knees became weak. The woman who'd cared for Joel before the State gave him to his pa had been his grandmother, and Joel never knew. *How could this be?* "Ms. Angel was Joel's grandmother?"

"Of course, child." Mr. Crutchfield chewed on his lip. "You know, I always wondered why you'd chose to work here or really work at all." He ran a hand over his balding head.

"What?" Hazel asked. "What do you mean?"

"Well, Ms. Angel had been an extremely wealthy widower. After her husband died, she and those two kids had plenty. As far as I knew, they never wanted for anything. You know, I think her husband had made it big in the oil business or something." He scratched a spot near his eyebrow. "You know that huge house, what's it called?" He tapped his boot on the floor and looked up to the ceiling. "The bed and breakfast on Pine Street."

Hazel thought, "The Sweet Rose Inn?"

He snapped his fingers, "Yeah that's the one. That used to be where she lived until the owners bought it after her death."

Hazel gasped. The house stood three stories high with clean white boards for siding and a beautiful, dark green door. It had a wraparound porch with a porch swing. It was one of the biggest houses in Waldron.

He frowned. "You didn't know."

She shook her head. "No, I had no idea. Joel didn't even know. His pa never said anything about it." She looked down at the floor. "They didn't really talk about things that had to do with his mother."

"Hmph," Mr. Crutchfield pushed his hands in his pockets. "Don't that beat all. I was certain you were working because you liked it here or needed to keep busy. I mean, Joel should have gotten his mama's part of the inheritance. I'd also thought possibly Joel was bad with money and had blown it all, or the inheritance wasn't as big as all the gossip had made it out to be."

Hazel felt her throat closing. "We didn't know," she said through pinched vocal cords. She had one more question, which made the tiny hairs on the back of her neck stand. She had to ask it, but deep down she already knew the answer. "Who sold the house on Pine Street? To the people who own it now."

Mr. Crutchfield looked at her like he couldn't understand why she'd ask such a simple question. "Why Hal, Joel's uncle, did of course."

When she looked up from her story, Ruthie's and Sandra's eyes were as wide as they had been the first time she'd told it. The whole thing grew more and more absurd, like she now lived in more of a fantasy world than her own reality.

Ruthie sat back in her chair, making it rock. "I can't believe it. All this time."

Sandra tsked. "It's so crazy! Why wouldn't Joel's pa ever tell him that Hal Sutherland was his uncle? It's like he just cut Joel's mother's family out completely from Joel's life. And why wouldn't Mr. Hal tell him after all this time working together."

Ruthie leaned forward, laying her elbows on the table. "Here's the rub to me. Hazel, surely dad knew. And Ms. Faye. They've been here their whole lives. Why wouldn't they tell us?"

Hazel shrugged her shoulders. She sure hoped her father hadn't kept such important information from her and Joel. She knew she'd have to talk to him about this, but the thought made her go weak in the knees. She swallowed. Her throat felt like she'd eaten sandpaper. She went to the kitchen to refill her glass with cool water from the sink. She took a sip, noticing the slight tremor in her hand. She turned to face Ruthie and Sandra. The question that had been plaguing her since her conversation with Mr. Crutchfield. "Do you think Mr. Davenport hated Mr. Hal so much because Mr. Hal stole Joel's portion of his inheritance?"

Chapter 23

RUTHIE

R uthie's trip to Vietnam had been a whirlwind of racing and waiting. On the airplane from Little Rock to Oakland, California, she'd already started writing a letter to Hazel about the experience. How her ears popped when they got up to a certain altitude. How it was hard to sleep and even breathe with all the cigarette smoke hanging in the air like gray storm clouds. But she did enjoy the people watching because everyone who got on the airplane dressed in their Sunday best. The men wore three-piece suits and ties while the women were in beautiful dresses and heels. She'd even seen some women wearing strands of pearls. She felt underdressed in her plaid skirt and white blouse. Her favorite thing about the flight, she scribbled to Hazel, was the food and drinks offered. She'd tried her first sip of champagne and tasted lobster—all for free! Still, even the food couldn't surpass the view when she'd looked out the window. She couldn't believe they were soaring above the clouds. The bright blue sky extending out endlessly into infinity. It took her breath away and helped her push aside the anxiety she felt every time she overheard angry conversations about the war from the nearby passengers.

When she landed in Oakland, her nerves were on edge. In the lobby, people pushed past her as if she didn't exist. She straightened her blouse. She needed to find where to go to catch her next flight—the one that would take her all the way to Vietnam. Since this would be a military flight, she found an airport bathroom and changed from her regular clothes to her dress blues, her nicest uniform. In her uniform, everything changed once she left the bathroom. Instead of going unnoticed, people began to glare at her as they passed her. Her body heated, feeling their angry eyes on her skin. She pressed on and ignored their stares.

Ruthie noticed a soldier dressed in faded fatigues. His thin frame looked ravaged by hunger or the environment. A chill ran down her spine because she'd be where he had been soon. She stopped him.

"Excuse me, sir," she said. "Can you help me?"

His hollow eyes met hers. "Ma'am, I should be saluting you. You outrank me." He gave her a lopsided smile and she noticed a dimple on the left side of his cheek.

"No, that's not necessary," she said, returning his smile. "I'm just trying to find where I need to go to catch the MAC flight. I'm a nurse." She wasn't sure why she felt the need to explain.

His face brightened. "Ma'am, you have no idea how much you are needed."

He pointed the way out to her. While she thanked him for his help, a woman in a green paisley dress with hair teased up into a tall bun walked up to him and spit on him. The spittle landed on the front of his chest in a white blob. "Baby killer," she hissed and stormed away.

The shock of it all sent Ruthie reeling. Without thinking, she took out a handkerchief from her purse and began to wipe the spit from his uniform. "I'm so sorry. So sorry," she apologized.

He grabbed her hand with the handkerchief and held it. His skin felt cool against hers, and they locked eyes. She'd not noticed before how empty and sad his eyes were.

"It's fine, ma'am. It's the third time already, and I'm still not out the door. But I'm home," he sighed. "But it sure doesn't feel like it."

A coldness spread throughout Ruthie's veins. What had she gotten herself into? She felt completely unprepared.

"Ma'am, no matter what happens over there or here. Remember the men need you."

With that, he staggered away and left Ruthie feeling alone and exposed. She kept her head down and her eyes lowered as she made her way to the area he'd pointed out to her. She realized too late; she'd never asked his name. But she said a silent prayer anyway for the sad soldier.

When she found the area, she saw mostly men waiting for the flight and about three women. To her surprise, she saw Patty.

Patty squealed. "Hallelujah! Ruthie! Am I glad to see you!"

They hugged, and Ruthie's jittery feelings calmed at seeing a familiar face. When they boarded, Patty sat next to Ruthie on the plane.

Ruthie squeezed her arm. "Before today, I'd never ridden in an airplane, and now I've been in two," she said.

Patty smiled, but it quickly disappeared. "Did you see the lines of people yelling and screaming at the men who came home?" she asked.

Ruthie swallowed. "It was like nothing I've ever seen before. I don't understand it. Those men fought for our country—their country. Some were on crutches, and one had a missing leg. I saw a women spit on one while he was still inside the airport."

Patty's face fell and her voice lowered. "I'm starting to regret volunteering."

Ruthie couldn't help it, but she'd had the same thoughts. She remembered what the sad solider had told her, "The men need you." Ruthie thought of Joel, Milton, and Ronnie. She took Patty's hand. "We're going to get through this together. The men need us, and that's all that matters."

Patty nodded, and a fragile resolve settled over Ruthie.

After the plane refueled in Honolulu and left the US, the reality started to set in. She felt excited. She felt like crying. Ruthie knew there was nothing she could do now—she was on her way to Vietnam.

The airplane filled with men and three women landed in Vietnam in silence. No one hollered an excited jubilant cheer when the wheels hit the tarmac. No one said a word. The eerie quiet of the passengers settled hard on Ruthie. She knew just like everyone else aboard the plane that when their time came for a return flight home, not all of them would be alive to take it.

She and Patty received their orders. They'd both been assigned to the 71st Evac Hospital in Pleiku. She'd overheard it was close to the Cambodian border, which was thick with combat action. No one told them what "thick with combat action" meant. Instead, she and Patty were whisked away and loaded onto a helicopter. Her stomach rose into her throat and Patty grabbed her arm, digging her nails into her skin, as the helicopter lifted.

Ruthie couldn't process everything happening. It felt unbelievable, she'd just left Waldron a few days ago, and now she was soaring over green hills and valleys in a helicopter.

Patty pointed and spoke into the huge headphones they'd given them to wear. "Hey, what's those small clouds near the trees?"

The passenger turned around to answer her. "They're firing at us. That's why we're gonna head toward the South China Sea. Safer to fly over. You ladies will get to see the sea."

Ruthie couldn't breathe. They were being fired at—with actual guns and bullets. She could die. Here, in this place. She could die and never go home. She'd been so focused on having an adventure and getting out of Waldron. She'd been so naïve. Now, all she wanted was to go home and see her sister and her dad, but she had a job to do, at least for a year.

When they landed, Ruthie noticed huge holes in the tarmac. Armed men helped them out and rushed them to a bus.

"Keep your heads down," they directed her and Patty.

Ruthie's heart pounded in her head. She wiped sweat from her forehead and, too scared to look around at her new surroundings, kept her eyes focused on the back of the man in front her. A bandolier of ammo stretched across his body. *All those bullets*, Ruthie thought. *He needs all those bullets.* Her legs felt like Jell-O, but she forced them to move and to follow.

She and Patty were loaded onto a bus. The stench of stale sweat and mildew permeated the enclosed area. Black chicken wire had been placed over the bus windows. She sat down on a bus seat in a daze. Patty sat beside her; her arms wrapped around her body. The heat outside suffocated her. "Why is there chicken wire on the windows," she asked the soldier who drove the bus.

"To keep the grenades out."

Fear poured over Ruthie, and she felt like she was drowning in it. Chill bumps broke out across her skin, and she forced herself to breathe as the bus pulled out and started on its way to the 71st Evac Hospital. She and Patty bobbed around on the bus's bench seat. The rough springs underneath digging into her backside. Between the tiny chicken wire holes, Ruthie saw the brilliant sky turning bright red and purple. Her first day in Vietnam was almost over. *Just three hundred and sixty-four to go.*

To get to the hospital, the bus had to pass between several fences topped with concertina wire. Huge guard towers manned the area. Ruthie leaned her head near the chicken wire, but she could barely see the guard moving around at the top of the tower with a huge rifle in his hands.

As they unloaded off the bus, Ruthie could hear the whoosh of helicopters landing not too far away and the roar of engines coming to life. The bus driver helped her and Patty off the bus, and as Ruthie's feet hit the hard earth below, she felt like she'd been transported to another world. Even in the dark of night, the heat and humidity pelted her face like she'd opened an oven. Although she was used to the humidity and heat of Arkansas, this heat felt different, and she imagined her body cooking from the inside out. The sliver moon sat high in the sky surrounded by stars. She squinted and, in the shadows, she could make out the different shapes of the base that would be her new home for the year—a few scattered palm trees, rounded buildings, tents, helicopters, and vehicles.

An extremely tall man approached them, rushing as if he was late for an important meeting. Behind him, a shorter man holding a clipboard followed.

"Welcome to the 71st, I'm Tom Wittmon, head nurse." He motioned to the man behind him. "This here is Darryl, my right-hand man and one of the best surgical nurses I know."

Darryl raised his hand. "Hello."

Where Tom was bald, Darryl had a thick head of dark red hair. Ruthie noticed that the dim lights around the area made the dark circles under Tom's eyes seem to stretch miles down to his sunken cheeks. Still, a broad smile spread across his face. Tom towered over Ruthie, Patty, and Darryl. He turned to walk, and they grabbed their rucksacks and followed him. Darryl made notes on the paper on his clipboard as they walked. "Darryl, you put a helmet and flax jacket in their hootch correct?"

Darryl nodded, "Yes sir. They have them on their beds."

Tom kept walking. "Good, now if you hear an alarm going off, you will wear them both. We are short-staffed, like all hospitals in Nam. I've assigned you both to triage. Connie Andrews will mentor you both. She's a short-timer though, so soak up everything you can from her quick. The hootches are right beside the hospital, and our shifts are usually twelve hours, but if there's a push, be prepared to work longer."

A push? Patty looked at Ruthie and she shrugged. She had no idea what he was talking about.

"Here's the hospital. Well, this is triage where you both will be working." Tom said, pointing to a long, dark building.

No light came from inside. The whole building sat in darkness. If Tom hadn't pointed it out, Ruthie would not have known that the building was part of the hospital.

"Where's the lights?" Patty whispered to Ruthie.

Ruthie felt a lump form in her throat. She wanted to know too, but if the answer was anything like the chicken wire answer, she wasn't sure she could handle it at this moment. She'd never wanted to go home so much in all her life.

A few feet more and they stopped. Tom turned to face them and extended his arm to a tiny hootch with sandbags piled waist high near the walls.

"And here's your hootch. Get some sleep. Connie will be waiting for you tomorrow at the hospital. Be there by eight. We'll get you started, and Darryl will show you around the area."

Darryl nodded and made a note on his paper.

"He'll help you get your money exchanged for script; we call it funny money. I'm sure you've been told not to drink the water around here without the tablets or from lister bags. The water the mess hall gives you is fine. You'll need to start taking CP pills for malaria. Connie will give you those tomorrow too. They may make you a little dizzy, but most people feel fine after them. So, you see there's lots to do. It's good to have you both. Get a good night's rest." He directed Darryl to hand them both a long silver flashlight, and then they were gone.

Ruthie and Patty stood in front of their dark hootch, unmoving. Panic started to rise from Ruthie's belly, and she bit her bottom lip. They were here. They might as well get on with it. "You want to go inside?" she asked Patty.

"Not especially, honey-pie," Patty said, and the old joke they shared made Ruthie's nerves settle somewhat. Patty reached for the door and opened it. They both clicked on their flashlights and shut the door. The room felt claustrophobic. Ruthie heard something scurry across the floor and she shined the flashlight in the direction of the noise, but whatever it was had disappeared. A shot of terror passed down her spine. She sucked in the stale, mildewy air. She and Patty passed their lights around the room. Two hospital type beds lined both sides of the walls with barely a foot of room to walk between them. At the back stood two metal lockers to hang their clothes. At the end of each bed were small bedside dressers with two drawers.

"Wow!" Patty exhaled. She threw her rucksack on the bed. "Sparse. And what made that sound? It almost sent me running for my life! I'm pretty sure I'm not going to sleep a wink."

Ruthie threw her bag on the bed too and picked the helmet up off the bed, leaving the flax jacket where it lay. She placed the helmet on her head then held the flashlight under her chin like she and Hazel had done a long time ago when they were children.

"Welcome to your worst nightmare!" she said and gave a cackling laugh.

Patty hooted. "You know what ol' Tom and Darryl forgot to show us?"

Ruthie knew exactly what Patty needed. "Yep, the bathroom."

Chapter 24

HAZEL

Hazel and Alice sat in warm plastic lawn chairs in Alice's front yard. Alice's daughter played on a blanket near their feet. They sipped homemade lemonade from glasses etched with tiny lemons. She sighed when her daughter stood up and ran across the yard. Alice set her glass on the plastic table between them. "Gracie," she hollered. "You get back on that blanket, you hear?" She shook her head. "Almost three years old and she's giving me a run for my money. I don't think I ever caused my mama this much trouble."

Hazel raised an eyebrow, "Oh, you gave your mama plenty of trouble."

Alice flashed her a smile, "Yeah, but most of it she doesn't know about."

Hazel laughed and Alice went to collect Gracie, returning her to the blanket.

Hazel laid her hand across her ever-growing middle. The baby inside moved and a brightness filled her.

"Only a few more months, right?"

Hazel nodded, "Yeah, June is just around the corner. I can't believe it. Time has flown by. I just wish..." she paused, feeling a lump form in her throat.

Alice reached over and touched her arm. "I know. But Joel and Ruthie will be back before you know it. And I'm here. And your dad and Sandra. You have people, Hazel. You're not alone."

Hazel blinked away tears. "I know. Thank you," she sniffed.

"And now you actually have more family than you ever knew about, right?"

Hazel nodded.

Alice blew out a huff of air. "I can't believe it. All these years Mr. Hal was Joel's uncle. Why do you think no one ever said anything? Maybe my mom and dad didn't know because they didn't move here until I turned four. But your dad and Ms. Faye, they had to know. And why wouldn't Mr. Hal and Mrs. Anne say something? I mean, they're the nicest people. Why keep something like that a secret?"

Hazel shrugged, "I don't know. It doesn't make any sense." She took a sip of lemonade. The sour sugary taste made her jaw clench. She remembered the conversation she'd had with Mrs. Anne before Joel left for Vietnam. Mrs. Anne had said Joel's pa had every right to hate her and Mr. Hal, and if they knew why, she and Joel would hate them too. "Maybe they did something wrong? To Joel's pa?"

Alice stood and picked up a doll Gracie left in the grass. Her tiny, chubby hands anxiously grabbed for it. Alice sat back down and looked at Hazel. "What if it's like what Mr. Crutchfield told you. What if it has something to do with the inheritance? It's hard to believe, but what if Mr. Hal did take it and kept it from Joel? But the only way to know for sure would be to get a copy of Ms. Angel's will."

Hazel bit her bottom lip. "I want to talk to Dad about it, but I'm scared because I'm so angry with him. I mean, he should have said something to Joel about this or at least to me."

Alice agreed, "It's so strange."

"How do I get to see a copy of an old will?" Hazel wondered.

Alice shook her head, "I don't know. I'll ask David when he gets home. Maybe he'll have an idea."

Hazel had just finished putting away the clean dinner dishes she, Sandra, and the boys had used when the telephone rang. She hurried to the telephone and picked up the receiver.

"Hello?"

"Hazel, it's Alice. I spoke to David about the will. He didn't know the answer, but he has an attorney friend who did."

Hazel's heart picked up its pace and the baby gave her ribs a kick. She patted her side as if that could comfort her unborn baby. "What did he say?"

"Okay, he said if Ms. Angel's house was sold, then the will had to have been, um, probated. Yes, I think that's the word. That means an attorney would have given a copy of the will to the court and it was probably filed in the record. He told David you can get a copy of the papers filed in the record. They are open to the public. He said you may have to pay for a copy though."

"I'll pay!" Hazel said. "Holy moly, Alice, this was so much help! Thank you! You have no idea."

"Hey now, I'm not doing it just for you. I'm invested. I'm dying to know what in the world is going on. You better dish about everything you find out."

"Yes! Yes, of course! Thank you again!"

When Hazel hung up, she closed her eyes. Before she went to the courthouse, she knew it was time to have a serious conversation with her father.

⁂

Before going to her father's house, she helped Sandra tuck in the boys. Sandra rocked little Mannie while Hazel read Mikey a story she'd written in the notebook Joel had given her. She read about a group of balloon-loving bears. Mikey giggled and listened intently. Just watching his eyes grow wide at the right spots in the story made her heart soar.

When Mikey and Mannie were both asleep in bed, she helped Sandra straighten all the loose toys scattered across the living room floor.

"You really should try to get your stories published, Hazel. They are delightful. You saw how Mikey loved the one you told him tonight."

153

Hazel stood up and stretched, placing her hand on her stomach. "Maybe, but they're just funny stories. I've made them up since I was little."

Sandra stopped and looked at Hazel, a firetruck in her hand. "Don't belittle what you do. It's a gift. A real God-given gift."

Hazel felt heat creep up into her cheeks and she nodded, unable to think of what to say.

Instead of going straight home, Hazel walked across the grass to her dad's duplex. She raised her fist and knocked on his door before she could change her mind. She straightened her shoulders. *I can do this; it's just my dad.*

When he opened the door, his eyelids were heavy and there were deep lines across the right side of his forehead.

"Fell asleep on the sofa again?" she asked.

He ran a hand down his face. "Yeah, I guess I did." His face cracked into a smile, but in an instant, it fell and his eyebrows raised. "Girl, are you okay? Is anything wrong?" he asked, looking down at her belly.

Hazel shook her head, "Everything is fine. I'm doing well."

"June, right?"

She nodded and she could visibly see the worry fall from his face.

"Oh, good, I thought we were going to need to rush to the hospital."

She chuckled, "Not tonight."

He opened the door wider. "You want to come in?"

"Yes, actually there's something I need to speak to you about."

"Of course," he said. He went to the sofa and rearranged the haphazard pillows.

Hazel followed him inside and shut the door behind her.

He patted the sofa, "Here sit. You don't need to be on your feet anyway. I think you're up on your feet way too much at the Piggly Wiggly."

She plopped down on the sofa, feeling the cushions give way underneath her. Her body felt more like a bowling ball than anything now. "I'm fine, Dad. Really, I am."

He sat down on the opposite side of the sofa. He grabbed one of the decorative pillows and flung it on a chair. "Ms. Faye," he shrugged. "She picked them out."

"They are nice," Hazel said. She knew what she had to ask, but the words felt like they were stuck to her tongue.

"You lonely?" her father asked. "You know if you ever feel lonely, you could stay the night over here."

Guilt passed over her, she was supposed to be angry with him. Still, when she saw his sleepy face at the door, her anger had evaporated, leaving only disappointment in its place.

She swallowed. "Dad, I really need to ask you something."

"Roger-dodger, ask away, girl. Whatever you need, I can help with."

The lump in her throat grew bigger. "I don't need anything, just answers."

He nodded and stared at her, waiting. Her body grew hotter.

"It's just that, well, I've found out some interesting information about Joel. And, um, it seems that he does have family." The anger began to bubble again inside her. "Actually, he's had family all along. Right here in town, and you knew about it and said nothing to us. How could you not tell us that Mr. Hal was his uncle?" Her voice sounded pinched. "You did know, didn't you?"

Her father's face crumbled into a frown. "I did."

Even though deep down she knew he had known, the confirmation of it felt like a slap on the face. She bit her lip and waited for him to continue.

"I'll start at the beginning."

"Yes, please do," she said, hearing the coldness in her own voice.

He flinched and nodded. "Ms. Angel was Hal and Sarah's mother. They lived in that huge house; you know the bed and breakfast on Pine Street."

She nodded. She already knew this part.

"When Sarah met Joel's pa, he was a kind and honest man. Everyone liked him. He'd just moved from somewhere up north. I can't remember where." He waved his hand in the air. "I don't think he was going to stay, but they fell in love and got married in a whirlwind wedding."

Hazel tried to picture the man she knew to be Joel's pa, Thomas, as her father described him. She couldn't imagine him really caring for someone and having a whirlwind wedding.

"Then the war happened. And Thomas and I were sent overseas."

"Did Mr. Hal go?"

Her father shook his head, "No, he had some issue with his back or something."

Hazel bit the inside of her cheek.

"We had a hard time over there, as you know. I got shot and lost a kidney and part of my liver. When we came back. We both were changed. Me physically and Thomas, well, something had changed in his head."

Hazel's eyes blurred and she blinked back tears. *Will Joel come back forever changed like his pa?*

"I don't think it was too long after we'd gotten home that Sarah became pregnant." He paused. His head hung down. "Well, you know what happened there. Poor Sarah. I think that was the last straw for Thomas. He'd lost everything then, including his mind."

Hazel's insides burned. "He didn't lose everything. He still had Joel."

Her father shook his head, "Yes, but a broken war vet and a crying newborn don't mix well."

Hazel's heart fell and she touched her stomach. Would that happen to her baby and Joel?

"Ms. Angel stepped in and took care of Joel. They lived in that big house. Thomas spent most of his time drunk. And that seemed to work for a while."

"What happened to Mr. Hal during that time?"

Her father looked up toward the ceiling then back to her. "I think while we were gone to war, Hal and Anne got married. I just remember him working for whoever owned the garage. Ms. Angel was big on letting her children make their own way in the world. She didn't spoil them or nothing." Her father scratched his head. "That was about the time Anne started having so many problems."

"What kind of problems?"

"I don't know how many, but I heard she lost a lot of babies. That had to be so hard for her and Hal."

Hazel's heart clenched inside her chest. She knew how hard it was to lose a baby. She and Joel had firsthand experience. Losing a baby felt like having all your insides ripped out and then shoved back in without them being put in their proper places. It changed you. Hazel wished Mrs. Anne would have told her about her troubles. It might have helped to have someone to talk to who understood what she was going through when she lost Madelyn Ray. Hazel swallowed. "When Ms. Angel died, why didn't Mr. Hal and Mrs. Anne take Joel in since they wanted a child? Why did they send him to live with, well, with a drunk?"

Her father shrugged, "I really don't know anything more. Hal and I are friends, but we aren't the kind of friends that talk about things like that."

"Did you know Joel probably should have gotten some of the inheritance from Ms. Angel's will?"

Her father's eyes grew large. "No, all I knew is after the baby went back to Thomas, Hal sold the house on Pine Street, bought the garage, and renamed it Hal's Service Center." He shook his head. "After that, I didn't really pay attention anymore. I had you, and later Ruthie came along. I was traveling out of town for work and then your mama left. Life got away from me, and I didn't even think about Joel until you girls brought him home."

Hazel folded her hands on her lap. She gripped them tightly together. How could her father forget about Joel?

"That time things got really bad with Thomas, you remember, when Joel stayed with us that winter?"

Hazel nodded her head. "I remember."

"I hoped Joel would agree to live with us, but he didn't want that, so I went to speak with Hal the next day. I told him Joel needed help. That it was too dangerous for him to be living with Thomas."

"What happened?" Hazel asked, feeling her body move to the edge of the sofa.

Her father shrugged. "Nothing. Not until that December. Hal came to me and asked if he could meet Joel. He wanted him to start working at the garage." Her father held out his hands, palms up. "That's all I know, girl. I'm so sorry if you feel like I've kept things from you. I just thought now that Hal and Joel worked together every day, surely, he'd tell Joel something, but I guess he never did, and I didn't feel like I needed to get in the middle of family business or whatever it was."

Hazel wanted to scream. "But Joel didn't even know that they were family."

Her father hung his head. "I'm sorry. I realize that now." He reached out and took her hand. "Hazel, I really am sorry. And I didn't know anything about Ms. Angel's will."

Her anger began to cool at the squeeze of his warm hand.

"So, what are you going to do now, sweetheart?" he asked.

Hazel took a deep breath. "I'm not really sure. Alice said that to sell the house, someone would have probated Ms. Angel's will. A copy of it would be in the record at the courthouse. I think I can get a copy. I'd like to see what it says." She told her father about the strange meeting with Mrs. Anne before Joel left for Vietnam. "She said if we knew what they'd done, we'd hate them too."

Her father's lips flattened into a straight line. He closed his eyes. When he opened them, they were watery. "I sure hope Hal hasn't done something he'll regret forever. Why don't you let me get a copy of the will and whatever other paperwork they have on the matter? It will cost money, and I'll pay for it. I'll bring it to you tomorrow afternoon once I finish up my woodwork."

"You sure?" she asked. "The only time I have is on my lunch break, and I was worried it might take a while, and I'd get back late."

He patted her hand. "Yes, girl. Don't you worry. I'll get it for you. We'll get to the bottom of this together."

She narrowed her eyes, "Dad, will you swear to me that you won't keep anymore secrets from me—ever?"

Her father's smile tightened. "I promise I've told you everything I know about this situation."

This situation? He didn't swear there were no more secrets. She opened her mouth to say something, but a huge yawn escaped. Whatever energy she had coming over here had long gone. Even though she could feel he was keeping something from her, Hazel's eyes felt heavy, and she could barely keep them open. She rubbed her stomach, and her baby kicked. It bumped her hand, and she couldn't help but smile. He or she had already started to boss her around and let her know it was way past bedtime.

Chapter 25

RUTHIE

Ruthie could not sleep. With the constant sound of roaring engines, helicopters landing and taking off, the intense heat, and the constant feeling tiny bugs were crawling all over her skin, there was no way in God's wonderful world that she could close her eyes and fall into the oblivion of unconsciousness she desperately craved. Last night, she and Patty had found the hootch set up for the nurses as a latrine and shower area. But they'd also found a rat and massive black bugs crawling up one side of the wall. She'd have preferred using the woods as a bathroom, but this was her home now, and she'd better get used to it.

When morning came, she and Patty got up early, neither able to sleep, and dressed in their green fatigues. They decided to do some exploring on their own. Patty strapped on her Polaroid camera. "In case I see something interesting," she said.

They easily found the mess hall by following a group of men. Ruthie's stomach growled as she picked up a metal tray and went through the line. Eggs, bacon, and a biscuit were put on her tray. She grabbed a glass of water while Patty got orange juice. They found a table in the back where two other women dressed in fatigues sat. Ruthie noticed the women's hair had been cut short and uneven, as if they'd cut it themselves. Dark circles under their eyes looked like permanent bruises, and the whites of their eyes were cracked red. She and Patty sat down across from them. Their thin faces brightened when they saw them.

"Hey! Ya'll just got here last night," one of the women said, reaching across the table to shake Patty's and Ruthie's hands. "I'm Diane, and this here is Mel."

"Short for Melanie," the other chimed in. "How'd you sleep?"

Patty and Ruthie looked at each other, and Mel and Diane started to laugh.

"That well, huh?" Diane chuckled. "Well don't worry, you won't be sleeping anymore anyways. We're the walking dead here."

"So they putting you to work first thing? What part of the hospital will you be working in?" Mel asked.

Patty took a bite of her eggs. "What are these things? They look like eggs, but they don't taste anything like eggs."

Diane and Mel chortled. "What? You're not used to fine dining?" Mel laughed.

Ruthie smiled. These nurses were a hoot. She took a bite of her biscuit, which mostly tasted like a biscuit.

"Wait until they runout of the normal stuff and start giving you C-rats. Those are the worst," Diane told them.

"They said we're to meet Connie this morning at eight," Ruthie said.

Diane's face fell. "Oh yeah, then you'll be in triage. Connie's DEROS came in and she's a short-timer now. Great nurse. You'll learn a lot from her."

"We're in surgery," Mel sighed. "Connie's great. You'll love her. We sure miss her in surgery. I guess we'll be having a going away party for her soon."

Diane nodded. "It's a revolving door around here. Once you get trained, you go home, unless you re-up."

"Re-up?" Ruthie asked.

"Yeah, stay another three hundred and sixty-five," Mel explained. "I did."

"Oh no! I can already tell you that's not for me," Patty said.

Ruthie thought the same thing even though she didn't say it. Diane and Mel chuckled.

"Well, we'll see," Diane said. "This place has a way of getting under your skin."

❧❧❧❧❧ ❧❧❧❧❧

After Ruthie and Patty ate breakfast, they walked back to the hospital. The place buzzed around them, full of activity. Trucks and boots kicked up the dusty, red dirt. Palm trees leaned to the side as a helicopter rose into the air. Ruthie shielded her eyes to watch it. Outside the rows and rows of concertina wire, Ruthie saw the shadows of rolling hills and a sky stained pink and red. They had some time to spare before they were needed at the hospital, so they walked farther, exploring their new surroundings. They found the mail room and the PX. They stopped in and exchanged their money for the funny money and bought a few essentials. Ruthie thought Darryl may appreciate them taking the initiative instead of waiting for him to show them around. They walked near the water tower and found a metal building with an awning and a swimming pool. A few women in swimsuits laid in beach chairs, sleeping. Ruthie wondered if that would be her soon enough—too exhausted to enjoy the water.

They stomped through tall grass to a large sign that Ruthie had noticed on their way in but couldn't read because of the dark. "The reason for our existence has just arrived, you, our patient," Ruthie read aloud.

"Get in front of it, Ruthie! I want to take your picture." Patty said.

"No, no," she protested, but Patty wouldn't have it. Ruthie posed in front of it and Patty snapped a picture. The camera spit out a square of cloudy, white film paper. Patty plucked it out of her camera using her fingertips and handed it to her.

"A souvenir," she said.

Ruthie took it and waved it in the air, watching as the shapes on the film started to take form. As she waved the photo, she watched a helicopter land on the helicopter pad. In the distance, they heard yelling.

"Let's go," Ruthie said, sliding the dried photo into the front pocket of her fatigues.

Patty sighed, looking at the small watch on her wrist. "But we've still got thirty minutes before we have to start our first shift."

Ruthie took off running. She yelled over her shoulder, "I think we're starting now."

⊱⊱⊱⊱⊰ ⊱⊰⊰⊰⊰

A push. That's what Connie had called the chaos. The helicopter, Ruthie quickly learned, was called a Huey. Hueys were supposed to only hold eight patients, but this one had brought sixteen—which wasn't a rare occurrence apparently. The men's bodies were thrown on top of each other like limp dolls.

"Another one's on the way," Connie yelled. "Filled up again. It's a MASCAL!"

Ruthie's head spun, and as if Connie could read her mind, she answered. "A mass casualty. Be ready."

But she could never have been ready for this. The smells, the blood, the screams and moans—all of it made Ruthie want to cover her ears and run. She didn't. Instead, she moved like a robot, letting the nurses who had seen this before direct her. She did exactly what they told her to do, helping where she could. The injuries were like nothing she'd ever seen in Waldron, but she had no time to think. Just do. Only do.

When the civilians started to arrive with children wounded and burned, Ruthie thought her heart may fall out of her chest. How was she going to make it through a whole year? She looked for Patty and found her holding a screaming little girl with a bloody mangled arm. Tears poured down Patty's face. Unable to process everything, Ruthie threw herself into quickly learning the routine and her new role in triage. She learned military personnel took priority over civilians. Those with abdominal wounds were examined first and rushed to surgery. Any head injuries where there might

162

be a possibility of brain trauma came last—mostly because those poor men usually did not survive. Patients with less severe injuries were moved to the back of the hospital away from the chaos until their injuries could be dealt with. Some men were already dead when they arrived. They were left until the still living were handled. Later they'd be identified, and their information and bodies taken to Grave Registration.

She watched the experienced nurses and doctors. They moved in blurs around her. Stop the bleeding. Sew and go. Move to surgery. The word "expectant" was being called out over and over.

"He can't breathe!" a doctor yelled. Connie brought over the equipment, and Ruthie watched as the doctor inserted a tracheostomy tube right in front of her and placed the wounded soldier on a ventilator.

In that instant, she decided this wasn't the place for her. She could never handle this. She turned to go—to leave this madness—when a hand grabbed her wrist, squeezing it. She turned to see a man. No, a boy, laying on a litter. His short blonde hair caked with dirt and blood. His blue eyes stared at her, huge inside his ashen face.

"Help me," he groaned. "Please help me."

All of Ruthie's fear evaporated, and she transformed into a nurse again. She began to look over him, to assess the seriousness of his injuries, starting with his head.

"Where are you hurting?" Ruthie asked and wished she could suck her words right back up. If she'd just looked down, she would have seen this boy was missing a leg. A wave of sickness passed over her, but she choked it down. *He's lost too much blood*, she thought, and moved quickly to stop it. If she didn't, this boy could bleed out right in front of her. She frantically patted her uniform pockets. She had nothing—no tubing, no clamps, nothing for a tourniquet. Her head whipped around. She didn't even know where they kept the supplies in this insane hospital. *This is my first day*, echoed through her head. *How can this be my first day!*

"Help!" she called. "He needs a tourniquet. Quick."

Dark hands moved to help her. "First day?" he asked as he started to expertly apply a tourniquet around the boy's leg.

Ruthie stared at the doctor. His hands moved quickly as he worked. His long face pinched. His black hair, shorn short against his scalp, had speckles of gray. She wanted to help him, but after he'd taken over, fear had seized her again, and she felt trapped in a nightmare. This couldn't be her life. Blood smeared on the floor, blood stained her uniform and the doctor's uniform, blood everywhere.

"Are you just going to stand there and watch me, or help me tighten this around his leg?"

His question jogged her back to reality. A boy lying in front of her needed her, or he'd bleed out.

"Oh yes, sir, I'm sorry."

The doctor chuckled. "I'm Gerry. Okay, hold this here," he directed her, and she did what he told her.

Just do, don't think, she told herself.

"All right, I think I've got this on now, and the bleeding seems to have stopped. Don't you agree, nurse?"

"Ruthie," she said. She looked at the expertly applied tourniquet and nodded. "Thank you so much for your help."

"Any time, Ruthie. Welcome to the 71st," he said, flashing her a brilliant smile. He leaned down to the soldier. "Boy, I'm going to take you to surgery now where I'll clear your wound of debris and get it sewn up. You got it? You're going to make it." He patted the boy on the arm.

The boy blinked. "I've never seen a Black doctor before."

Gerry laughed. "Well, there's not many out there, son. Count yourself lucky." He looked at Ruthie and waited for her to meet his eyes. "You're going to be fine here, I promise. First days are always the hardest."

She watched as he moved quickly to help the boy to surgery, and she hoped Dr. Gerry was right. That she would be okay here. Oh, dear Lord, how she hoped he was right.

※※※※ ※※※※

After the MASCAL, Ruthie, Patty, Connie, and the nurses she'd met earlier at breakfast, Diane and Mel, sat propped up on the hospital beds with tubes running from their arms as blood drained into pouches.

"Wow, what a first day," Connie said. "A MASCAL and now you're giving blood."

"Do you have to do this often?" Patty asked.

"Only when our blood supplies run low. We were already low, and today drained us of the rest of our supply."

"I have a question that I've been scared to ask," Ruthie said.

Connie looked at her with one eyebrow raised. "Shoot."

Ruthie swallowed. "When we got here last night, all the lights were off, and the place was completely dark. Why is that?"

Connie let out a sigh. She looked over at Diane and Mel. They nodded at her. "Well, if you got here last night, then you got here on the quietest night we've had here since I arrived twenty-two months ago."

"You re-upped!" Patty exclaimed.

Connie nodded. "Yep, I couldn't leave the guys. They needed me. But now my mom is in poor health, so it's time. I'm going home."

"What do you mean quietest night?" Ruthie asked.

"There are mortar attacks here constantly. If the lights are on, we become a target. It's safer to work with the lights off. You just need to keep clamps and extra tubing in your pockets. It's difficult in emergency situations, but it's better than being sitting ducks."

"Oh," Patty said, slinking down in her chair.

Ruthie felt a lump form in her throat. Even though she always knew dying here was a possibility, the reality of it, of this place, sent a chill running through her.

"Well, I think that's enough blood for now," Connie said, and she helped Ruthie and Patty remove their tubes and collect the blood they had given.

Chapter 26

RUTHIE

Ruthie and Patty were in their hootch, asleep, when the first mortar hit. Ruthie's eyes popped open, and her body became alive. She leaped out of bed at the same time as Patty. Their foreheads knocked together.

"Ouch," Ruthie said, rubbing her head. But before she could apologize, another mortar hit, and she fell to her knees in the small space between their beds. She reached and grabbed her helmet and flax jacket that lay ready on the end of her bed. She slipped them on, and she and Patty crawled under her bed, not caring about the bugs or varmints underneath.

"This is insane!" Patty said over the sounds of explosions.

Ruthie nodded. "I think we're supposed to find a bunker, but I'm too scared to leave."

They stared at each other for an hour. Their eyes grew wider with each explosion. When the explosions sounded close, they covered their ears with shaking hands. *Is this how I'll spend my last night on Earth*, Ruthie thought. *Under a bed with Patty and the bugs?*

"How long do you think it will last?" Patty hollered.

Ruthie didn't have an answer. She had no idea. Her mind went into overdrive, repeating over and over—*Mrs. Battalou was right*. She'd ruined her life when she came here. But then came a few moments of silence, and Ruthie realized the attack might be over. She and Patty crawled out from under the bed and took a deep breath, filling her lungs with air.

"Let's go see if they need help at the hospital," Ruthie said.

Patty's shoulders drooped. "But we already did our twelve."

Still in pajamas, helmets, and flax jackets, Ruthie grabbed Patty's arm and pulled her outside of the hootch. A cool wind blew, and Ruthie shivered. In the distance, near the edges of the camp, gray smoke and red flames rose into the air. Men ran toward the area.

"They missed the ammunition dump, thank the Lord, but got a few of the supply sheds," one of the men told the other as they passed by Ruthie and Patty, heading toward the fire.

"I heard the village took a hit too," the other soldier said.

Ruthie wanted to stop them and ask what village. Had anyone been hurt? But the men moved so fast and were gone before she could even process the words. Patty and Ruthie rushed to triage. Inside, wounded men were on the floor under their beds where the nurses had put them for their safety. Others that couldn't be moved had thin mattresses thrown over their bodies.

"Hey! You must be the new nurses," a short, too-thin nurse in green fatigues hurried toward them. Her brown hair had been cut in a short bob which made her look like a teeny bopper and not a hair over fifteen years old.

"I'm Lucy. Could you help me get these men back into their beds? Everyone went to help put out the fire, and I heard we may be getting some villagers in, so I need to make some room."

Ruthie looked at Patty. Her face downcast. Ruthie nudged her. "Well, we weren't going back to sleep anyway."

Patty quietly nodded, and she and Ruthie got to work helping Lucy with whatever she directed them to do.

Ruthie felt like death hung over the next day. She and Patty grabbed coffee and breakfast before heading back to triage to do their twelve. She'd lost count already how many hours she'd been on her feet. They pulsed and ached inside her boots. Ruthie was surprised to find the nurse they'd met last night, Lucy, still working. She'd not had one break, even though Ruthie and Patty had encouraged her to take one. Lucy's stained fatigues hung off her body, and Ruthie felt sorry for not thinking to bring her something from the mess hall.

Lucy stood near a woman from the village, wrapping the burns on the woman's arms. Lucy looked up and gave them a tired smile. The memory of the woman being rushed to triage last night with raw red arms, holding her severely burnt son to her chest sent a sharp pain through Ruthie's insides. The boy died a few moments after they'd arrived. There had been nothing they could do. When the boy passed, Lucy had tried to communicate with the woman to release her son's charred body so they could care for her arms. But the woman screamed at them in Vietnamese. Ruthie's stomach roiled as she remembered the woman's high pitch screaming and the smell of burnt flesh. She couldn't understand. Didn't the Viet Cong know they were hurting their own people?

"We should have brought you something to eat," Hazel said to Lucy.

"Yeah, I can go back and get something right now for you," Patty said.

Lucy shook her head. "I'm almost finished here. I'll run and grab something. I'm dead on my feet."

Ruthie motioned toward the new dressing on the woman's arms. "How'd you get her to let you care for her?"

Lucy's eyes were cracked with red lines, and she yawned. "She fell asleep briefly while you both went to breakfast, and I gave her a shot of morphine. I gave her enough to make her loopy. She's pretty out of it."

Ruthie looked at the woman closer. Her eyes were partially open as she battled the effects of the medicine, but they continued to droop.

"I was able to debride the burnt skin, apply some ointment, and get her wrapped before her eyes ever started to open."

Ruthie marveled at how quickly Lucy had been able to care for the woman, and she wondered if she would develop those skills over time. Then Ruthie realized the woman's dead son was gone. She swallowed. "What happen to her son's body?"

Lucy finished wrapping and gently laid the woman's arm beside her body on the bed.

"They took his body."

Patty gasped. "They took that poor woman's son while she slept?"

As soon as the question left Patty's lips, Connie, their mentor, walked from the back, holding a small bundle wrapped in white gauze. "I've got some men coming to help move her to Ward Five. That ward is used as ICU and recovery for the civilians," she explained to Ruthie and Patty. "When she's released today, she'll be able to take her son's body and bury him." Connie laid the small, wrapped body on the woman's chest and laid her wrapped arms over him.

They all stood there in silence, looking at the sleeping woman holding her dead son. Ruthie felt a part of her break. When this woman woke up, she'd have to relive the nightmare all over again.

Connie touched Lucy's arm. "You need to go get some rest."

Lucy nodded. She turned to Patty and Ruthie. "Thank you again for all your help last night."

When the men came, Connie directed them. They carried the woman and her son out on a litter. Patty held the door open for them. After they'd gone, Connie smiled and said to Ruthie and Patty, "Look, I know you guys have had a rough start. We're having a small party tonight at the O club. Why don't you both come? You need to unwind and let your hair down."

Ruthie blinked. Other than birthday parties, she couldn't remember ever going to any actual parties in Waldron. But she thought Connie could be right, they did need to unwind. Her back muscles were strung so tight, she thought they might pop.

Patty yipped, pulling on Ruthie's arm. "Yes! We'd love to go! Right, Ruthie?"

Ruthie smiled. "Yeah, thank you for inviting us."

After the news about the party, Patty's mood had lifted somewhat. She'd spent the day bouncing on her toes and humming "Wouldn't It Be Nice" by The Beach Boys. When their shift ended, Patty wanted to go straight back to take a shower and get ready, but Ruthie wanted to do something before the party.

"I won't be long," Ruthie told her.

"Don't you want to shower and have time to fix your hair?"

Ruthie looked down at her wrinkled and stained fatigues. "Yeah, I'd love to take a cold shower again," she said, remembering her first shower here and the freezing-cold rivulets of water that trickled from the shower head.

Patty laughed. "I know, right? They don't leave you much choice. The shower stall with bugs crawling up the wall or the ones that barely drip enough water to wet your hair. I hear, though, there's one shower that works right, and I aim to find it."

Ruthie laughed and promised Patty again that she wouldn't be long, and she'd have plenty of time to shower before the party. Outside, even in the dark of night, the heat still bore down on her. She hurried, trying to remember the way from triage to ICU in the dark. She heard the whoosh of a Huey taking off. She wondered where it was going. Patty would be crushed if the party had to be canceled due to another MASCAL. Ruthie lifted her chin into the air. Brillant stars speckled the night sky. She'd spent the whole day inside working, only leaving to grab a quick lunch, and she already missed the sun on her face. She hoped they'd switch her to nights before the rainy season started so she could enjoy a little outside time.

She found the long building used as ICU. Sandbags were piled so high along the front that they nearly touched the mesh-covered windows. She stepped inside. Hospital beds lined both sides of the walls. Almost all the beds were filled with injured men from yesterday morning's emergency. Metal IV stands beside the beds pumped liquid medicine into those who needed it. A man in a wheelchair rolled up and down the free space.

She spotted the person she'd come to see at the far end of the room. He sat up in bed. His face and blonde hair clean of dirt and blood now. A thin blue blanket covered his lower body, but still she could see the empty space where his right leg should have been. For all that had occurred, he seemed alright. She wasn't surprised at all to see Dr. Gerry sitting beside the boy, playing cards.

"So, can I get dealt in?" she said.

"Of course, but new nurses have to pay a double ante," Dr. Gerry said.

"Doc G you know that ain't fair. This pretty lady helped save me. I'm John by the way," he extended his hand out for her to shake.

Ruthie shook his hand, thinking this kid doesn't look a day over eighteen. She pulled up a chair and took the cards Dr. Gerry dealt her.

"So what are we betting?" she asked.

John pushed part of his pile of cotton balls toward her.

She laughed. "Wow! Pricey." Ruthie looked at her cards. She'd been dealt a pretty good hand—two of a kind. She tried to keep her face from revealing her luck.

"I get to go home," John told her.

She wondered if she should warn him, thinking about the soldier at the airport in California who'd been spit on right in front of her. Surely John already knew how the tides had changed, and how people hated the war, which in turn meant they hated him. But as she looked into his face, so young and innocent. If he didn't know, she decided she couldn't be the one to crush him. She smiled and said, "That's great. I'm sure your family will be glad to have you back."

"How have your first days been?" Dr. Gerry asked, quickly moving the subject away from home.

It almost took her breath away to think that everything she'd seen and done had all happened in less than forty-eight hours. She didn't have words to describe it. The MASCAL, John losing blood and nearly dying in front of her, the explosions, the burnt woman with her dead son. Her throat closed up and her eyes blurred as she stared at her cards in her hands.

"That bad, huh?" John said, peering over his cards.

She nodded but couldn't speak.

Dr. Gerry reached over and patted her arm. "I won't tell you it will get better. Cause it might get worse. But you're strong, and you'll get through this. And you'll get to help save lives."

"Like me," John piped up.

Ruthie nodded, still unable to speak. She took her two new cards from Dr. Gerry and smiled because now she had three of a kind.

Chapter 27

RUTHIE

After a few more hands of cards, Dr. Gerry showed Ruthie the way to the officers' club, but he called it the O club like Connie. It surprised Ruthie that the building was nothing more than a hut. Inside, flames flickered from kerosene lanterns and a scuffed rectangular table had been set up in the back as a makeshift bar. The bartender stood bare chested, passing out drinks to men and women. Other than a few tables and chairs, there wasn't much to the O club. But everyone inside it acted as if it was everything. In the back, a band made up of two guitar players and a drummer played and sung "The End of the World" by Skeeter Davis. On the wall behind the band hung a sign that read, WE'LL MISS YOU LUCY!

"Wait!" Ruthie shouted over the music. "This is Lucy's going away party?"

Dr. Gerry nodded. "Yep, she leaves tomorrow."

Ruthie felt her throat close. *But we just met.*

Ruthie watched the eerie shadows move as nurses and doctors danced, arms raising up and down. Thoughts of prom and Ronnie entered her mind. She thought about how he held her close. She wondered where he was right now and silently prayed for his safety. Ruthie noticed Lucy standing to the side and she went to her. Lucy's face lit up when she saw Ruthie. She grabbed Ruthie, hugging her tight.

"I can't believe this is your going away party. Why didn't you tell me you were a short-timer?"

Lucy smiled. "Well, we kinda had our hands full and I didn't want to sound like I was bragging. Which I would have been."

Ruthie laughed, even though it hurt her heart. She'd only met Lucy and still it felt like she was losing a friend.

Lucy pointed toward the table being used as a bar. "That shirtless hunk is Mark. He's a surgeon. Go get a can of Thirty-Three from him. It's a game some of the guys came up with so everyone can get to know each other."

"Thirty-Three?"

Lucy nodded and took hold of Ruthie's arm and walked her to the table. "It's a Vietnamese beer. Sometimes it's good and sometimes it's not, and sometimes it tastes more like vinegar than beer."

Ruthie crinkled her nose.

When they got to the table, Ruthie felt her cheeks heat. She couldn't take her eyes off the sweat that glistened across Mark's bare torso. When he winked at her and gave her a half grin, it made his left dimple pop, and she felt as if her whole body blushed in response. Hazel would have died. But her best friend, Margarette Ann would have gone wild. The thought of Hazel and Margarette Ann made her smile. The way Mark danced as he passed out beers made Ruthie laugh because it was so close to scandalous. She knew Hazel's face would have turned as bright red as a newly ripened tomato.

Lucy introduced Ruthie to Mark. "You ready to play?" he asked.

Ruthie instinctively shook her head no, which made him hoot.

He handed a beer to Lucy, who pushed it into Ruthie's hands. The chill of the beer surprised her, and she shivered. Ruthie turned the beer can over in her hands, confused. The pop top was gone.

Mark laughed as he watched her inspect the can. Turning it upside down. He yelled above the music, "If you want to open it, you have to get the church key from the key keeper."

Ruthie frowned, "A key keeper?"

"It's the game," Lucy told her. "You have to go up to each person asking if they are the key keeper, but they can't give you the answer until you tell them something about yourself."

Mark nodded like he approved of Lucy's recitation of the rules. "It's a way for us to get to know each other," he said, shrugging.

"Oh," Ruthie said, feeling instantly too tired to play a game. Why should she get to know people anyway, if they were just going to leave like Lucy? Ruthie looked down at the beer in her hand. She didn't really want it. "Who's taking care of the patients tonight?" Ruthie asked, thinking she'd feel more comfortable skipping this party and going back to triage to help out.

Lucy furrowed her eyebrows. "Hey! No leaving my party. Plus, it's being covered, don't worry. You need a break. Don't you dare think about leaving until you drink that beer. Now go find yourself the key." Lucy sashayed off to join the other dancers.

Ruthie looked around for Patty. She spotted her across the room. Apparently, Patty didn't have to be told twice. She held the same type of beer in her hands and sipped it as she easily made conversation with some nurses Ruthie had never met. Maybe this would be a good way to get acquainted. Still, Ruthie held the beer, feeling awkward. *What's wrong with me?* In Waldron, she'd been the happy, outgoing McKay girl. But here, she didn't feel like herself. She doubted herself and everything she did.

"Ruthie, I'm glad you took my advice and came."

Ruthie turned and relief washed over her. "Hi Connie! Thank you for helping me when we were giving blood. Best stick ever."

Connie laughed. "Plenty of practice."

Ruthie felt her chest tighten. "Aren't you a short-timer too?"

Connie smiled. "I've got just a couple months left."

Connie had pulled her straw-colored hair into a French twist. She wore a dress with large dark and light pink blocks outlined by thick white lines.

Her cheeks were a matching rose pink. The pink made Connie's face look flushed.

Connie pointed to the beer in Ruthie's hand, "You looking for the key?"

"Yeah, did you find it?"

She frowned, "No, I just got here and haven't made it to the bar table yet." She fanned herself. "It's stifling in here though."

"Too many bodies in a tight place," Ruthie commented. She tried to think of conversation topics but only one came to mind. "Do you like triage?"

A grin spread across Connie's lips. "I love it, but it's brutal. Still, I think that's every job here. I used to be in surgery, but now I assess the men that come in and determine whether they are going to live or die."

"Are ya'll talking about work?" Mark asked, leaning between them. He stood so close to Ruthie's face that she could smell him—sweat mixed with a woodsy scent. At least he'd put on a T-shirt.

Connie's face fell. "I-I better get back," she stuttered.

Ruthie reached out for her arm but missed. "Already?" she pleaded, not wanting to be left alone with the gyrating, beer-giving surgeon. But Connie had already gone, squeezing between the dancing bodies.

Mark looked at her beer. "You are horrible at this game."

Ruthie rolled her eyes. "Give me a break. I haven't had a chance to start." Her eyes scanned the crowd. Everyone moved around, not staying in one place, dancing and laughing. She held out her hand. "How could I even begin? It's impossible."

Mark laughed. "I could make this easy on you if you'd dance with me."

Ruthie rolled her eyes. "Don't tell me you have the beer key."

"I have the beer key."

Ruthie groaned. *Of course you do,* she thought. Mark reminded her too much of Greg with an air of arrogance surrounding him like a cloud. But what could one dance hurt? Especially if it got her out of here and back to her hootch so she could finally sleep.

She opened her mouth to tell Mark she'd dance with him, but an explosion rocked the building and made her wobble. Mark reached out, grabbing her arm to steady her.

"Get to the bunker," he directed.

Lucy and Patty ran beside her. Lucy looped her arm into Ruthie's and Patty's, pulling them to the door. "Well, Charlie couldn't say good-bye without a bang, I guess. Let's get out of here."

They pushed their way through the O club's door and ran into the darkness. A whizzing sound above sent a shot of coldness through Ruthie's veins. Lucy led the way, and Ruthie was glad to see the bunker wasn't far. The bunker blended into the ground—half buried under the dirt and half covered with sandbags and netting. It reminded Ruthie of one of those old tornado shelters in Waldron. *Home.* What wouldn't she do to be there right now? Ruthie followed Lucy and Patty inside the bunker. The area was sparce, and the air smelled stale. Benches lined the walls, and a few cots had been pushed in the corners. Patty went deep into the bunker and plopped down on a bench farthest from the door. Ruthie followed her, but Lucy found Mark and they began to talk near the entrance.

"I want to go home," Patty moaned.

Ruthie looped an arm around her friend's shoulder and pulled her close to her side. "It's going to be okay."

"How can we make it a whole year? With this all the time?"

Ruthie glanced over at Lucy and Mark. Their appearance showed no sign of fear—just caution. To her, it looked like they were waiting out a bad storm.

"Maybe you get used to it," Ruthie commented.

Patty groaned. "I'll never get used to it."

After hours of sitting and waiting, the attack ended. Ruthie blinked as she came out of the bunker. The sun had started to rise, and a tinge of pink began to appear on the horizon. Ruthie sighed. She'd have to work her shift again with no sleep. She prayed there would be no emergencies today.

Patty pointed. "Look!"

Ruthie followed Patty's finger. A gray cloud of smoke filled the air. Breath left Ruthie's lungs, and she sprinted with the others toward the smoke and the hospital. She thought of John and the other patients helpless in bed. Bodies pushed and jostled her as they all ran in the same direction. Their feet pounded the red dirt. When they got to the fire, she pushed her way through the crowd. She had to see. Her heart slowed when she made her way to the front and saw the hospital still intact. But her blood ran cold when she realized the fire was coming from a nurse's hootch a few feet from the hospital. It had been completely destroyed. Smoke smoldered off charred wood planks. The twisted metal of the beds poked out from underneath the destruction. No one could have survived, she thought.

Lucy ran beside her. Her shoulders slumped forward, and she started to cry. "All the presents I'd bought my family to take home. All my things—destroyed."

"This was your hootch?" Ruthie asked.

Lucy cried. "Yes."

"Where's your roommate?" Ruthie asked, feeling a cold dread seize her.

Lucy raised her head to look at Ruthie. "Oh! She's gone to Hong Kong. She left two days ago for R&R. Did you think someone was in there? I'm so sorry. I'm upset because of all my things, and you thought someone died." Lucy wiped her tears away with the back of her hand and grabbed Ruthie in a fierce hug. "I'm so sorry!"

Over Lucy's shoulder, Ruthie watched the smoke rise from the destruction. She decided she and Patty would never hide under their beds again.

Chapter 28

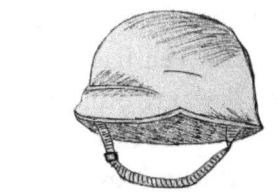

JOEL, MAY 1969

The 101st had been called out to a skirmish around a village not far from a section of the Ho Chi Minh Trail. Before they headed out, Joel heard the men there had already taken some heavy fire and were low on supplies. Since the main goal of the 101st was to add assistance where needed, Joel and his platoon were loaded up with rucksacks full of M16 ammo, M60 ammo, and grenades. He and the other men divided themselves into groups of six and boarded three different Hueys for the forty-five-minute flight to the location. They had no idea what they were really being flown into. They were just told to go, and they went.

His feet dangled out the helicopter's open door. He felt jittery as the wind blew his hair to the side and chill bumps dotted his sweaty skin. He could see plumes of white smoke among the green foliage below and knew they were being fired on. A rocket could take them all out in a millisecond. Even though he tried not to think about that, his body knew, and his mouth went dry. It was hard for him to not think about Hazel and the baby and what would happen if he never came home. His life could be so easily ended by one sniper's bullet. He tried to force himself to push the thoughts of Hazel away. He had to be hyperaware of what was going on if he had any chance to make it out in one piece.

He looked over at Chad sitting beside him. His face tight. The usual smile gone. Joel glanced behind his shoulder at Pen. He sat with his knees to his chest. His face pale white and eyes closed shut so tight, the lines around them seemed to fold over. Joel hoped the landing zone would be guarded this time, and they wouldn't have to make a run for it. The last air assault they'd been to had so much fire at the landing zone, the Huey couldn't land, and they'd had to bail from about ten feet in the air. He and Chad had made it unscathed. But Pen had landed right on his face, and he and Chad had to run back dodging bullets to help him. Joel shivered as he remembered the shots hitting the dirt beside his feet as he and Chad grabbed Pen's arms and skittered with him to the trees for cover.

Joel thanked the Lord this time the landing went smoothly, and everyone was able to regroup once they were on the ground. The men gathered around Lieutenant Roberts. "Let's head this way," he said, motioning toward the east.

In the field, there were no salutes, no "Yes sirs," no acknowledgment of superiors. The Viet Cong loved to take out officers, so everyone just nodded and let the point man chosen for the day, Bill Warwick, lead the way.

When they made it to the village, Lieutenant Roberts looked around. There were no other forces here, just people from the village. His face turned a bright shade of red. Whatever issues there had been in this area were long over. Joel wasn't angry though, his body relaxed. There'd be no shooting today. His heartbeat started to return to a normal pace. Roberts told the platoon to wait while he called in for further orders.

"Well, that was a big to do about nothing," Chad said, positioning his M16 over his shoulder. "I was ready to rock and roll."

"Do you think we'll head back to base?" Pen asked. Joel could see the hope in his eyes.

Chad shrugged. "Who knows."

Joel took in the village. It was rare they got a moment to look around without fear that they might step on a bouncing betty, trip a booby trap, or fall into a pit with a punji stake. Joel shuddered. He'd seen the wounds of a man who'd fallen into one of those pits, where the spears were sharpened to a point and covered in human feces. The wounds were terrible and the fear of infection far worse. He swallowed and pushed the thought away.

The village sat nestled in the center of the jungle, surrounded by thickets of ferns and foliage and the large leaves of the elephant grass. The huts of the village stood off the ground on round wooden stilts. The walls looked thin and yellow. Dried palm leaves were woven and stacked together to make a roof. Joel noticed how the people of the village eyed them suspiciously. He couldn't blame them. Women pulled their children close to their sides, and men paused to let them pass. He'd heard a little about US soldiers burning down villages, and he wondered if they'd heard the same reports passed around by wandering travelers or NVA soldiers.

Lieutenant Roberts marched back toward them. "We're staying here for a while. Let's set up camp in the center of the village. We'll start our daytime reconnaissance patrol and leave a two-man team at the camp to guard the supplies. We'll sleep at night in the village. Four men perimeter guards will rotate and monitor the area about a hundred feet around village while the others catch some Zs. Looks like we may be here for a while, so get comfortable and don't cause any undue trouble for the villagers."

Joel bit down on his cheek. Staying in a village could be dangerous as some villagers were friendly by day but turned into enemies by night. He wondered how that enemy would feel when they were sleeping not ten feet away from their huts.

"What's the purpose?" Danny Barnes asked. "Why are we staying out here."

Roberts shrugged. "Do you honestly think I know?" He laughed, but it came out too harsh. "I figure that the Viet Cong has been using this village for supplies or recruits. And we're gonna keep that from happening. As you can see, the 3rd Battalion has already left, so it's just going to be us left to guard this area."

Pen's body deflated. "No hot meals for a while," he whispered to Joel.

But Pen had been wrong. Three weeks into their stay, the village people had welcomed them in, sharing hot food, sweet rice cakes wrapped in banana leaves, and fresh fruits. For the food, the men of the 101st traded C-rations, old uniform buttons, small sewing kits, and anything that wouldn't get them in trouble with the uppers. Joel's favorite hot meal came from a woman who they all had started calling simply "the rice lady." Her rice practically melted in his mouth.

Joel finished up his patrol shift and made his way up the wobbly stairs of the rice lady's tiny hut. When he knocked on her flimsy door, he could already smell the rice cooking, and his stomach growled.

"Come in," she said, her English getting better each day they were here.

He opened the door and ducked under the low door jamb. He'd eaten better here than he had at the Phu Bai Base. He lowered his head to the women. Her deep wrinkles made mountain crevices across her face. Her white hair hung in limp thin strands across her slumped shoulders. She handed him a wooden bowl with a toothless smile. A clump of rice sat in the center.

"Thank you," he said, nodding. He handed her the few extra uniform buttons he'd found in the bottom of his rucksack. She took them eagerly as payment. Joel had found she liked many things the soldiers traded for food, but buttons were her favorite.

Joel made his way under the hut to sit in the shade. He leaned against one of the stilts. He placed the wooden bowl on the ground beside his leg and dropped a couple purification tablets into his canteen. He shook it up, and while he waited, he reached into his pocket to take out the newest letter from Hazel. At least once a week, a chopper had come and landed in the landing zone that he and the men had leveled out about a hundred yards from the village. The choppers would drop off a few supplies and mail. Late yesterday, Warwick and Barnes had left on the chopper for R&R and were replaced with two new guys, one a medic that Joel hadn't met yet.

He stared at Hazel's letter. He'd read it three times already away from Chad and Pen. He felt bad for them. Chad never got letters from his parents, and Pen's girl had stopped writing him after she'd broken his heart. Her last letter came during the first days of being at the village. Pen had read it out loud to him and Chad.

"I can't do this anymore. Have a good life." Pen turned the letter over, but the back side was blank. He'd stared at Joel and Chad with watery eyes. "That's it? Two lines?" he'd asked as if they had any answers.

"Another letter?"

It was Pen. Joel's chest deflated. He shouldn't have gotten it out to read, but his fingers itched to hold the paper, and his eyes ached to see the words. He missed Hazel so much. He hurriedly pushed the letter back into his front shirt pocket.

"Oh, he gets letters all the time," Chad said, plopping down under the hut near them with two clumps of rice in his hands.

"How'd you get two helpings?" Joel asked, raising one eyebrow.

Chad shrugged, "What can I say, the rice lady likes red heads." He inhaled the rice and looked at Joel. "Did you read your love letter already or what?"

Joel's face heated, but he laughed. "Yeah, I've read it."

"And what'd it say? Come on, you know I have to live through you." Chad lifted his knees to his chest and dusted his hands on his pants before wrapping them around his legs.

"She just said she was doing well. The baby is growing, and she made a joke about how she's getting bigger every day." Joel wished deeply that he could be there, watching all the changes she was going through.

"That's great news," Pen said. He smiled, but the smile didn't touch his eyes.

"Yeah, it is. So why the long face Davenport?" Chad asked him.

Joel blinked. Had he been frowning? "Well, her sister Ruthie is a nurse, and with all the complications with Hazel's last pregnancy, I would kinda rest easier, you know, knowing Ruthie was with her. But Ruthie's here now, and although Hazel has people around her, none of them are nurses."

"Here?" Chad asked, tilting his head to the side.

"Yeah, in Vietnam. She volunteered to be a nurse. So, she's not there with Hazel anymore. And I'm so far away." Joel picked up the wooden bowl and downed the rice so he wouldn't have to talk about it anymore.

"Everything will be great, man. You're going to be a father. It's far out. Another life. A copy of you and your girl."

Joel nodded and choked down the rice.

"Good luck cake for your happiness?" a soft voice said.

A woman stood in the fading sunlight near the shade of the hut. The glare made it hard for Joel to see her, but she held out a basket. He, Chad, and Pen stood, stooping to come out from under the hut to see what she had inside the basket. Her basket contained round, colorful cakes, some green, yellow, and a light shade of purple, all dusted with a white powder.

"Bánh pía for much happiness," she said.

Joel looked up at the woman holding the basket. She smiled without showing her teeth. Her eyes were big and round. Her black hair pushed behind one ear; the rest hung over her face to conceal a long, raised red scar that ran down her cheek to the middle of her chin. Joel realized he'd never seen her before. They'd been at the village for nearly a month, and he'd never seen her. She pushed the basket closer to him. The sweet smell filled his nose. He thought about not taking one, but he also didn't want to offend her.

"How much?" he asked.

Her smile brightened and she giggled. "Free to you. For happiness."

Joel thanked her. He reached inside the basket and picked a bright yellow one. She quickly lowered her gaze and bowed her head.

"Many days of happiness," she said.

"To you too," Joel said, holding the cake up awkwardly.

She nodded.

"I'd think twice before eating that, hickory dickory."

Harvey Davis walked toward them. His arms folded in front of him. He glared at the woman with the basket. She lowered her chin and glided past him to take her cakes to other men sitting around in groups. Davis's eyes hardened and followed the woman's movements.

"Leave her alone," Chad said.

"Yeah," Pen echoed. "We're not supposed to cause issues for the villagers."

"Stuff it, you idiots. Do you think she's one of these villagers? Have you ever seen her before? You think you can trust her? She'd like to have all your heads on platers." Davis started to head toward the woman, and in one swift movement, Joel caught Davis's T-shirt from behind, pulling it back. Davis reared around, but Joel kept a tight grip on the back of Davis's shirt.

"She was being kind. After all these village people have given us, you think you could show some civility. But you're nothing but low. Lower than low."

Davis whipped his shirt out of Joel's grasp. He gave Joel a hard shove back. "I'm just trying to warn you, daddy. Hate for your child to end up fatherless before the little tyke is even born."

Joel's blood boiled inside him. He started to charge Davis, but Chad and Pen grabbed his arms and held him back. He struggled against their hold, sending the small yellow cake flying in pieces.

"Well look there, you've ruined it," Davis said, motioning to the ground. He shrugged. "Don't worry you're pretty little heads. I'm leaving." He motioned toward Joel. "You boys better keep a close eye on this one, he gets all riled up for nothing."

When Davis was out of sight, Pen and Chad let Joel go. He yanked his arms away.

"You should have let me go," he yelled. "Why didn't you let me go? I could have ended him." Joel's chest heaved up and down.

Chad shook his head. "Yeah, and Roberts would have ended you. I know Davis is annoying, but he's right. You gotta get ahold of yourself, man. What would your girl say if you got put behind bars or court martialed?"

Joel's body went limp. His arms hung at his sides. He had too much of his pa inside of him. He remembered how close he'd been to ending up behind bars so many years ago before he and Hazel married. He'd let his anger at his pa get the best of him that day, and it nearly cost Hazel's father his life. Chad was right. He had to get it together. He couldn't let anger control him like it had controlled his pa. Harvey Davis wasn't worth it.

He kicked the dirt, sending red dust plumes in the air. "Yeah, you're right." He looked up at Chad and Pen. "I don't know what to say. Sorry I... I..."

Pen held up his hand. "Don't apologize. We get it."

With that, they sat back under the hut. Chad told stories about his farm back home in Oklahoma. Joel tried to listen. He tried to get his mind off what Davis had said, but no matter how hard he tried to push it away, his words kept repeating in the back of his mind like a broken record. If Joel died here, he'd leave his child fatherless. He'd never know his son or daughter. Never hold his baby. Never get a chance to be the father he hoped he'd be.

❦

Joel, Chad, and Pen lucked out with first guard duty, and they'd made it back to the village before dark had even fully set in. Joel tried to sleep, but he tossed and turned as he lay on the hard ground with just his poncho as a barrier. His small tent seemed to trap the heat from the outside, making it hard to breathe. He threw the mosquito net over his body and tried to close his eyes, but his mind reeled, never fully allowing sleep to take hold. So, when he heard rustling noises, he thought for a brief second the camp had been taken over by a herd of unknown animals. But then he heard men groaning and crying, and he knew something had to be terribly wrong. He crawled out of the tent, blinking his eyes to help them adjust to the darkness. The light from the half-moon barely illuminated the village. When Joel's eyes adjusted, he gasped at what he saw, men crawling out of their tents and across the ground holding their stomachs. Some ran to palm trees or outside the camp into the huge elephant grass to vomit or worse. The sounds and smells of sickness surrounded him. Joel covered his own mouth to keep from being sick. Chad and Pen ran up beside him, both wide-eyed, their faces pale.

"What's going on?" Pen asked.

Before Joel could respond, the sound of gunfire ripped through the dark night. A scream sent chills down his spine. Another shot exploded, then another.

"We're being ambushed!" Harvey Davis screamed, running by them shirtless. His unbuckled pants hung open; his rifle flung over his shoulder.

Joel's eyes darted around. Men were everywhere, sick and unable to protect themselves. He ran to this tent, grabbed his M16, and threw on his helmet but had no time for his boots. Chad and Pen ran to their tents to grab their rifles.

"Where's Lieutenant Roberts?" Pen asked.

"Not sure," Chad said.

"Whatta we do?" Pen yelled over the sound of gunfire.

"We protect our men. I'll go this way," Joel said, pointing to a field of tall elephant grass. He'd seen many of the sick men crawl toward the grass before the gunfire started. "Chad, you go that way," he pointed to a group of palm trees. "Pen, you stay here, guard the camp."

Pen nodded, and Chad took off running toward the palm trees. His bare feet slapped the ground. Shots rang out, but Joel raced toward them and the screams.

In the field, he slowed his pace. His heart beat hard against his chest, and the blood rushed between his ears. The men were scattered throughout the field, so he had to force himself to slow down. If he shot, he couldn't be wrong. He couldn't make a mistake and hit one of his own. He slowed his breath and moved the tall grass with the barrel of his rifle. The grass felt rough under his bare feet, but he made himself take slow, deliberate steps. On the ground in front of him, the moonlight reflected off of skin. The elephant grass looked broken and trampled. Joel bit his lip to keep in a scream. He moved closer to the body. It was one of his men. Blood oozed out of holes in his bare chest, his head resting in a puddle of vomit. Bile burnt the back of Joel's throat.

The grass in front of him swayed and rustled. He held his breath and crouched down low near the body. The smell of vomit made his eyes water. A Viet Cong soldier stood not a foot away from him, his back to Joel. The Viet Cong soldier's head darted side to side, looking around. Joel could see him holding some sort of rifle. He had rows of huge rounds of ammunition attached to his helmet like a circular crown. When he turned around, the only thing Joel thought before he pulled the trigger was that he looked young. The report from the gun rang in Joel's ears, and the soldier grasped his chest. His eyes stared at Joel, unfocused, before he crumpled to the ground, dead. Someone yelled something in Vietnamese. He heard running before he saw them. There were four or five, but he couldn't be for sure. They were running away, the grass swaying and swooshing with their movements.

Joel's mind blurred, and he let anger take control. He ran after them, screaming and sending a spray of bullets in their direction. One fell, Joel ran past the body, continuing the chase. He fired again and again. Another fell and he kept going, pushing through the sharp stitch in his side. He barely noticed the sharp stones his feet hit as he ran. Another fell, but the last one had gotten so far ahead that Joel lost sight of him. Joel stopped. He lowered himself back down into the tall grass, his breath sawed in and out. He'd taken out three on the run. He had to stop. It was too dangerous to go any farther on his own. When he could breathe and real thoughts began to formulate in his head again, he knew he had to confirm the ones he'd gotten were dead and that no more danger would come from them tonight. He scanned the area and found the last two bodies easily. One of the bodies was a young boy, probably no older than seventeen. All Joel's anger evaporated. He'd killed a kid, but what could he have done. He'd have killed Joel if he'd gotten a chance. Joel shook off the desire to chug some hard liquor and focused on finding the last body.

He didn't have to look hard. The bent and broken grass showed the way to where the body lay. He squatted down to check for a pulse, and the Viet Cong soldier's helmet rolled off, long dark hair spilled out onto the ground. Joel's breath caught in his chest. He saw the red puckered line, running down the side of her face across her cheek to her chin. His anger returned in full force. Davis had been right. She'd given so many of the men her cakes. What had she said, "For your happiness"? She'd made them all sick so they could ambush them. Fear clutched his heart. She'd tried to give him one of the cakes. He'd almost eaten it too. He could have been killed tonight.

He walked back to the village. Around the tents and huts, bodies lay strewn across the ground. Soldiers. Villagers. Viet Cong. All dead. His eyes darted around to find Chad and Pen. "Sutton?" he hollered for Chad. "Pen?" he yelled. He began to run around. His heart raced in his chest. "Sutton! Pen!" He didn't want to think about it, but what if he'd lost them? He made himself examine the bodies lying on the ground. He recognized a man from the village and a young blonde soldier that had replaced Warwick while on R&R. Joel felt a huge weight on his chest. He didn't even know the kid's name.

"Davenport!" he heard his name. It came from above him.

He lifted his chin. In the rice woman's hut, Chad stood in the doorway, waving his arm. Joel sucked in a breath. He felt his heart starting to return to a normal pace. Joel took the stairs to the door two at a time. The thin door of the hut hung open at a crooked angel. Inside the hut, children and women whimpered and cried. Joel followed Chad inside. The women stood in a corner of the hut, holding their children close. Tears streamed down their faces. In the middle of the floor, the rice lady lay. Her thin, white hair splayed out in a fan around her. Pen kneeled over her body. His head in his hands. His body racked with sobs. Joel looked at Chad's pale face.

"What happened?" Joel asked.

Chad grabbed his arm tight and pulled him back outside, down the stairs, and away from the crying. Under the hut, Chad ran a hand roughly down his face. Joel could barely make out his shadow as he paced back and forth in the darkness.

"He killed her," he said almost so low Joel couldn't hear the words.

Joel's stomach twisted. "What? Pen?"

Chad stopped pacing and nodded.

"What? Why?" It didn't make sense.

Chad shrugged, "It was an accident. So much was going on. She opened the hut door. Why she'd open the door when people were shooting, who knows, but it startled Pen. He'd shot three or four times before he realized it was her."

Joel's knees gave out, and he lowered himself to the ground. Chad sat beside him, clutching his knees to his chest. She'd been a kind woman who did nothing wrong but open the door at the worst possible moment. *What have we done to this village? What have we done?*

Chapter 29

JOEL

It'd been two days since the ambush. Chad, Pen, and Joel loaded the last poncho-covered body onto a chopper to be transported to Grave Registration where they would be processed and hopefully returned to their families. Eight men from his platoon had been killed. Medevac choppers had already taken six other wounded men to hospitals to be cared for. The wounded villagers, which included children, were flown out on Chinooks with their family members to field hospitals. The villagers clung to each other during takeoff, fear smeared across each of their faces.

Right after the ambush had happened, Joel had volunteered and recruited Pen and Chad to help the villagers bury their dead. Joel shivered when he remembered that night. A little boy, maybe two years old, crying for his mother. She'd been shot in the chest, and there was nothing they could do to help her. The boy had crawled near her body and stayed there. It almost broke Joel to have to remove him so they could bury her. Another woman had ripped the boy from his arms. Joel had no idea if she was related to the boy or not, and he hoped the boy hadn't been left an orphan. He wondered how many children this war had left as orphans.

The rest of the men not on burial duty had taken the Viet Cong's dead and flung them into the field beyond the village to rot in the sun and as a warning sign for any other Viet Cong or NVA. Because of the action, men from the 3rd and 9th Battalion had been called in for reinforcements. They'd started patrol of the area. Already Joel had heard that during their sweeps in the jungle, they'd located newly planted booby traps.

Later that day, Lieutenant Roberts called the remaining members of the 101st together. The morning had been cool, but now as they stood in a much smaller group than they'd started with, the blazing heat of midday warmed the top of Joel's head and sent sweat running down the middle of his back.

"Look, I've spoken to the higher-ups. And I agree with their assessment, we all need some R&R, so we are heading to Eagle Beach tomorrow morning. We'll stay a few days there. At least until they send us some new cherries."

Joel shook his head. Cherries—new recruits to replace the dead and wounded. Everyone was replaceable here.

Some of the guys including Harvey Davis and Chad let out some whoops and hollers about heading to Eagle Beach. Chad looped his arm around Joel's neck and shook Joel. "We're heading for some beach time!" Then he tried to loop his other arm around Pen's neck, but Pen pushed him off and walked away. Joel and Chad watched him go.

Pen had said maybe two words since the night of the ambush, and Joel hadn't seen him eat much either. It worried him. Maybe a few days on a beach near the South China Sea, away from the stress and violence of the war, would be good for him. At least, Joel hoped so.

Chapter 30

HAZEL

I t had taken her father over a month to get the paperwork from the probate office at the courthouse. Apparently, Mrs. Abernathy was the only one who could find anything in that office, and she and her family had passed around a stomach bug for weeks before going on vacation to see her cousins in Chattanooga. But now she had them. The documents lay on her table. She'd read them last night with Sandra and then a hundred times after that to remind her of Mr. Hal and Mrs. Anne's betrayal. Each time she read Ms. Angel's will, she burned inside. She and Joel had loved them deeply, and the whole time they knew they had wronged Joel in the worst way.

Hazel passed the table, trying not to let her eyes glance again at the white sheets of paper as she went to the kitchen to make herself some toast and jam before work. Her stomach couldn't handle anything greasy. It had flip-flopped all night after her and Sandra had pored over the papers.

"I can't believe it," Sandra had said, sitting back in her chair. Mannie was cradled in her arms.

Hazel held Mikey. His arms wrapped around her neck and his soft snores tickled her skin. Holding Mikey had been the only thing that had kept her calm. She and Sandra flipped through the same pages over and over again. They'd read them front and back many times, hoping they'd missed something.

But the will had been clear, Ms. Angel's estate was to be halved, leaving half to Mr. Hal and half to Joel. It appeared Ms. Angel had her lawyers prepare the will not long after Sarah, Joel's mama, had died. Hazel had been confused. If Joel was supposed to receive half of the estate, why didn't that happen? That's when Sandra pointed out that the executor of the will was Mr. Hal, and as executor, he would have been responsible for making sure all the debts and taxes were paid, and the money was properly distributed to any heirs—himself and Joel. But he didn't do that, and what it looked like to her and Sandra was he'd only distributed the estate's assets to himself.

What am I supposed to tell Joel? She knew she would have to tell him what she'd learned, but when? He already had so much to worry about, and she didn't want to send a letter telling him someone he loved and trusted unconditionally turned out to be a liar and thief. Even though she didn't want to believe it, the proof lay on the table in typed black letters.

She bit her bottom lip. She dipped a butter knife into a nearly empty jar of blackberry jam to spread on her toast. Her mind was a whirlwind of thoughts as the knife clinked inside the glass jar. Reading those words had made her heart break. Mrs. Anne had been right. She did hate them. Especially if they'd done what it looked like they'd done—taken all the money and given nothing to Joel. They'd taken his part of the estate and left him with an alcoholic, abusive father. She wondered now if all their kindness had been fake or if they were trying to make themselves feel better for all their past wrongs.

Hazel went to spread the jam across her bread when a sharp tightness in her rounded stomach made her drop the knife. Jelly streaked across the countertop. She stepped back from the counter and laid her hands across her middle, forcing herself to breathe. After a few moments, the tight pain left. Hazel closed her eyes tight, waiting for more, but nothing else happened. *What in the world?* she wondered. She took in a few more deep breaths to calm herself. *I'm fine, this is normal. I'm not due until the end of June or early July,* she told herself. She wet a wash rag to clean up the small mess. She sighed. She didn't feel like eating now. Even though she told herself to be calm, she couldn't. Her hunger had evaporated as her worries increased. She needed Joel. She ripped the toast into tiny pieces and tossed them to the birds on her way out.

⁂

When she'd arrived at Piggly Wiggly, she'd seen Officer McConnell coming out of the drugstore across the street, a cup of coffee in his hand. He'd nodded at her. She forced herself to nod back. His words about wanting to speak with Joel when he came home still haunted her. She swallowed, feeling it stick in the back of her throat. Every day, she tried hard not to worry for the baby, but how could she stop herself when there was so much to worry about. She worried about Joel's safety, Officer McConnell's vague threat, and on top of all that, she had to deal with Mr. Hal and Mrs. Anne's betrayal.

In the store, she easily made her hands busy. The monotonous day's work of straightening the shelves, sweeping the floor, and ringing up and bagging groceries made her forget everything for the time being. By three-thirty, it was almost time for Hazel to go home, and she couldn't wait. Louanne had been in rare form all day. Everything about her today drove Hazel batty.

"I mean, we'd gone out on three dates," Louanne said, puckering her pink lips. "Then Annalise sees him out with a girl from Greenwood. Can you believe it? After the second date, he told me he loved me. Men are big fat liars."

Hazel sighed. *Some men are big fat liars,* she thought. Mr. Hal's face popped into her head. As if her thoughts had conjured him, she heard a throat being cleared across her checkout counter. She almost gasped when she saw Mr. Hal standing there. Her body froze. Louanne stopped talking mid-sentence. The air felt charged between them. Mr. Hal cleared his throat again and pushed a carton of milk and three apples toward her. She couldn't help herself. She glowered at him. Her heart pounded in her chest. She wanted to pick up one of those apples and launch it at his lying face, but she picked up the milk instead. The faster she got him rung up and he paid, the faster he'd be gone.

He ran his tongue across his teeth and clucked it. "So, I heard your daddy was looking for information from Mrs. Abernathy down at the courthouse."

Hazel's heart skipped a beat. Of course he'd have heard. What did she expect in a small town? Her thoughts went in a million directions, and she pushed her shoulders back. She wouldn't lie. She'd face this head on, like Ruthie would do. "Yep, what business is it of yours?" Hazel said. Out of the corner of her eye, she saw Louanne's mouth drop open a foot. Hazel gripped the paper milk carton so tight she left indentions in the sides.

Mr. Hal coughed, "I see. So... I guess you've seen the will then." He looked down at the floor before glancing back at her with pleading eyes. "I can explain."

A thousand horrible words passed through her thoughts, each one inappropriate to say to a customer, but before she could choose the right one to launch at him, a gush of water released from somewhere inside her. Liquid ran down her legs, wetting her shoes.

She gasped as an onset of tightness gripped her. It started in the center of her belly and wrapped its way around to her back. She grabbed the cash register and held it, gritting her teeth.

Louanne squealed. "What's wrong with you, Hazel?"

She felt Mr. Hal's rough hands on her arms. "Hazel, we need to get you to the hospital."

She twisted her head, "I'm not going anywhere with you." Hazel meant for her words to sound cruel, but they sounded breathless. Her stomach muscles tightened and squeezed her insides. The pain ran from her front to her back, and she could hardly take a breath.

"Help! Help!" Louanne started to holler. She waved manicured hands in the air frantically. "She's having a baby!" She looked at Hazel. "Don't you dare have that baby here. Not in the checkout line of Piggly Wiggly. Oh Lordy, I think I'm gonna be sick."

Hazel twisted her head. "Shut up, Louanne!" she snarled.

Louanne's eyes almost popped out of her head. "Well, I've never."

Hazel had no idea when Mr. Crutchfield arrived, but suddenly he stood beside her. "Breathe, Hazel," he yelled near her face.

The words made her suck in a breath.

"Call Arvel and Sandra Lewis," Mr. Hal directed Mr. Crutchfield. "I'll get her to the hospital."

"I-I said I'm not going with you," Hazel panted.

"You've got to go with him, Hazel, or you're going to end up giving birth right here on the Piggly Wiggly floor," Mr. Crutchfield pleaded. "Don't worry, I'll call your dad and Sandra. But go now, and let Hal get you to the hospital quick."

Hazel wanted to refuse again, but another wave of pain shot through her, and she started to worry for her baby. It was too early for her to be in labor. She couldn't handle losing another child.

She released her death grip on the counter and allowed the two men to help her to Mr. Hal's truck. Inside the truck, she closed her eyes and started to focus on managing the pain. *Women have babies all the time*, she told herself. *I can do this.* When Mr. Hal's door closed with a slam, it made her jolt, sending a wave of pain through her back. She groaned.

"Don't worry, I'm gonna hurry," Mr. Hal told her.

She didn't reply.

After they were on their way, she closed her eyes again, trying to take long, slow breaths, but the pain made her whole body tighten as the pressure in her pelvis increased. If he didn't hurry, the baby would be born right here in his passenger seat. The thought sent a chill down her spine. *Too early*, she thought.

"Look, I know you probably have some questions about what you saw in the will. And I'd like to explain," Mr. Hal rambled.

Hazel huffed. "I don't care to hear any of your explanations right now." She gritted her teeth.

Mr. Hal nodded and tightened his grip on the wheel. His foot pressed harder on the accelerator.

When he swerved into the Waldron Memorial Hospital parking lot, Krissy Maxwell stood near the door with a wheelchair. Her bright red hair was pulled back in a bun, and her nurse's cap sat straight on her head.

"Hazel! Come on, let's get you inside," she said.

She quickly wheeled Hazel through the emergency doors. Hazel tried to push the terrible thoughts of losing Madelyn Ray out of her head and just breathe. Hazel noticed Mr. Hal had seemed to have disappeared, and she felt grateful for that. Krissy rolled the wheelchair toward the waiting room where her dad and Sandra were already waiting for her. They rushed to her side.

"How are you doing, girl?" her father asked, his brows drawn together, making his forehead wrinkle.

She panted and tried to give him a smile, "Not too great, Dad."

"I'm going with her," Sandra said to Krissy.

Krissy nodded. "This way then."

"Good luck, sweetie. I'll be here praying for you," her dad said as Krissy wheeled her toward the birthing room, leaving him behind. Sandra picked up her pace and reached for Hazel's hand. "You're going to be fine. Just keep breathing."

"Too early," Hazel panted.

Sandra squeezed her hand. "Everything will be fine."

Hazel wanted to believe her.

The next hour swept by in a blur. The pain. The crying, mostly from her. Krissy and Mrs. Battalou encouraging her to push. Sandra gripped her hand and wiped her forehead with a soft cotton hand towel. Suddenly, it was all over, and she heard a sound that set her heart on fire—her baby's cry. She had no idea a feeling like this existed. Love spread over and warmed her from the inside out, erasing all her pain and fear. When Dr. Sullivan held up her baby, tears blurred her eyes, and she blinked them away.

"He's a boy!" Dr. Sullivan announced.

"Congratulations, Mama," Sandra said, leaning over to give Hazel a hug.

"A boy," Hazel said out loud. Even though she heard the words, they felt so dream-like. *Can it be true?*

"He's a tiny one. But he looks healthy," Dr. Sullivan told her. "Let her hold him, Mrs. Battalou, and then get him in the oven."

"Oven?" Hazel asked.

Mrs. Battalou smiled. "Incubator, dear." She wrapped the baby and handed him to Hazel. "We'll get him cleaned up and in the oven in a bit. But here you go, Mama." She passed the small bundle to Hazel.

He looks healthy. Dr. Sullivan's words clung to her soul as she looked down into her son's tiny face. He looked so much like Joel. Oh, how she wished Joel were here. Her most wonderful moment tinged with sadness.

"He's so handsome," Krissy commented, and Sandra agreed.

Sandra leaned over and delicately touched his cheek. "Did you and Joel ever pick a name?"

Hazel shook her head. "No, but I've already decided one for myself. His name is Aaron Thomas Davenport. Aaron is Joel's middle name."

Sandra smiled, "And Thomas after Joel's pa?"

Hazel sniffed, "Yes. I hope Joel doesn't mind."

Chapter 31

RUTHIE

Ruthie felt blessed every time she went to the mail room and found she had a letter from someone. She'd received countless letters from her father, Hazel, and Sandra. And although she loved hearing about home, all of their letters felt glossy and full of partial information, as if her family wanted to protect her from the turmoil happening in the United States. Her father talked about the weather, missing her, and how proud he was of her. Hazel spoke about how her pregnancy was coming along, about how the baby loved to kick her in the kidneys, and the many trips to the bathroom she'd make during the day. Sandra wrote to her about Mikey and Mannie and how they were growing like weeds. Only her best friend, Margarette Ann, wrote her the truth. Through Margarette Ann, she'd learned more about the protests at college campuses and people marching through the streets with signs and loud screams. Margarette Ann would tell her about the news and the constant rise in the death toll. They didn't hear about that here, but she'd suspected the information they received from the government that they were winning the war might have been skewed. Ruthie didn't understand why no one could be honest with what was going on.

She didn't fault her father, Hazel, or Sandra for trying to protect her because in all actuality, she did the same to them. Her letters weren't just filled with partial truths, she filled them with flat out lies. She could never tell them yesterday she'd pushed a soldier's guts back inside his stomach and held his hand until he breathed his last breath. Or in just the few short months of being here, she'd cleaned and applied pressure to so many gunshot wounds, she'd stopped counting. Or that she'd already held many amputated legs and arms. Or listened to screams and moans until she didn't even notice them anymore. She only told her friend, Margarette Ann, the truth about these things. It had gotten increasingly hard to write lies, so around the end of April, she'd went to the PX before work and purchased a tape recorder and extra tapes. She found it much easier to tell lies than to write them. She'd pinch her cheeks and jump in place a few times in her small hootch to get her energy up, then push record, making her voice sound upbeat. By the time she pushed stop, she'd swear she should have gone to Hollywood and become an actress. She didn't even feel bad about the lies. She loved her family too much to make them worry more than they already did about her.

Before work, she decided to run to the mail room to drop off her latest cassette. The mail clerk took it. "Hey McKay, you got another letter."

Ruthie bounced on the toes of her boots. "Well don't just stand there, Boyd, let's see it."

He rolled his eyes and found the letter. She swiped it quickly from his hands. "You get the most letters and care packages of anyone I know," he laughed.

She did a little flip with her hand. "I'm a lucky girl, Boyd. A very lucky girl."

Outside she wasted no time and tore into Hazel's letter. Seeing the curly handwriting on the sheets of notebook paper made her heart leap in her chest. Her eyes pored over the words. Hazel had the baby! She'd named him Aaron. Ruthie loved the name, but her heart fell. It was too early for Aaron

200

to come. Hazel would have only been around thirty-two weeks along. She kept reading. He'd weighed nearly five pounds when he'd been born. That made Ruthie feel somewhat better. She read Hazel's description of the incubator and how it looked like a small cooking oven. Hazel explained how Aaron had trouble keeping his temperature up and feeding, but now he could latch on easily. Hazel wrote lately he'd gained ounces almost every day. She said Mrs. Battalou and Krissy had set a rocking chair by the incubator and let her sit there all day if she wanted. Mrs. Battalou even taught her how to crochet so she could make Aaron a baby blanket. Ruthie smiled when she read that their father had picked the brightest blue and yellow yarn for the blanket. At the end of Hazel's letter, she promised Ruthie everything was good, better than good, and she didn't need to worry. She also said when Aaron came home, she'd play the cassettes Ruthie sent for him so he would recognize his Aunt Ruthie's voice. Aunt Ruthie. The thought made tears spring to Ruthie's eyes.

She reached for the hospital's door and Connie burst out. Connie's eyes were red rimmed, and her fatigues stained. Ruthie could hardly believe her mentor would be leaving in the next few weeks. She'd miss Connie, but it wasn't just about missing her. Triage had been short-staffed for a while because Patty had been moved to surgery. How were they going to survive with another nurse gone? They'd gained a few new doctors over the last weeks, which Ruthie thought would be a good thing, but quickly learned the new doctors moved too slow. Dr. Gerry tried to teach them to sew and go, which was the best method for MASCALS, but the new doctors wanted to pontificate and think too much about treatment when each second that ticked by was a matter of life or death. Just the night before, Ruthie had packed up to leave for the day when she'd heard the familiar sound of multiple Hueys, and she knew she'd have to stay and help. Twenty wounded men were rushed in—all with various injuries. Ruthie watched as one of the new doctors stood by a young soldier with dark brown hair and skin. The soldier clutched the doctor's hand, begging the doctor to save him. But it was impossible, once the military anti-shock trousers were removed, Ruthie saw a wide gaping hole in the young man's abdominal area. His stomach and most intestines were gone. The doctor stood there staring cluelessly while blood spilled on the floor onto his shoes. She'd ended up pushing him out of the way and making the call herself.

"Expectant," she called because his life expectancy was short.

Other nurses moved in and took the dying soldier to the back to make him more comfortable for the few minutes he had left to live. The new doctor thanked her, but she shook her head. That night, she'd made all the calls. She'd felt like an executioner, deciding who went to the back to die, who went to surgery, and who could wait to be cared for. She had to tell herself over and over that she didn't cause this, the war did, and she had a job to do.

Connie stood in front of the door. She blinked her eyes and held up a hand to shield them from the sun. "Can you believe we finally have a day with some sunshine?" Ruthie asked.

With May had come torrential rainfalls like nothing Ruthie had ever seen. She hated it. Everyone did. It made the work at the hospital ten times harder. They'd have to sweep mud and water out the door almost every hour, and everything around them stayed wet. Her fatigues never felt dry—always moist. She and Patty had stretched a wire across their hootch to hang their clothes on, but it didn't matter. They never fully dried. But this morning, the perpetually gray sky had opened just enough for a little morning sunlight to poke through the clouds.

When Connie didn't respond, Ruthie reached out to touch her arm. "Rough night?" she asked.

Connie shrugged. She ran a hand through her frazzled, blonde hair. Tears began to spill down her cheeks. Ruthie took Connie in her arms.

"I have time to get some coffee before I start my shift. You want to sit with me and talk?"

Connie shuddered. "Yeah."

Ruthie and Connie grabbed a biscuit and bacon from the mess hall and found a dry area available near the pool under the metal awning. They ate in silence. Ruthie didn't want to pressure Connie to talk, so she stretched her legs out and watched the breeze send the pool water sloshing above the cement edge. If it didn't stop raining before long, there'd be no pool at all, just a muddy lake. *At least Connie has quit crying*, she thought, popping the last bit of biscuit into her mouth.

Ruthie realized she couldn't handle the silence. She needed to get to work soon. She decided to start with an easy question. "Are you excited about going home?"

Connie sniffed. "Yeah, I am. I'm ready to get out of this place." She pulled her knees to her chest and wrapped her arms around them. "So many nurses re-up, but I'm not. I can't do it a second time."

Ruthie nodded. "I think when my time's short, I won't ever re-up. I miss home too much."

"I do feel bad about leaving. The men need us. It's just," Connie gulped. "My mom needs me now and I can't stand seeing him anymore. And he's staying. He decided to stay another year."

Ruthie frowned. She had no idea what Connie was talking about. "Who's staying?"

"Mark."

Ruthie thought about Mark, the bartending surgeon, always dancing around the O club with his T-shirt off, showing off his muscular frame. Mark had dark brown hair, cut short. His icy blue eyes stood out against his tan skin. He always smiled. After the first night, when she almost agreed to dance with him, they'd never really spoken much. He was a surgeon, and she was busy in triage. On the nights Ruthie felt like hanging out at the O club, she never paid much attention to him. He reminded her too much of Greg, the pompous arrogant guy she'd dated in Waldron.

A wind blew and the puddles surrounding them rippled. Ruthie pushed lose strands of curly blonde hair out of her face. She swallowed. She couldn't understand why it mattered to Connie if Mark stayed. Connie glanced over at Ruthie as if she could see the wheels spinning in Ruthie's head.

She sighed. "You don't know, do you?" Connie rubbed her forehead. "I thought everyone knew or gossiped about it." She chuckled. "Well, I guess it's good to know that I'm not always the topic of conversations."

"What happened?" Ruthie asked.

"It feels like a hundred years ago, but it also feels like yesterday." Connie let out a groan. "I was stupid. I never had a real boyfriend. I'd gotten here at the same time as Mark. We met the first night at the O club. Both scared out of our minds."

Ruthie nodded. She understood completely.

"Like always, there was an attack, and we had to hide in a bunker. I clung to him, and he clung to me. That night..." she paused. Connie's cheeks burned red.

Ruthie reached over and touched Connie's arm. "You don't have to tell me the rest."

"I was in surgery when I first arrived here. Did I tell you that?" Connie asked.

Ruthie nodded. She'd heard that.

"Well, let's just say, after that first night, Mark and I spent many months together before I found out he was married. I thought he loved me. After I found out, I spoke to him about it, and he dropped me like a hot potato. He wanted nothing else to do with me. Barely spoke to me, other than to ask for surgical tools when I assisted him during a surgery." Connie huffed. "I didn't understand. I felt like I was the one who should be mad, not him. But..." her voice trailed off. "But I didn't feel mad. I felt broken. I really did care for him. Every time a new nurse caught Mark's eye, I'd have to watch him flirt and carry on with her right in front of me. He did it on purpose. I know he did. I asked Tom if I could transfer. He was kind and did it without even asking me why. Now I hear that Mark's found someone new again."

Ruthie gulped; a tightness formed in the pit of her stomach. "Patty?"

Connie nodded. "Yep, it's hard to watch. When I bring patients to surgery, I see it. He's so flirty with her, touching her, and I've even seen them sneak a kiss when they thought no one was watching. I'm glad I'm leaving soon. I don't think I could stand it much longer."

"I'm so sorry, Connie," Ruthie apologized. She'd hardly been able to talk to Patty since she'd started working nights in surgery, but Ruthie would make time today. Even if it meant she got no sleep at all. She'd find Patty and warn her about Mark. Ruthie just hoped it wasn't too late.

Chapter 32

JOEL

Eagle Beach was like nothing Joel had ever seen. Joel sat on the warm sand and watched the waves lap onto the shore. The South China Sea sparkled under the bright sun. This place felt like a vacation. He'd never been to a summer camp, but the hootches reminded him of cabins. The war didn't exist here. He couldn't wait to write Hazel and tell her he'd learned to water ski. There were basketball courts and volleyball nets that weren't made from mosquito netting. The first hamburger he ate nearly made him cry. He and the men from the 101st played the jukebox and movies at night. He hoped Pen might loosen up and maybe talk to him and Chad. But that was a no go. Pen's communication had been reduced to audible grunts and shrugging.

Chad sat down beside him. "Hey, you seen Pen lately?"

"Yeah, I saw him," Joel huffed, laying his whole body flat against the soft, warm sand.

"Oh, that good, huh?"

Joel opened one eye and turned his head toward Chad. "He volunteered again to guard the weapons and equipment. That's his fifth time. I think he does it on purpose, so he won't have to hang with us."

Chad sighed. "I think he's tired of us asking him if he's alright."

Joel rolled over on his side and propped his head up with his elbow. "But he's not okay, is he?"

Chad shrugged. "Dunno."

"Do you think we need to report him? They could take him for a psychiatric evaluation or maybe he could just go back and stay at the base."

Chad plopped down on the sand and laid his arm across his eyes. "Yeah, I wish I knew what to do. He's our friend, and I'd hate to do something to make him feel like we've turned our backs on him. His girl already broke his heart."

Joel swallowed. He understood how Chad felt, but he also understood that someone in a bad frame of mind could be dangerous, and not just to themselves, but to everyone else too. Joel almost said something when a wet tongue licked the bottom of his foot, making him jolt up from the sand. The mangiest dog he'd ever seen stood there wagging his tail. His matted hair bunched up around his eyes. Joel laughed and reached over to rub his knuckles across the mutt's dirty fur.

"He begging for a hot dog or something?" Chad said. He leaned up, and the dog walked to him. Chad patted his head.

"Let's go get him one and maybe he'll let me cut those matts around his eyes with my knife."

Chad laughed. "You're such a softy."

That night, Warwick and Barnes returned from R&R. They'd been quickly filled in about what had happened at the village. With them came the new guys, replacing the dead and wounded. They all worked together to build a huge campfire on the sand near the water. The men gathered around it, laughing and drinking beers. Joel watched the flames twist and pop as they leaped into the blackest sky.

The new guys talked about everything happening in the US. The talk of protests set Joel's teeth on edge. He agreed—send them home—but the stories about how the other men were treated when they arrived back was more than he could stand. He turned away and tried to focus on Warwick's and Barnes's stories of their time in Hong Kong on R&R.

Pen joined the group, holding a guitar in his hands.

"Play us a song!" one of the new guys yelled.

Pen shook his head and handed the guitar to Chad. "I can't play, but I thought you might want to entertain us."

Chad's face brightened when he saw Pen. He took the guitar from him. Pen sat beside Joel and Joel gave him a good slap on the back. "Hey man. It's good to see you. You done with guard duty?" Joel asked.

Pen looked down sheepishly. "Yeah, Lieutenant Roberts said I couldn't volunteer again. He said the duty had to be shared."

One of the new guys, who went by the nickname Slam, chuckled. "Duty."

Pen rolled his eyes. "I saw the guitar in one of the supply sheds. Someone said it'd been left here. And I remembered you played."

Chad held the guitar close like a long-lost friend. He leaned over it and began to tune the strings as he lightly strummed. Joel noticed that Pen's smile didn't quite meet his eyes, but that was alright for now. It was something, he thought.

Chad raised his head and looked at Joel. "Okay, Papa, you get to choose the first song tonight."

Joel couldn't help but beam. He'd gotten a letter this morning from Hazel. She'd had the baby! Early, but everyone was doing fine. He had a son, Aaron Thomas Davenport. He couldn't think of a more perfect name.

Joel laughed. "Hmm, let me think. Don't rush me."

Chad snickered. "Fine, while we wait all night for you to pick a song, I got a good joke for ya." He raised his voice so everyone around the fire could hear him. "This one's for all of ya'll." Chad cleared his throat. "Okay, okay, what has more letters than the alphabet?"

The men looked at each other.

"Is this some 'Okie from Muskogee' joke?" Harvey Davis called.

Chad burst out laughing. "Nope. But don't worry, you won't figure it out. You gotta be smarter than a rock for this joke."

Harvey almost choked on his beer. Warwick and Barnes hooted. "Oh man, I missed you guys," Barnes laughed.

Harvey shook his head. "Yeah, yeah. Tell us. What has more letters than the alphabet?"

"The post office," Chad said.

Guys moaned and picked up handfuls of sand to toss at him. Chad laughed so hard his face almost matched the color of his hair.

"That has got to be the worst joke I've ever heard," Warwick said, tossing another handful of sand at Chad.

"What, come on! That was great!" Chad protested, giving the guitar a good strum and sending a melodic chord through the night air.

Joel glanced at Pen. He stared into the flames. His face solemn.

"Sing 'Cathy's Clown,'" Pen said, making the laughter come to an abrupt halt.

Chad blinked and sucked in a breath. "Well, okay, I was hopin' for something a little livelier, but I guess 'Cathy's Clown' will do." He closed his eyes, letting his fingers strum the chords. He lifted his chin into the air, and his tenor voice filled the air. Everyone, including Joel, joined in on the chorus. The sad lines touched Joel to the core. He'd missed the birth of his child. A moment that he could never get back was gone. They all felt like clowns here in one way or another. But the difference between the song and them were that these clowns had no choice.

Part 3

THE WAR TAKES AND GIVES IN THE STRANGEST OF WAYS.

Chapter 33

JOEL

Joel felt the warm breeze through his hair. A warm spray of water hit his face. Chad drove the boat, whipping it around to jump the biggest waves. Joel and Pen bounced in their boat seats. Thousands of gray clouds hovered above them, and the sound of thunder boomed in the distance. They'd have to head in soon, Joel thought. But for the moment, he just enjoyed the wind across his face and the broad smile spread across Pen's. It sent a jolt of hope coursing through his body. But that happy hope shriveled away when Pen pointed toward the sky. Joel followed his finger to see three Hueys hovering in the air. Their propellers whipped around in circles, making the palm trees bow to the side. The men on beach laying on towels stood to watch the Hueys land.

"What do you think is going on?" Chad yelled over the roar of the boat engine. "Think we should head back?"

"Look," Pen said, pointing toward the beach.

Men from the 101st were waving their arms frantically, motioning for them to come to shore.

"I guess that answers your question," Joel said. A coldness ran through his blood. It looked like their last days at the beach would be cut short.

By the time they made it to shore, everyone was getting dressed, loading up equipment, and packing up to go.

"What's going on?" Pen asked Harvey Davis as he passed by dressed in his fatigues, a heavy rucksack flung over one shoulder and his M16 on the other.

Harvey gave them a hollow-eyed stare. "We're on. No more fun. We're heading to A Shau Valley."

In ten minutes, Joel, Chad, and Pen were dressed and loaded with a rucksack full of M16 ammo, M60 ammo, and grenades. They jumped into the open belly of the last Huey. Joel's stomach leaped into his throat when the chopper rose into the air. How quickly he forgot the sensation.

They were heading to the A Shau Valley not far from the Ho Chi Minh trail. That alone made the hairs on the back of Joel's neck stand on edge. The trail had been used by the NVA and Viet Cong to transport supplies like food and ammunition. He and all the men had heard of the dangers and deaths that had happened near the trail, and now they were heading there. Before they left, Lieutenant Roberts had told them men from the 3rd Battalion had been humping close to the trail and located a network of enemy tunnels that led to enemy bunkers, huts, and discarded communication wires. From there, a fire fight had ensued near Hill 937, and the 3rd Battalion had been ordered to take it. Joel swallowed. Taking it hadn't gone as planned, and now the 101st were the reinforcements.

Joel's squeezed his hands into fists, and he swallowed down the lump in his throat. He made himself look at each face sitting on the chopper floor around him. Chad, Pen, Danny Barnes, Harvey Davis, Warwick, and their new NCO, Sergeant Jameson. Joel prayed to God they all made it back in one piece, and the new commanding officer knew what the heck he was doing.

"Hey, we're here, but we can't land," Danny Barnes yelled to them. "Too much fire. Whatta we do, sir?" he asked, looking at Jameson.

Sergeant Jameson shook so hard his whole body seemed to vibrate with the movements of the chopper. "I-I-I..." Jameson stuttered.

Harvey Davis rolled his eyes. "Looks like we're gonna have to jump, men! Get ready. Once your boots touch dirt, be ready to rock and roll."

Everyone nodded. The helicopter circled the area, gradually getting lower so they could jump. Joel's heart hammered against his chest. As they circled, he took in the hill they were supposed to take. From the top to the bottom of the hill, plumes of white smoke billowed to the sky. Joel's arms went weak. The fighting was everywhere. Brown limbless trees stretched toward them like witches' fingers. Bomb craters pocked the ground and were filled with water. The situation looked so much worse than he could have ever thought. How long had the 3rd Battalion been fighting without help? Six or seven days? He couldn't imagine the horrors those men had endured. But it wouldn't be long until he wouldn't have to imagine anymore.

As the chopper lowered closer to the ground, Joel sucked in deep breaths, knowing it may be the last ones he ever had the opportunity to take. Hazel's face flashed into his mind. He breathed a silent prayer that no matter what happened, she and their new son would always feel his love.

"Ready?" Chad yelled.

Joel nodded. While the chopper hovered above the ground, everyone bailed out. Joel landed flat-footed onto the dirt. The landing jarred his bones, but he didn't let it stop him. He grabbed Pen by the back of the shirt to keep him upright, and they took off running, returning fire by unloading twenty rounds of ammunition in three seconds while they both screamed at the top of their lungs.

"This way!" Warwick screamed.

The men followed behind him, sprinting toward cover. Joel's lungs burned as he raced with the others. Pen panted hard beside him. They quickly found the rest of their platoon.

Roberts directed them to form a single file line. "Watch for snipers. I heard they're everywhere."

Joel instinctively pulled his helmet lower on his head.

Roberts pointed to the north. "We're rendezvousing with the 3rd at the base of the hill. All I've got to say, men, is say your prayers now. I hear it's a real mess up there. May God be with us."

They made their way to the ridge and followed a trail, heading to the base of the hill. On the way, they passed discarded cartridge cases and bandoliers. Two dead NVA soldiers' bodies had been pushed to the side of the trail. Their bloated bodies lay at odd angles. Foamy blood leaked from their noses and mouths. Joel looked away and covered his nose until they passed. At the base of the hill, the first thing Joel noticed was the stench. The area smelled of excrement, rust, and sweat. Members of the 3rd Battalion were sitting down, their backs against the bare-limbed trees. They stared out vacantly. The dark circles under their eyes almost sat on their hollow cheeks. Their uniforms were covered in dirt and blood.

Roberts left to meet with their commanding officer. Joel and others from the 101st stood unsure what to do.

From behind him, Joel heard a familiar voice, "Now if that don't beat all. I asked the good Lord to send me a sign, and he sent me Joel Davenport."

Joel spun around. "Milton? Is that you?" Joel could hardly believe his eyes.

Milton stood there. The broad smile across his face reached up to his bloodshot eyes. He flung his dark arms around Joel's neck, squeezing him. Joel squeezed back.

"I can't believe it's really you," Milton said, slapping Joel on the back.

Although Milton smiled, the stains on his uniform worried Joel, and seeing Milton's face made the memories of home rush back.

"This is crazy, man!" Joel agreed. "Guys, this is my neighbor, Milton Lewis, from back home."

The 101st greeted Milton and he shook hands with the ones closest to him. "Follow me. Let me fill you in," Milton said, taking them to a space where they could sit.

Milton took a seat on the ground next to a mortar-scarred tree. Joel, Chad, Pen, Harvey, Warwick, and Barnes gathered around him. Milton shook his head. "There's no other way to put it, but this endeavor's been nothing more than a blood bath. After we found the hidden NVA bunkers, we realized there were many more up the hill. That's when we were ordered to take it." Milton's throat moved as he swallowed. "First it started with the snipers. They started taking out our NCOs and gunners first. You need to tell yours," he motioned to Sergeant Jameson, "to take off anything showing his rank, or they'll go for him first." Milton pointed toward an area. "A sniper took out one of the men sitting right beside me before we got him. Shot my man right in the head when he took his helmet off to scratch." Milton sighed, and his body seemed to slump forward.

Joel looked behind him to where Milton pointed about a hundred yards from the area. A dead NVA soldier laid at the base of a tree in a tangle of limbs and branches. Loose ropes hung from the top of the tree. It looked as if maybe he'd tied himself to the tree to snipe at the men below but fell to the bottom once Milton's men got him.

Milton continued. "At first, we tried to take the hill. We'd get so close to the crest, and then the NVA would pop out of places we'd never seen and start shooting. In a minute, we were surrounded. They were like those groundhogs back in Arkansas. One minute there was just dirt behind you, and then next minute you were being shot at." He ran a hand down his face. "I lost a lot of men, and some we still can't find." He hung his head. "I'm sure they're gone too."

Joel reached out and laid a hand on his shoulder. Milton smiled. "You have no idea how good it is to see your face."

"What happened after that?" Joel asked. "This place looks like the moon with all the craters."

"Oh yeah, well that's when things really started to buzz. They sent in air strikes. They dropped bombs and napalm all over this place. It was the craziest thing I ever saw. You could feel the heat from the blasts from down here. They did that for four days straight. The destruction was brutal. But that still didn't end it. At night, you can see all the NVA's small cookfires on the top of the hill. I think they light them up to taunt us, and it's not a few either. There's plenty of NVA still up there." He shrugged. "I guess that's why they called ya'll."

"Any ideas what the plan is for tomorrow?" Harvey asked.

"Nah, but I'm sure they'll drop a few more bombs before we get started," Milton said.

They all sat there for a moment. The silence between them hung thick with fear and uncertainty. What could the 101st add to the effort except more blood? Joel wondered.

They didn't advance that day. Instead, Joel watched from his sitting position in the dirt as the higher-ups conversed together in small groups.

"So many big wigs here," Chad commented.

Milton huffed. "Yeah, now they show up."

"Maybe they want a piece of the action," Pen said.

"Or the glory," Joel commented, making the others laugh.

"No glory in this," Milton said. He slapped Joel on the back. "You have no idea how good it is to see you, man. Sandra wrote me and told me Hazel was pregnant. Congratulations."

Joel's insides burned for home. "I actually got a letter not long ago. She had the baby. A boy—Aaron Thomas Davenport. He was early, but she said everyone is doing well." He swallowed down the regret he felt for not being there with Hazel and the baby.

Milton pulled Joel into a tight hug. "That's great, man! A strong name too. Welcome to fatherhood."

Joel chuckled and he blinked back the tears that threatened to spill out.

"Did you know that Joel's sister-in-law is over here in Vietnam?" Pen asked.

Pure shock appeared on Milton's face. "What? Ruthie's here?"

Joel nodded. "Yeah, she volunteered as a nurse."

"Didn't she join the Army Nursing Corps?" Chad asked.

Joel raised one eyebrow. "Wow, you really do live vicariously through my mail."

Chad laughed, "Yeah, it's not like my family ever writes me. So, I gotta pretend I'm part of yours."

Joel leaned over and laid a hand on Chad's shoulder and squeezed. "You ain't got to pretend." Chad gave Joel a half smile.

"Why doesn't your family write to you? If you don't mind me asking." Milton said.

Chad looked up into the darkening sky. Tiny pinpricks of stars were beginning to appear.

"My mom's blind, and my father... well, he only finished the fifth grade. He can't read or write. I helped them with that stuff because my sisters and brothers all moved off. No one wanted to work the farm, so it was up to me." His throat bobbed and he rubbed a hand through his red hair. "I just hope they are managing without me there."

"I'm sure they are," Pen said.

Chad nodded but didn't say anything more.

At night, Joel slept beside Milton, Chad, and Pen. The cracking and breaking of mortared trees made Joel uneasy. He stared at the black hill, unable to sleep. Milton had been right, hundreds of tiny cookfires burned near the top of the hill. Each one flickered in the wind. He wished he could extinguish them between his forefinger and thumb and be done with this, but nothing in war was that easy.

The next morning, Joel felt relief when they were told they wouldn't start their advance that day either. Instead, he and the others cheered and watched as F-4 Phantom jets dropped a barrage of bombs and napalm all over the hill. He felt the heat from the napalm on his face as the ground shook and giant fireballs filled the sky. They slept under the stars again. The anticipation for the next day made everyone antsy. Pen tossed and turned beside him.

"You alright?" Joel asked.

"No," Pen said. His answer was short, but poignant. Joel felt the same. How could anyone rest knowing they may be dead tomorrow?

Chad rolled over on his side. "I can't sleep either."

"Why don't you sing," Joel suggested.

"Do you have any last requests?" Chad's joke rang hollow, and he sighed. "Sorry, anything you wanna hear?"

"Do you know, 'Abide with Me, 'Tis Eventide'?" Milton asked. "It's my favorite hymn."

"Sure do," Chad said. "All good Baptist boys do."

Chad's melancholy voice filled the air around them as he started the first verse and moved into the chorus. Joel closed his eyes, letting the words sink deep into his soul, and he hoped God was with him. He hoped God was with them all.

Chapter 34

JOEL

As the sky tinged pink, the men stood in silence, loaded with ammo and M16s. Joel's blood vibrated inside his veins. His heart raced inside his chest before he'd even taken one step toward the hill. Milton, Pen, Chad, Warwick, Harvey, and Barnes stood beside him.

"It's time," Milton said.

Joel hardly heard him. His blood thrummed through his temples.

"Use the craters as trenches to fire from," Milton advised. "It's safer than being out in the open."

Joel tried to speak, but he couldn't formulate any words.

"You okay, hickory dickery?" Harvey asked, bumping him with his elbow.

Joel blinked and gave a quick nod. Harvey's old nick name sent an odd calmness over him. "I'm good, jerk."

Harvey grinned and moved to the front of the line. Then the ascension to take the hill began.

They made it about a hundred yards before the firing started.

"Rock and roll!" Harvey yelled as he rapidly fired toward a group of NVA they'd stumbled on. The NVA soldiers began to run away up the hill. Harvey chased after them.

"Don't follow them!" Barnes screamed, chasing after Harvey. "They want you to follow them."

Warwick took off after them.

"Follow me!" Milton said.

Joel, Pen, and Chad moved low behind Milton, using the thin trees as barriers.

"See that crater up there?" Milton pointed. "The VC's using it to fire on the men below. Let's take it."

"How?" Pen's voice shook as he asked.

"Divide and conquer," Milton said. "Two will be decoys and the others will sneak behind and take it."

"I don't want to be a decoy!" Pen exclaimed.

"I'll do it!" Chad said.

"I'll go with you." The words were out of Joel's mouth before he could stop them.

Milton nodded. "Okay, you two start shooting toward the lip of the crater. Pen, you follow me. We're gonna make a large loop around to the back."

Joel and Chad watched as Milton and Pen started to walk, crouched low and away from the crater.

"You ready?" Chad asked.

"Ready as I'll ever be. Let's go there?" Joel pointed to a fallen tree about forty feet away from the crater.

Before Joel could say go or count them down, Chad started to run up the hill toward the downed tree. Joel made his legs move. *Pop-pop-pop*. He followed behind Chad. The dirt beside him exploded as bullets hit near his feet. A *whiz* passed by his ears. He stumbled and fell. A burning sensation spread through his thigh. His boots scrapped dirt as he scrambled up. Chad made it to the tree seconds before him. Joel threw his back against it beside Chad.

"Well, that was exhilarating," Chad said. His breath sawed out of him.

"I think they got me," Joel said. His chest heaved up and down. He looked down at his thigh. The leg of his fatigues was ripped on the side, like someone had taken a knife and cut them open. Blood dripped down his pant leg.

Chad leaned over and opened the rip. "Grazed."

The relief Joel felt was brief. Bullets hit the tree above their heads and sent splinters of wood raining down on them.

They both rose up and returned fire before hunkering down behind the log again. After three more times of returning fire, an unease settled on Joel.

"They should have been there by now," he said to Chad.

"Yeah, something ain't right. What you want to do?"

Joel covered his face to block the falling pieces of wood. "Let's give em' a lemon." He took a grenade shaped like a lemon from a cylinder tube and handed it to Chad.

"You fire, I'll throw," Chad directed.

He didn't even bother to countdown. Joel hefted himself above the safety of the tree and screamed at the top of his lungs as he pulled the trigger to release a spray of bullets.

Chad leaped to his feet. "Arg!" He yelled, heaving the grenade into the crater.

Joel and Chad dropped to the ground with their hands covering their ears. The explosion rocked the ground. They didn't wait. They took off running toward the crater and threw themselves in it. Smoke billowed into the air. The stench of charred flesh burned Joel's nose. He and Chad sat with their back against the dirt wall of the crater among the body parts of the two dead NVA soldiers, coughing from smoke.

"We've got to find Pen and your friend Milton," Chad said, before breaking into a coughing fit.

Joel moved his hand in the air to clear out some smoke. "I'm gonna look around."

"Watch out, those snipers will try to take you out when your head pops out from the hole."

Joel swallowed. Even though his leg burned, he gripped the edge of the dirt crater, feeling the grit under his fingers, and lifted himself to look out.

He sucked in a breath. Fifty yards above them to the right, Milton and Pen were pinned behind thin trees. At least five NVA fired a barrage of bullets at them. Pen sat on the ground. He covered his head with his hands and rocked in place. Milton looked to be praying.

"They're in trouble," Joel yelled. He lowered himself back down, putting his back against the crater. He dropped his empty magazine to the ground. Before he could reload, a VC soldier ran toward the crater screaming. Chad shot him down right as Joel clicked a new magazine in place. "Let's go!" Joel said.

Chad didn't hesitate. He lifted himself out of the hole beside Joel. They ran toward Milton and Pen. Joel felt insane. His heartbeat pulsed through his ears and no real thoughts went through his mind. Chad hurled a lemon toward the NVA while he and Joel unleased an unearthly amount of metal toward the men.

The explosion sent bodies flying through the air. Milton twisted his body around the tree and returned fire to help Joe and Chad. Joel had almost made it to Milton when he heard him scream, "Watch out!"

Milton tackled Joel, knocking the wind out of him as an explosion erupted beside them. Joel's ears rang. Pieces of dirt and earth fell on top of them. *Pop-pop-pop.* Shots rang out around them. Milton's body crushed him into the ground. Milton's body tensed and he let out a loud groan.

"Milton?" Joel yelled.

Chad threw another lemon and raced beside them, firing back. "Get up. Get up. Get up," he screamed. He grabbed the back of Milton's fatigues and hefted him off Joel. "Pen, we need you! Help us!"

Joel hurried to his feet. He wrapped his arms around Milton's chest and dragged him back toward the crater they'd just left. They fell in the hole. Joel's backbone hit the ground hard, and he groaned. Milton's body crushed him. He gritted his teeth and pushed Milton off of him before helping the man set up beside the crater wall. Inside the crater, all time seemed to stop. Joel heard nothing. He focused on Milton. "Where does it hurt?" he asked.

"My back," Milton grimaced. "My front. Everywhere." He tried to give Joel a half smile, but the corner of his mouth drooped.

Joel felt all the air leave him. He couldn't let Milton die. Mikey and Mannie would not be fatherless. He dropped to his knees beside Milton and tried to assess the damage. He lifted Milton's shirt. Blood oozed out of a big hole in his stomach. He turned him over and Milton gasped. "Sorry man, let me look." The shot came from the back. The hole in the back looked manageable. The exit wound in the front looked dire. Joel couldn't breathe. He couldn't lose Milton. "Medic! We need a medic here!" he screamed over and over until he couldn't breathe.

In the distance, he heard shots all around them. Were they being surrounded by the NVA and VC? Were they advancing on the hill? He had no idea, and it didn't matter. All that mattered was keeping Milton alive. His training began to kick in. He ripped the bottom of his shirt and began to plug the wound. He pushed to apply firm pressure, ignoring Milton's screams.

"You're going to be okay, man. I've got you." Joel said.

Milton grabbed Joel's arm. "Tell Sandra and my boys I love them."

Joel felt the back of his throat burn. "You'll tell them yourself."

Joel had no idea how much time had passed when he heard a rustle at the top of the crater. He grabbed his M16 and pointed it up. Chad's red hair appeared, and when he saw Joel, his mouth broke out into a huge smile.

"He's here!" he yelled over his shoulder. "Barnes, we need a medic here!"

In a few moments, Danny Barnes leaped down into the crater to assess Milton's wounds. He gave him a hit of morphine before pulling away the bloody material Joel had used to apply pressure. Milton's tense face softened.

"We took the hill," Chad told him as they watched Barnes work. His face went serious. "But we lost Warwick and our new NCO. It's terrible, I can't even think of that guy's name right now. How's your leg?"

"It's fine. Where's Pen?" Joel asked.

Chad huffed. "He's at the top. They've dropped off food supplies and he's eating. He almost got me killed." Chad shook his head. "He was terrified, but who wouldn't be. I can't really blame him."

Milton groaned. He opened his eyes and looked up at Danny Barnes. "So, what's the verdict, doc?" he asked.

Barnes smiled. "Oh, you're gonna live, and you've definitely earned a ticket home. Let's get him down the hill. The medevac choppers are on the way. He needs to get into surgery."

Chad and a man from the 3rd Battalion grabbed Milton's arms and began to pull him out of the crater while others pushed his legs from below. Milton grimaced. While they worked, Joel grabbed Danny Barnes's arm and pulled him to the side. "Were you being straight-up? Or what?"

Barnes laid a hand on Joel's arm. "He's going home, Davenport. The faster we get him down the hill and on a chopper to surgery, the more chance he has that it won't be in a box."

Joel nodded, understanding. Barnes looked down at Joel's leg. "You're bleeding too."

"It's just a graze."

Barnes tried to look at it, but Joel stopped him. "After we get Milton on a chopper and heading to surgery."

"Fine, but it will need to be cleaned and stitched up right after, you hear me? We can't have any infection setting in."

Joel leaped out of the crater, his leg burning. "You got it!"

Joel and Chad held Milton's arms, and two other men took his legs. Together they carefully maneuvered him down the hill. At the base, Joel saw a sign that had been tacked onto a limbless tree. It read *Hamburger Hill*. Joel couldn't think of a more fitting name to describe this hellish place. But they'd taken it, the hill was theirs.

Chapter 35

RUTHIE

Ruthie never got a chance to talk with Patty, because a constant coming and going of evac helicopters began bringing in wounded from A Shau Valley. She usually never cared where the wounded men came from—her main goal was to save as many lives as she could, but today, she couldn't help listening to Dr. Gerry talking with one of the pilots named Jake. She'd helped Dr. Gerry clean and bandage a graze wound on the side of Jake's arm.

"The 71st is too far to be bringing them here," Dr. Gerry argued with Jake as he wrapped the bandage around his arm. "The faster they get medical attention, the better their chances of survival. You've gotta start taking them to a closer hospital."

Jake shrugged with his good shoulder. "I'm just following orders, doc. It's bad out there. We've been transporting them to all the hospitals we can in a hundred-mile radius. Everyone's full. The hill looks like the moon so many craters have been blown into it. The men are being chewed up and spit out."

"So there's going to be more?" Dr. Gerry asked.

"Loads more."

Jake had been right. A relentless, steady stream of wounded men were brought in over the next eleven days. Ruthie and the other nurses were on high alert. They took off only to grab a few bites of food or get a couple hours of sleep before heading back to the hospital. Ruthie's legs ached and her feet throbbed in her boots. On somedays, she and the other nurses worked nearly sixteen-hour shifts just to keep up. Even Tom, her boss, had to pause his managerial duties and assist in triage.

"Craziest push I've ever seen," Tom had said to her.

On the eleventh day, another Huey arrived with more wounded men. Tom had already left to get some sleep after pulling an all-nighter, leaving Ruthie to step in to make the calls. The choppers brought only one dead and one expectant this time. Some of the men were immediately rushed to surgery where Dr. Gerry and Mark were waiting. She and the other triage nurses helped to clean the wounds of the others and get them moved to ICU.

Ruthie examined the wounds of a soldier with short auburn hair and olive skin. He lay on his stomach, his body stripped bare. Two bullet holes in his back—one on his right shoulder and the other wound went in and out in his lower left side. He folded his good arm under his head. His skin and hair were caked with dirt. After she'd gotten the bullet wounds to stop bleeding, Ruthie pulled Dr. Gerry over to examine him before he headed out to surgery. Dr. Gerry gave him a quick assessment and determined the bullets had missed his vital organs.

"I guess I'm pretty lucky, huh?" the soldier said, turning his head to the side so Ruthie could see his brown eyes. His slender face needed a shave, and a red scrape raced across the bridge of his nose.

She smiled. "Yes, you are. Very lucky," she said.

"Did you hear, we took the hill? We got Hamburger Hill."

"Hamburger Hill?" Ruthie asked.

"That's what we called that piece of dirt because for a while, we were being chewed up like hamburger meat."

The thought made Ruthie shiver. Her mind went to Ronnie, Joel, and Milton, and she prayed they were nowhere near Hamburger Hill.

She swallowed down her worry. "Well, I'm glad it's over. What's your name?"

"I'm Andrew, but my family calls me Andy."

"Well, Andy, I'm going to get you cleaned up and your wounds bandaged. You're probably going to have to stay on your stomach for tonight until the doctors can look at you again tomorrow. It might hurt some while I'm cleaning, so let me know, okay?"

Andy talked nonstop while she scrubbed his skin until it turned a rosy pink. He talked mostly about his family in Baltimore. He had a little sister in eighth grade, and she'd already decided she wanted to become a nurse. He talked about riding his bike down the sidewalks and playing baseball with his friends in the streets of their neighborhood. Ruthie listened to his stories as she worked to debride his wounds of any dirt and dead tissue with her forceps. By the time he started talking about his girlfriend and how hard it had been to leave her, Ruthie had already cleaned all the dead tissue away and flushed his wounds with a syringe filled with saline solution.

After she bandaged him, she leaned down by his face, so Andy wouldn't have to stretch his neck to see her. "All right, I'm all finished. I'm going to go find some men to help move you to ICU."

Andy's chin began to quiver. Ruthie's heart fell. Had he been in pain the entire time and hadn't let on? "Are you alright? Is there something you need?"

Andy sniffed. His words were thick. "No, just talking about home really got to me, I guess. Do you think..." his voice cracked. "Do you think they'll send me back home now?"

At that moment, Ruthie felt the weight of the last eleven days on her, crushing her. She shook her head. "I don't really know." She saw the pain in his eyes. "But maybe," she said, not wanting him to lose all hope. How could she tell him she'd seen so many patch and go jobs in the short time she'd been here. More than likely, he'd be forced to go back out in the field. If only one of the bullets had hit something vital, then he'd for sure have been sent home if he survived. She watched the men move Andy to a litter to transport him to ICU. She waved to him.

"Thank you," he called out to her.

She smiled, but in the back of her mind, she wondered just how unlucky Andy truly had been.

❧❧❧❧ ❦❦❦❦

A week later, on Connie's last night at the 71st, Ruthie decided to host a small going away party for her. She decided to have the party at her and Patty's hootch and invite only the female nurses who'd worked with Connie. The day of the party, Ruthie snuck into the O club and took some drinks. After she'd secured the drinks, she walked around and asked other nurses if she could borrow some cassette tapes for music.

She and Patty worked together to drag her bed outside to make more room in the small space. She hoped the rain would hold off. She didn't really want to sleep on a soaked mattress. She ran her arm across her damp forehead. "This thing is so small. I had no idea it would be this much trouble," she said.

Patty laid a hand on her side. Her chest rose and fell quickly. "I feel like I'm getting a workout, and I don't want a workout, babe."

Ruthie laughed. It felt good to spend time with Patty. They'd barely spent any time with each other since they were on different shifts. This had been the first free moments they'd gotten to spend together in such a long time. She considered talking to Patty about Mark but decided against it. The stress of the last few weeks had exhausted her, and she needed this time to unwind. She wanted to enjoy the party and laugh with Patty, not worry about stupid Mark. Ruthie flopped on the bed, feeling it sink deeper in the mud. "I forgot to tell you, sugar. I've got a surprise."

Patty leaned over, putting her hands on her knees. "What's the surprise, doll?"

"I got something from home today."

Patty's eyebrows went up. "And…"

"Ms. Faye, my dad's girlfriend, sent me two packages of Vienna Fingers and three packages of Chocolate Pinwheels."

Patty acted like she might pass out. "Whoa! You've struck gold, hot mama."

Ruthie shook her head. "Hot mama, that's the worst."

Patty giggled, "Yeah, it's bad. Want to break into those Vienna Fingers now? I feel like we deserve a reward after all this work."

Ruthie stretched her arms above her head. "No way, I'm using them as refreshments for Connie's party tonight."

Patty frowned. "All of them?"

"Yeah, I think it'll be nice. And it's almost enough for everyone to have a few."

Patty stood upright. She propped a hand on her hip. "If you want my two cents, I think you should save some and not waste them all on Connie."

A bead of sweat ran down Ruthie's back. She looked at Patty, not really believing what she heard. "Well...I don't feel like it would be wasting them. Is something wrong? Don't you like Connie?"

Patty rolled her eyes and shrugged. "Let's just say, I've heard some things about her, but she's about to be gone anyway. So, what does it matter. I think you should save some and not waste them on her. But suit yourself." She looked at Ruthie's bed. "Since we're done here, I'm going to go grab a quick shower."

Ruthie watched Patty enter the hootch to grab her shampoo and a change of clothes. *That wasn't like Patty at all*, Ruthie thought. Ruthie hoped there wouldn't be any issues at Connie's party.

❧❧❧❧❧ ❧❧❧❧❧

At the party, Ruthie blasted "Help Me, Rhonda," by the Beach Boys from her small cassette player. The nurses danced together all scrunched in the hootch. Others sat on Ruthie's bed outside, drinking beer and talking. Ruthie felt like a real hostess in her khaki shorts, flowered shirt with bell sleeves, and army boots. She walked around holding out the packages of cookies. It made her happy to see the women's eyes light up when they saw them. Some even hugged her. It made Ruthie happy to share a little piece of home with them.

Ruthie made sure to keep a close eye on Connie and Patty, and to her relief, there'd been no issues. But it didn't escape her notice that Patty moved outside when Connie came into the hootch. Ruthie wondered what Patty had heard about Connie and if whatever information she'd heard came from Mark.

"Ruthie!" Connie squealed, jarring Ruthie from her thoughts. Connie danced, her hands waving in the air. Connie smiled, it spread across her face and made her eyes dance. Her mouth opened in a laugh. Connie's whole demeanor had changed in the days leading up to her departure back to the US. This time tomorrow, Connie would be home with her mom. It was hard not to feel envious of her. Ruthie picked up a Vienna Finger from the package and downed it in two bites. The buttery cookie and vanilla flavor exploded on her tongue, and she closed her eyes and licked her lips. *Thank you, Ms. Faye.*

Connie looped her arm around Ruthie's shoulders. The smell of alcohol and sweat on her skin. Ruthie held out the box of cookies and Connie took one. "Thank you for the party. It's wonderful. You have no idea how grateful I am."

Ruthie leaned into Connie. "Just don't forget me while you're home. Send a letter every now and then and let me know how you're doing."

Connie took a bite of her cookie. "Of course!" But Ruthie never heard from Connie again.

Chapter 36

Hazel, June 1969

Hazel shot up in bed. Her heart fluttered and her mind whirled. Her bedsheets tangled around her feet. She looked at the clock on the nightstand. The small hand pointed to the six. She had two hours until she had to be at work. She fell back against her pillow. She didn't have to go to work. Mr. Crutchfield had given her until mid-July to rest, recuperate, and spend time with Aaron. She closed her eyes and tried to go back to sleep. Her eyes popped open. *Aaron! He's usually up by now.* She twisted in her sheets to look inside the basinet near her bed. She nearly screamed when she saw only a thin, rumpled sheet and no baby.

She scrambled out of the bed, looking around the basinet, around the floor. Her breath quickened and she hit the bedroom door running into the living room. She heard a sound in the kitchen and raced to it. Her body shuttered to a stop when she saw her dad sitting at the kitchen table, a bottle in his hand, feeding Aaron.

Her father raised his head. "Hey sleepy head, I let myself in to check on you both and heard this little guy getting restless. I thought I'd let you get some sleep. Sandra said he's been keeping you up all night."

Hazel's chest deflated and she sank into the kitchen chair near her dad. She watched him cradle her son. She understood his desire to hold him. She loved feeling Aaron in her arms, rocking him, breathing in his baby scent.

"Was he getting restless? And you got him without waking me up?"

Her father beamed. "Sure did. I'm really getting good at this baby thing again. I thought I'd plumb forgotten how to do it. Now, I don't mean to brag, but it looks like I'm a natural."

Hazel chuckled. "I must have been exhausted to not hear anything." She reached over and rubbed Aaron's little head. His skin felt soft, and the baby fuzz on the top of his head felt velvety under her fingertips. She stared at Aaron's tiny pink lips suckling the bottle. His cheeks moving with each gulp. "What are your plans today, Grandpappy?"

He shook his head, but she saw the corner of his mouth turn up. "I told you I'm Papa." Her father sniffed. "Hmm, I think maybe somebody needs a new diaper."

Hazel smiled. "I heard you were a natural. Want to give it a go? I've got some clean cloth diapers right over there," she said, pointing to the sofa where she'd left the clean clothes after she folded them last night.

Her father shook his head. "Oh no, that's a kind offer, but I better mosey on. I've got to bring some rocking chairs to a couple in Arkadelphia today."

She took Aaron from his arms and sniffed, *definitely needs a new diaper.* "I know they will love them. I sure love the one you made me."

Hazel looked up, hearing knocking coming from the front door. "Hello?" Sandra's voice called.

Sandra came into the kitchen in a beautiful navy-blue dress with huge white buttons down the front. She had on makeup and her dark hair was styled with the ends curling near her cheekbones. She looked beautiful. She had Mannie and Mikey with her. They clung to the hem of her dress.

"Hi," Hazel said, confused. "Did I forget about something? Why are you dressed so nicely this early in the morning?"

Hazel's father walked past her. "Good morning," he said with a hearty voice, bending down to give the boys a hug.

Hazel furrowed her eyebrows, "Is something going on that I don't know about?"

Sandra's face broke into a huge smile and her eyes became watery. She touched the corner of her eyes with her fingertips. "Oh my, I can't start crying again. I'll mess up my makeup." Sandra motioned for Mikey and Mannie to go play with the toys Hazel kept for them. They went straight for the Rock 'Em Sock 'Em Robots and started banging the buttons, making the robots arms jerk out to punch each other.

Hazel's father took Aaron from her arms. "I guess this grandpappy does need to practice his diaper skills." He grabbed a clean diaper from the top of the pile and headed for Hazel's bedroom."

Sandra went to the living room and sat on the sofa. She motioned for Hazel to join her. "I wanted to tell you last night when the telegram came, but you'd already gone to bed. Your dad said you were exhausted." Sandra fanned herself with her other hand. "Oh, my gracious. I just can't hold it in." Tears began to stream down her face. "I got a letter from Milton. And he's been shot."

Hazel sucked in a breath. Her knees grew weak, and she was glad to be sitting. "Shot? Is he alive?"

Sandra grabbed her. "Oh dear, I guess I shouldn't have led with that because all the blood just ran from your face, Hazel."

Sandra's face split into a huge grin. Her white teeth glowed. Hazel shook her head. "I don't understand. You look so happy."

Sandra patted Hazel's hand and chuckled. "Well, I'm not happy he was injured. But he said in his letter he's doing good. He lost a kidney, but his recouperation has gone quick. They are sending him home. He should be home in a month. Two at the most."

A surge passed through Hazel's chest. "Home? That's crazy! He just got to Vietnam."

Sandra laughed. "I know! Can you believe it? Milton's coming home."

Hazel's arms felt weightless as she wrapped them around Sandra's neck. "Oh, my goodness, I'm so happy for you and the boys!" Hazel squealed.

They held each other until Hazel's father cleared his throat. "Girl, I hate to interrupt, but I better get going." He gently passed Aaron to Hazel.

"Dad, will you be back by dinner?"

"Sure will," he said, bending down to give Mannie and Mikey a good-bye hug.

"Great! Then tonight, let's celebrate."

Sandra nodded. "Yes, let's make a special dinner."

"Spaghetti," Mikey yelled.

Everyone laughed.

"Spaghetti it is," Hazel said.

Sandra stood, "I better get going too. I'm going to be late as it is."

Hazel tilted her head, "Where are you going?"

Sandra smiled, "I called a special meeting at the church to personally give whoever can make it the good news."

The tightness in Hazel's chest loosened. Milton was coming home! Now they just needed Joel and Ruthie to come home, and everything would be right in her world.

Chapter 37

RUTHIE

R uthie sat on her bed unable to sleep. She held her flashlight up so the light was focused on the notebook paper covered in slightly smudged blue ink. She half wished she'd never gone to the mail room this morning to drop off the last cassette she'd recorded for her father.

"You gotta letter again, McKay. Will your popularity never end?" Boyd, the mail clerk, had jested.

Ruthie did a little dance. Boyd's smile made his cheeks tinge pink and pop out like little apples.

"Well, I'm glad I could start your day off right," he said.

A bolt of lightning flashed across the sky and a boom of thunder made the little mail room rock.

Boyd sighed. "Another day in paradise. Man, this rainy season is for the birds. So many packages get ruined, and the letters are damp."

She waved her letter in the air. "This one is going in a safe spot," she said, sliding it in the waistband of her fatigues.

Boyd wiggled his eyebrows, making Ruthie laugh. She bolted from the mail room door, holding her arms above her head. Rain pelted her head and body. Her boots sloshed through the mud and muck. She laid a hand against her side, feeling the edges of the letter poke her skin. She pressed it hard to keep it in place. At the hospital, she shook the rain off her and sighed. She'd spend another workday in a wet uniform. She carefully removed the letter from her pants, folded it, and put it in a small plastic bag before sticking it in her pocket. She'd wait until afterwork to read it. She wanted time to savor it.

⚜

After work, she slid out of her damp clothes and into a T-shirt so worn, some places were almost translucent. She slipped on a pair of men's shorts she'd bought at the PX and slid into bed. The metal frames creaked underneath her. She'd saved Hazel's letter all day for just this moment. The thought of reading it had energized her, making the day pass quickly. Now she read Hazel's words, feeling like she'd been donkey kicked in the chest. She couldn't catch her breath. She squeezed her eyes shut tight, feeling them burn under her eyelids. Tears escaped from the corners of her eyes. She shook her head. She shouldn't be so upset. Everything had turned out fine, but she didn't feel fine. She bolted to her feet and paced back and forth in the small space between her and Patty's bed. She wished Patty wasn't working nights. She desperately needed someone to talk to, to tell her she wasn't overreacting. Someone who would understand how she felt. She forced herself to read the letter one more time—like a car wreck she couldn't keep her eyes off of. Her legs shook underneath her.

Dearest Ruthie, I sure do miss you. Dad and Ms. Faye are doing well. Still no word on if they'll ever get married. The weather is already insufferably hot here. I hope you have better weather there. Aaron got to come home at the end

234

of May. I have never been happier, and sleep deprived all at the same time. He's really grown. He's seven pounds now. I wish you were here to see him. You will be head over heels for him when you do. I promise to send pictures soon. I've been playing your cassettes for him, so he'll recognize your voice when you come home. It also helps me to imagine you're here and not a million miles away. I don't get a lot of letters from Joel. But in the last one I got, he said he was doing well. I hope that's true. I'm not sure he would tell me the truth. I pray for you both every night. I've been rambling, filling this page with words, because I hate the real purpose of this letter. But don't worry, everything is good. Milton was shot. He lost a kidney, but he's alive, and that's all that really matters. He's alive and he's coming home. Sandra received a military telegram. He should be home in July. Wouldn't it be outstanding if he made it home by the 4th? I thought you'd like to know. I love you! We all miss you terribly! Please send more cassettes when you can. Be safe Ruthie. I'm counting down the days until you return. Hazel

Breathe, Ruthie told herself, but she couldn't. Milton was okay and he would be heading home. Still, the space in the hootch felt too small, like the walls were closing in on her. Her chest rose and fell rapidly, and she felt like she might suffocate. Because of America's hatred of the war, President Nixon had sent twenty-five thousand soldiers' home. Who got to pick? Who got to be the lucky ones? What about Joel and Ronnie? And why didn't Milton get to go home before he could be hurt? She balled up her fists, crinkling Hazel's letter, and pressed her fists hard against the sides of her head. She couldn't stop the flood of panic rising inside of her. Nearly every day, when blood ran through her fingers, embedding in her nails, she never allowed herself to think that somewhere one of the men she cared about and loved could be bleeding on a bed somewhere. Their blood staining another nurse's hands. Even though Milton lived, the whole matter hit too close to home. Were Joel and Ronnie safe? The reality of the danger they could be in made her stomach roil.

Ruthie couldn't handle it anymore. She needed to talk to someone. She needed her friend. Ruthie grabbed a flashlight and barged through the hootch's door. The rain had stopped, but the wind whipped the material of her T-shirt and shorts around her body. The smell of earth and oil hit her in the face. She held her flashlight out and began to trudge through the red muck toward surgery.

"Hey Ruthie," Dr. Gerry said. "You okay?"

She ran a hand through her tangled curls. "I'm just looking for Patty. I really need to talk to her."

His face fell. "I'm sorry. I think she went on break."

Ruthie felt her chest collapse. She left surgery, not wanting to keep Dr. Gerry occupied when he had his hands full. She went back outside. The wind blew her hair back from her face. She trudged through the mud, not caring where she was going, and took a path she'd never been on before through tents and scattered palm trees. She dodged puddles and potholes. She'd always wanted to explore more of the area within the wire, but she never had enough time. Ruthie passed through an area with rows of tents on either side of the red road. A loud laugh floated from one of the tents. Ruthie froze in place, her boots sinking in the mud. She knew that laugh—Patty. She followed the sound until she found the right tent. The door flap stuck to the side of the tent because of the wind. Dim light made a semi-circle on the ground in front of her. Ruthie stayed in the shadows, straining to hear.

"Want another drink?"

Ruthie sighed. Mark. Patty was in there with Mark.

"I'm so jealous. You get this huge tent while we have to share a tiny hootch. It gets so hot in there during the day when I'm trying to sleep. I feel like my skin is cooking."

"You can always come here to sleep," Mark replied. "I'd share my bed with you."

Patty giggled and Ruthie heard the distinct sound of kissing. A wave of anger rolled through Ruthie's body. Mark is married! Married. He took advantage of Connie, and now he's moved on to Patty. Ruthie couldn't let this happen.

She threw herself into the tent. Patty and Mark were sitting on the edge of Mark's bed. His arms wrapped around her. When Patty saw Ruthie, she gasped.

Mark's eyes went wide, and he popped up from the bed to put some distance between himself and Patty.

For a moment, Ruthie worried about how crazy she must look with her worn T-shirt and shorts, hair wind-blown and crazy, and a flashlight and letter in her hand. But she shook her head. Why should she be worried about how she looked? Mark should be worried about how he looked and what he was doing. "I-I needed to talk to you," Ruthie stuttered the only thing that came to her mind.

Patty bit her bottom lip. Her eyes looked down to the floor. Mark spoke first.

"We were on a break and needed to get away from the hospital. You know how it is, McKay. Needing to get away."

Ruthie met his eyes. She wanted to slug him in the face. He knew as well as she did that if Tom caught Patty in here, in Mark's tent, kissing him, she'd be dishonorably discharged from her duties and sent home. Since he's a doctor, all he'd get would be a stern lecture, if that. She glared at him then looked toward Patty. Patty kept her eyes focused on the floor.

"I need you to come with me. I need to talk to you," Ruthie spoke to Patty, ignoring Mark.

Redness began to creep up Patty's neck. She stood and dusted off her fatigues even though there was nothing on them. "We need to get back to work. Our break is almost over." Her words were clipped. She met Ruthie's eyes. Her lips pulled together in a tight line.

"But..." Ruthie started but stopped.

Patty's glare burned a hole in Ruthie's chest. Her voice dripped acid. "But nothing, Ruthie. We were on break. And we need to get back. I will talk to you later. I do not have time for you now."

Ruthie felt like she'd been gut punched. The air escaped from her lungs. Patty pushed past Ruthie and left out the tent's door. Mark laid a hand on Ruthie's shoulder.

"It's not what you think, McKay."

Her throat burned with the words she wanted to scream at him, but instead she shrugged off his hand and left, stomping through the mud all the way back to her hootch.

❧❧❧❧❧ ❧❧❧❧❧

After the Mark tent incident, Ruthie didn't see Patty for the rest of the week. Every morning, Ruthie woke up and waited for Patty to come back to their hootch after she got off work. Ruthie had nearly been late several times because she waited as long as she could, even skipping breakfast. But Patty never came to the hootch, and Ruthie positively knew Patty was avoiding her. Ruthie's sadness and need for a friend morphed into anger—red-hot anger. She tried not to let it, but she couldn't help it. She blamed Mark, but she equally blamed Patty. Ruthie sat on her bed and huffed, pulling on her boots. A knock at the door made her jump.

"Come in," she shouted.

Darryl poked his head through the door. "Can you step out?"

Ruthie's mouth went dry. "Darryl, what are you doing here? Am I in trouble?"

Tom's assistant shook his head. "Not that I know of."

Ruthie hurried and rushed outside. Darryl whistled; his hands pushed deep in his pockets. He rocked back in forth to the tune.

"What's up?" she asked. She'd just taken a shower, but her underarms already felt damp.

Darryl looked up to the sky. "Gonna rain again," he said more a statement than a question.

Ruthie looked up too. A dark, endless gray spread above them with low hanging navy clouds. She wondered how long it had been since she'd seen the sun.

"I think that's all it ever does now," she said. She took a hair tie off her wrist and pushed her fingers through her wet hair to work it into a low bun, securing it with the tie. "What does Tom want?"

Darryl shrugged. "Dunno. But he said he wanted to talk to you before work. You better make your way to his office. But you better deal with those first." He pointed down to the ground.

She followed his finger, but all she noticed was red mud. "What?"

"Your laces. Wouldn't want you to trip. See ya later, McKay." He gave her a smile and then walked toward surgery.

Ruthie's boot laces had pooled around her feet in the mud. She bent down, the mud squishing under her knee. Her hands trembled, making it difficult for her to tie them. What could Tom want to speak to her about? The only thing she could think of was Patty. What if he wanted to ask her something about Patty and Mark? Had he already found out Patty had been in Mark's tent? If not, she couldn't rat Patty out. It would ruin her. But could Ruthie lie to her boss?

Tom's small office sat near the hospital to the right. Wet sandbags dripped left over rain near the front entrance. The huge droplets made plop sounds as they hit the ground, matching the rapid beats of Ruthie's heart. The office's thin wooden planks were splattered with red mud. Ruthie walked up to the door and forced herself to breathe. *Geeze Louise!* She needed to get ahold of herself, but she couldn't shake the feeling she'd been called to the principal's office. She lifted her fist and gave the door a few short raps.

"Enter," she heard Tom call through the thin door.

Ruthie's body went numb, and she couldn't move. She closed her eyes tight, swallowed hard, and forced herself to open the door.

Tom sat behind a small desk. Two gun-metal gray filing cabinets filled the wall behind him. His chair creaked as he swizzled to face her. The light above his head made a halo appear across his bald head.

"Ruthie! Come in, come in, have a seat." He waved a hand toward the wooden chairs positioned in the front of his desk.

She plopped down in a chair. It squeaked and the sound set her teeth on edge. Her head felt fuzzy, her heart pumping too hard. She gripped the armrests of the chair to keep herself steady. What was she going to say if he asked her about Patty?

He picked up the manilla folder lying in front of him and laid it back down before looking at her. "So, you've been here for about four months now."

She nodded, trying to swallow the excess saliva forming in the back of her throat. *About eight months to go*, she thought.

"How are you doing?"

Ruthie blinked. "Good, I'm doing good."

"Good," he parroted her words. "Triage can be a very difficult area, and you've handled yourself well. I know recently you've been asked to help in ICU some, and it appears you've done a good job there as well."

Ruthie felt her chest loosen somewhat. "Thank you, sir."

"But you've been on the day shift only, I see," his eyes glanced down at the folder on his desk. He made eye contact with her. "I'd like you to move to the night shift in ICU for a while."

"The night shift?" Thoughts of working in darkness during mortar attacks with only flashlights as her guide made her skin prickle, and a shudder passed throughout her entire body.

Tom nodded. "Yes, I think you are perfectly capable of handling it. And we're short-staffed in ICU."

Ruthie couldn't agree less with Tom, she didn't feel capable. Every day, she worked on autopilot.

"But before you start the night shift in ICU, I have another proposal for you. I spoke with Gerry. He didn't know if you'd be interested, but he thought you could handle filling in for Patty in surgery for a few weeks while she goes on R&R."

Ruthie scratched her head. "R&R? But we've not been here six months yet."

Tom frowned. "Yes. That's when I advise nurses to take their R&R, but she gets two weeks, and she gets to choose when she exercises them."

Ruthie could tell by Tom's terse words that he didn't like Patty going on R&R so soon.

He shook his head. "Look, if you don't want to, it's fine. Gerry said you are an excellent nurse, and you'd do wonderful in surgery. But if you're not interested, Darryl said he doesn't mind going back to surgery. He's been working in ICU since we were shorthanded, and it will also free him up to assist more in other wards that are down personnel."

Ruthie's mind swirled. Why was Patty leaving for R&R so soon? Flames ignited in Ruthie's belly. Patty was going above and beyond to avoid her. All Ruthie had tried to do was save her from Mark, and now Patty was deserting her. Ruthie pushed the thoughts away and quickly considered the offer to work in surgery for two weeks. Just thinking about working in the same building with Mark made her stomach flip-flop. "That's very kind of Dr. Gerry and maybe one day I'd like to try surgery, but not right now."

Tom nodded. "I understand. I'd like you to start tonight then on the night shift."

Ruthie tried to swallow, but it stuck in her throat.

Tom continued. "Go get yourself some breakfast then head back to your hootch and try to get some sleep. Night shift starts at six."

Ruthie thanked Tom and left his office. The gray sky had darkened, and a soft drizzle began to batter her shoulders. She'd been told to expect at least three more months of rain. A big drop of rain plopped on the top of Ruthie's head and ran down the side of her face, tickling her cheek. She roughly brushed it away. She couldn't believe Patty! They'd always said they would go somewhere groovy together like Hong Kong for R&R. But now Patty was splitting without her. What a flake she'd turned out to be.

Ruthie rushed to the mess hall and grabbed a biscuit, the only thing she thought she could stomach right now. The junk with Patty and changing to nightshift had her stomach all tied up in knots. She downed her biscuit and hurried back to the hootch to try and get some sleep even though she knew it would be impossible.

A puddle the size of a lake sat in front of the hootch's door. Ruthie kicked the door open with her boot and jumped through the threshold, trying to avoid the mud pit. Her boots hit the slick floor and slipped. She fell back, catching herself on the doorframe. Ruthie winced when her arm scrapped against the wood.

Patty whipped around, clutching her chest. "What are you doing? You scared the blessed daylights out of me."

Ruthie held her arm up to examine the damage. "I was trying to avoid the mud." She turned her arm. She saw no open wound, but a bright pink scrape ran from under her forearm to her bicep. While she examined her arm, she snuck hurried glances toward Patty's bed. A suitcase lay half open full of clothes. It reminded her so long ago of her mother's suitcase and Hazel begging their mother not to go. A pain clutched Ruthie's heart.

Without asking if Ruthie was alright, Patty turned back to her bed and picked up a shirt. She smoothed it against her body and began folding it. "I thought you'd be at work," Patty said, not turning her head to look at Ruthie.

"Tom asked me to move to nights in the ICU. I'm supposed to try and get some sleep before I start."

Patty nodded and placed the shirt in her suitcase. She picked up a plaid green skirt and started to fold it.

"So, I heard you are going on R&R," Ruthie said, throwing it out there. She sat on her bed and began carefully removing her muddy boots.

"Yep."

Ruthie sighed. She couldn't handle it anymore. "Patty, what is going on with you? I feel like you've been avoiding me ever since I caught you in Mark's tent."

Patty spun around, her face scarlet red. "You humiliated me that night in front of Mark. I think you thought you were trying to save me or something, I don't know. I can handle myself. I'm not a child, but you acted like I was one, just like my parents do."

Ruthie sucked in a breath. "I was trying to help you."

"Help me? How?" Patty said, grabbing her bathing suit from the small dresser at the end of her bed. She threw it hard into the suitcase.

Ruthie couldn't contain it any longer, she shouted, "Mark's married, Patty! He's married. He led Connie on and now he's moved on to you. And what if Tom or Darryl caught you in his tent? You could get sent home!"

Patty's nostrils flared. She pointed at Ruthie. "Did Connie tell you that he led her on? Did she say that before she left? Well, that's nothing more than a big fat lie." Patty straightened. "Connie was jealous. She had the hots for Mark, and he didn't like her. She followed him around like a lost puppy dog. When he turned her down, she began spreading vicious lies."

Patty looked down at Ruthie sitting on the bed. "Mark told me you had the hots for him too, but he'd turned you down as well."

Ruthie's jaw dropped open. Her blood boiled so hot in burned in the back of her throat. "That's not true! I never cared about Mark."

"Of course you'd say that." Patty's voice snapped like a rubber band. "He's an excellent surgeon. You're just jealous because I have someone who loves me, and you don't. You never had a boyfriend and now you want mine. And so what if he's married? He won't be for long. He told me when he gets back to the States, he's getting a divorce. He's already sent his wife a letter telling her he wants one. He told her he's in love with me."

Ruthie's hand went to her mouth, covering it.

"What? Nothing to say now?" Patty sneered. "That's right. He loves me."

Ruthie's chest tightened. "You knew he was married?" Ruthie shook her head side to side. "He doesn't love you, Patty. He's using you."

Patty waved her off. "That's what Mark said you'd say. That's why I'm going to Hawaii." She let out a sickening laugh. "All this time, I thought he was wrong. I thought you might actually be happy for me. But he was right. You're just jealous like Connie." Patty slammed the lid of her suitcase closed. She grabbed the handle and headed for the door. Before leaving, she lowered her voice. "When I get back, I'm going to ask to be moved to another hootch. Good-bye Ruthie." Patty slammed the door so hard it rattled.

A pain seared through Ruthie's insides. She stared at the closed door. If she thought it would do any good, she'd rush out and confront Mark, but what good would that do? Patty believed him over her. After all this time, she believed him and not her. The thought ripped at Ruthie's heart. A cold chill settled over her, and she curled into a ball on her bed, burying herself under the thin sheet. She began to wail—for Milton, for Joel, for Ronnie, and for herself. She cried and cried until her head pounded. She prayed for sleep and the sweet relief of feeling nothing, but no relief came.

Chapter 38

RUTHIE

Ruthie uncurled herself from the bed. Her head pounded between her temples, but she had to get ready for work. In the short while that she slept, she'd dreamed of her father. He'd hugged her tight and told her to keep going and not give up. She found comfort in his words, and even though it was only a dream, for a brief moment she'd been home. She gathered her things and went to shower. Outside the world had gone dark. A damp and musty smell mixed with sharp scents of oil and gasoline made her crinkle her nose. The familiar rumblings of motor engines and the woosh of helicopter blades made her marvel at how this place never stopped. It continued to hum twenty-four hours a day. Everyone here kept plugging along, kept moving, and maybe she could do the same.

In the shower, the cold water drizzled on her skin. She still couldn't wrap her mind around how terribly things had ended with Patty. Ruthie kept repeating their argument over and over in her head. She heard light rain begin to patter the shower hootch's roof. She quickly dried off and dressed. She ran back to her hootch to put away her shampoo and grab her helmet and flax jacket. It was time to start her first night in ICU.

Inside ICU, only a few lights were lit. She'd been here countless times, and in the dimness, everything looked different. Darryl walked up to her. "Don't worry. You're going to be fine," he said.

"I wasn't worried," Ruthie said.

He laughed. "Oh really, that's why that little line between your eyebrows looks more like a mountain crevice."

Ruthie's hand went to her face, and she touched the place between her eyebrows. "I don't have a crevice." She frowned. She looked around, noticing there were a few extra patients than the last time she'd been here. Some slept and others played cards using a dim lamp. Darryl began to give her the rundown.

"I volunteered to stay with you tonight since it's your first night."

"I thought you were going to surgery?"

Darryl scratched his head. "Yeah, tomorrow. But I wanted to make sure you were set up first. Of course, you know this place is like triage in that it goes from rush to boring in a hot second. Sometimes if there's a huge push in triage, some of the nurses here go to help there."

Ruthie nodded. She knew all that.

Darryl continued, "Alright, to get started, if I was you, I'd keep some Penrose tubing for the IVs and spare Kelley clamps in your pockets. If things go full dark, which they often do, you'll be glad you've got them close."

Darryl took her to where the supplies were kept. She followed his lead and filled her pockets with supplies.

"Now we don't have a lot of patients. There was a push earlier today, but most didn't make it."

Ruthie's body sagged to think that while she slept after her and Patty's argument, men had been dying.

"The two that did make it will need their dressings changed during the night."

Ruthie nodded.

"Other than that, there's not much new. Oh, except this guy right here," Darryl strode over to a bed with the form of a body lying on it. The man laid completely hidden under a pile of blankets. The mound of blankets shivered. She could hear the man underneath moan. A glass IV filled with fluids stood on a stand next to the bed, but there were no tubes."

"He's got malaria and jungle rot on his feet."

Ruthie grimaced.

"He's vomited three times already, so I set up an IV. He'll probably need some fluids. He wouldn't give me his arm. Try again later and see if you can get an IV in him, and if not, we may have to shoot him up with some meds so we can work with him. He wouldn't even let me remove his boots."

"How do you know he's got jungle rot then?" Ruthie asked.

"His friends told me. They carried him here today—probably about ten miles or so. He looked like a sack of potatoes being hauled with two men holding his arms and two on his legs. They said they'd all run out of CP pills weeks ago. They're lucky the rest of them haven't gotten malaria too. I hooked them up with more." Darryl motioned to the pile of blankets. "They said he's been sick for a while but wouldn't tell anymore. He got really bad today, so his commander forced him to come in. They've been in the jungle for months on some search and destroy mission."

Ruthie laid a hand on the pile of blankets. It shook under her fingers. The poor man had to be suffering. Malaria was a terrible disease and could even be life threatening. "He needs some chloroquine," Ruthie said.

"Good luck getting it in him," Darryl commented. "Okay, I think that's about it. One more thing, we are out of disposable syringes, so the glass ones are in the back. I think that's it. Don't worry. I'll be here with you tonight if you need anything. Got any questions?"

Ruthie smiled. "Yeah, I actually have one question."

Darryl raised an eyebrow.

"Is there anything I need to know about when the lights go out? I mean really go out, during the mortar attacks?"

Darryl's mouth flattened. "There's not much to know really. Always keep your flashlight clipped to your belt and extra supplies in your pockets. Help the ones you can get under their beds and cover the others with mattresses then pray and hope for the best."

The memory of the hootch completely destroyed after being hit during an attack on one of her first nights sent a shudder through her. The explosion had twisted the metal beds in that hootch into crazy shapes. She blinked the memory away. There would be nothing they could do to save the patients or themselves from a direct hit.

The door to the ICU opened and Dr. Gerry rushed in, bringing rain and mud with him.

"I'll go grab the broom," Darryl sighed, seeing the mess. He headed to the back of the ward where the cleaning supplies were kept.

Dr. Gerry gave a half grin, the skin near his brown eyes creasing. "Sorry, Darryl," he apologized.

"What are you doing here?" Ruthie asked.

He held out a circular metal tin. "My wife sent me some cookies and I wanted to share some with my favorite nurse."

Darryl cleared his throat from the back.

"You can have some too, Darryl."

Ruthie laughed.

"I also wanted to wish you good luck on your first night. Even though I'm on nights too, I won't be able to come visit much. We're short-staffed since Mark went to Hawaii on R&R, and I was afraid I wouldn't get another chance to bring you some."

Ruthie's head spun. "Mark went on R&R to Hawaii?"

Dr. Gerry nodded. "Here take a few." He popped the top of the tin and held it out so she could see it was filled with pinwheel cookies. The sweet smell made her nauseous.

Ruthie forced herself to smile and took some of the cookies. Mark and Patty went to Hawaii for R&R together. She took a bite of a cookie, and it turned to sawdust in her mouth. The weight of this information pressed on her chest. Patty knew Mark was married and still she chose to go with him to Hawaii. How foolish Ruthie had been to think she could protect Patty from Mark. Patty didn't need her protection. She knew exactly what she was doing, and she didn't care. A blaze of fury brushed any speck of regret she had about her and Patty's damaged friendship away. She picked up another cookie. "Thank you for this. I needed it."

Dr. Gerry narrowed his eyes. "Are you alright?"

She gave a quick nod of her head. "Yep. I'm good."

After Dr. Gerry left, Ruthie looked around. Darryl seemed to have already checked on most of the patients, so she decided to focus her attention on their newest uncooperative patient. She grabbed some clean, powder blue pajamas with snap buttons the hospital used instead of gowns. She needed to get him cleaned and changed, fluids in him, and his boots off. If he had jungle rot, she'd need to treat the infected ulcers and clean them. She also needed to know how severe the infection had become to determine the amount of antibiotics to give him.

The heap of blankets shook, and she began to remove them one at a time, folding them, and laying them to the side.

The soldier groaned. "Leave me alone. Don't take my blankets! I'm freezing!"

Ruthie heard Darryl chuckle, and she rolled her eyes. "You're freezing because you have malaria. If you let me help you, I can get you cleaned up and comfortable a lot quicker than if you fight me."

Over his protests, she'd picked up and folded every blanket on him until she made her way to the last one. She removed it, leaving only a thin sheet covering his body. He lay on his side with his back rounded into an arch—the bones from his spine visible through the thin material. He shook violently. She began to remove the sheet, and he clung to it in a white-knuckled death grip.

"Leave me alone." His voice sounded more fragile than angry.

He clawed at the material with dirty fingernails when she tugged on it. Finally, the sheet slipped from his fingers, and she pulled it off of him like a layer of onion. She saw the man still wore his stained fatigues and a stench of dirt and sweat wafted from him. She cringed. It looked like he hadn't washed in months. Dried mud caked around the bottom of his boots, and some of the dirt had fallen off in clumps onto the bed. She sighed. She'd have to get the whole bed changed too. The man moved, wrapping lean, muscular arms around his bent legs as if he was trying to fold himself into a ball. He gripped his legs tight, but his body continued to tremble from the fever.

She touched his shoulder, and he jumped. "Don't touch me!" he screamed.

She moved to the other side of the bed and bent down to see his face. His long, dark hair flopped to the side. Apparently in the jungle there was no time to get an official army cut. A beard covered his chin and looked like he'd tried to trim it with rusted scissors. The soldier's eyes were closed tight, making deep lines across his face. A single tear seeped from the corner of his right eye and ran into his scraggly beard.

"Look, I can't help you if you don't let me," Ruthie said, making her voice sound calm. "I need to get you cleaned up and you need fluids and antibiotics. You could die if you don't let me help you. So please, let me help you. Don't make me hog-tie you to do it, because I will. I mean it. But that's exhausting and I'm already exhausted. Plus hog-tying a patient on my first night in ICU might make my boss a little testy."

One of the man's eyes popped open. Green—his one green eye stared at her. It focused in and out and she couldn't tell if he was all there mentally. She laid a hand across his forehead. He flinched then stilled, pushing his head into her hand. It must have felt cool against his fiery skin.

"You'd really hog-tie your prom date?"

His words made her jerk her hand back from his head. She stared down at him. Both green eyes stared back at her. She tried to picture him how he was in high school before the war.

"Ronnie?"

He gave her a half grin then winced as if it hurt.

"Ronnie! Oh, my goodness, you're sick!"

A fter Ronnie recognized Ruthie, he allowed her to take care of him and get him cleaned up. His face reddened when she had to give him a bed bath. She'd found a bucket and filled it with water that browned after just a few swipes at his dirt-caked skin. She even found herself blushing as she passed a damp cloth across his arms and bare chest. She couldn't get over it. Ronnie was right here in front of her. A lightness blossomed inside her, and she realized being here and talking to him would be the closest to home she'd get for a while.

"So where have you been?"

His teeth chattered while he spoke. "In the jungle for months. We marched near La Drang Valley and Chu Pong Massif. The jungle was dense and hard to get through lots of times. When the rainy months started, we never got dry."

"That sounds terrible."

He shrugged one shoulder. "Yeah, it was."

He didn't continue and she decided it might be best to change the subject. She smiled. "You know, Hazel is going to be so excited when she hears that I've seen you."

The ends of Ronnie's lips turned up. "So how is everyone at home? I got letters from Joel when he was first drafted before he left for Nam, but I haven't heard from him since."

Ruthie stopped washing him. Her chest grew tight.

"What is it?"

She bit her bottom lip. "Hazel hasn't heard from Joel much lately. The last we heard he was doing good, but that was quite a long time ago. And I got a letter from her recently that Milton..." her voice trailed off.

Ronnie grabbed her hand. "What happened to Milton?"

Ruthie swallowed the lump in her throat. "They sent Sandra a telegram. He's been wounded, but he's doing okay. He's going to get to come home. It's just, I think about how it could have so easily gone the other way." She felt her eyes fill with tears, and she rapidly blinked them away. She moved and began to wash Ronnie's legs. Focusing on removing the caked-on mud without pulling his leg hair. Earlier when she'd undressed him, she'd removed his boots and wet socks. Ronnie had tried not to wince, but she could tell he was in pain. Ruthie had found three of the hardest pillows she'd ever seen and used them to prop up his raw, ulcer-ridden feet. She bent down, wetting the washcloth in the bucket beside her, and passed it across his shin. "You know, I've got to clean your feet too."

"Yeah, I know." He frowned. "I hate Milton was injured. He and Sandra are good people. It's good he gets to go home."

Ruthie nodded, wondering if she heard a tad bit of envy in his voice. "They're the best people. Did you know Hazel had a baby?" she said, trying to switch the topic from going home.

Ronnie smiled. "A baby Davenport, that's exciting!"

"Little guy came early, but he's doing good. His name is Aaron. Joel had already left when she found out she was pregnant. After I clean your feet, I'm going to get you hooked up with some fluids and antibiotics."

Ronnie did a little salute. "Yes sir."

"Well, I came over here to see if you needed any help with the uncooperative patient, but I see you've already whipped him into shape," Darryl said, walking to stand beside Ronnie's bed.

"She threatened to hog-tie me," Ronnie said.

Ruthie laughed. "And I would have too. Darryl, I'd like to introduce you to my high school prom date."

Darryl's eyes widened. Ronnie shook his head. "It's true. It was my senior prom."

"So what was Ruthie like in high school?" Darryl asked and began to help Ruthie clean Ronnie's infected sores.

"Oh, no one wants to hear about that," Ruthie said, feeling her cheeks heat, but she knew Darryl was trying to distract Ronnie from the pain in his feet.

Ronnie gritted his teeth for a few seconds before he said, "She was a spitfire. A cheerleader and a good friend."

"A cheerleader, huh?" Darryl said and gave her a wicked smile.

Ronnie told Darryl about the night so many years ago when he'd found her dateless outside the high school gymnasium in her prom dress. He told stories, some that Ruthie had never heard, about him and Joel hunting rabbits in the field by his parents' farmhouse. Before long, she and Darryl had Ronnie's feet clean and ready to be wrapped in gauze. She got the gauze and gave it to Darryl. While Darryl finished with Ronnie's feet, Ruthie inserted a needle into his arm to start fluids. She handed Ronnie an antibiotic pill and he swallowed it down without water.

"It looks like you're all set," Darryl said to Ronnie after securing the last bandage.

"How long do you think it will be before I can get back in the field?"

Ronnie's question pierced Ruthie's heart. She didn't want to think about Ronnie leaving and going back out into the war where bullets and bombs rained down on everyone equally. She shivered.

Darryl looked at Ruthie and scratched the side of his head. "Malaria can get very serious. Even life threatening, and you have a serious case. But you're getting fluids now and you've started antibiotics. You'll need a few weeks of that. Your feet are in bad shape too. I'd say all in all, you're probably looking at about a three month stay, maybe longer."

Three months or more, Ruthie thought. *I've got at least three months to spend with Ronnie.*

Chapter 39

JOEL, JULY 1969

J oel held his rifle over his head. The water came to his chest. He waded
behind Chad. After Hamburger Hill—that's what they all called it
now—the 101st had been sent back to Camp Hochmuth. Joel couldn't
think about all the people they'd lost on that hill. They'd lost Warwick and
fifty or so other men they knew about. There were still twenty-five men
unaccounted for, three from his own division, and more wounded than he
could count. They'd only got three weeks of respite at camp before being
shipped out again into Huế's rough terrain. The word passed around was
the Viet Cong had several strongholds in the area, and Joel and 101st were
to only engage when directed. He had no idea why they were even being
sent to such a dangerous area if they weren't allowed to engage.

Under the brown murky water, the mud sucked at Joel's boots, making
every step an exertion of energy. Twigs and debris floated beside him and
sweat stung his eyes. A Vietnamese woman grabbed her wash and fled
when she saw them. He wanted to tell her they meant no harm, but
memories of the village and the red puddle pooling behind the rice lady's

back made him bite the inside of his cheek. Sometimes in his dreams it wasn't the rice lady, it was Hazel. Other times, Hazel would be standing on Hamburger Hill—alone while napalm dropped all around her. He shivered. He hated his dreams.

At least at camp he'd been able to check on Milton. Danny had been right. Milton would be fine, and after recovery in a hospital in Japan, he'd be going home. He hated Milton had been wounded, but Joel couldn't stop thinking how lucky Milton was to be alive and going home. What Joel wouldn't give to see Hazel's face again and his new son.

A burst of lightning spread fiery tendrils across the sky. The thunder rumbled so close, he felt it inside his chest. Some days it would be ninety-five degrees, and the sun beat down on their backs, making the hours of marching insufferable. Then the skies would open, and rain would pour from the heavens, leaving them all soaked to the bone. He snuck a peak behind him at Pen. His face expressionless between his raised arms, holding his rifle above the water. He had started to turn a corner at Eagle Beach, but the hill ruined it. Pen had stopped eating again and tossed and turned in his sleep. Every day, his eyes looked more and more vacant, like he'd checked out of his head. Joel wanted to report Pen to Lieutenant Roberts. He wanted him to get help or stay at camp. If his mind wasn't right, he could be dangerous to them all. But Chad had talked him out of it again.

"He'll feel like we betrayed him, man," Chad had said. "I couldn't live with myself. He needs us."

Joel had agreed to stay quiet. Still, Pen grew more irritable each day just like the rest of them. Joel worried one wrong move or word to him and Pen would ignite like a powder keg.

Something bit Joel's neck and he swatted it. He'd taken his malaria pill this morning and hoped it would do the trick. Marching at odd times had started to wear on everyone in the 101st. They'd march for a full day and sometimes at night. Now they stayed away from most villages and slept in the dirt in shallow trenches that they dug themselves. Sometimes they'd huddle together, soaked to the bone under ponchos to keep the pouring rain off. In the Viet Cong area, no one could trust villagers even if they appeared harmless. The VC used women and children to dupe foolish and trusting grunts. He'd heard some sold poisoned drinks to the soldiers.

Joel shook his head. Being here was maddening. But he had to think the government had some reason for this craziness and he at least hoped men weren't dying for nothing.

Chad waded up next to him with his rifle over his shoulder. He motioned for Pen to catch up.

"You good?" Joel asked when Pen moved beside them.

Pen didn't respond.

"Hey, are you good?" Joel asked louder.

Pen shook his head, "Yeah, sure. I'm good. What's your deal?"

"Man, we just want to know if you are okay," Chad said angrily. "You've hardly spoken to us. You barely eat."

"I'm fine," Pen snipped.

"Shut up, you are not," Chad's voice grew stern.

The men in front turned around to look at Chad.

"Cool it," Joel whispered.

"Maybe if I punch him in his fat face, he'll quit lying and talk to us."

"Chad, give it a rest," Joel growled.

They were surrounded by bugs buzzing near their ears. Joel knew being hot and wet constantly was not doing them any favors. Everyone's nerves were set on edge.

"What are you numbskulls doing?" Harvey Davis asked as he sloshed up from behind them. "You're supposed to be in a single file line, idiots."

"Shut up, Davis," Joel snapped.

"Don't start with me today, hickory dickory." He moved past them, making the water splatter Joel's face.

Joel's stomach tightened. He wasn't sure how he felt about Harvey anymore. Part of him still wanted to punch his ugly arrogant mug, but another part of him felt like he owed him his life. He'd saved Joel from eating that tainted bread the woman gave him. If Joel had eaten it, he could have been one of those corpses shipped home in a pine box.

Harvey turned around, sloshing backwards in the water. "Did you dip wads hear about Hamburger Hill? I caught wind of it before we left camp. Some of the pilots were talking about it." He held a hand up to block the sunlight from his eyes. "Yeah, not long after we left, they let the NVA have the hill back." Harvey gave a forced laugh. "Warwick dies fighting to

255

take a hill, and our government lets them have it back. No problemo. No resistance. Just here you go. Those idiots are able to land on the flippin' moon, but they have no clue how to win this war."

Joel's stomach twisted.

"Shut it, Davis," Chad said. "That can't be right. They wouldn't give the hill back."

"It's true. I swear it. You and I and all these other stupid fellows," he raised his hand, pointing to the men wading through the water in front of them. "We're the poor, dumb idiots. Apparently, we're just a dime a dozen. Disposable combat troops. And Lieutenant Roberts must be the biggest idiot of all because they made him the king of the disposables."

Harvey turned around and trudged his way in front of them. Joel slowed to allow Chad and Pen to pass so he could follow behind. The cool water did nothing to stop the anger boiling inside him. Was his life—all of their lives—so meaningless to the American government? What was even the point of all the death and destruction if they were just going to give it back? They could have left the hill alone and Warwick would still be alive. He gripped his rifle tighter. He wasn't disposable. Maybe to his superiors, but he had people who loved him. People who needed him. He had a son. *Doesn't that mean anything to anyone?* He blew a rush of air out of his nose. He guessed that to the ones who sent him here, it really didn't mean anything at all.

❧⟞⟝❧

Joel sat on the ground, tired and wet from the march. He pushed his arms above his head and stretched, feeling the tight muscles in his back lengthen. Heavy gray and black clouds filled the sky. The air around him smelled of rain. They were all wet, soaked to the bone and sour from the information Harvey had spread that afternoon. Joel took off a boot and pulled off a sock. He wrung out the water in it.

"You better get some dry ones. You don't need to get jungle rot," Danny Barnes told him. He kneeled on the ground behind Chad. Chad's white butt in his face. Danny gritted his teeth as he tried to remove a leech from Chad's backside.

256

"I know. I know," Joel said. "But where are we going to find dry socks. I used my last pair yesterday and they're still damp. We can't light a fire to dry them because we'll alert the VC, and they'll come a running."

Chad laughed, "I bet they'll come fast because they have dry socks."

"Be still!" Danny huffed. "I'm never going to get this leech off your butt if you keep moving. Do you think I want to keep staring at your hairy backside!"

Danny had already removed two leeches from Chad's skin. Joel watched in horror; thankful he didn't have any. Chad had tried to pull the slimy critters off himself, but Danny practically bit Chad's head off when he saw him.

"You're gonna make bigger wounds. And out here they'll have more chance of getting infected!" he'd said, waving his arms around. "Let me do it. You just need some heat."

Chad turned his head to look down at Danny. "I thought my backside gave you joy."

Danny looked up at him. "Not a chance, Sutton. It stinks worse than your breath."

Joel laughed. It felt good to laugh. He still couldn't shake what Harvey had told them. They were disposable men. He looked at Chad and then at Danny. These men had families. Homes. A life before the war. They weren't disposable. He felt his chest tighten. In one of Hazel's letters, she'd said people in the US were angry with them. He couldn't understand what he'd done wrong. He'd been forced to come here. If he hadn't, he'd have been thrown in jail. What was he and the other men supposed to do? The government told them they were winning this war, but he couldn't see how that could be true.

Danny removed the last leech from Chad's skin just as flashes of lightning flamed and popped around them like firecrackers.

"So much for trying to dry my socks," Joel said, slipping the wet sock back on his foot right before the heavens opened and rain poured down on top of them. He pulled his poncho over his head, but it was like trying to stop a flood with his hands. The rain soaked into his already damp clothing, saturating them.

The thunder shook the ground, and the rain blew sideways, pelting his face with stinging drops of liquid bullets. The men began to move together in a huddle, their green plastic ponchos mashed together. Joel saw Pen on the outside of the huddle. His wet poncho stuck to the side of his face. Joel started to move toward him and wait the storm out, but Lieutenant Roberts stopped him.

"Davenport, Sutton, you're up for patrol," Lieutenant Roberts said, walking behind the huddle of bodies. "Do a perimeter check."

"Yes sir," Joel said, yelling to be heard above the storm. They did not salute. Saluting could end a superior's life faster than anything, especially if NVA or VC were watching.

Joel put his helmet back on his head. Large drops of rain ran from the helmet and into his eyes. The wind swept his poncho around like a dog slinging a bone. Joel looked at Pen. "We'll be back," he yelled.

Pen nodded. His eyes were blank pools staring back at him. Joel couldn't help but worry about Pen. His behavior had started to really tick Chad off. If only he'd talk to them. But they'd tried, and he pushed them away. Joel worried that Harvey's news today about Hamburger Hill had done more damage. After hearing Harvey's news, Joel had decided when they made it back to Camp Hochmuth, he'd secretly speak to one of the doctors about Pen's mental state and not tell Chad. If Pen or Chad hated him after that, then so be it. But Pen needed help. Help neither he nor Chad could offer.

The rain and darkness made it difficult to do a proper perimeter check. He and Chad made slow circles around the huddled bodies, gradually extending the circle with each pass around.

"Watch out for those bouncing betties," Chad hollered to him.

"How? I can't even see two inches in front of my face," Joel hollered back.

The rain pelted them as they progressed slowly away from the huddle and into a clearing. Joel pumped his cold hands into fists to get the circulation going.

"I hate the rain," Chad said, the wind swallowing his words.

Joel nodded and tried to unstick the side of his poncho from his face. He twisted his head to the side, and out of the corner of his eye, he saw a flash.

He froze. His blood pumped hard through his veins. He reached out and grabbed Chad's arm, pulling him close.

"Did you see that? Straight ahead."

Chad wiped rain from his eyes. "What?"

Joel leaned in closer. "There was something over there. I saw a flash beside one of the stones. What is that? Some kind of man-made graveyard of sorts."

"A flash?" Chad's brows dipped. "You sure?" He pointed to the sky. "Could it have been lightning?"

Joel shook his head. "It was something else." His heart thumped hard in his chest. He knew what he'd seen, and it had nothing to do with the storm. He pointed out the headstone or whatever it was that had been the source of the flash.

Chad looked hard and long. "I think you're right. It looks like a graveyard. I wonder if there's a village close by." He shook his finger toward the area. "You take the right. I'll take the left."

They split apart, hunched over, rifles raised. The hairs on the back of Joel's neck raised, and even though exhaustion had taken its toll, he felt his body more alert, more alive than he'd felt in days. They skulked toward the piled stones like hunters on the prowl. Although the rain and wind chilled him to the bone, his body felt on fire. The blood pushed through his veins.

Five feet from the stones, they paused. Joel couldn't see Chad's face through the rain, but he could see his hands. Chad began to count down with his fingers. Three, two, one. When he got to one, they rushed to the pile of rocks, rifles ready to fire. They rounded the makeshift grave together. Joel's finger moved to the trigger, but there was nothing there. Only a small mound of raised dirt.

The air left Joel's lungs in a rush. "What the heck?" The heat of embarrassment hit his cheeks. "I'm sorry, man. I really thought..." he sighed. "I thought I saw something."

Chad laughed, looping his rifle over his shoulder. "Look, we can barely see. No harm no foul."

Chad patted the mound of raised dirt behind the rough grave with his boot. Joel's stomach jumped in his throat when Chad let out a loud yell. It happened like a movie in slow motion—Chad's boot broke through the dirt, sending him wobbling to get his balance. Loose dirt swallowed his boot and leg, and before either could do anything, they were swept up in an avalanche of rubble and ground.

Joel wasn't sure how far they fell. He landed hard on his backside. A sharp pain radiated from his tailbone to his neck. His rifle lay in front of him covered in dirt. He scampered to it, feeling every muscle in his body protest. He grabbed it and leaped to his feet. Pain soared up his spine. He spun around pointing his rifle as he wiped mud and rain from his eyes. He couldn't see Chad. He couldn't see anything. He blinked and rubbed his eyes until they ached.

"Sutton," he whispered.

He heard a groan. "I'm here."

Flashes of lightning illuminated the area around him for brief seconds. In those moments, he took in everything he could, trying to make sense of what happened. Joel heard a click, then saw the round glow from Chad's flashlight. Chad sat on the ground, rubbing his head. He passed the light around the area then pushed himself up with his hands, groaning.

"You hurt?" Joel asked.

"Nah, but where are we?"

"Looks like we broke through to an underground tunnel or bunker of some kind."

Chad panned the light around the area again. They saw stacks of stolen supplies, broken helmets, belts, and used cans of C-rats. A row of firearms had fallen over.

"There has to be twenty or thirty rifles," Chad said.

"Yeah, and look. Point your light there."

In front of them, Joel saw a dark opening like an entrance to a cave. Part of the bunker that hadn't collapsed. Joel had been told that the tunnels and bunkers the VC created could be miles long. The light from the flashlight only illuminated part of the tunnel before them. The darkness inside extended way past the light.

"Whoa, it has to go way back," Chad said, making a low whistle sound. "How far you think it goes?"

Joel didn't get a chance to respond because a sound somewhere deep inside the darkness echoed and reverberated off the tunnel walls. The sound of laughing and talking made Joel's knees go weak. He felt Chad tense beside him, and he switched off the light.

"I don't think we are alone," Joel whispered. His arms became like lead and his stomach twisted. "We've got to get out of here."

Chad nodded. Using only the quick flashes of lightning to guide them, they tried to assess the steepness of the tunnel's wall.

"I think we can do it. Lift me up," Chad said. "I'll pull you out."

Joel squatted down. His back ached and his thighs burned, but he held the position as Chad placed his heavy mud-covered boot on Joel's thigh close to his groin.

"Ready?" Chad asked.

"Yeah, hurry," Joel said through gritted teeth.

Chad pushed all his weight against Joel's leg and bounced off it toward the top of the wall. His hands frantically tried to reach the edge.

"It's slippery," Chad said, his words strained.

Joel's legs trembled and he thought he might lose his stance.

"I got it. Push me," Chad said, panting.

Joel grabbed Chad's legs, heaving them hard over his head. He heard scrapping sounds and Chad grunting. Joel's head whipped to the side toward the dark hole. Joel's blood ran cold as the laughing grew louder. He looked up with a flash of lightning and saw Chad's boots completely disappear above him over the edge. Joel turned to face the tunnel, holding his rifle ready. The laughing and talking so loud he could almost make out words.

"Give me your hand," Chad called, leaning over the ledge with his arm extended.

Rain pelted Joel's face. He reached high for Chad's hand. His arm extended until he felt like it might pop from his shoulder. Their wet fingertips slid over each other.

"I can't reach you!" Chad cried.

Blood rushed through Joel's head. He would die down here. If he didn't get out, he would die. He ran to the other wall away from Chad.

"What are you doing, man?" Chad called, his voice frantic.

"I'm gonna get a running jump at it."

As the words left his mouth, a bolt of lightning flashed, and Joel saw him. He stood in the entrance of the tunnel, shock plastered on his face. The shock was short lived, and in another burst of light, Joel saw his face twist with rage. The man screamed words Joel couldn't understand. He raised a gun and pointed it at Joel. Joel didn't wait to see if he fired, Joel took off running and leaped for Chad's hand. His hand reached into the air, finding Chad's arm. He dug his fingers into Chad's skin. Over Chad's howls, he heard the gun behind him explode. The blasts rang in his ears. Chad jerked him up so hard, Joel felt like he'd popped his arm out of its socket, and then he went over the edge. They wasted no time. He and Chad scrambled to their feet and ran.

"We've got to get back, to the others," Chad screamed. "They're shooting at us!" Hurry!"

Joel couldn't respond. He heard the pops and bullets whizz by his head. His chest heaved and his arms pumped hard. His legs were on fire, but he couldn't stop. He didn't know how far he'd ran until he saw the others running toward them. The 101st coming with raised rifles, returning gunfire. The reports echoed and bounced around him.

"The calvary," he said to Chad between breaths. He looked over his shoulder to smile at Chad, but all he saw was open field. Joel stopped running. Confused, he reeled around in circles. Lieutenant Roberts ran to him, getting in Joel's face to be heard over the gunfire and storm.

"What is it?"

Joel sucked in air. "A hidden tunnel." He sucked in another breath. "At the graveyard."

Lieutenant Roberts nodded and barked out commands Joel didn't hear. Harvey Davis ran near him, following the rest of the men. Joel lurched out and grabbed his arm, pulling Harvey to him. He yelled. "Chad. Where's Sutton?"

"Haven't seen him," Davis said, shrugging him off.

Joel felt his heart stop. He tried to think, but the blood pounded between his temples. Chad yanked him from the tunnel then they'd ran. He saw Chad running. *He was running with me, beside me, wasn't he?* Joel felt like a madman. He turned and raced back toward the graveyard, not caring about the bullets whizzing past his body.

"Sutton!" he screamed. "Chad!" Fear clutched his throat.

"Here, here!"

Joel spun around. Pen stood about a hundred yards away, waving his arms hysterically in the air. Joel sprinted toward Pen. When he got there, he took a step back. The air left his lungs. Chad laid on the ground, clutching his stomach and wailing in agony.

"Give me a light, Pen," Joel said.

Pen searched for the flashlight on his belt, his hands trembling. He pointed the light toward Chad. The beam bounced across Chad's face, midsection, and legs.

"Hold it still!" Joel screamed.

Chad's face grimaced. Pen grasped the light in both hands. Joel fell to his knees beside Chad. The light finally rested on Chad's middle. Chad held his stomach and Joel saw long, spidery red streaks run between his fingers.

"Is it bad?" Chad asked.

Joel pulled his hands away and raised Chad's shirt. Chad balled his hands into fists and grimaced. A hole in his stomach gurgled and bubbled blood. Joel put his hands over it, forcing Chad to lay back on the wet ground. Joel's body went cold when he saw the second, larger hole. He placed one of his hands over it, pressing with all his might. Chad screamed.

"Medic," Joel shouted. "We need a medic!"

Chad coughed and blood gushed from between Joel's fingers.

"It hurts, man. Don't let me die. I'm not ready to die."

Chad's terrified eyes looked at Joel, pleading.

"You're not going to die. Give him morphine!" Joel yelled. Danny Barnes ran beside Joel and plunged a needle into Chad's side.

Chad screamed, "I can't feel my legs!"

Danny gave Joel a worried look.

"Give him more!" Joel yelled.

Danny gave Chad another stab of morphine.

"Let's turn him over. I need to see his back," Danny directed.

Joel nodded and motioned for Pen to help him. Together, they gingerly moved Chad onto his side. Chad cried out as Danny assessed his wound. He looked up from behind Chad to Joel. His face went slack. He shook his head.

"Get the MAST," Danny ordered Pen. "They'll compress the abdomen and help with blood loss."

Pen nodded and scrambled up to his feet. He hightailed it back toward the area where they had been huddled.

"It's his spine. I think it's severed," Danny said in a low voice for only Joel.

Joel's heart fell. Danny and Joel laid Chad back down, and Danny laid his hands on Chad's wounds, pressing them to stop the blood flow. Joel grabbed Chad's hand and squeezed it tight.

"We're getting you help, Chad. Hang on. Hang on please."

"Mama," Chad cried. "I want my mama. Mama!" he screamed.

Chills passed through Joel's body.

Chad whimpered; his breathing grew faster.

"Come on, Sutton. Don't give out on me. Hang on."

The rain pounded them.

"It's so cold," Chad said, his whole body trembling.

Joel's insides crumbled. He squeezed Chad's hand. Chad let out a soft moan, his breath leaving him, and he went still. His hand hung limp in Joel's hand. Chad's eyes stared out, empty.

"Chad?" Joel asked. "Chad?"

"He's gone," Danny said.

Joel heard something behind him and turned. Pen stood there with the MAST in his hands. Joel reached up and gently closed Chad's eyes with his fingertips. Pen hung his head.

"I didn't make it," Pen said. His voice so tiny Joel could barely hear it over the wind.

"They probably weren't going to work anyway, Pen," Danny said.

Pen threw the trousers to the ground. Anguish spread across his face, and he rubbed at his collarbone. "Well, now we'll never know, will we." He turned and stormed away.

Joel didn't go after him. He couldn't make his body move from where he sat beside Chad. He couldn't leave him. Danny stood, placing a hand on Joel's shoulder. He gave a light squeeze before walking off.

Rain drops pooled and streamed down Chad's lifeless face. He thought about Chad's poor father and mother, his brothers and sisters. He'd never be able to help them on the farm again. What were they going to do without him? What would he do without Chad? No more dumb jokes. No more singing. Chad never got the chance to meet a girl and have a family of his own. Joel felt the world crumbling away around him. Why were they even here? He squeezed Chad's cold hand and prayed. He did his best to say good-bye to his best friend.

Chapter 40

HAZEL

A safety pin stuck out of the side of Hazel's mouth. Strands of her dark hair fell into her eyes as she battled with her son. Aaron lay on the sofa and kicked his little legs in the air. He refused to let her put a diaper on him. For a little guy, he sure knew what he wanted, she thought, and he wanted to be naked. She couldn't blame him. It had to be a hundred and fifty thousand degrees outside. Even indoors, the fans and window air conditioning unit couldn't keep up with the heat. Sweat tickled the side of her face, but she took the pin and secured the side of his cloth diaper. He looked disappointed that she'd finally succeeded.

Sandra, Mikey, and Mannie burst through the door, bringing the heat with them. "Oh my! What a handsome boy," Sandra exclaimed. She went to the sofa and picked up a half-naked Aaron. She nuzzled him and he cooed. She held him down so Mikey and Mannie could see him and give him a quick peck on his cheek before running to the toys to play. Hazel loved how Aaron's cheeks were finally filling in. He'd put on a good number of pounds and rounded out since he'd been home. He wasn't that tiny, skinny baby she'd brought home anymore.

"I can't believe I have to go back to work soon," Hazel said, feeling a lump rise in her chest. "I don't think I can do it."

"I know it will be hard, but you know Mannie and I will be with him and then Mikey too when school is out. He'll be just fine."

Hazel fanned herself with her hand. "Are you sure you can handle all three boys?"

Sandra pretended to find something on Aaron's neck and tickled it. He smiled. It melted Hazel's heart to see her baby smile. "It will be no problem at all. I do suspect, though, I won't be alone. Your father and Ms. Faye will be over here a lot. Have you talked to him lately? About the situation with Mr. Hal and the will?"

Hazel leaned back on the sofa, melting into it. "He read the will before he gave it to me. He looked disappointed and confused mostly, but we never talked about it. I don't think he really knew what to say. I don't know how I'd feel if I found out my closest friend was a liar and thief."

Sandra nodded and held Aaron in the air so she could get his feet with her mouth. He giggled, and it sent joy radiating through Hazel's chest. "You know," Sandra said. "Milton will be home next month, and he'd be a good one to talk to about it. God has blessed him with such insight and wisdom." She gave Hazel a sly look. "But don't you ever tell him I said that."

They both cackled at Sandra's joke. A knock on the front door startled them all. Mikey and Mannie ran to Hazel and Sandra. Mannie held out his arms and Hazel picked him up, holding him close.

"You expecting someone?" Sandra asked.

Hazel held Mannie closer. "No," she said, feeling her breakfast turn solid inside her stomach. Her heart began to beat wildly. She wondered if all wives and mothers felt this fear when there was an unknown knock on their doors. Bad news from the war came in all different shapes and forms, but the worst was when someone personally delivered it.

"I can answer it," Sandra said.

Hazel shook her head. "No, I'll get it. It's nothing. It's going to be nothing," she repeated, mostly for herself. She had to force her weak knees to work so she could stand. She shifted Mannie to her hip and made her way to the door. He wrapped his arms around her neck, and she leaned into him, kissing his head. She couldn't help it, but her hand trembled. She turned the doorknob and peaked out the crack. The air left her. It wasn't a soldier or officer from the Army. She opened the door wider. Sandra came to stand beside her. Hazel blinked at the man standing on her stoop. He looked familiar, but she couldn't place him. He looked toothpick thin in his collared shirt and khaki pants. His sandy blonde hair cut short against his scalp. In his hands he held a gift wrapped in blue paper with a puffy golden bow.

"Hi!" he said, looking awkward. She stared at him, speechless. He held up the gift in his hands.

"This is for your new baby."

Sandra and Hazel met eyes then looked back at the man, who seemed completely out of place.

"Oh, you probably don't remember me. I'm Oliver Holland. I'm your mother's... I mean Elizabeth's husband."

Mannie wiggled in Hazel's arms, and she set him down. He ran to the toys to grab a truck. Sandra backed away from the door and Hazel heard her whisper. "We'll be right here if you need us."

Hazel nodded, stepped outside on the stoop, and closed the door behind her. Her bare feet cooked against the hot cement, and she rotated them, propping one on top of the other to keep them from burning.

"Boy, it's a scorcher, isn't it?" Oliver commented, wiping his forehead with his hand. He pushed the gift toward her.

Hazel swallowed. "I'm not sure I want it."

Oliver's eyes widened. The honesty in her words even shocked her.

He lowered his chin. "I understand. It's just a crib mobile with clouds and the moon. I think it plays 'Twinkle Twinkle Little Star.'"

She felt bad for not taking it. She hated this. Why was he here? She took the gift from his hands, thinking maybe if she'd just take the stupid gift, he'd leave. "Thank you," she said, her voice flat.

He ran a hand across his face. "I'm sorry about this. I know this is strange. But your mother wanted me to bring it to you."

Her anger got the better of her and she snipped, "Too bad she couldn't do it herself."

He reached out and touched her arm. His touch made Hazel flinch.

"She did want to bring it herself. I promise. But she couldn't."

Hazel watched, horrified, when Oliver's eyes began to grow watery.

"A while back, she was diagnosed with breast cancer. She doesn't have much longer, Hazel. She's dying."

Hazel wondered how a normal person would feel about learning their mother had cancer and didn't have long to live, because she felt nothing. Not a pang of sadness. Not a flash of longing—nothing.

"She knows she doesn't deserve your forgiveness, but she wanted me to ask you to come to the house and see her. She'd like to apologize in person if you'd let her."

Chapter 41

RUTHIE

At the end of Ruthie's first night in ICU, she didn't want to leave. She wanted to soak up more time with Ronnie. But his eyelids began to dip down and almost close. His voice slurred and she knew he needed to rest. He needed to get sleep—sleep was a healer of many things. When the nurses for the day shift came in, Ruthie snuck a quick peck on Ronnie's forehead. His skin felt clammy and warm under her lips, but not fiery like he had been when she first started caring for him. She whispered good-bye and then left to grab some breakfast and a few hours of rest.

The painted sky looked beautiful as it spread above the large patch of red dirt surrounding the hospital. Morning light already reflected off the metal hootches. On the day shift, she'd rush to work, never taking in the beauty of the morning, and ended her shift in the dead of night. She stretched her arms above her head, letting the muscles in her back stretch and her bones pop. The tightness embedded in her body since her fight with Patty eased some. The land around her looked flat, but in the distance beyond the hootches, tents, trucks, and concertina wire, she could see the outline of huge mountains almost navy under the clouds. The guard on the tower closest to the hospital already stood armed and alert. His eyes turned toward the mountains. It was hard to process that beyond the peaceful-looking mountains there were people fighting a war. But even with that knowledge, she felt calm, a feeling she almost didn't recognize any more. It had to be because of Ronnie. It was like having a little piece of home here with her.

She looked toward the helicopter landing pad area and saw a figure in full gear running toward her. She tilted her head to the side and squinted her eyes. It looked like a pilot. *But why is he running?* Something had to be wrong. Her calmness vanished like in a magic trick—poof. Worried he may be hurt, she rushed to him, meeting him in the middle between the landing area and the hospital. When they reached each other, he doubled over, panting with his hands on his knees. She immediately recognized him but couldn't remember his name. He was the pilot whose arm had been grazed months ago. Dr. Gerry had spoken to him during one of the worst pushes they'd ever had. She reached down to pat his back.

"Are you okay?" she asked. Her eyes were already scanning every inch of his body, looking for wounds or anything abnormal.

He nodded his head. "Come," he panted. "Come quick."

She frowned. "What?"

He stood up. Sucked in air. "I need you to come quick. Our flight nurse got sick, and a village was just bombed with napalm. They were trying to hit a Viet Cong encampment but hit the village too."

Ruthie's body went rigid and the blood in her veins ran cold.

"We were ordered to transport as many villagers as we can," he panted. "Transport them here to the hospital."

She remembered the mother holding her burnt child in her arms on her first nights here. Ruthie shook her head violently from side to side. There was no way she could handle this—a whole village burned. And she'd never even been past the concertina wire. She stuttered, "I-I just got off my shift."

He grabbed her arm, pulling her toward the medevac helicopter. They were so close she could feel the air against her skin from its blades whirling in blurry circles, the helicopter waiting to soar into the pink and blue sky. It sent chills down her spine. Her boots dragged in the dirt, making paths behind her. He wasn't listening.

"I really can't do this. I have to get it approved by my supervisor. I'm not a flight nurse."

He tightened his grip on her arm. "There's no time. We've got to go."

Near the right of the helicopter, Ruthie saw the flight nurse doubled over. He vomited onto the ground.

The pilot noticed her looking. "He's new. He drank the water. He'll be fine, eventually," he yelled over the noise. He pushed her inside the belly of the helicopter like she weighed nothing. The loudness overtook her. She scrambled to her seat. The pilot motioned for her to slide the headphones over her ears, and she did, noticing the little microphone that ran near her mouth. He then ran around the helicopter to hop in the front seat. She saw another crew member sitting in the passenger seat. He looked back at her. Sweat dotted his dark skin, but he flashed her a smile and gave her a little salute. Before she could say anything, the helicopter lifted into the air. Her stomach rose into her throat. She laid a hand on the side of the helicopter. Her other hand gripped the seat. The sensation of soaring made her dizzy.

She heard the passenger talk in the headphones to the pilot. "She's gonna be sick too."

The pilot sighed. "We don't have time for this."

Ruthie wrapped her arms around her. "I'm not going to be sick. It just surprised me."

The passenger looked back at her. "You sure?"

She nodded.

"I'm John. If you need anything." He motioned to the pilot. "This here's Jake. Just hold on, pretty lady. It's gonna be a bumpy ride."

She gripped her arms tighter around her middle and stared out the window. They soared over the mountains. The ones she had been staring at only moments ago. She felt the shift as they started to descend. Lower, lower, until she could make out the tops of trees.

Her stomach flipped. "We're not landing in the trees, are we?"

Both John and Jake started to laugh. John turned back to look at her. "No way! What do you think we are, amateurs? There's a grassy clearing up ahead."

She rose in her seat a little to look out the front. She saw a large clearing beyond the trees. She sat back down, pushing her back against the seat. She felt queasy and started to take long, deep breaths through her nose. They were almost there and even though she'd worked a straight twelve-hour shift, she still had a job to do. She began to look around the space inside the medevac helicopter.

"What kind of medical supplies do you have on hand?" she asked.

John looked at her and smiled. "Now you're talking! We've got basic stuff like bandages, but we've also got some medications, morphine, IV tubing, and fluids. Enough to stabilize most patients until we can get them to you at the hospital."

Ruthie nodded. "Alright. Are there any others?"

"Do you mean any other medevacs coming to help with the villagers?" Jake asked.

"Yeah, other than us. I mean there's probably room for only eight people in here," Ruthie said.

John looked over at Jake.

"I've gotten fifteen soldiers in here before," Jake said as he maneuvered the helicopter closer to the clearing.

Ruthie's mouth hung open and John bellowed into her headphones.

"Is she shocked?" Jake asked, never taking his eyes off the clearing in front of them.

"Oh yeah, she's shocked," John replied.

Jake laughed and then his laughter abruptly stopped. "Listen," he said, and the tone of his voice made her mouth go dry. "It's going to be bad out there. You stay close to John. He'll keep you safe. Our job is to get there and assess the situation. If there's more survivors than we can handle, we call for a second chopper. But..." his voice trailed off.

She felt the hairs on the back of her neck stand up.

"With what I heard, there may not be many survivors."

Ruthie's stomach dropped with the helicopter as it landed in a green grassy area.

"Keep your head down and walk behind me," John directed her.

She grabbed a medical bag that lay near the open door and leaped out of the helicopter. Her boots hit the ground and sank into the mud and wet grass. She followed close behind John. He held a machine gun, aimed and ready. The sight of it sent her heart in overdrive. *What if there are Viet Cong out here with their own rifles waiting for us?* She brushed the thoughts aside, focusing on John's back, the weight of the medical bag in her hand, and the slurping sound of her boots as she picked them up from the wet ground.

The scent of earth and rain after a storm reminded her of the forest near her old home in Waldron. They hadn't walked far before the clearing ended, and they entered a lush forest. Palm trees and thick brush surrounded her. A chattering sound echoed all around. "What's that sound?" she asked John.

"Mongooses," he said. "Keep moving. It's not much farther."

She smelled it before she saw it. It burnt the inside of her nostrils, making her eyes water. The smell of cooked meat and smoke made her want to vomit. She steeled herself. She came to do a job. These people needed her. John pushed a huge palm frond out of the way, and she saw it. The gasp escaped her before she could stop it.

"I know," John said. "Let's get busy."

She wanted to cover her ears and close her eyes tight. But there was no time. A few huts remained intact, but most of the village lay in ruins. Blackened piles of bamboo and palms sent billows of black and gray smoke into the air, making it hard to breathe. Dark craters pocked the earth. She refused to look at the burnt corpses strewn everywhere and instead concentrate on the living or still living. Women rocked dead children in their arms while other children stood naked and crying, burns all over their small bodies. Ruthie went to them first. She wondered if they even had parents anymore or if their parents were some of the corpses lying on the ground. She examined a little boy with dark red and brown burn splotches running down both arms. Yellow blisters already dotted the burnt areas. Tears streamed down the side of his cheeks. He needed to go to the hospital. She couldn't adequately care for the burns here. They were too deep.

"He needs to go," she said to John.

He nodded. "Can you give me a quick assessment of how many need to go?"

She looked around, making herself focus only on the injured and not the dead. "Thirty. There's thirty that need to go."

He got on his hand-held radio. "Jake, we've got thirty at least. Get some more help here!"

The radio squawked back. "Will do."

She and John gathered some who needed medical attention. Ruthie tried to explain to the villagers the best she could by using hand signals and pointing to the red cross on her bag. John tried the few Vietnamese words he knew, but the villagers were leery of them, even the ones that needed the most medical attention. They were able to convince two men, three women, and eight children—all suffering from deep second- and third-degree burns to follow them to the clearing where Jake waited in the helicopter. The two men carried one of the women, whose shin bone stuck out of her skin. The bigger children carried the smaller ones, although they were wounded too. John led the way with his machine gun pointed and ready. Ruthie followed in the rear, holding a girl, maybe one year old, with burns and wood embedded in her legs. Ruthie hoped the other helicopters would be able to convince the other villagers to come to the hospital with them. Ruthie held the girl and her medical bag. Her damp hand pulsed from gripping the handle so hard. The small girl whimpered, her deep black hair clinging to her wet face. When they made it to the clearing, a second helicopter landed, and men leaped out and ran toward the village.

Near the helicopter, the men carrying the women, as well as the others, hesitated. One of the women grabbed a child to hold them back. Ruthie could clearly see the terror on their faces. They'd probably never been in a helicopter before. Ruthie tightened her grip on the little girl and the bag. She pushed her way around the group. She held up the bag so they could see the red cross sign again and made her way to the helicopter. Jake rushed to her and helped her and the little girl inside. She looked out of the open door. One of the women bit her bottom lip, but her pain must have been greater than her fear because she made her way to the helicopter and crawled inside. After her, the rest followed. John and Jake helped the men load the woman with a broken leg. Then before Ruthie knew it, the heavy Huey lifted into the air and turned to head to the hospital.

Ruthie worked six more hours, helping in triage. She focused on the little girl, who clung to her neck. She held her tiny body and caressed her hair while another nurse debrided the burnt skin from her legs and removed chunks of wooden splinters from her legs. After that, Ruthie took over cleaning and bandaging the girl's wounds. The little girl's brown eyes followed her every movement. Ruthie's heart broke for her. She had no idea if anyone in the girl's family was left to wonder where she was. Ruthie had spotted her sitting alone near the smoking remnants of a blackened and charred hut. The girl seemed so small—too small to be alone, and she was hurt. So, Ruthie picked her up. The little girl didn't cry but wrapped her little arms around Ruthie's neck. Since she had no idea what the little's girls name was, she called her Daisy, after the little flowers she'd always loved. Before Ruthie finished bandaging her wounds, Daisy had already fallen asleep from the pain medication and stress. Ruthie stared at her beautiful, peaceful face. She prayed Daisy would live a good life, safe from the war.

Ruthie helped transport many of the stable villagers to Ward Three to recuperate and rest. She helped the woman with the broken leg get comfortable on a small cot. The woman stared vacantly past Ruthie.

"Ruthie! There you are," Darryl said, running toward her. His face flushed.

"What's wrong?"

"The little girl you brought in is crying hysterically and she won't let anyone touch her."

Ruthie followed Darryl back to triage where she'd left Daisy sleeping. Once she entered the door, she could hear Daisy's piercing screams. She rushed toward her. Daisy's face flushed bright red, and tears stained her cheeks. When her brown eyes saw Ruthie, they lit up and she stopped screaming. She reached out her arms. Ruthie grabbed her, hugging her to her chest. Daisy linked her arms around Ruthie's neck. She squeezed so tight, Ruthie could barely breathe, but she didn't care. Ruthie looked over at Darryl. His eyes had grown watery. He walked over to her. "Maybe you could take her to your hootch and get some sleep. Come back to work when you're ready, after you both sleep and eat. She'll need to be rebandaged by then."

Ruthie mouthed "thank you" and Darryl smiled. In her hootch, she and Daisy cuddled together in Ruthie's hospital size cot. What was she going to do with this little girl? Ruthie knew she would need to find her family, but that may take some time. Before then, Daisy needed to be cared for; she needed to be cleaned, to sleep, to eat, and not in that order. Ruthie's mind felt full of mud. She tried to think of everything a little girl would need, but the warmth from Daisy's body sprawled out across her chest, and her rhythmic breathing pulled Ruthie into a deep sleep. The last drop of Ruthie's adrenaline slipped from her body, and she slept.

Chapter 42

RUTHIE

A huge explosion woke Ruthie. She felt dazed. She looked down at her chest and met Daisy's huge eyes, staring back at her. Black strands of hair stuck to her forehead. Ruthie moved. Her back ached from being in the same position, and she shifted. Daisy whimpered. Ruthie could hear the patter of rain, hitting the roof.

"It's okay, little one. It's just thunder."

The second explosion rocked the small hootch. Daisy's hands went to her ears. She started to wail. Fresh tears streamed down her face. Ruthie wrapped her arms around her. It wasn't thunder. They needed to get out of here and fast. She scurried off the bed, sitting Daisy back on the mattress so she could slide on her boots. Daisy screamed as another explosion echoed loud and hollow in the distance. Ruthie put on her flax jacket and set her helmet on Daisy's head. The helmet covered almost all of Daisy's face. All Ruthie could see was her tiny pink mouth. She stopped screaming and patted the helmet with her hands. It looked adorable, but there was no time to stop, they were being attacked. She and Daisy needed to hightail it to a bunker.

She grabbed Daisy in her arms and burst through the door, not waiting for a fourth mortar to hit. Rain pelted them. Ruthie fought the wind. It pushed her sideways, and she struggled to raise her leg against it. She held Daisy close. The poor baby had been through so much in her short life. A blaze of fire ignited in the distance on the other side of the base where the trucks were kept. Men rushed around her in herds, yelling about the fire. With the wind and the crowd, she felt herself being pushed away from where she wanted to go. Her heart pounded in her chest as she tried to fight the chaotic mess. She had to get Daisy to safety. She felt a strong hand on her shoulder.

"Let's get you both to a bunker," Dr. Gerry screamed over the sound of the chaos. He helped push her toward where she needed to go.

Once inside the bunker, Ruthie's heart began to return to a normal pace. She moved to the back to sit on the bench seats, cradling Daisy on her lap. Both drenched, they shuttered. A searing thought ripped through Ruthie, and she nearly screamed out. Ronnie was in ICU! She needed to get there and help. As if Daisy could read her mind, she wrapped her little arms around Ruthie's body and gripped her tight.

"The hospital," she said. "We need to help at the hospital. The patients." But what she really meant was she needed to help Ronnie.

Dr. Gerry sat down beside her. "The staff is there. You need to stay here with her," he motioned toward Daisy, who buried her wet face in Ruthie's chest. "There's nothing you could do anyway if they hit the hospital. But I've been here a long while and they never do. Oh, they get close sometimes, but they never do."

Ruthie looked over at him. His calmness seemed to spread to her.

"She's really taken a liking to you," Dr. Gerry said, patting Daisy on the back.

Ruthie nodded. "Yeah, she's been stuck to me like glue."

"What are you going to do?" he asked.

Ruthie looked down at the top of Daisy's head. Her long, black strands of wet hair were plastered to her face and back. "I don't really know other than take her back to the village and see if we can find her family."

"What if there is no family left?"

It was a question Ruthie had tossed around in her mind but tried not to dwell on. Daisy had to have some family left. Someone to love her and take care of her. She closed her eyes. "I don't know yet."

Outside the bunker, except for the drumming of rain on the ground, all had grown quiet. The attack had ended. She felt her lungs finally fill with air.

"I got my DEROS yesterday," Dr. Gerry said.

Ruthie's head whipped to the side to look at him. She felt as if she'd been punched in the gut. She knew she should be happy for him. He'd re-upped once before and now his second year had finally come to an end.

"I'm going to go home this time. I'm not re-upping again. My wife needs me. America hates this war, and I don't see that changing. I can't handle seeing these poor men torn to pieces. And..." he swallowed. "And not being able to put many of them back together has started to get to me. In the eyes of our country, their lives mean nothing. But they mean something to me, and I feel guilty for wanting to leave them."

She reached out and took his hand in hers, giving it a firm squeeze. "I understand. And it's okay." She knew that's what he wanted to hear. Still, the words felt like ash on her tongue. She wanted to be selfish and beg him to stay. He was her lifeline—a comforting friend, and she didn't know if she could deal with life here without him. Instead, she said nothing at all, just pressed her palm harder into his.

<hr />

After the attack, she learned only a truck had been hit. Ruthie took Daisy back to the hootch to grab her shower items. She needed to talk to her boss, Tom, about Daisy soon. But first, they'd shower and eat. Because of the rain and mud, Daisy's bandages were a mess, so Ruthie gingerly removed them to examine the little girl's burns and wounds. The stitches she'd received looked good, still intact, and nothing was bleeding.

Ruthie decided she'd take Daisy to the hospital first, after they'd showered, and apply fresh bandages then grab food from the mess hall.

Ruthie watched Daisy splash the water that pooled around her on the shower floor. No smile on her face, just splashing. Ruthie wondered what was going on in this little girl's head. Did she miss her family? Was she still in shock? Ruthie didn't have any clothes to dress Daisy in, so after she dried her, she put her in one of the army-green T-shirts she'd bought from the PX. It swallowed Daisy. Her head and hands were the only things visible. Daisy stood still while Ruthie brushed her hair. She was careful not to pull the knots. It felt eerie how quiet Daisy stayed, but Ruthie didn't know what to expect. Daisy had been through so much.

Once they were ready, she picked her up and headed to ICU. Darryl scowled while he swept mud and water out the front door, but his face brightened when he saw them.

He bent over until he stood eye level with Daisy. She turned, hiding her face in Ruthie's shoulder.

"Wow! She's really taken to you."

Ruthie felt a swell of pride blossom in her chest. Daisy had taken to her. She didn't know why, but she felt honored that a little girl who had suffered so much could find some kind of solace in her.

"I need to rewrap her legs and get her some food. I think she's starving even though she doesn't act like it. Her little stomach was growling the whole time I bathed her."

Daisy turned her head to peer at Darryl from under her long hair. He held his hands out, but she whipped around, wrapping her arms around Ruthie's neck and choked her.

Darryl shook his head. "Well, I won't be of any help. She seems to hate me."

Ruthie grinned. "She doesn't hate you. She just doesn't know what a wonderful, funny guy you are yet. Give her some time."

Darryl moved so Ruthie and Daisy could come inside and avoid the mess he'd been sweeping. "Hey, I wanted to let you know that I heard Patty has come back early from R&R. Had to be a record trip. It was like she got there and turned around—hopped on another plane and came right back."

A heavy feeling settled in Ruthie's stomach. "Really, why would she do that?"

Darryl shrugged. "Don't know, but she went straight to talk to Tom."

Ruthie bit her lip. "I need to speak to him too. Soon." She hugged Daisy.

Darryl nodded. "If I can help." He motioned to Daisy. "Just let me know."

Ruthie started to walk toward the back to grab fresh bandages for Daisy. Her mind reeled from what Darryl had said about Patty. Part of her worried something could be wrong, but then her fury with the situation bubbled up and she remembered she didn't care. Patty had made her choice.

"Hey, hey! Calling nurse Ruthie."

The sound of her name brought her back to herself. Ronnie sat up in his bed. A huge smile on his face. She felt a calmness wash over her just at the sight of him. She went over to him and laid the back of her hand across his forehead.

"Your fever is down. Did Darryl give you more antibiotics?"

He waved her question off. "Yeah, yeah. Is something wrong? You looked like you were deep in thought. And more importantly, who is this cutie?" He puffed out his cheeks and crossed his eyes.

Daisy giggled and the sound stole Ruthie's breath. "That's the first time I've ever heard her laugh."

Ronnie ballooned his cheeks again then pushed air from his lips, making them sound like a deflating balloon.

Daisy rocked in Ruthie's arms and giggled.

"I guess I'm just a funny guy," Ronnie shrugged.

He held out his hands and Daisy immediately went to him. Ruthie stood there, empty handed and stunned. "I can't believe she went to you."

Daisy sat on Ronnie's lap, staring at his face, which Ruthie noticed had been cleared of stubble. Daisy took a little finger and slowly poked at his puffed cheeks.

"Do you care to hold her while I get the bandages for her legs?"

Ronnie made a trumpet sound with his lips while nodding his head. Daisy slapped his cheeks, not even turning her head when Ruthie left them to get the bandages. On her way to the back, Ruthie made a quick assessment of how the other patients in ICU were doing. It looked like

Darryl, of course, had things under control. The room had been returned to normal, and all the patients returned to their beds after last night's attack. The patients looked well—some slept, some played cards or talked. She felt her tight chest ease. She wanted to care for Daisy, but she also had a job to do, and even though she knew Darryl would help her, she didn't like people taking up her slack. How would she be able to work and care for Daisy too? She shook her head. She'd worry about that after she talked to Tom. She grabbed the bandages and watched Ronnie teach Daisy patty-cake. Daisy's smile brightened her whole face. Ruthie stood and watched them for a beat. *Ronnie will make a great father one day*, she thought. His eyes caught hers and her cheeks heated. "Okay, you keep doing what you're doing, and I'll get her legs cleaned and bandaged."

Ronnie took Daisy's hand and made her do a little salute. "Aye aye, captain."

Daisy's happiness was contagious. The whole ICU stopped what they were doing to watch Ronnie and Daisy play while Ruthie worked. It took no time for Ruthie to have the medicine cream spread and her little legs rewrapped. "What a good patient you are?" she said, bending down to nuzzle Daisy's cheek. Daisy closed her eyes and nuzzled back. Her stomach growled.

Ruthie leaned up. "She's so hungry. Do you care to watch her some more and I'll go grab some food and water?" Ruthie looked down at Ronnie's feet and noticed his bandages were not white, but a dusty gray. "When I get back, I'll need to apply some fresh bandages to your feet too. How'd they get so dirty?"

He sighed. "The mortar attack, I had to help Darryl get some of the patients under the bed. Maybe Daisy can help distract me while you do it."

Ruthie smiled, but guilt built up in her chest. She should have been here. Ronnie shouldn't have been the one helping Darryl get patients under the bed. It should have been her.

Ruthie slipped out as Ronnie and Daisy played. Ronnie wadded up pieces of paper from a notebook and he helped Daisy throw them in a trash can Ruthie had placed near the bed. Another patient in a wheelchair, who had been shot in the side but mending quite well, helped collect the wadded balls that didn't make it into the goal.

On her way to the mess hall, she decided to stop by Tom's office first. She stood in front of the door and took in a big breath before raising her hand to knock.

"Come in," she heard him yell behind the door.

Tom sat at his desk chair. His scowl disappeared when he saw her. "McKay! Just the woman I wanted to see. Take a seat."

She plopped down in the familiar seat across from his desk. It always felt like she was in trouble when she came here.

"I heard you have a cute stowaway."

Ruthie cleared the lump in her throat. Of course he'd already heard about Daisy, probably from Darryl. She nodded. "Yes sir."

"What are your plans?"

The question sounded so abrupt and open-ended. This was the Army. She didn't get to make plans. Plans were made for her.

"My plans?" she said, but it came out a soft whisper.

Tom nodded. "Yes. Jake and John filled me in on the condition of the village. They also told me how they pulled you on board after your shift. They had nothing but good things to say about how you did in the field. We need some good flight nurses. You interested?" he asked, his eyebrows raising high on his forehead.

Ruthie tensed. "No sir. I don't think I'm cut out for that kind of adventure."

Tom laughed. "I'm sure you are, but I get it. So, what are you plans with the little girl?"

Ruthie's throat almost closed. With his one question, every idea she had vanished immediately from her mind and all that remained was a deep longing she'd barely admitted to even herself—she wanted to keep her. But was it even possible? And if so, would she be a good mother? And how could she work and take care of a little girl? She had a job to do.

"If you will give me permission, I'd like to ask John and Jake to take me back to the village to see if she has any living family."

The smile left Tom's face. He leaned back in his chair. The squeak of the springs resounded in the office, sending chills down Ruthie's arms.

"And what are you going to do if she has no family left?"

Ruthie felt lightheaded. She swallowed. "I don't want to take her from her country, her culture, but if she has no one, I don't want to put her in an orphanage either."

Tom shifted. Ruthie watched his jaw work. "That's good to hear. Did you know, before I took this position, I was a flight nurse?"

Ruthie shook her head.

Tom swallowed, "Yes, and I'll tell you I saw a lot of orphaned children. And I saw the orphanages they lived in. They aren't safe, and they barely have enough food to feed the children." His eyes looked past her; a deep pain set behind them as if he was remembering something.

Before she could stop herself, what she really wanted to know escaped from her lips. "Could I adopt her? Take her home with me?" She braced herself for a look of pity, but it didn't come. Instead, Tom's face brightened.

"I already started looking into this for you, just in case. I'd even thought I might try to adopt her if you didn't want to."

Ruthie's breath left her in a rush. "You were?"

He smiled. "Yeah, McKay. I'm not heartless. Plus, my wife is an angel sent from heaven, and she wouldn't mind. I investigated the adoption process, and it's actually been done before. Now, it's not an easy process, but I'll help you. But you must finish your tour. And you may have to re-up if the process isn't complete by next March when your DEROS would come in."

She opened her mouth, but he held up a hand, stopping her.

"I know what you're going to say. How am I going to be able to do my job and take care of Daisy. Is that what you've named her?"

Numb, Ruthie nodded.

"I think I've got a plan for that too. I order you to go find and talk with Patty. She was here earlier and left, heading to get some food. Go. Find her now."

"But..." Ruthie stammered.

"Get out of here, before I sign the papers and make you a permanent flight nurse."

Ruthie went straight to the mess hall. Not to find Patty like Tom has ordered. She needed to get Daisy food. She didn't care if Patty was there and she didn't care if Tom had ordered her to speak to her, she wouldn't do it. This was one directive she wouldn't obey.

Ruthie slipped inside the mess hall and grabbed a metal tray, making her way to the line. The lunch for the day looked pretty good, and her stomach began to cramp. She realized she couldn't remember the last time she'd eaten either. In the line, she skipped the creamed ground beef on toast and chose roasted chicken, vegetables, two rolls, and two pieces of apple pie. The man with a scruffy face wearing a white, stained apron stared at her when she asked him for chicken and vegetables for two. But to her relief, he didn't ask questions or give her any trouble. He took his tongs and picked up another piece of chicken and put it on her tray. She thanked him.

At the end of the line, she grabbed a handful of napkins. She opened them and spread them across the tray to keep the bugs and any rain off. When she turned to go, her eyes locked onto Patty sitting at a table near the back with other nurses. Patty had pulled her hair into a messy bun. Dark circles sat under her eyes. She looked half asleep as she took a bite of pie. Ruthie tried to hurry and leave before being spotted, but it was too late. Patty looked up. When they made eye contact, Patty's face flushed. She began to scramble out from the table and Ruthie quickened her pace to the door.

"Wait!" Patty called after her, but Ruthie didn't stop. She shoved the door open with her shoulder and left the mess hall.

"Wait, please. Ruthie, please!" Patty pleaded.

Ruthie could hear Patty's boots thumping the ground behind her. Patty panted hard. She pushed her way around Ruthie and stood in front of her, blocking her way. Ruthie tried to go to the right, but Patty moved quickly to block her again.

Ruthie huffed. "Get out of my way."

She held out her hands. "Look, I'm sorry! I was wrong. I didn't listen. Please let me explain."

Ruthie looked down at the tray of food in her hand. "I've got to get this to ICU for..." her voice trailed off. She didn't know if she wanted to tell Patty about Daisy.

"For the little girl?" Patty said softly.

Ruthie opened her mouth, the moment of shock passed, and she knew Tom had told Patty everything. "Yes, for her—Daisy," she said curtly. She didn't like the thought of Patty and Tom discussing her or Daisy.

"I'll walk with you." Patty insisted.

They began to walk. Ruthie concentrated on the space ahead of her while Patty spoke quickly. Words spilled out of her like she needed to get everything out before Ruthie could run away.

"You were right about Mark. He told me he loved me and said he'd leave his wife and marry me. But the very first night we were in Hawaii, he snuck out of the room. I think he thought I was sleeping." She reached back to straighten her bun. "I wasn't. I followed him. I don't know why, but I did. I found him in a telephone booth with the door wide open. He never saw me, but I could hear everything. He had called his wife. He told her how much he missed and loved her. How she meant everything to him, and he couldn't wait to see her again. I felt duped. I thought about Connie and who knows how many other women he'd done it to. So, I left. I went back to the room we shared, packed, and left before he ever came back. I spent the rest of the night at the hospital there. I told them how we were low on supplies. I did the whole *Petticoat Junction* thing. They loaded me up with everything we needed, and the next day, I caught a plane back. Ruthie, I'm sorry." She held out her hands. "It's just this place is horrible. We see death every day, and I just wanted to feel something, you know, something other than scared all the time. I thought that it was love and he felt the same way, but I was wrong. So wrong."

Ruthie swallowed, unable to answer, because she understood. Even while she played cards with a patient, danced at the O club, or laughed with friends, there existed this underlying fear buried deep inside that this day could be her last. Ruthie knew that fear because although no one ever spoke about it, it ran deep within her veins and everyone's here—a sure constant.

Patty sighed. "I'm most sorry about believing what he said about you. I should have known. I've never had many girls for friends. And I sure don't want to lose you. Can you ever forgive me?"

Ruthie's eyes watered. She wanted to stay mad at Patty. Oh, dear Lord, how she wanted to stay mad, but being mad took so much energy, and she didn't have any energy to spare. All her energy needed to be focused on the little girl she now needed to care for.

Patty swallowed. "Tom told me about the little girl. Daisy, right? Do you want to adopt her?"

The abrupt change in topics made Ruthie stop. Patty stopped too.

"I'm sorry if I overstepped. But I think I can help."

Ruthie sucked in a breath. She wanted to talk to someone about it, but she didn't know if Patty was the right one anymore. Still, Ruthie's options for conversation were thin. It wasn't like she could pick up the phone and call Hazel or Sandra, or even her best friend, Margarette Ann. She let out a long sigh, and without thinking too much about it, she forgave Patty and all the words she had bottled up poured out. "I've never thought about being a mother until I woke up today with her cuddled to my chest. It broke something inside of me and I want to keep her safe. I want her to have a good life away from the war. I know we need to go back to the village and see if she has any family left. Because if she does, then that's who she needs to be with, but..." her voice dropped. "But I feel like an evil person because a part of me hopes there's no one left." She clutched the metal food tray tighter. "It's horrible I know."

Patty shook her head. "I understand. Even though its wrong, it also feels right."

Ruthie met Patty's eyes. Maybe she did understand. *Help me dear Lord if it's wrong*, Ruthie silently prayed, *because it does feel so right.*

Patty reached out and touched Ruthie's hands clutching the metal tray. "Come on. Let's get Daisy some food and I'll tell you my plan as we walk."

On the way back to ICU, Patty told Ruthie what she'd discussed with Tom. She wanted to move back in the hootch with Ruthie. She would be moved out of surgery and to ICU. She admitted that move was a little selfish on her part, but also safer for everyone in surgery because if she ever had to work with Mark again, she'd stab him in the eye with a needle.

Patty said Tom had agreed to put Ruthie and Patty on a swing shift where they worked odd hours, so they could both care for Daisy. They'd still be required to help with pushes. Ruthie listened, taking in everything Patty said. She had something like hope growing in her heart. She tamped it down. Daisy belonged to her family, and if they were still alive, she would go back to live with them. The thought of letting Daisy go almost made it impossible to breathe. Ruthie wondered how it could be possible to feel love for someone you just met, but she did. She loved Daisy. The thought made her want to weep. Because of the love she felt, she wanted the best for Daisy and the best thing would be returning her to her family. In the meantime, until they received news about Daisy's family, Ruthie would care for the sweet little girl and love her for as long as she could.

Chapter 43

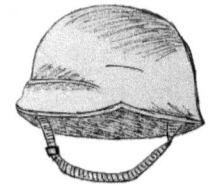

JOEL, AUGUST 1969

Joel woke up with a start. He leaned forward, rubbing his face. Sweat covered his body. The dream felt so real that he could still smell Chad's blood running through his fingers. He pressed hard on bullet wounds, but they wouldn't stop bleeding. The raw metallic smell lingered in the recesses of his mind. The wind blew his poncho-made tent, making the sides flap. It didn't seem real. Even when he watched the chopper take his friend's body away, reality wouldn't set in. *How can he be gone?*

The night after Chad had died, Lieutenant Roberts had promised they'd head back to Camp Hochmuth. Joel needed to get back to camp. He needed to write Hazel—his lifeline. They'd not received any mail since they'd left, and he needed to know if she and the baby were okay. An overwhelming feeling that the universe wasn't done screwing him settled on his shoulders. If he could just know that she and the baby were fine, then maybe he could survive the pain he felt filling up his lungs since Chad had been killed. Nothing seemed fair or right. He balled his fists and pressed them into his forehead. But they weren't going back to camp. Lieutenant

Roberts had informed them plans had changed. *Lies and more lies.* The new orders Lieutenant Roberts received kept them on a path toward the Ho Chi Minh trail. They were to keep humping toward the trail while looking for more Viet Cong hidden tunnels and bunkers.

It didn't matter to the higher-ups that his friend had died or that Pen was unstable. Joel had tried to talk to Pen several times after Chad died, but he refused to speak to him. Joel laid back down against the solid ground, covering his face with his arm. Now he didn't have Chad to help pull Pen out of whatever funk he was feeling. A heaviness settled in Joel's chest. *How can I help Pen when I can't even help myself?*

After the 101st had eaten a small breakfast of C-rats, they began to gather up their gear for another long day of humping. At least it hadn't started raining yet, Joel thought and wadded up his poncho. He stuck it in his rucksack. As he swung it over his shoulder, he saw some men pointing toward his direction. When the men parted, he saw Lieutenant Roberts heading his way. Joel's heart rate spiked and the hairs on the back of his neck stood.

"Davenport," Lieutenant Roberts said, approaching him.

Joel wanted to breathe, but he couldn't. He knew what was coming.

"You're the point man today. We leave in ten."

There was no offer of condolences for recently losing his best friend, no look of sympathy, no words of encouragement, just an order, and then Lieutenant Roberts was gone. Joel knew he should be terrified, but the anger he felt made any fear a reasonable man would have felt evaporate.

"What a tool."

Joel's head snapped to the side. He hadn't realized Harvey Davis stood beside him. Harvey slugged him in the shoulder hard. Joel frowned and rubbed it.

"You're gonna be fine. You know what to look for. Just take your time."

Joel held out the hand-held metal detector while using his other hand to swing a machete to cut through the brush. It was a slow, arduous process. Sweat ran down his face and stung his eyes. He paused to wipe it away with his arm. He sucked in air. Mongooses chattered in the brush, and a pungent smell of moist leaves rotting filled his nostrils. He tilted his head up to see a canopy of limbs and green blocking most of the sunlight.

In just a few more yards, it felt like he landed on the moon. There was no need to hack at vegetation anymore. The leaves on the trees had shriveled and died. Black limbs rose into the sky. The smell made him wince and he covered his nose. He stopped, making all the men behind him stop with him. The wasteland spread before him for at least a mile.

"What's going on?" Lieutenant Roberts said, coming to stand beside him. "Oh, I've heard of this," he said.

"What happened?" Joel asked.

"Agent Orange. Kills the foliage so we can spot the Viet Cong and NVA."

"Has it worked?" Joel asked, taking in the devastation. He thought about the beautiful forest he, Hazel, and Ruthie had grown up in.

"Sure, sure. Now hurry and hump through here. We'll be exposed, so rush it."

Joel nodded and continued. Black leaves swirled around him as they dropped from dead limbs. *This looks like something out of a nightmare.* He picked up his pace even though his muscles ached. When they hit green again, he'd never been happier to hack away at the foliage with his machete.

By the time the sky had turned red and purple, exhaustion had set in, and the hand holding the machete had started to go numb. He heard a hollow caw from a bird in the distance, and a muscle cramp shot through his hand, causing his fingers to lose their grip on the machete. He instinctively lunged forward to catch it but thought better of it. He pulled his hand back sharply, not wanting to grab the wrong end and be forced to have Danny Barnes sew him up out here in the field.

He watched the machete fall, as if in slow motion. It tumbled to the ground in front of his feet. When it hit the ground in front of his boot, dirt caved in. Joel thought of the grave and being sucked in the hole with Chad. He froze. His legs refused to move. Before it was too late, someone from behind grabbed the back of his fatigues. His body leaned far over the hole, his boots barely on the ground. Joel heard a sickening snap and metallic crack as metal hit metal.

"It's a booby trap!" Harvey yelled.

Joel felt the grip on the back of his shirt tighten. The collar cut into his throat. He wanted to scream. His boots started to slip. His feet fumbled to find traction. The heavy metal detector started to send him over the edge.

"Help me!" Havey screamed. "I'm losing him!"

In a fraction of a second, hands grabbed Joel's arms, and everyone pulled him away from the dark hole. Danny, Harvey, and Joel fell back onto the dirt inches from the deep cavity. Joel clawed at his shirt, pulling it away from his neck so he could breathe. "It's one of those bear trap ones," he said between gasps.

They dropped to their knees and crawled as close as they could to examine it, careful not to get too close to the edge. They cleared away large leaves and grass. The hole had been made to look like regular ground, part of the jungle floor. Anyone could have mistaken it, until they stepped on it. *I could have stepped on it.* Joel shivered. Like his machete, his leg would have disappeared into the hole. Joel's stomach clenched when Danny shone his flashlight into the darkness. At the bottom were boards filled with jagged metal pieces and nails. The mechanism had been triggered when the machete hit it. The boards and jagged metal pieces had snapped together, just like a bear trap. The machete handle lay in two pieces. *That could have been my leg.* Goose pimples spread across Joel's arms even though he wasn't cold.

"Good thing you're clumsy," Harvey said.

"Let's break for today and set up camp," Lieutenant Roberts called out. "I want a thorough perimeter clearing. Let's make sure there's no more of those booby traps around here, or God-forbid a stray toe popper."

Chapter 44

HAZEL

Hazel rocked Aaron in the wooden rocking chair her father had made for them. Aaron's tiny mouth twitched in his sleep. *The Lucy Show* played on the television for background noise. She barely ever turned on the television anymore, but afterwork, with Sandra and the boys still at church, everything in the house was quiet—too quiet. Last week, the war had stopped being the headline news and the murder of seven people by a group of teens became the top story. Violence didn't just exist across the ocean. Instead of watching television, when Aaron slept, Hazel usually wrote her stories, but tonight she was exhausted. Louanne had called in sick to work, so Hazel had not had a chance to sit down all day long.

After *The Lucy Show* ended, the nightly news theme music began to play. Hazel frowned. She didn't want to watch the news. She tried to stand to flip the television off, but Aaron fussed in her arms. She sat back, not wanting to wake him. She looked up at the screen as a man with a grave face appeared.

"Sadly, we begin our broadcast with news of the war. Last month turned out to be another bloody month, with five hundred and thirty-seven men giving their lives for the cause."

The number made Hazel's blood run cold. *So many—dead. In a month! And the newscaster only said "men?" What about Ruthie?* Surely, there were other women there like Ruthie. Hazel hoped that by not mentioning women, it meant none had died and they were all safe, but she knew deep down that couldn't be true. It was war. *But if some women died or were injured, would there be any mention of it?* A sob stuck in her throat. She worked her way off the rocking chair, trying not to wake Aaron. She couldn't listen to this anymore. Not when Joel and Ruthie were still there.

Hazel gently laid Aaron in his baby bed. The mobile her mother had sent him made a tinkling sound when she laid him down. The hanging moon and clouds swayed. She still hadn't decided if she'd visit her mother, and it had almost been a month now since she'd found out from Oliver she was dying.

"She doesn't have much longer," Oliver's words came back to her.

Why did she feel so guilty for not going? The woman had been awful to her before leaving her and Ruthie—two small girls without a mother. Hazel stood and lightly ran her finger down Aaron's soft arm. He sniffed. She could never leave her son. But what would it hurt to say good-bye? She knew her mother didn't deserve it, but if it would get rid of this guilt that ate at her, wouldn't that alone be worth it?

⁂

The next day, Hazel had mentioned going to see her mother to Sandra. Sandra didn't voice an opinion on whether she thought Hazel was doing the right thing or not. Sandra only promised to look after Aaron while Hazel made the trip to Mansfield.

Hazel parked in front of her mother and Oliver's brick house. She wasn't exactly sure how she ended up here. She gripped the steering wheel, her knuckles white. She remembered when Ruthie and she had been little, Ruthie telling her, "I hope she never comes home." And their mother never did; she'd made a home here without them. This felt like a bad idea. Her hands still firmly in place on the steering wheel, she stared out the windshield at the beautifully manicured lawns of the neighborhood. She couldn't do this. She needed to go, but before she could turn the car back on, something knocked on the passenger side window. Hazel screamed. Oliver leaned over and Hazel tried to calm her nerves. She rolled the window down.

"Olivia, my daughter, saw you sitting out here. Do you wanna come in?"

Hazel bit her lip. "I-I don't think so."

He sighed. "She's really doing poorly today."

Hazel could see the pain in his face. It radiated from his eyes. They were dull blue with black rings sunk deep below them. She wondered if they had once been bright and full of life. Had he been happy with the life he had shared with her mother? She couldn't help but think that he had been part of the reason her mother left them. The thought made her stiffen.

"I won't stay long," her voice sounded harsher than she intended.

He blew out a breath. "Thank you," he said, closing his eyes briefly.

Oliver led the way, and Hazel's stomach flipped inside her with each step they took toward the front door. He opened the door and held out his hand for her to go on in.

Inside, the smell of air freshener hung thick, attempting to cover the smell of sickness, but the smell still lingered in the air. Hazel's eyes burned. She squeezed them closed and blinked them quickly. Oliver walked past her, leading Hazel farther into her mother's home. She glanced right and left, taking in everything. The kitchen entrance sat on the right. Hazel peered in. The floor had black and white tile squares and turquoise appliances and cabinet fronts. Hazel wondered if her mother had spent time in there cooking dinners for her new family. Hazel grimaced. She had to stop. Her mother was dying.

"She's in the living room," Oliver whispered. "She can't make it up the stairs anymore to the bedroom. I tried to carry her, but I have a bad back." His cheeks pinkened.

In the living room, her mother lay on a forest green sofa. The wooden legs dark against the white shag carpet. Thick blankets covered her mother's thin frame even though it felt stifling inside the room. Hazel looked at her mother's face. Her eyes were closed. Her thick blonde beautiful hair was gone. Now it hung limp and thin with patches of scalp showing through. Her cheeks were sunken in, and she looked older than Hazel knew she was. Oliver went and gently touched her shoulder. Her eye lashes fluttered, and she gave him a dazed, sleepy look.

"Dear, you have company."

Her words slurred. "How do I look?" She tried to sit up on her own but couldn't.

He leaned down and kissed the top of her head. "You look wonderful. Like always. Let me help you."

Oliver helped position her with her back propped against a huge fluffy pillow. It seemed to swallow her frail frame. She had always been slender, but now she appeared skeletal. The sight made Hazel wince. When her mother was comfortable, she looked toward Hazel. Her thin eyebrows furrowed, making the lines in her forehead deeper.

"Oliver?" Every word seemed difficult to form. "Who is this?"

Hazel's breath caught in her chest. Her mother didn't recognize her. Hazel took a step back. Oliver put out his hand, mouthing the words please wait.

"It's Hazel, dear. You remember," he prodded.

Her mother closed her eyes. Hazel could see her eyes moving side to side under her lids, as if searching her mind for a relic of the past. When she opened her eyes, she looked directly at Hazel.

"Of course, I remember," her eyes began to grow watery, and tears began to spill out of them. "My eyesight is poor. The sickness. I'm sorry, so sorry, Hazel." The tears poured and dripped from her chin. Oliver wiped her face with a handkerchief, put it in her hand, and laid it on top of the blankets covering her.

"I'll leave you two alone," he said. Before he left, he pushed a wooden chair with matching green cushions closer to the sofa. He motioned for Hazel to have a seat. She worked her bottom lip with her teeth, wondering if she should sit or just leave. She looked over at her mother. Her face wet with tears, and Hazel sat down.

After he left, a thick silence spread between them. Hazel couldn't think of anything to say, so she stared at her hands and worried with a hangnail. Her mother began to cough. The cough sounded deep in her chest. It racked her whole body. Hazel's head shot up.

"Do I need to get Oliver?"

Her mother held up her hand and shook her head. When she'd regained her composure, she wiped her mouth with the handkerchief Oliver had left.

"How are you?" she asked after a few minutes passed.

"I'm fine," Hazel said not feeling the need to say more.

Her mother pushed her head back into the pillows. "I heard your boy is doing well."

Hazel didn't want to talk about Aaron with her mother. She had come to see her, but her mother didn't deserve more than that. "Yes, he's well."

Her mother swallowed and winced. She licked her cracked lips, but it did nothing to help. "I heard about Ruthie. Why'd she volunteer to go to Nam as a nurse?"

Hazel glared; heat flushed through her. "What do you care anyway?"

Her mother flinched at the question. Hazel closed her eyes and gripped the bridge of her nose with her fingers.

"I'm sorry." Hazel sighed. "I'm trying here."

Her mother started to twist the handkerchief in her hands. "Your question is a fair one," she said weakly. "I deserve it and probably this cancer rotting me from the inside out." She gave Hazel a half grin.

Hazel didn't respond. She felt angry with her mother, but she didn't hate her, not anymore.

Her mother closed her eyes. "I need to tell you something. I don't know if your daddy ever will. But I think you girls deserve the truth. You need to know why I did what I did." She looked at Hazel. "I wanted to tell both of ya'll together, but I don't think I'll make it until Ruthie comes home."

Ruthie coming home. The thought made Hazel's insides loosen somewhat, and she sure wished her sister was here right now.

Her mother continued. "Your father and I were young when we married. Too young. I wasn't ready," she sniffed. "I couldn't handle it. Everything in that old house needed fixing, and we didn't have enough money to do it. Then you came along, and your father was smitten with you," she looked over at Hazel and smiled. "Any extra we had went to you." Her mother wiped her mouth with the handkerchief. "We started to fight about money. Then your father got that job working the roads. It made more money, but it meant I was alone, on my own for the week. Too young, to be left all alone with a baby. And the woods out there, well they're isolating."

Hazel bit her tongue. She wouldn't scream at a dying woman. This woman had left her and Ruthie alone in those isolating woods, but to them it hadn't felt like that. When they'd met Joel, the woods felt like home.

"You were two, maybe a little older. It's hard to remember now. It's been so long. A lifetime ago," she breathed in deep. Her breath rattled in her chest as she wheezed. "That's when I met Oliver. He had a good job. He came from a fine family. I enchanted him," she held out a finger, "those are his words mind you. I think I was jealous of you, Hazel. How crazy is that? Because you were the apple of your father's eye."

Flashes of her mother calling her ugly and telling her she had horsehair ran through her head.

"Then Ruthie came along," her mother looked back down at her hands. "When I told your father I was pregnant, he knew immediately what I had done."

Hazel folded her arms in front of her to keep from covering her ears. She didn't want to hear any more of her mother's story, but like a horrible catastrophe, she couldn't stop herself from asking, "What did you do?"

Her mother let out a huff of air. "Ruthie isn't your father's daughter. She's Oliver's. Your father knew from the beginning, but he didn't care."

"What?" Hazel sprung up out of her seat. "Ruthie is Oliver's daughter!"

Her mother started to cough, "Please sit. I can't handle the moving around. It's too much for me. Please let me finish."

Hazel made herself sit back down. She felt lightheaded.

"I don't understand. Then why didn't you just leave then when you found out you were pregnant with Oliver's baby?"

Her mother squeezed her eyes closed. "Sorry, sometimes a wave of nausea hits me." She reached up and touched her thin hair like she wanted to twirl it with her fingers before remembering most of her beautiful hair was gone. She dropped her hand back on the blanket. "You don't understand. If people knew I had an affair and gotten pregnant, I'd have been an outcast. Your grandmother would have disowned me."

Hazel gasped. "Grandmother never knew about Ruthie?"

Her mother shook her head. "No one did but your father and Oliver. Your father said he'd take care of me and the baby. He'd act like the baby was his so no one would know. So I... I..."

"Wouldn't become the town outcast or disowned because you were easy," Hazel finished her sentence for her.

Her mother cringed at her words. "Yes." She swallowed and Hazel could see how difficult it was for her. "When Ruthie was born, he did exactly like he promised. He raised her as his own. He loved you both so much. And I think we were happy for a time."

Hazel gritted her teeth, "Then why'd you leave?"

Her mother looked up at the ceiling, "I ran into Oliver again years later. He'd started his own dentist practice here in Mansfield. He'd never married. Said he couldn't get me off his mind. I felt like it was fate. And we fell in love all over again." Her head lobbed to the side. Her glassy eyes met Hazel's. "I don't expect you to understand. But love makes you do strange things."

Hazel felt a tightness in her chest. "You're right. I don't understand. Because I know I'd do anything in the world for my son. I'd have died if it meant Madelyn Ray could have lived. All I see when I look at you is a selfish, spoiled brat who loved the idea of having a nice house and prestige more than she loved her own children. I need to go. I wish I never came here."

Hazel tried to stand and leave, but her mother began to cry. "I'm sorry. I realize that now. I'm so sorry. I treated you girls so wrong."

"There's one thing I don't understand. Why didn't you take Ruthie with you? When you left us. If she was Oliver's, why didn't you take her?"

Her mother took a shallow breath. "I tried," she wiped the corners of her mouth. "Your father wouldn't let me. He said she was his daughter and your sister. It didn't matter to him if she wasn't his blood. He wouldn't let me split you both up, and I couldn't take a chance he'd fight to get her back and cause a scandal because of my affair. So, I left her."

Her mother nodded and Hazel stood up. She couldn't handle any more.

"I better go. I need to get home."

Her mother put out her hand. It hung there in the air, thin and spotted. Hazel hesitated but then took it. It felt like bones in her hand.

"I wanted you to know everything. Before I was gone." She closed her eyes. "I did a lot of wrong by you and your sister. I see that now. I don't know why it takes dying to help see all your wrongs more clearly," she chuckled then coughed. "I can't ask for Ruthie's forgiveness because she's not here." Her mother's cloudy eyes looked up, meeting hers. "I know I don't deserve it, but I'm asking for yours."

❧❧❧❧❧ ❦❦❦❦❦

H azel drove straight home, but instead of going inside her duplex, she walked over to her father's. She knocked on the door. Ms. Faye opened it. Her smile spread wide across her sweet face.

"Oh, Hazel, what a pleasant surprise. Arvel," she called inside. "It's Hazel."

Her father came to the door. "What are ya doin' standing out here? Come on in," he said, looking confused.

Hazel shook her head, "Nah, Dad, can we talk?"

His mouth pulled into a tight line, "Yeah, girl, of course. Is everything alright?"

"Out here," Hazel motioned at the stoop in front of the door.

He looked at Ms. Faye and she nodded. He walked outside and Ms. Faye closed the door behind him. Hazel heard it click.

She plopped down on the stoop and her father dropped down beside her with a grunt.

"I'm getting too old to get this low."

His big body filled most of the space on the stoop. She looped her arm inside of his and laid her head on his shoulder. They sat there for a moment. Hazel listened to the wind blow the chimes Joel had hung in front of their door before he left for the war. The shimmering notes played a soft sad song.

"Why didn't you ever tell me?"

Her father laid his head on her head, "Tell you what, girl?"

"I went to see Mama today."

He didn't move his head, but she heard him suck in a deep breath. "She's got cancer, I heard," he said softly.

"She does."

He sighed, "She told you about Ruthie." It wasn't a question.

"Yeah, she did."

"Girl, no matter what she told you, Ruthie is my daughter. Just like you're my daughter. Blood or no blood, you both were mine."

"I understand. She said you wouldn't let her split us up."

He didn't respond. He didn't have to.

"Mama asked me to forgive her for leaving us."

Her father turned, taking her in his arms. She laid her head against his chest like she did when she was little and breathed in his woodsy cologne smell. She wrapped her arms around him.

"I did. I let go of all my anger, Daddy," she said, the sobs rising up in her throat, choking her. "I did it. I forgave her." She pulled back from her father to look in his face. "But please tell me there's no more secrets out there. I don't think I can handle any more."

Her father chuckled and wrapped her in his big arms. "There are no more secrets, girl. You know them all. Now, how do we tell your sister?"

Chapter 45

RUTHIE

R uthie worked with Tom to arrange a trip back to the village. He suggested not bringing Daisy because the trip might be dangerous. He'd told Ruthie the woman with the broken leg from Daisy's village was still in Ward Three. With the help of a local Vietnamese woman named Mai, who worked in the kitchen, Ruthie visited Ward Three and spoke to the woman. A clean plaster case surrounded the woman's broken leg. Ruthie spoke to the woman while Mai translated. The woman told Ruthie that she knew Daisy's parents and grandparents and she agreed to go with them to the village to find Daisy's family. Ruthie felt excitement mixed with dread start to rise in her chest. They could find Daisy's family and then she'd have to give her back. *It's for the best*, she kept repeating to herself.

Ruthie asked the woman the question she'd been dying to know ever since she'd seen Daisy's big, dark brown eyes. "Do you know her name? Her real name?"

Mai relayed the question to the woman and Ruthie's nerves vibrated waiting for an answer. The woman closed her eyes and shook her head. She apologized. She said she did not, but remembered hearing her grandmother call her Hoa nhỏ, which Ruthie was happy to learn meant little flower. The woman told Ruthie that she wished to leave the hospital and return to her village. She missed her home. Ruthie nodded and promised to speak to Darryl about the woman's wishes. Darryl reluctantly agreed to allow the woman to stay in the village, but before they left, he instructed the woman on how to properly care for her broke leg and explained when she could remove her cast.

The morning of the trip, Ruthie stood with Mai and the woman from Daisy's village, waiting near the helicopter pad. The woman leaned on her crutches, and Mai stood close beside her. Neither spoke, and both squinted into the air, waiting for their ride. Ruthie could practically feel the nervous anticipation radiating off the women. She tried to hold it together for them, but her stomach roiled inside of her. Today could be the day that changed her life and Daisy's life forever. Ruthie tried to calm her nerves and thought about how sweet Daisy looked when she left the hootch this morning cuddled next to Patty. She knew if they found someone in Daisy's family, it would be a good thing, but it would crush her.

The sun peaked out behind dark storm clouds. The pink sky stretched across the horizon. Ruthie hoped the rain would hold off until they returned. Mai pointed into the air. Both Ruthie and the village woman stared where she pointed. In the distance, a small dark dot moved in their direction—their ride. Ruthie felt a fresh batch of chill bumps break out across her skin and her stomach twisted harder.

⚘⚘⚘⚘⚘ ⚘⚘⚘⚘⚘

Ruthie had not been surprised to see Jake and John were the ones picking them up. Their bright smiling faces calmed her. When the helicopter landed, John leaped out and ran to give her a huge hug, squeezing her so tight she felt her bones rub together.

He yelled over the whooshing helicopter propellers. "Your chauffeurs have arrived." After he helped her and the other women into the helicopter, he showed them all how to buckle in. Both women's hands shook as they snapped their buckles in place. The women held hands, gripping so tight Ruthie could see their knuckles turn white. In an instant, Jake lifted off, Ruthie's stomach rising with the motion. The women let out gasps of air and squeezed their hands together tighter.

The trip to the village felt like it took ages. Ruthie bit her fingernails then forced herself to stop by sliding her hands under her jiggling legs. She needed to trust that God knew what was best for her and Daisy. Ruthie prayed for Daisy's family to be alive because she knew deep down, even though she'd miss Daisy like crazy, that this would be the easiest route for them both. She closed her eyes and pictured happy images of Daisy reuniting with her family. She imagined smiling faces and tears. The thoughts made joy blossom in Ruthie's heart. But, three hours later, the happy images of Daisy being reunited with her family were gone.

The destruction of the village took Ruthie's breath away. Even though she'd been here right after the bombing happened, she'd been more focused on caring for the people. Now she stood frozen, taking in the complete devastation of the area. Heaps of charred huts laid crumpled on the ground. Craters caused by mortars pocked the area, making deep valleys near the few huts that remained intact. The villagers sat dazed around cookfires like they were unsure what they should do now. Ruthie had brought some medical supplies with her, and with Mai's help, she began asking if anyone needed medical attention.

Ruthie worked on cleaning and wrapping wounds while the village woman hobbled on her crutches asking questions of the villagers about Daisy's family. John and Jake stood close to Ruthie with guns held ready to protect her.

"Do you think she's having any luck?" John asked.

Ruthie shrugged, trying to concentrate on the patient in front of her. The man sat on the ground. His long white hair fell into his eyes and his scraggly beard hung long on his chest. The wrinkles along his face were deep like the crevices of a river. Ruthie had examined him, and he seemed to be in mostly good condition. He had superficial abrasions on his arms and legs. Healing burns covered the palms of his hands and his arms. Ruthie rubbed some ointment on his burns, but what she worried most about was a piece of wood embedded in the man's leg. The skin had already turned red around the area and felt warm to the touch. Ruthie knew if she didn't get it out and clean the area, the infection would get worse. She asked Mai to tell him everything she said. "Let him know I've almost got it. And to hold very still. Once I remove it, I've got to clean the area, and it might burn some."

After Mai told him, the man nodded and said something in response. In broken English, Mai said, "He says he knows the family she is looking for." The man stretched his arm out and pointed to the woman with crutches. "He says he's known the grandmother all his life. They grew up together. And he knows the rest of the family too."

Ruthie's head shot up to meet his eyes. Her heart pounded between her ears. She stammered, "Are they alive? W-w-here are they now?"

Mai relayed her questions to him in Vietnamese. The man responded and pointed in another direction. Ruthie's mind reeled and she wished she could understand.

"He said when you are finished, he will take you to them."

Ruthie nodded. Her arms felt heavy, but she made her hands work. She pulled out the piece of wood and cleaned his wound and wrapped it. So, this is it, now he'd take her to Daisy's family. Even though Ruthie's heart broke into a million pieces, she felt happy. Daisy would be reunited with her loved ones. But loneliness settled in the pit of her stomach. She thought about Hazel and how depressed she'd felt after she lost Madelyn Ray. Ruthie knew this wasn't the same, but it still felt like she was losing someone she loved. Ruthie's fingers fumbled with the wrap. When she was done, she looked at him. "Will you take me to Daisy's family now?"

Ruthie, Mai, Jake, and John followed the man. They walked through burnt remnants of his village. The man talked as they went, and Mai told them what he said.

"He says after the bombs, most people that survived left to be with family in other villages."

"What's he going to do? Is he going to leave to be with family?" Ruthie asked.

Mai asked him, and the man laughed and spoke. "He says he is too old, and he has no other family. He has nowhere else to go. He will stay. A few, he says, will stay."

Ruthie looked out at the mounds of charred huts and craters scarring the earth. There wasn't much left to stay for. They followed him to the edge of the village where the openness ended, and they entered the jungle. The shadows from the huge palms and canopy of trees darkened everything around them. Ruthie pushed large leaves away with her hands. Bird calls echoed around them.

"Hey, now, we're not going far in here," Jake said, gripping his rifle tighter as the man continued to walk deeper into the brush.

"We can't, too dangerous," John said. "Who knows who could be hiding behind those trees."

Ruthie's eyes darted side to side. Was this man leading them to danger? Was he secretly a part of the Viet Cong?

Mai relayed what the man said as he motioned with his arms. "He says what he wanted to show you is right up here. Very close."

Ruthie looked at Jake and he shook his head. Ruthie pleaded with him. "He said it's close. Please just a little farther." Ruthie felt desperate. She needed to speak to someone in Daisy's family. She had to meet them. Jake frowned but he didn't stop them from following the man. In a few short paces, they stepped out into a small area that had been cleared of brush. In front of them lay a huge space of overturned earth. It looked like someone had dug a huge hole and filled it in with dirt. The smell of earth and rot hung in the air. Ruthie covered her nose. The man pointed to the loose dirt pile and spoke.

"Here," Mai translated. "He says the family you are looking for is here."

A heavy feeling settled in the pit of Ruthie's stomach. "I don't understand," she said. "I thought he was taking us to them."

The man spoke slowly so Mai could translate. "He agree. He take you to them. This is where they are. They are dead. He said after the bombs, the Americans came and helped clean the area and they buried the dead here. All of them here. In the same grave."

Ruthie's knees buckled and she fell beside the dirt. "How? How did Daisy survive if all her family is dead?"

She didn't mean for Mai to ask him, but she did. The old man stood near her. The story he told gave Ruthie chills.

"The night was calm. The rain had stopped. I remember everyone was happy. The children played under the stars. It was Minh's đầy năm. When the first bomb hit, many of the older children grabbed the younger ones and ran for the trees to hide. I remember explosions all around them. Some of the children made it through. But others hid in their huts." The man shook his head. "They should have all gone for the trees."

Ruthie wiped away tears.

"He says he remembers when it was over. A boy covered in blood brought her back to her hut. But it was on fire. The little girl was so small, but her screams were so loud. Her family was already gone. They had all hidden in the hut. Her legs were bleeding, but she tried to crawl into the fire. He pulled her away himself." The man looked at the burns on his palms. "He asks if she is alright."

Ruthie nodded. "Yes, yes," Ruthie said, trying to speak over the thickness in her throat. "She's doing fine."

He smiled a toothless smile. "Good, good." He looked at Ruthie and said something. She looked toward Mai. "He says don't bring her back here. There is nothing for her here."

Chapter 46

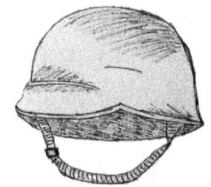

JOEL, SEPTEMBER 1969

Joel jolted awake. He'd dreamed of Chad again. He felt the hard ground under his body, and he tried to center himself back into reality. His chest heaved and his body trembled. The dream, like all the others, felt so real. This time he dreamed Chad had been the point man. Chad's foot raised over a toe popper he didn't see. Joel opened his mouth to scream for him to stop moving, to not take another step, but only high-pitched sounds came out. He remembered Chad's head turning to look at him, then placing a long finger over his mouth before he stepped on it. Joel had awakened before the explosion. Joel touched his throat. He felt intact.

As he and the other members of the 101st packed up their gear, dark clouds loomed in the sky. A crack of thunder shook the ground. Before he could even finish packing, rain began to pour. Lieutenant Roberts called over the gale for them to continue to get ready.

"We're not going to let a little rain stop us, men," he yelled out.

Joel shook his head. Pen walked by. "Can you believe this?" he asked, trying again to talk to Pen. "After yesterday with the booby traps, he's going to make us march in a downpour."

Pen paused and looked over his shoulder. Joel hoped he'd say something, hoped he'd engage, but Pen didn't reply or even nod. His vacant eyes stared right at Joel. Joel hoped he could see his desperation reaching out to him, but Pen just turned and walked away. Joel's limbs went weak. Pen needed help, but out here there was nothing anyone could do. He needed Chad.

Joel watched Pen walk away from the other men and stand on the outskirts of the group—alone. A coldness spread over him when he spotted Lieutenant Roberts walk toward him and start talking. He watched Pen nod. Joel's heart hammered in his chest, and he took off in a sprint toward them.

"What's going on?" he asked, breathlessly when he reached them.

Lieutenant Roberts looked at Joel and frowned. "Giving out the day's duties is all, Davenport."

"What duties did you give Pen today, sir?"

Pen snarled, "What's it to you?"

"He's point man today," Lieutenant Roberts replied, ignoring Pen.

Joel hardly recognized his friend anymore. His soft, kind features were long gone. There was no life in Pen's sunken eyes. The dark rings underneath them seemed to stretch to the tips of his pointed, sharp cheek bones. He looked like he hadn't eaten in weeks.

Lieutenant Roberts stared at Joel. Joel's eyes bounced from Lieutenant Roberts to Pen's twisted face. Pen's neck muscles stretched taut. Joel wiped rain from his face. *What do I do?* His stomach roiled. *What can I say? Pen's gone off the deep end and it'll be safer for everyone if you didn't make him point man today?* Joel looked at Pen, and even though the man standing before him looked nothing like his friend, he knew he couldn't say anything to cause him trouble. He bit the inside of his cheek so hard he tasted metal. Chad wouldn't want Pen to get in trouble. And who's to say Lieutenant Roberts would care anyway. With the number of booby traps out there, he still wanted them to hump in this pour.

"I-I was just going to say," Joel stuttered, feeling the resolve of what he needed to do. "Maybe instead of Pen being point man today, I could do it for you, sir. I'm a whiz at using the hand-held metal detector." The words sounded dumb, and Joel knew it. But it was all he could think of to say.

Lieutenant Roberts looked baffled. "You want to be point man?"

Joel shrugged, "Yes sir." Joel didn't look at Pen, but he could feel his fiery glare on him. It made his skin crawl.

"Everyone has to have a turn, Davenport. I'd think you'd had enough of it, at least for a while, after finding that booby trap and all."

Joel swallowed down bile in the back of his throat as he remembered how close he got to losing his leg. He shook his head. "Just wanna do my part." He took his thumb and motioned toward Pen without looking at him. "And Pen didn't get much sleep last night, so I'll fill in for him."

"I got plenty of sleep," Pen spit out. "I don't need you doing my part for me. I'll do it, sir."

Lieutenant Roberts's eyes passed from Joel to Pen and then back to Joel. "Well, I guess that settles it. Pen, you're point man."

Just as the declaration was settled, the rain stopped as suddenly as it had started. Lieutenant Roberts tilted his head to the sky. "And lookie there! You'll have some clear weather for a while."

When Lieutenant Roberts had walked out of earshot, Pen turned on Joel with vengeance. "I don't need you helping me. I don't need you at all," he said, the muscles working in his jaw.

Joel's eyes blurred and he blinked. Where had his friend gone? "Pen, this isn't like you. I was just trying to help."

"If you want to help, you will stay as far away from me as you can today."

"What does that mean?" Joel asked, as fear ran its icy fingers down the back of his neck.

Pen gave him a smirk then walked away, whistling the melody to "Stairway to Heaven."

Chapter 47

RUTHIE

A few weeks after she'd returned from Daisy's village, Ruthie sat in the squeaky chair across from Tom in his office. He paced behind his desk—back and forth. His hands rubbed his bald head.

"I guess it's official. You do want to adopt her?" He paused and looked at her.

She thought the decision to adopt would have made her happy, and she was happy, but knowing Daisy had lost everyone crushed Ruthie. She'd learned at the village that Daisy's entire family, her father, mother, sister, brother, and grandmother, had taken shelter in the hut. One bomb had killed them all. If it wasn't for the boy who picked up Daisy and hauled her to the forest to hide, she'd have been killed too. A shiver passed through Ruthie's body. Daisy had no family now. Ruthie shook her head. *No*, she told herself for the hundredth time. *She has me*. She straightened her shoulders. "Yes, I'm going to adopt her. What do I have to do to make that happen? Is it even possible?"

Tom plopped down in his chair. He wiped dots of perspiration off his brow. "I made some telephone calls. It's possible, but it's not easy. I've already arranged for you to meet an attorney. His name is Sang Le. His reputation is good, and he speaks fluent English. He is located in Qui Nhon. That's a good way from here, but we'll get you there, don't worry about that."

Ruthie's breath hitched. A meeting with an attorney. This was real. Chills spread over her arms. "When's my appointment?"

Tom folded his hands and laid them across his chest. His brows furrowed. "Have you even sent your family a letter to discuss this with them first? Being a single woman, I'd think you'd like to ask your father or a relative for advice first."

Ruthie shook her head. She couldn't even image how she'd start a letter. How could she ever explain to her family everything that had happened since she'd been here and her desperate need to adopt Daisy. They'd think she'd lost her ever-loving mind. "There's nothing to discuss. Daisy needs me, and I'll do whatever I have to do so she can have a good life."

Tom shrugged one shoulder. "Suit yourself. Your appointment is set for October fifteenth."

Ruthie slumped in the chair. "But that's a month away."

"Yes, it is. And I have no idea what an adoption will entail. It could take a lot longer. I just don't know. You may have to be willing to re-up to see it through."

The thought of staying in Vietnam another year made Ruthie's stomach hurt. Every part of her wanted to go home—to be away from here. She swallowed the bile slowly rising. She wouldn't leave Daisy though, not for anything. "Like I said, I'll do whatever it takes."

Ruthie's nerves were on edge. Tom said he thought the adoption was possible, but she knew he didn't have all the answers. She wouldn't get her real answers until she met with the attorney, but the meeting was ages away. She felt jittery. She bit her nails. She couldn't go back to the hootch where Patty and Daisy were waiting for her—not yet, not until she worked through some things in her mind. Instead, she headed to the

ICU to talk to Ronnie. She needed someone from home. She opened the door and saw Ronnie sitting straight up in his bed, writing in a notebook. His complexion looked normal, and his feet were unwrapped. They stuck out from under his blue blanket. Pink scars dotted the bottom of his feet from his healed wounds. He smiled when he saw her. Ruthie's heart sank. Ronnie would be leaving soon. Darryl had told her yesterday Ronnie had only three more days left, and he'd be heading back to the jungle to meet his platoon. She didn't want him to leave. She wanted him here with her. Not out in the jungle where bouncing betties and bullets waited around every corner.

"What did he say?" Ronnie asked, laying down his pencil. "Can you adopt her?"

Ruthie made herself smile.

"You can! You can do it!" he said, not giving her a chance to respond. He let out a triumphant holler, making everyone in ICU look at them. "Hey everyone, Ruthie here's going to be a mother."

Everyone who could applauded, and Ruthie's face heated.

Darryl walked over. "We need to celebrate."

Ruthie sighed. "No, we don't. Tom said he thought it might be possible. I have an appointment with an attorney, but it's not until October. We don't need to celebrate anything yet."

Ronnie reached for her hand. He took her fingers and held them. The simple gesture made Ruthie shiver. His eyes grew soft. "Listen to the man, Ruthie. I know it will happen. You'll have a daughter soon, and I want to celebrate with you before I go."

Darryl nodded. "Right, Bob Hope..."

A man from the back of the room yelled, "Will never come here. Too dangerous."

The rest of the men raised their voices in agreement.

Darryl raised his hand to silence the men. "Exactly! He'll never come to the 71st, it's too much of a hot spot. But that doesn't mean we can't have a concert here too. We've got some guitars, and I'm sure we could find some singers. We could do it right in the center near the pool. We could build our own stage."

Cheers all around the room rose up.

Ruthie frowned. "Did you forget we are in the midst of the rainy season? You'll never be able to do anything outside."

Ronnie pulled her closer to him and caressed her arm. She felt the heat from her face move to the tip of her ears. Some men whistled.

Ronnie laughed. "We've been wet before haven't we, men!"

The men's voices rose in agreement and Ruthie knew she was losing the argument.

"Please, Ruthie, let a poor soldier, who took you to the prom mind you, celebrate with you before he has to leave." His eyes pleaded, and Ruthie's old feelings for him started to resurface. She tried to push them back down. They were friends. Only friends. She had no time for love. She was going to be a mother.

Darryl hushed everyone and continued. "And our beloved Dr. Gerry is leaving. We can celebrate Ruthie's news and give him the biggest going away party we can! With a concert under the stars!"

Excited murmurs of agreement bubbled through the air. She'd lost the argument. Ruthie leaned down and lightly kissed Ronnie's forehead. "Fine, you win." She laughed. "You all win."

The men's cheers echoed throughout the ICU, and Ronnie's smile stretched from ear to ear.

Chapter 48

HAZEL

Milton came home on a Saturday. Hazel and Sandra had the radio on, dancing around the kitchen to Stevie Wonder's "My Cherie Amour" while they finished dinner—pot roast with baby carrots and tiny golden potatoes. They had moved Aaron's bassinet into the kitchen. Mikey and Mannie laughed and scrambled to catch the rattles Aaron tossed from his bed. After Hazel pulled the pot roast from the oven, she grabbed Sandra's hand and spun her around before letting out a scream. Milton stood in the entrance of the kitchen, a broad smile on his face. Everyone froze in place, staring at him like he couldn't be real.

"You don't have to stop on my account," he chuckled. "I was rather enjoying the show. I guess you didn't hear me knock, so I let myself in."

Sandra raced to him, leaping into his arms. She peppered his face with kisses.

"Daddy!" Mikey yelled and ran to him, grabbing his legs and squeezing.

Mannie toddled to him; his arms high in the air. Milton kissed his wife deep, then picked up both his boys, one in each arm.

"You're home," Sandra said, tears streaking down her face. "I didn't think you were coming until next week."

He leaned over and between his sons kissed her again. "They found me an earlier flight and I took it." He sniffed the air. "Something sure smells good."

Hazel walked over and hugged him, squishing the boys too. They giggled. "It's pot roast. It's so good to have you home."

"Well, if you don't mind, this guy right here could use a home-cooked meal."

Hazel hugged him again, feeling a sense of peace. Milton was home. Before long Joel and Ruthie would be home too, and then everything would be alright. "I'll make you a plate."

Milton winced when he sat the boys on the floor. He must have seen worry in Sandra's eyes because he grabbed her hand and gave it a squeeze. "I'm fine, baby. Just fine. I'm home."

She wrapped her arms around his neck and began to sob.

***

The next morning at work, Hazel tried to focus on the fact that Milton was home and push from her mind the huge number of recent war deaths she'd heard announced from Mr. Crutchfield's office radio. Goose bumps prickled her skin, and she shook her head. *Concentrate on the good*, she told herself and picked up a can of corn to move it back to the canned vegetable aisle. Hazel moved to straighten the canned carrots. Her mind wandered to Aaron. He looked so cute this morning in Milton's arms while Sandra made breakfast and the boys built houses out of blocks. She bit back the jealousy she felt. She'd rather be home, holding Aaron, but she needed her job.

Her mind flitted to Ms. Angel's will. She had no idea how much Mr. Hal had stolen from Joel. What if it had been enough to allow her to stay home with Aaron? Red hot fury flamed through her. Hazel felt her insides twist when she remembered her father telling her Mr. Hal had stopped him at the coffee shop a few days ago. "And what did he want?" she'd spat out.

Her father had shrugged. "He said he'd like to talk to you and explain. I told him it was your decision whether you wanted to hear any explanation or not."

Hazel bit the inside of her cheek. "He tried to talk to me at the store before I went into labor." The memories of him giving her a ride to the hospital made her wrap her arms around her middle.

"He mentioned that. Well just don't be surprised if he tries again."

The bells on the front door clinked together, knocking Hazel from the memory. She hurried to finish straightening the carrots and get back to her cash register.

"Hazel," Mr. Crutchfield stood at the front of the store. "Mrs. Crutchfield reminded me to bring this to you. Apparently, I'd forgotten it for weeks now, and if I didn't remember it today, I could find supper elsewhere." He chuckled and handed her a box wrapped in blue paper with a huge white bow.

"Oh, thank you," she said, smiling.

The front bell chimed, and an older woman walked into the store.

"Do you want me to put it in your locker?" Mr. Crutchfield asked.

She handed the present back to him. "That would be super. Thank you."

"But if you see Mrs. Crutchfield, you be sure to tell her I gave it to you."

Hazel agreed. "I promise."

Mr. Crutchfield flashed Hazel a grin and looked over at the other cash register where Louanne stood, looking at her red fingernails. "Did I ever tell you how much we missed you when you were gone? Didn't we Louanne?"

Louanne examined her fingernails closer. She blew on them. "Yeah, sure. We missed you."

"Thank you," Hazel said, feeling her cheeks heat.

She took her place by her cash register. When she'd returned after having Aaron, she'd been amazed how she hadn't forgotten a thing. It felt like she'd never left and nothing in the store had changed except for the addition of Daniel to the Piggly Wiggly team. He'd been hired to help out while Hazel was gone. Hazel liked Daniel, just barely fifteen with an enthusiastic bright smile. It made her chuckle the way his cheeks flushed when anyone spoke to him. He turned out to be a sweet kid, lots of help. Louanne had told her Daniel was Mr. Crutchfield's nephew, and that's why he got hired. But Hazel didn't care, she thoroughly enjoyed having someone other than Louanne to talk to during working hours.

The bell on the top of the door jingled again. This morning was turning out to be a busy one. Hazel looked at the door and her body broke out in chills when Mr. Hal walked inside. Their eyes locked for a brief second before he looked away. He walked quickly past her without saying a word.

"Wow," Louanne breathed. "I thought ya'll were family friends. That look you gave him was plain frosty. Spill it, sister. What's going on?"

Hazel glared at her. "I don't want to talk about it." Hazel silently prayed Mr. Hal wouldn't try to talk to her here, not today.

The bell on the door jingled again.

"This place is really hopping today," Louanne sighed as a loud group came through the door.

A woman with very long, board, straight brown hair wearing blue jeans and a turtleneck walked up to Hazel's counter. "Do ya'll sell markers and poster paper in here?"

"Yes ma'am, in the back near the school supplies," Hazel said, pointing toward the back of the store.

"Great!" she said.

Someone in the group laughed loudly and they disappeared through the aisles. Although Hazel couldn't see them anymore, she could hear them. Their laughter and cackling resounded from the back of the store. Daniel stood beside her ready to bag groceries. His eyes were big, and his brows crinkled.

Hazel shook her head, "Strange group."

Daniel's cheeks pinkened and he nodded.

It didn't take the group long to find what they needed. They approached Louanne's register, but before they got there, Louanne quickly set out the small, register closed sign.

"I'm on a break. This lane is closed," she said, not even glancing at Hazel before walking off.

A man, wearing plaid pants and a turtleneck, shrugged and moved to lay his markers and poster paper on Hazel's counter. Hazel glared at the back of Louanne's head as she sauntered off. *The nerve!* Hazel flashed a look at Daniel. He frowned and looked down at his feet.

The woman with long hair laid down another stack of markers and poster paper. Hazel made herself smile at them. She began to punch the prices into the cash register and hand the items to Daniel. He stared at the items like he didn't know what to do.

"Just bag the markers," Hazel whispered to him.

He nodded.

"I'm going to write on my poster, 'Get the hell out of Vietnam,'" a man in the group said.

Hazel sucked in a jagged breath. Protesters. Her hands started to tremble each time she pressed the numbers on the cash register. She didn't like the war either and wanted it to end. She hoped this group didn't blame the men there, like so many others. Hazel took in a breath and tried to focus on what she was doing, not on what they were saying.

"I'm going to write on mine, 'Get out of the war before the war gets you,' in block letters," a different woman with the group said, her cropped hair swinging loosely around her face.

Hazel began to feel dizzy. She tried to hurry so they could leave.

"I'm writing, 'Burn draft cards not children,'" said the man, wearing the turtleneck. He laughed.

Hazel felt the muscles in her back stiffen. She gripped her hands into tight fists. She had to hold it together.

"Yeah, I like that one," said the long-haired woman. "Tell those stupid baby killers off."

"That's it!" Hazel screamed.

Daniel jumped. Unable to control herself, she leaned over the counter and pointed her finger in the long-haired woman's face.

"My husband and sister are not baby killers! They are there fighting this war for their country. Your country! American soldiers are dying every day for you and you," she said, pointing to the others in the group. "And you spout off all this garbage. Not realizing their sacrifice. Whether you agree with the war or not, they are sacrificing. My husband may never get to see his baby! And you don't care. You don't care!"

Hazel felt huge hands on her shoulders. Mr. Hal turned her around. "Come on, Hazel. Come with me. It's okay," he said, speaking calmly.

He walked her to the back of the store toward the employee area. Hazel's feet shuffled along. Her head hung forward. Her chin almost touched her chest. She couldn't believe what she'd done. All the months of her pent-up fear and anger had just exploded out of her, and now she felt deflated.

"I think maybe she needs a little rest; you know, being a new mother and all," Mr. Hal said.

"Yes, it seems so," Mr. Crutchfield replied.

A coldness spread over her body. She hadn't been back that long, and now look at what she'd done. Mr. Crutchfield would fire her for sure. What other choice did he have after such an outburst? She'd screamed at customers. She never screamed or bit back, that was Ruthie. *What's gotten into me?*

Mr. Crutchfield lowered himself so he was eye level, but Hazel wouldn't raise her head. Her face flamed, and she couldn't make herself meet his eyes.

"Hazel, can you hear me?"

She nodded, feeling her bottom lip start to tremble.

"Why don't you go home and get some rest. Let's try again tomorrow, okay?"

Her head shot up. "I'm not fired?"

Mr. Crutchfield's face cracked into a half-grin. "Heck no, child. All you did was voice what all of us here were too chicken to say."

Chapter 49

RUTHIE

It was nearly three in the afternoon by the time Ruthie made it back to the hootch. Patty would need to head to work soon. The swing shift Tom and Darryl had come up with allowed both Ruthie and Patty time to sleep at night while being able to take care of Daisy during part of the day. She looked up into the sky filled with rain clouds. The constant rain couldn't squelch the warmth blooming in her chest. She felt lucky. Tom had done so much to help her. She'd never had a boss like him, someone who really cared.

Ruthie opened the hootch's door. Daisy sat in the small space between her and Patty's beds playing with the wooden blocks she and Patty had made for her from wood scraps they'd found near the burn pile at the back of the base. They'd sawed the wood into small squares then sanded them to remove any rough spots. Dr. Gerry had located some paint, and they painted them with the only colors he'd been able to find—gray, green, and black. Daisy looked up from her blocks. Her eyes lit up when she saw Ruthie. Tears formed in Ruthie's eyes, blurring everything around her.

"What happened? Is everything okay?" Patty asked, and Ruthie could hear the concern in her voice.

Ruthie wiped at her tears. "Everything is good. Very good."

Patty laid a hand on her chest. "Oh, thank goodness. I thought maybe there had been a push or something."

Ruthie smiled. "Nope, let's pray not at all today."

"Amen to that!" Patty agreed. "I'm ready for the celebration tonight."

Ruthie bent down and gave Daisy a hug. She breathed in the clean, floral scent of Daisy's hair from Patty's shampoo. Daisy would be her daughter. Her eyes began to tear up again; she'd been doing that a lot lately. With the adoption, Ronnie leaving tomorrow, and Dr. Gerry leaving too, she was surprised her eyes weren't constantly pouring water like fountains. She knelt down and, to Daisy's delight, began stacking the blocks with her.

Patty sat down in the space between the beds and started to stack blocks with Daisy and Ruthie. Her eyes focused on the blocks while she spoke. "Ruthie, I've been thinking about something for a little while. And I'm going to tell you, but I don't want you to do anything to try and persuade me differently, you hear me?" She looked up, meeting Ruthie's eyes. Her face serious and unsmiling.

Ruthie's fingers quivered when she picked up a block and set it on a tall stack, making it sway. She cleared her throat. "Well, someone once told my sister when something is uncomfortable, just spit it out like ripping off a Band-Aid."

Patty nodded. "I thought about what Tom told you, that you might need to re-up to see this thing with Daisy through. And I've decided if you have to re-up, then I will too. I want to help you and help this precious girl right here." She reached over and tickled Daisy's cheek, making her giggle.

Ruthie didn't know what to say. She sat there, stunned. "B-but you hate it here," she stammered.

"I can't deny that." Patty smiled. "But I love my friend and this little girl more."

An overwhelming feeling of thankfulness spread through Ruthie. She reached above Daisy to Patty, pulling her in to hug her. "Are you sure?"

Patty pulled away and slugged her softly in the arm. "I said don't try to persuade me differently!"

They laughed. "Thank you," Ruthie whispered, and Patty nodded.

They returned to helping Daisy stack blocks again. Patty coughed, interrupting the silence. "On another subject, I saw Mark today."

Ruthie's body froze. "And?"

Patty shrugged. "He ignored me and walked past me like he never saw me. But I know he saw me because I stood right square in his path and wouldn't budge. He had to walk around me to get by. I don't know what I was thinking. It's not like he'll ever apologize for what he did."

"What a jerk!" Ruthie said.

"Jerk," Daisy echoed.

Patty's mouth fell open and Ruthie covered her mouth with her hand. She looked down at Daisy, stunned. Daisy stared back up at her—big, brown eyes and smiling. Lately, Daisy had begun to babble, but Ruthie had no idea if she was speaking Vietnamese or just repeating sounds.

But Daisy had never said a word Ruthie understood—until now, and boy there was no mistaking the word she'd said.

"Did she just say…" Patty trailed off, her mouth falling open again.

Ruthie sucked in a breath. Her daughter's first English word was jerk! She'd have to add this to the long list of things she needed to tell her father and Hazel. She imagined Hazel's face when she told her, and Ruthie couldn't help it, laughter burst out of her. Daisy looked shocked at first and then began to giggle and Patty joined in. Ruthie laughed so hard her side began to ache. She hadn't laughed like this in such a long time, and it felt good.

"I hope this isn't a sign of what kind of mother I'm going to be," Ruthie said.

Patty hooted. "It means you're going to be a great mother."

❧❧❧❧❧ ❧❧❧❧❧

Before Patty left for work, she'd already started humming "I Want to Hold Your Hand" by the Beatles in anticipation of the party. Ruthie felt excited too, even if she thought celebrating Daisy's adoption before the first meeting with the attorney felt presumptuous. If she dwelled on it too much, she'd start to feel twitchy. They were in Vietnam, and nothing went like it was supposed to go. Sometimes she couldn't shake the feeling that something dark and sinister waited for her in the future.

After Patty left, Ruthie tried playing with Daisy more. But no matter how she tried to concentrate on being in the moment, she couldn't shake the feeling something bad was about to happen. The small hootch's walls started to feel like they were closing in on her. When she couldn't take it anymore, she picked up Daisy and planted a kiss on her cheek. Daisy smiled and squinted her eyes.

"Let's get out of here for a bit," Ruthie said.

Daisy grinned. It calmed Ruthie to see Daisy smile. She'd been sullen and quiet for so long. It seemed like overnight she'd turned into a bubbly, happy girl.

Outside, the sky had grown darker. Ruthie could practically smell the rain coming. She looked around. There weren't a lot of places on base where she could take Daisy. Dangers loomed around every corner—helicopter blades, truck tires, sharp edges. Ruthie worried about the future, when Daisy became more adventurous and wanted to start running and exploring. Ruthie gave Daisy a tickle, making her laugh. The safest place she could think of visiting was the mail room. Ruthie propped Daisy on her hip and headed that way. Tom's words came back to her, and Ruthie wondered if maybe she should write to her family now and tell them about Daisy.

The air inside the mail room made it feel like she'd walked into a hot box. Even Daisy noticed. Her brow crinkled, making Boyd, the mail clerk, laugh.

"Yeah, I know the feeling," he said. His hair glistened with sweat and his pink cheeks were damp from perspiration. Boyd rubbed his forehead with the back of his forearm. "What can I help you with? The faster you tell me, the faster you can escape."

Ruthie fanned herself and Daisy with her free hand. "How do you deal with it?"

He shrugged. "It's not so bad all the time. Good thing you came in tonight, McKay. I've got a letter for you." He rolled his eyes. "Like always."

That made Ruthie hoot, and her heart leaped in her chest—a letter from home! She quickly thanked Boyd and headed to the only person who'd want to hear news from Waldron—Ronnie.

Chapter 50

RUTHIE

Patty frowned when Ruthie and Daisy came into the ICU. "Is something wrong?" she asked, taking a glass thermometer from a soldier's mouth and glancing at it. She smiled at him, waving it in the air before placing it in the pocket of her fatigues. "Perfect. No fever today." He smiled back and she patted his shoulder before rushing to Daisy and Ruthie. Patty laid a hand across Daisy's forehead and bent down to kiss her cheek.

Ruthie sighed. "No, nothing is wrong. I got a letter today and wanted to read it with Ronnie in case it was news from home."

Patty narrowed her eyes, a sly grin on her face. "Oh, I see. You wanted to read it with Ronnie." The way she said it made Ruthie's face heat.

"Yep, that's right. She can't get enough of me." Ronnie said, pushing a man in a wheelchair. Ronnie's blue hospital pajamas blew behind him as he raced the man down the open space between the beds. The man's smile extended from ear to ear, but the top of his head and eyes were wrapped in white gauze. Ruthie remembered the push a couple of days ago. She'd pulled shrapnel (parts of C-rat cans, glass, and whatever else the Viet Cong could find to fill the dirty explosives) from the man's face. Later she'd found out from Dr. Gerry that surgery couldn't help him, and he'd lost both his eyes. He'd be getting a plane ride home soon. Ronnie rolled the wheelchair near Ruthie and Daisy. He leaned down. "How'd you like the ride, Ben?"

Ben nodded. "Thanks. I needed that."

Ronnie smiled and Ruthie felt her face flush hotter. She needed to get ahold of herself. She and Ronnie were friends. There couldn't be anything more—not right now. But the thought of maybe one day, when they were both back home, had started to take root in her mind, which bloomed into thoughts of maybe they could raise Daisy together. Ruthie tried to tamp the thoughts down. Ronnie would be leaving tomorrow. But then Daisy lunged in her arms toward Ronnie. His face glowed when he took her in his arms and spun her around. Patty gave Ruthie a wicked smile, like she could read her mind.

Tomorrow Ronnie would be back with his platoon. Her eyes glanced down at the white gauze wrapped around Ben's head and a shiver passed through her.

Patty walked toward the back of Ben's wheelchair. "You ready for an afternoon snack?" she asked him.

"Are there any of those chocolate chip cookies left over?"

Patty winked at Ruthie and Ronnie. "Let me see what I can find," and she wheeled Ben off.

Ronnie took Daisy to his bed and plopped down. They began to play patty-cake. "So, you gonna read that letter or not?" he asked Ruthie.

Ruthie felt a jolt. "Oh yeah," she quickly pulled it from her pocket. "It's from Hazel." She opened the envelope and removed the notebook paper. She held out the letter and quickly let her eyes scan the words. "Oh my!"

Ronnie's head jerked up from his game with Daisy. "What? What is it?"

Ruthie could hardly speak, joy radiated through her.

"Ruthie what is it? Is it Milton? Is something wrong?" he asked, worry in his voice.

She shook her head. "No!" she laughed. "No, nothing's wrong. Milton's home and he's doing great. He's great," she repeated the words, and they sounded joyous to her ears.

"I bet his boys are so glad to have him home," Ronnie said. "Milton's always been the kind of father I hoped to be one day." He looked at Ruthie and her body heated right to her core.

***

That night, everyone gathered around the makeshift concert stage. It looked unstable to Ruthie. All plywood planks and cinder blocks, but the musicians and singers didn't seem to mind. Ruthie and Patty had enlisted the help of other nurses and doctors to push wheelchairs filled with patients well enough to attend toward the front of the stage. The patients that could walk on their own came, and others hobbled on crutches. Nurses laid out unused bedsheets and blankets on the ground for the patients to sit on. Ruthie shook out a blanket for her and Daisy.

Ruthie crossed her legs and Daisy sat in her lap. Ruthie leaned her head back, feeling a needed cool breeze against her skin. It prickled her with goose bumps, and she shivered. Ruthie squeezed Daisy closer to her. She hoped it wouldn't rain on everyone. They would all be drenched by the time they got the patients back to the hospital.

"Got room for one more on your blanket?"

Ruthie's body warmed at the sound of his voice. Ronnie's now-strong frame loomed over them. She smiled. Internally repeating, *we are friends, only friends.* Her dreams of them living in Waldron, near her family, raising Daisy together after the war were nothing more than dreams—dreams she shared alone and would never tell Ronnie, not in a million years. Daisy began to bounce on her lap. Ruthie tried to make her voice sound casual. "Of course there's room for you."

Ronnie winked at Daisy. When he sat, Daisy bounced over to him almost making him topple over. "Whoa! Now, there's my favorite girl!" He looked over toward Ruthie—their eyes locked on each other. "One of my favorite girls."

Ruthie's heartbeat quickened and she felt breathless. She wanted to say something. To make a joke to keep things light, but the way he looked at her made her mind buzz with thoughts that made her blush.

"Hey what do you think about Dr. Gerry's cake?" Patty said, walking over with a huge three-layer cake in her arms.

Ruthie quickly averted her eyes from Ronnie's gaze, grateful for Patty's interruption. Patty bent down so they could see it. Ruthie tried to focus on the fluffy white icing. On top of the cake the words "We'll Miss You" were written in blue and red.

"It's perfect," Ruthie said, her voice thick.

"Here he comes! The man of the hour!" the singer said, pointing from the stage.

Everyone turned to look and laughed. Tom and Darryl pulled a smiling Dr. Gerry toward the stage, his head shaking side to side.

"What is all this?" he said, chuckling.

Tom patted Dr. Gerry on the back. "We're going to miss you. There's never been a greater doctor."

Patty walked toward Dr. Gerry with the cake while the band broke out into "For He's a Jolly Good Fellow." Everyone joined in singing and Daisy clapped her hands. Ruthie closed her eyes and sang along, feeling tears pressing to escape. When the song ended, Ruthie touched Ronnie's arm. Electricity seemed to pass through her fingertips. She forced herself to act normal. "You good with her for a little bit?"

He kissed the top of Daisy's head. "Yeah, I've got her."

You really do, Ruthie thought. *You could have us both*. She blinked. "Thank you," she said, hurrying to get up and put a little space between them.

Ruthie walked over to Dr. Gerry. He pulled her in a tight hug. She inhaled. "I already miss you! How am I going to survive being here without you?"

Dr. Gerry released her. Taking her hands, he gave them a tight squeeze. "Ruthie, it has been a pleasure working with you. And you have turned into one of the finest nurses I know. You don't need me." He waved a finger at her. "Now, I expect letters from you letting me know how everything is working out with you and the little one, you hear me?"

Ruthie nodded. "And I expect you to send me some of your wife's cookies."

Dr. Gerry hooted. "You got it!"

The band broke into "Sittin on the Dock of the Bay" by Otis Redding. Ruthie gave Dr. Gerry another quick hug before going to help Patty. Patty stood at the wooden table they'd set up earlier for the food and drinks. Patty worked to cut the cake while Ruthie held out the plates they'd confiscated from the kitchen.

"This was a really fun idea," Patty said. "The band's not half bad too."

Ruthie laughed. "They're not half good either."

Patty chuckled. "True. They're no Bob Hope that's for sure."

"Let's just hope they make better mechanics than musicians," Ruthie said, making Patty giggle.

They both picked up a few plates with cake and began walking around passing them out. Ruthie brought two plates of cake over to Ronnie and Daisy. She lowered herself beside them. Daisy's eyes were drawn to the plates. Ruthie handed one to Ronnie and then pinched a little piece of cake off from her plate and fed it to Daisy. Daisy's eyes grew huge like round saucers. Ruthie and Ronnie cackled.

"I think she likes it," Ronnie said.

Daisy reached her hands out for more.

"You better eat yours before she goes for it next," Ruthie said.

Ronnie smiled. "She can have it all."

Ruthie sat her plate down in front of Daisy's little legs and watched as Daisy grabbed the cake, smooshing it in her fingers. She licked her fingers and pushed cake into her mouth. In a few moments, she'd eaten it all and reached for Ronnie's plate. Ronnie sat it down and Daisy went to town.

"Is that her second piece?" Patty asked, joining them. "I'm never gonna get her to sleep."

"I know. I think we've created a cake monster," Ruthie said.

Patty looked down at Daisy. She shook her head and sighed.

"Hey Ruthie, do you think I could talk to you for a minute?" Ronnie asked.

Ruthie felt her pulse quicken. Patty gave her a half grin. "I've got our girl," she said, watching Daisy plunge a hand into Ronnie's cake and bring it to her mouth.

Ronnie got up and stuck out a hand toward Ruthie. She stared at his palm for a moment. Her mind whirled in a million directions. She slid her hand inside his and he gently pulled her from the ground. She could feel Patty's eyes watching them. Heat radiated through her center. She let Ronnie lead the way. As he held her hand, she tried to maintain her composure, to continue breathing, but all her nerves fired with electricity. Ronnie walked until the music from the band was nothing more than background noise. Finally, he stopped near a metal awning that housed an M48 Patton tank. He pulled her into the shadows under the awning.

They stood facing each other. She couldn't see his eyes or make out his facial expressions. All she could see was the outline of his face in the darkness. The air felt charged and the space around them heated. She wanted to reach out and touch his face, let her fingers trace his cheeks, his mouth. But she stopped herself, if she touched him, the feelings she'd pushed down since high school might flood in and overtake her.

Ronnie cleared his throat. He fidgeted on his feet. *He feels nervous too.* The thought made her smile.

"We've known each other for a long time," he finally said.

She swallowed but couldn't speak. He reached out for her. His hand slid down her arm until he found her elbow. Ruthie's knees became weak. He pulled her close to him. His hand found the back of her head, gripping her hair in a fist, he brought his warm mouth to hers. She parted her lips, letting him feel the space with his tongue. Their kiss felt hard and frantic. Ruthie's arms slid around Ronnie's neck, and she clung to him. All the feelings she'd pushed down and tried to forget rose to the forefront. She needed him. She wanted his mouth on her mouth. His hands pulled her until her body pressed against his chest. His mouth tasted of sweetness from the cake, and she wanted more. She wanted all of him. When his grip around her loosened, she pushed her body closer to him.

Between kisses, he mumbled, "Ruthie, we've got to slow it down."

She shook her head. "I don't want to." She stood on her tiptoes, her lips urgently seeking his.

He broke the contact and took a step back. "I'm sorry."

Instantly the heat left, and Ruthie shivered. She crossed her arms around her body. Shame blazed across her cheeks, and she felt glad to be hidden by the darkness. He reached for her, trying to loosen her crossed arms so he could take her hand. She didn't have the energy to fight. She gave him her hand and he rubbed his thumb across her fingers. Still, even filled with embarrassment, his touch made her want to fold into him.

"I'm sorry," he said again.

"I'm not," Ruthie snapped.

He let out a long sigh. "I didn't mean I was sorry about kissing you. I meant I'm sorry about all of this."

Ruthie didn't understand.

Ronnie blew out a huff of air. "See, I've liked you since high school, Ruthie."

The words made Ruthie sway. She could hardly process what he said. "What? That's not true. That can't be true. In high school, I made it so obvious that I cared for you, but you made it very clear you wanted only to be friends. In your letters once you left and joined the Army, you said you cherished our friendship."

His voice dropped to a whisper, and she had to strain to hear him. "At my senior prom, when I saw you outside alone, I felt so grateful in that moment. I should have just asked you, but I couldn't get up the nerve, and there you were all beautiful and alone. When we danced," he swallowed, "all I could think about was the way you felt in my arms, the smell of your perfume."

Ruthie's stomach fluttered. "Then why didn't you ever say anything?"

He gripped her fingers tighter. Ruthie's skin tingled where he touched her hand. She took in a shaky breath when he passed his thumb across her knuckles, releasing a thousand butterflies in her belly.

He whispered. "That night at prom on the dance floor, I felt terrified."

"Why?" she couldn't understand why he'd be scared.

"I knew if I told you how I felt. If I let myself kiss you, then I wouldn't be able to stop. I would never let you go. I'd never join the Army. So I said nothing. I did nothing. Later at Hazel and Joel's wedding, I thought about approaching you, but I got cold feet. Plus, I thought I'd never see you again.

You'd move off. Get married. But we ended up here... together. And all those old feelings came back."

Ruthie understood what he meant. When she'd wrote to him, she had to force herself to be happy with just being his friend, but she didn't want to be Ronnie's friend. She wanted to be his, to belong to him, to love him.

"Look," he said, breaking her train of thought. "I brought you out here to tell you how I feel before I leave tomorrow," his voice trailed off. "I wanted you to know."

She felt the prick of tears sting her eyes.

"I leave tomorrow at zero-six-hundred."

Ruthie felt like she'd been kicked in the chest. He pulled her closer to him and she resisted the urge to jerk away to protect herself. He kissed the top of her head. "I wanted to ask you. When all this is over and we're back home, if I can visit you and Daisy. Spend time with you both. I want to give us a chance like I should have all those years ago."

Ruthie slipped her hands around his waist, burying her face in his chest. She breathed in the smell of him—sweat and soap. She nodded, unable to talk; she missed him already. Oh gracious, how she already missed him. She nodded yes into his chest.

"Then kiss me, Ruthie," Ronnie whispered. "Kiss me again."

When his lips met hers, warmth flooded through her veins. Ronnie wanted a future with her after the war. A real future with her and Daisy. A hopefulness blossomed inside her, taking root in her heart. She kissed him hard back, knowing she'd remember this moment over and over again as she waited for the day when he could be with her and Daisy again. If she'd only known how her life would change, she'd have never let him go.

Chapter 51

HAZEL

The end of September had not cooled. Instead hot, sticky heat made the sheets cling to Hazel's leg, making it impossible to sleep. Aaron lay in his crib beside her bed. The mobile from her mother silent and still. She listened to his soft baby breaths. She looked over at him. It had been nearly five months, and she still couldn't believe he was here with her. He was a handsome boy, a tiny version of his father. Her body ached in pain at the thought of Joel. She'd thought the passing days would make it easier to deal with him and Ruthie being gone, but it didn't. Every day without her husband and sister were exactly as hard as the first. She kept busy and that helped some, but nights were the worst when the sadness started to creep in. It had been such a long time since she'd received a letter from Joel telling her he was alright. A chill ran over her, and she wondered what that meant. She flopped back into the mattress, laid an arm across her eyes, and tried to go back to sleep.

Her mind wandered and she remembered Officer McConnell at Piggly Wiggly this afternoon. She was sure he'd made it a point to come to her cash register. He towered over her and Daniel in his wrinkle-free uniform. She picked up a package of steaks wrapped in clear plastic and began to key the price into the cash register. She didn't acknowledge him. She passed the steaks to Daniel to bag.

Officer McConnell cleared his throat. "Heard from Joel lately?"

Her head went fuzzy, and she swayed.

He reached across the counter to steady her. "Whoa, don't fret now. I'm just asking as a concerned individual." His warm hand gripped her arm, making the hairs on the back of her neck stand. The last time she'd seen him, he had attempted to make a veiled threat toward Joel right in front of his pa's hospital door.

Daniel bagged his steak and shoved it in his direction. Hazel jerked her arm from his hand.

"Have a good day," she'd forced herself to say. He looked at both of them, shook his head, and left.

Hazel pushed her head into her pillow and rubbed away the tears leaking from the corner of her eyes. *Joel. Joel. What are we going to do when you return? Your friend, Mr. Hal, is a liar and thief, and your pa told Officer McConnell everything before he died.* She knew her father would continue the lie and deny Joel had shot him. It had been a horrible accident, but Officer McConnell wouldn't stop. Not until he knew the truth about that day long ago in the woods.

On top of all of this, how could she tell Ruthie that Oliver was her real father? *Ruthie and Joel, what horrible surprises you're going to have when you return home.*

Hazel sighed. She knew she'd never get back to sleep, and she couldn't handle laying here anymore and dwelling on all the awfulness surrounding her and her family. She carefully and silently swung her legs over the bed. She tip-toed to her vanity and quietly pulled out the chair, trying her best not to wake Aaron. When she sat down, the chair cushion let out a small squeak and he stirred. Hazel sucked in a breath, waiting, hoping he wouldn't awaken. After a few beats of her heart, she slowly pulled out the vanity drawer. She smiled. Inside the drawer lay the notebook Joel had bought her along with the three other ones she'd bought herself after she'd filled Joel's with stories. She picked up the newer notebook and her pencil and started to write like she did every night she couldn't sleep. She drowned her worry and loneliness in stories filled with flying children, pirates, dancing dogs, and parading forest animals. She glanced up at her reflection in the vanity mirror. The dark rings under her eyes looked deeper. If her insomnia continued, she'd have enough stories to fill a library. She couldn't help but smile at the thought. She loved how every night Mikey requested her to read to him and Mannie a story from her book before bed. That's what he called it, "her book." She sighed. *Maybe one day.*

Chapter 52

JOEL

As Joel marched, anger boiled inside of him. He tried to focus on Hazel. Even though the day dawned for him and the men of the 101st, it would be nearly bedtime for her. He tried to concentrate on her—imagining her rocking the son he'd never seen and putting him to bed. He desperately wanted to be with them. But his focus would break each time he'd catch sight of Pen, marching ahead as point man, recklessly throwing his machete from side to side. Something wasn't right with him, and it left Joel feeling irritable and jittery.

He blew out a puff of air. "Dang it!" he said, mostly to himself. He had to deal with Pen. He couldn't let him get himself and all the rest of them killed. He pushed his way from the back to the front. His feet ached and his body protested with each quick step. Pen's last words echoed through Joel's head. "If you want to help, you will stay as far away from me as you can today."

By mid-afternoon, Joel had made it to the front. He pushed his way around Harvey Davis.

"Hey, watch it, hickory dickory," Harvey said. "There's just more trees and brush ahead, what's your rush?"

"I need to speak to Pen."

Harvey gave a low whistle. "He's in a mood today."

A tremor passed through Joel. "What do you mean?"

"Look." Harvey motioned toward the front.

Joel careened his head, so he could see around the few other bodies in front of him. Pen's body sagged, as if his pack weighed a thousand pounds. He continued to aimlessly swing his machete in front of him, chopping through the overgrown brush and palms. The pace he took was quick—too quick. He never took any time to look at the hand-held metal detector that hung from his right hand.

"He's liable to get us all killed," Harvey said, his jaw clenched. "He's not even trying to be careful."

If Chad were here, he'd smack Pen beside the head. Maybe now, the duty belonged to Joel. "I'll talk to him."

Harvey grabbed Joel's arm and jerked him close. "Something's wrong with him, hick. You'd do better to stay as far away as you can. You need to think about your wife and your kid. You don't owe him anything. If he wants to get himself killed today, so be it."

Harvey's words were sharp and stung him like a wasp, but the truth of them settled over him. He didn't owe Pen anything. He owed Hazel everything. He tried to help Pen, but he had refused his help. If Pen was going to act a fool, why should Joel jeopardize himself? All Joel wanted was to see Hazel's brown eyes again, to hold her and their child in his arms and never let them go. Joel gritted his teeth. Thoughts of Chad eating rice under the rice lady's hut, laughing around the campfire, strumming a guitar on Eagle Beach, and helping carry Milton down Hamburger Hill all ran through Joel's mind. He knew what he needed to do, but he didn't want to do it. What would Chad do? What would Hazel do? She'd held his father's hand as he died because family—real family—stood beside each other even when it was uncomfortable. And isn't that what he, Chad, Pen, and all the men of the 101st had become? They were the most mismatched family that ever existed, but they were still family. And one of their family members needed help right now. Joel just hoped it wasn't too late.

"Thanks for the warning," he said, flashing Harvey a smile. Then he forced his feet to move, pushing his way closer to Pen. He heard Harvey sigh loudly, but Harvey didn't try to stop him.

When he made it close to Pen, he noticed Pen had begun to pick up his pace even more, swinging the machete wildly, mumbling something Joel couldn't hear.

"Slow down!" Joel called to him. "You gotta watch for mines and booby traps. A slow and steady pace wins the race."

"Like I care," Pen's words came out in a huff.

Joel's anger boiled in his veins. "Pen stop! You're being an idiot! You put all of us in danger when you act without thinking."

Pen whipped around. He held the machete out, pointing it at Joel. The blade inches away from Joel's nose.

"I'm the point man today. You'd do good to shut your mouth."

"What?" Joel blinked.

The whites of Pen's eyes were cracked with tiny, spidery red lines. They shook inside the sockets above dark, deep circles. A sense of terror passed over Joel, chilling him to the bone. For the first time, he realized he wasn't speaking to Pen. Not the Pen he knew, the kind, awkward, C-rat-loving guy. The man before Joel now was a crazed lunatic.

Joel held his palms out and spoke gently. "Look, man, I'm sorry. I know it's been hard." He bit his bottom lip. "Chad's death. I miss him too. Every day. He was my friend. But we're friends too, Pen. Right? Please, please just get behind me. I'll take over from here. Or let's do it together. I can't have anything happen to you." His throat grew thick, but he choked out. "I need you."

Pen let out a hideous sounding laugh. Joel clenched his jaw. *He's gone mad.*

"You need me?" Pen pointed the end of the hatchet toward himself.

"Why'd we stop!" Lieutenant Roberts shouted from somewhere behind them.

In an instant, Pen's grimaced face changed, his scowl turned soft. His eyes became watery, and he looked at Joel as if pleading. His madness switched off momentarily. Joel reached out his hand and touched his arm.

"I can't do this," Pen whimpered. "I can't handle this anymore."

"I know. Let me take over."

"Get moving, Pendleton!" Lieutenant Roberts screamed. The other men jeered from behind.

"Don't listen to them, Pen," Joel consoled.

Pen shook his head wildly from side to side. Then stopped and stared Joel dead in the eyes. He cupped his hand beside his mouth and yelled, "Sorry, sir. Davenport's holding me up. Going now."

Joel felt like he'd been sucker punched. The air left his lungs. Pen glared at him as he turned around and began hacking through the brush again. Joel stood there frozen in place.

"Better get moving, hickory," Harvey chided behind him.

Joel sucked in a breath and ran a hand across his stubbled face. Harvey was right. The faster they got to where they were going, the faster this day would be over.

They'd only marched a few paces when Pen's body went rigid. If Joel hadn't been watching him closely, he'd have rammed into his back. Joel held up his hand to make the others behind them stop.

"What is it, Pen?" Joel whispered.

He heard him mewl. "A mine."

"How close?" Joel said, doing his best to stay calm, but his insides felt like jelly.

"Inches."

Joel's senses grew heavy, weighed down with fear. He tried to think. "Okay, is it small? Like a toe popper?"

Pen shook his head, "Bigger."

Joel's throat tightened and he couldn't swallow. His heart began to race, and his breath came out fast and ragged. "Don't. Move." Joel told him then slowly turned to Harvey. "We need a marker. Got a mine. Big one ahead."

Harvey put a hand beside his mouth to shout down the line, but before he could say anything a shot whizzed by his head, exploding the tree trunk behind him.

"Get down!" Harvey screamed.

Joel squatted down, grabbing his rifle.

Pen didn't lower himself. He stood frozen in place with his hands over his ears, crying. "I can't do this anymore."

341

"Hold on, Pen!" Joel said, maneuvering beside him. He had to get him away from the mine. "Back away, just back away from the mine," he said, positioning himself in front of where the bullets came from to protect Pen from any incoming shots.

The 101st shot back at the unseen assailants. Joel lifted his rifle and shot at the brush in front of him. The reports bounced off the trees, echoing around them. It sounded like they were surrounded by thousands. The palms and long grasses moved and swayed.

"They're everywhere!" Harvey yelled, turning to shoot behind him.

Joel saw a Viet Cong soldier run toward them. The man's gun was raised ready to fire. Joel raised his rifle and shot. The man's shoulder whipped backwards as if performing a grotesque dance move. He fell to the ground. Joel watched where he fell.

"I'll be right back," he told Pen. "I'm going to try and get closer to that tree. I think some are hiding there." He didn't wait for Pen to reply. Joel belly crawled through the tall weeds. A shot hit the ground beside him. Joel flinched. His hands trembled, but he raised his gun to shoot off a few rounds. He stopped to reload. He wasn't going to be able to make it any farther—the action around him was too hot. *This is it. It's over for us all.*

"Someone radio for help!" he heard Harvey scream.

Joel looked over his shoulder at Pen. Time seemed to slow. Blood pounded between his ears and the sound of gunfire disappeared around him. Pen's foot swayed over the mine like he wanted to step on it. Joel forced out a scream. "Pen, move. Get down! Get down!"

Joel knew he should run in the opposite direction of Pen. To his right, Danny threw a lemon. It exploded, and Joel scrambled to his feet. His eyes met Pen's eyes—madness, all he could see was madness. Tears streamed down Pen's face and Joel raced toward him.

"I can't do it anymore. I'm sorry!' Pen screamed over the gunfire.

Joel's heart pounded hard against his rib cage. His leg muscles tightened but he pushed them harder. A shot whizzed past his head, sending him to his knees. "Pen, no!" he choked out, trying to get back to his feet.

Pen looked at him. "I'm sorry," he mouthed then shook his head and started to lower his foot toward the mine. Joel felt like he moved in a slow motion. All he could hear was his heavy panting as he tried to run on

342

weighted legs. He leaped in the air, hoping to shove Pen away from the danger. He extended his left arm, hoping to snag Pen. But before he could reach him, Pen stepped forward onto the mine.

The blast blew all other noises away and set off a loud siren in Joel's ears. *I'm flying*, he thought. His body soared away from the blast through the air like a ragdoll. He hit a tree and fell hard to the ground. His skin seared with the heat of the blast. He felt his body cooking from the outside in. His head pounded with the sharpest pain he'd ever felt. He opened his mouth to scream, but only a sickening gurgle came out. He tried to open his eyes, but layers of skin hungover one of them. He could smell burning flesh. It made his stomach turn. His head lobbed to the side, and he saw an arm. For a minute, it appeared comical, a lone arm without a body. But horror seized his heart when he saw the small metal band on the left finger. It was his arm. He tried to breathe, but his lungs felt charred.

I'm going to die, Hazel. Memories played through his mind. His and Hazel's first kiss, the day he proposed, their wedding day, he, Hazel, and Ruthie running through the forest when they were young kids.

"Hickory?"

Joel thought he heard something, but his mind felt fuzzy and confused. Pain consumed his body. He never knew pain like this existed. He needed it to stop. He wanted something to ease the suffering.

"Davenport?"

A blur appeared in the corner of his vision. He groaned. "I'm dying," was what he tried to say, but it sounded more like a garbled mess. He felt his body lifting. Sharp pains shot through him. He tried to scream.

"Shut up, idiot. I'm getting you out of here."

"Leave me," his words came out as a gurgle. His head lolled backwards.

"I'm not letting your child grow up fatherless. The choppers are coming. They've called in an air strike. They're about to light it up."

"My arm," Joel said, feeling his body bounce, each movement sending an electric fire through him. The pain sharp like knives. He thought he might still be on fire. He couldn't take it. His mind started to go in and out.

"Your arm? It's gone," Davis said, huffing. "I tied you up the best I could to stop the bleeding. Half of you got blown away, and you're still a heavy hick."

A shot rang out. Harvey groaned, falling forward. Joel hit the ground. He let out a raspy scream. Agonizing pain spiraled through him. Harvey scurried back up. He grabbed Joel and hoisted him in his arms. Harvey moaned.

"They got me in the side," his breathing sounded thick and heavy, and his movements began to slow.

"Leave me," Joel said, forcing the words from his charred throat.

"If you say that one more time, I will."

Joel felt blackness and cold spreading over him. He tried to push it back, but he felt weak. He just wanted the pain to stop.

"Stay with me," he heard Harvey yell. Joel felt like he was falling.

"Lay him down," he heard someone say. "Tourniquet?"

"I did the best I could," Harvey explained.

"You're injured too?" the voice asked.

"My side."

Joel's good eye flickered. He heard the hum of the whirling helicopter propellers. The wind from the propellers hit his burned skin and he screamed. Then he felt like he was rising into the air.

"Get me more morphine."

He felt something squeeze his right shoulder. "I'm here," Harvey said.

"Stay down. You've probably been hit in a vital organ."

"Don't you and your ugly mug go dying on me. Not after all I've done to save you."

Chapter 53

HAZEL, OCTOBER 1969

Hazel opened her front door, letting the cool, crisp breeze inside. The smell of fall hung in the air. Mikey and Mannie's giggles filled her ears and Hazel's heart soared. Milton raked leaves in their front yard into a pile over and over so Mikey could race and jump into them. Mannie toddled behind him, stopping at the pile and laughing before hopping into it. The last few weeks with Milton home had been a salve to Hazel's frazzled nerves.

"Hey there!" Milton called, raising his hand. A bright smile stretched across his face. He winced slightly as he raked the leaves back into a big pile.

"Where's Sandra?" Hazel asked.

"She went to get some candies for the candied apples. She should be back soon."

"Hazey! Watch me, watch me!" Mikey called.

"Sure buddy. Let me go grab Aaron, and I'll be right back."

She ran inside and scooped up Aaron, who laid on his tummy on a baby blanket on the floor, gnawing on a teething ring. He kept hold of the ring in his little fists and pushed it into his mouth. She propped him on her hip and rushed to the kitchen to grab the small carved pumpkin she'd just finished. The pumpkin smiled at her with three jagged teeth. She picked it up to set outside on the stoop.

Hazel sat down beside the pumpkin with Aaron on her lap. He watched Mikey and Mannie play. His eyes followed their movements, and a spit bubble escaped from his smiling lips. She made his little hands clap when Mikey and Mannie jumped into the pile. His cackling laugh made her feel light and her whole body relaxed.

Out of the corner of her eye, she saw her father come out of his duplex. She turned and made Aaron's little hand wave. "There's Papa, Aaron."

Aaron giggled, but he didn't take his eyes off the whooping and hollering boys. Hazel couldn't take her eyes off her father. The fold of his mouth made her skin prickle, but she didn't know why. He rushed toward them, something white in his hand.

"Dad, is everything okay?"

Her father ran a hand down his beard, and she could tell something wasn't quite right.

Milton stopped raking and walked toward them. "What's wrong, Arvel?"

Sandra pulled up in her vehicle. They all watched her grab a grocery bag from the passenger seat and walk toward them. She smiled. "Hey, ya'll, I got some caramels and apples." Her smile faltered when she took them in, and she looked at Milton. "Dear, is something wrong?"

Hazel's father took Aaron from her arms and handed him to Milton. "Here, could you take the little guy?" Milton nodded and dropped the rake. He cradled Aaron in his arms. Mikey and Mannie stood beside his legs, their eyes bouncing from grown-up to grown-up.

Hazel's heart began to thump hard in her chest. "Dad, you're starting to scare me. What's wrong?"

Her father rested a hand on the back of his neck. "Hazel, I ran into Billy in town."

Hazel's body went rigid, and her stomach clenched. Billy had graduated two years ahead of her and now worked for Western Union. Hazel knew part of his duties included delivering telegrams for the military. Billy's wife told Hazel once in Piggly Wiggly that delivering the telegrams from war,

346

the ones where the soldiers died, had broken him in so many ways, and now he dreaded any time a telegram came in.

Her father held out the white piece of paper in his hand. "He said to give this to you. He couldn't do it. I'm so sorry, Hazel. I read it." A tear ran down his cheek and into his beard.

Hazel didn't reach up and take it. She stared at it, hanging there in his hand. She shook her head. "I can't. I don't want to know." She pulled her knees up to her chest and wrapped her arms around them, rocking on the stoop. "Please don't make me read it. Please don't."

Her father's knees hit the ground beside her, and he wrapped his arms around her. He squeezed her close. "Hazel, listen to me. He's alive. He's still alive."

"What does it say?" Milton asked, and Hazel could hear the fear in his voice.

Hazel's eyes flickered up to Milton. He bounced Aaron in his arms. An empty feeling formed in the pit of her stomach, and she felt sick. Hazel could barely breathe. "He's alive?" she whispered.

"Yes," her father said. The word had no certainty to it. Hazel's chest tightened, and she thought she might be having a heart attack.

"Please read it," she pleaded with her father. "I can't do it."

Her fathers wallowed. Mikey linked an arm around Milton's leg. Sandra scooped up Mannie and held him close. They all collectively sucked in a breath when her father started to read.

"Mrs. Davenport, this is to confirm that a report was received at headquarters on October 3, 1969, stating that your husband, Joel Aaron Davenport, U.S. Army has undergone a surgical procedure due to an amputation of his left arm above the elbow at the Bien Hoa hospital. His present condition is serious as he suffered severe burns on over half of his body. His prognosis is now critical. We realize your concern

347

and assure you that he continues to receive the best care possible. If he stabilizes, he will be shipped to the U.S. Army hospital in Saigon. We will continue to update you when more information is received."

Hazel heard someone screaming. It took a while for her to process that it was her. Aaron started to wail. Hazel buried her face in father's shoulder. Her body racked with sobs. No one said anything. She heard Sandra and Milton praying. But no one dared promise her everything would be okay because that was a promise no one knew if they could keep.

Chapter 54

RUTHIE

Ruthie left early while Patty and Daisy slept cuddled together in the hootch. Today she'd take the one-hundred-and-twelve-mile ride to Qui Nhon to meet the attorney, Sang Le. Tom had arranged for her to ride with a convoy heading to the Qui Nhon Airfield. She'd stay two weeks, working in triage at the 67th Evac Hospital there on the base. She'd help fill in the gaps until the new nurses arrived, then she would head back on a truck, bringing mail and medical supplies. Ruthie's heart hurt to leave Daisy for so long. How much would she grow while she was gone? Still, she had to go. Darryl had volunteered to help Patty care for Daisy while Ruthie was gone. It had taken awhile, but finally, Daisy had warmed up to him. Ruthie had no doubt it was all the sweet treats he'd sneak to her when he thought no one was looking.

Ruthie stared out the truck's window as the area she knew so well faded away in the distance. Her and Patty's conversation from last night as they watched Daisy sleep played in her head.

"Ruthie, you are going to be a wonderful mother."

"But how do you know?" Ruthie had asked.

"Because you're willing to do everything to keep her safe."

Ruthie's face flushed. "Thank you, but I haven't done everything. I haven't even told my family yet."

Patty smiled. "From what I know of your family, they will welcome this little one with open arms. Mine, on the other hand, would cast us out into the streets."

Ruthie hadn't replied. She'd reached out and touched Patty's arm. From what Patty had told her about her family, she knew Patty spoke the truth. They'd disown Patty if she'd brought Daisy home as her daughter. She wasn't exactly sure what her family would do when that day came, but she knew they wouldn't do that.

※ ※ ※

Qui Nhon was like nothing Ruthie had ever seen before. Buildings made up of tin, concrete, and bamboo were pressed together without much space between them. Palm trees shot up all over the city, and the air smelled of the salt sea and exhaust. In the distance, Ruthie could see the outline of dark blue mountains rising high into the air, but when she turned her head in the other direction, all she could see was the blue of the South China Sea. How different this place was from where she'd come. The land looked different, but when they pulled onto the bumpy road and passed the concertina wire leading to the Army Airfield and the 67th Evac Hospital, all the buildings looked relatively the same as what she'd left. She found comfort in that, that things here wouldn't be so different.

Ruthie wondered where Ronnie was right now. After he'd left, she'd received one short letter from him that she'd brought with her. On notebook paper he'd written, "*The memory of our kiss is what gets me through the rough nights. I can't wait until we are home, and you and me and Daisy can start a new adventure together. Yours always, Ronnie*"

The days after he left, Ruthie had hardly any time to be depressed. Her days had been filled with work and caring for Daisy. At night though, without the hustle and bustle to distract her, a deep sadness settled over her. She cared for him, possibly even loved him, and she wanted more than anything this future he wrote about—all three of them together.

The truck stopped and Ruthie rocked in her seat. She flung her knapsack onto her shoulder and stepped out. The smell of saltwater hit her so hard, she could almost taste the salt on her lips.

"Second Lieutenant McKay?"

Ruthie turned to see a woman in green fatigues. Her choppy brown hair blew in the breeze. The lines around her big, brown eyes crinkled when she smiled.

Ruthie nodded. "Yes, that's me."

The woman put out her hand. "Lieutenant Lois Shelton. But call me Lois. I'm here to welcome you to the 67th."

Ruthie shook her hand.

"I'll show you to your hootch and get you set up at the hospital. I hear you'll be helping for a couple of weeks, is that right? We sure could use the help. And you've got an appointment of some kind set for tomorrow in town with a lawyer?"

Ruthie kept in stride beside Lois. A warmth spread through her. Tom had kept the reason for her appointment with an attorney private. "Yes, that's right," she said, not offering more.

Lois narrowed her eyes but didn't press. Ruthie continued to follow her, listening to the waves lap against the shore. She'd never lived so close to so much water. She wondered how it would feel to dive into it headfirst.

"Our hospital has about three hundred and twenty beds. We're air-conditioned, so that helps."

Ruthie thought of something. "Does the night shift have to work in the dark?"

Lois laughed. "Work in the dark? No, that's crazy! Wow! I can't even imagine how difficult that would be." Then Lois's laugh stopped abruptly. "Wait, you don't have to work in the dark... do you?"

Ruthie swallowed. "Yeah, we do. It's safer that way. Too many mortar attacks."

Lois shook her head. "Unbelievable. What a crazy war."

Ruthie thought Lois didn't know the half of it.

❦

Ruthie dropped her stuff off at her temporary hootch. It had a little more space than what she and Patty shared, and although there were two beds, Lois had told her she'd have the whole place to herself. Lois then took her straight to the hospital to show her around.

The hospital's walls were painted a corral blue, which Ruthie liked. Like triage at the 71st, beds lined both sides of the walls. In the back, a blue sheet hung that reached to the floor. Behind it, Lois told her were the supplies she'd need: tubes, glass IVs and stands, medicines, towels, and extra sheets. There were only a few patients laying in the beds. Ruthie made a quick assessment with her eyes and noticed they seemed to be doing fine.

Lois must have read her mind. "Both had severe sinus infections and have been treated. There's no need to send them to ICU. They'll be heading out after we give them their antibiotics." Lois held out her hands. "Okay, so that's pretty much everything. Do you want to go back to your hootch and rest, start fresh tomorrow after your meeting?" Lois asked.

Ruthie considered it for a few minutes. She really hadn't had a chance to rest for such a long time. But the thought of being alone made her nervous. She knew she wouldn't sleep. Her mind would wander and whirl. If she stopped moving, her heart would feel like it was trapped in a vice, the sadness of leaving Daisy squeezing it. She knew her thoughts would bounce from Daisy to Ronnie and would overwhelm her. She shook her head. "It's okay. I want to get started right away."

Lois shrugged. "Okay, suit yourself."

At that moment, the hospital door slammed open. The loud pop of the door hitting the wall made Ruthie jolt.

"Help! Help!"

A soldier in a swimsuit and bare chest rushed in. Water dripped from his hair and body. His arms wrapped around the waist of another soldier in a wet swimsuit. He hauled him toward Ruthie and Lois. The soldier he carried looked ashen. He grimaced.

"Get him on the bed," Lois ordered. "What happened?"

"We were swimming," the soldier tried to explain, but his explanation was cut short as the wounded man's face contorted and he moaned. "My leg. My leg."

Ruthie's brain tried to process what could be wrong. She quickly moved down to his leg which was swollen and red. She touched his skin, still damp from the South China Sea. She turned his leg over and he screamed. On the side were puncture wounds she'd never seen before in Vietnam, only maybe in Waldron during the summer months when people explored the forests.

"Snakebite? On base?" Ruthie asked, her breath catching in her chest. "How?"

Lois sighed heavily. "I'll be back. We need to clean the wound and administer some antivenom. Hopefully it's not too late."

"Snakebite?" Ruthie repeated not believing what she saw.

"Yes ma'am," the soldier who carried his friend in said. "There's sea snakes out there in the South China Sea."

***

Ruthie's first night away from Daisy ended with no sleep. She tossed and turned. She'd think about the man with the snakebite but force her mind to picture happier things like Ronnie and Daisy sitting together on a blanket under a cloudy sky. But inevitably, her mind would wander to her appointment with the attorney. What if it went poorly? What if he told her she couldn't adopt Daisy? They wouldn't let her stay here in Vietnam permanently to raise her. What if they lost the war? Things weren't looking good, that's what Margarette Ann's last letter had said. Her mind wandered to her family and to Milton. He was safe, but Joel and Ronnie were still out there. When she couldn't handle it any longer, Ruthie got up and dressed.

Outside the hootch, Ruthie breathed in the salt air. Although she knew there were snakes in the water, she walked through the hootches and past the 67th hospital until she reached the banks of the South China Sea. Brilliant pinks and oranges reflected off the water. It lapped on the shore near her boots. The peaceful sound of the rolling waves made her fluttering heart calm. Even in beauty there was danger, she reminded herself. She spent a few more seconds watching the yellow glow of the sun in the distance rise higher into the air before making her way back to the hospital where a truck waited for her.

Lois walked out of the hospital. She smiled at Ruthie. "Ready?"

Ruthie nodded. She hoped with every fiber of her being that this meeting would go well.

"We're gonna ride to the main street then take a pedicab to the attorney's office. What's his name?"

"Sang Le," Ruthie said.

Lois knocked on the truck's door and Ruthie heard the locks pop. Lois opened the door and climbed in, and Ruthie followed her.

The drive to the main street in Qui Nhon took about twenty minutes. Ruthie couldn't believe how busy the city was even in the midst of war. On the side of the road, people sold fish and other items from wooden carts.

"Don't buy any drinks or food from the street venders," Lois told her.

"What? Why?" she asked.

"You never know who's working with Charlie. Many of our men have gotten poisoned from spiked drinks and food."

"Oh!" Ruthie exclaimed. They passed an old man wearing a nón lá. The conical shaped hat shaded his face, but Ruthie could still see the wrinkles from his warm smile. He held a fish in the air to show a woman. She examined it closely. *Could that man, who looked like a kind grandfather, be the enemy? Could he be working with the Viet Cong to poison and kill American soldiers?* The thought sent a chill through her.

When they got to the stopping point, their driver got out and helped Ruthie and Lois secure a pedicab. Ruthie told the pedicab driver where she wanted to go, repeating the attorney's name and showing him the attorney's address on a piece of paper Tom had given to her. He nodded his head and motioned with his hand for her and Lois to sit. The pedicab had three huge wheels, bigger than any bicycle she'd ever seen. The seat in the front for passengers was long enough for her and Lois. The seat padding looked worn, and Ruthie could see the plank of wood beneath it in places.

The driver took his position in the back to pedal. He motioned again for her and Lois to sit. *This is it*, she thought and sat down on the hard seat.

They rode through the town, the wind hitting her face. They rode by areas that smelled of fresh flowers and fish, then they rode by areas that smelled of urine and rotting garbage. They bumped along the uneven road until the pedicab stopped in front of a small metal building. Ruthie frowned; this couldn't be it. It didn't look like an attorney's office to her. The pedicab driver hopped off the back seat and walked toward them, holding out his hand. Lois took it and he helped her out. He then held his hand out to Ruthie. She paused and the driver motioned to the building. "Sang Le," he said. She nodded and took his hand, letting him help her. He waved his hand at them and pointed to his pedicab.

"I think he's saying he'll wait for us," Lois said, trying to interpret his gestures.

They both thanked him, and Ruthie walked up to the door. Without the wind from the moving pedicab, the air around her felt hot and stale. Sweat dampened the small of her back. Her nerves were already a jangled mess, and her head hurt from the sharp shards of anxiety, threatening to overtake her. She half considered jumping onto the pedicab and pedaling away just to avoid this meeting and any bad news the attorney would tell her, but she straightened her shoulders. She could do this. She had to do this... for Daisy.

Her knock on the door sounded hollow, but in no time, a thin man with thick, gray hair appeared. He opened the door wide. If she had to guess, she thought he might have been her father's age. In broken English he said, "Ruthie McKay, you here for your appointment?"

She forced herself to meet his bright smile with a smile of her own. "Yes sir. That's me."

"I'll be right outside the door," Lois said. "In case you need me."

Sang Le welcomed Ruthie inside his small one-room office. The office had two chairs, one filing cabinet, and a typewriter sitting on a rickety-looking table. Ruthie had never seen such a sparce office. He motioned for her to sit in one of the chairs while he took the other one across from her. He wasted no time with pleasantries but got down to the crux of the matter, which she appreciated.

"You would like to adopt?" he asked.

She nodded.

"In war, it is hard."

Ruthie felt her shoulders slump forward.

He held up a finger. "But not impossible. Paperwork is very easy." He then began to explain to Ruthie how she would need to obtain guardianship of Daisy in Vietnam, and then when they reached America, she could complete the adoption process.

"So the adoption doesn't happen here?" she asked, shocked.

He shook his head no. "Guardianship then adoption in America."

She swallowed, feeling the words she wanted to ask get trapped in her throat. But she had to know, she needed to know for her family and for herself. She forced the question out. "How long will it take?"

"When you leave?" he asked.

"Next March probably," she told him.

The corners of his mouth turned down, creating wrinkles along his chin. Ruthie's stomach twisted.

"Hmmm, might be possible. But can you stay more?" he asked.

"Longer? Stay longer here in Vietnam?" she asked and Sang Le nodded.

She breathed out. She could. She could re-up if she had to for Daisy. "Yes, I can stay as long as I need to," she said, sounding more resolved than she felt.

Chapter 55

PATTY

Patty pulled extra Penrose tubing for an IV and Kelley clamps from her fatigue pockets. Her fatigues were blood-splattered again. She rushed as fast as she could to get fluids into the boy lying on the bed, but her hands shook. How long had it been since her hands had trembled so much? She'd left Daisy with Tom after Darryl had run through the hootches, calling every nurse to come help in triage and surgery. Daisy had cried when she left her with Tom, but what could she do? They needed her help. She rushed to triage, avoiding surgery. During the chaos, for a second, she wished Ruthie were with her, helping her. Ruthie had only two arms and two hands, but in a crisis, it seemed like she had twenty. Then Patty remembered what was behind the curtain in the back, and she hoped Ruthie stayed away forever.

The soldier in front of her looked so young, she thought, and slid the IV into his skin and secured it with tape. He'd lost both legs and had already been through surgery. He moaned out in pain, and she shot pain medication into his arm. He groaned and laid his head back. *Okay*, she thought, *now onto the next one*. She spun around to see what she could do next, but it seemed like finally everything was under control. Men filled every bed. *So many*, she thought. She rubbed her head with her hands. Her body felt bone-tired. Daisy hadn't slept well since Ruthie left and now this. She'd need to sleep for a week, no, a month, to catch up. She went to the back to grab a mop and bucket. She forced herself not to look at the bed next to the curtain. She shook her head. She couldn't dwell on that now. She had blood to clean.

Darryl opened the door to let in some light. The sun had begun to rise, and rays of sunshine flooded into the dim room. Tiny particles danced in the rays of the sun and Patty lost herself, watching them, wishing for a better time.

"Hey Patty," Darryl said, waving a hand in front of her face.

She startled. "I'm sorry. I think my mind was wandering."

"What day is Ruthie due back?"

Patty thought about it, but her mind churned slowly. "I think, um, Sunday maybe." The thought seized her. Ruthie came back on Sunday. A cold sensation spread throughout her body. She turned to Darryl, grabbing him by the shoulders. "What day is it?"

Darryl frowned. "It's Sunday, Patty. Are you okay?" He pointed. "There's a truck coming down the road."

Sharp needles of panic shot through Patty, and she bolted for the truck. She waved her arms frantically in the air. She had to stop the truck. She couldn't let Ruthie come any closer to the hospital.

Chapter 56

RUTHIE

The truck bounced along the road, through the concertina wire, and past the guard towers. She never thought she'd be so happy to see the entrance of the 71st Evac Hospital. Today there was not a dark cloud in sight, and the sun filled the air. She leaned closer to the truck window to feel the warmth on her face. She'd see Daisy soon. She wanted to hug her and feel her small body in her arms. She couldn't wait to get back to being a parent, brushing Daisy's hair, snuggling with her at night, feeding her, and playing games with her. Ruthie thought about what the attorney had told her. It was possible—Daisy could be hers, and she couldn't wait to tell Patty, Darryl, and Tom. It may take a while, but it was possible. She just needed a Vietnamese court to grant her guardianship during a brutal war—that's all. No problem. All's groovy. She shook her head. She didn't want to get discouraged. Sang Le had said it would be difficult, but it could be done. Still, his words made her breath hitch.

"Sometimes things don't work out," he'd said. "But this country has too many orphans. The government cannot feed and care for them all. It would be good for orphans to have a home."

With the unknown, she wondered if she should tell her father and Hazel anything yet. Tears stung her eyes, and she blinked them away. She missed her family. Missing them felt like an ache inside her chest. She could use their advice, but why give them the news if there was a possibility things wouldn't work out. The thought of not being granted guardianship tore her up inside. Then what would Daisy do? Would she end up starving in an orphanage that couldn't care for her or protect her?

"What in tarnation is going on?" the driver said.

Ruthie blinked away her terrible thoughts and followed his eyes outside of the truck's windshield. A woman in fatigues ran toward them waving her arms wildly in the air. "Patty?" Ruthie whispered.

"What is that crazy woman doing?"

Fear flooded through Ruthie, zapping through her veins like electricity. *Daisy! Something is wrong with Daisy.* "Stop the vehicle!" she yelled.

"What?" the driver asked, looking at her confused.

"Stop now!" She screamed and started to open the passenger door, not waiting for him to slow down.

"Hang on! I'm stopping, I'm stopping!" he yelled at her.

She flung the door open. The truck's brakes squealed, but she didn't take the time to wait for it to fully stop. She leaped from the vehicle, feeling her bones jar as she hit the ground flat-footed and raced toward Patty.

Ruthie nearly tackled Patty when she reached her. Her words came out in pants, loud and filled with terror. "Daisy! What's happened?"

Patty shook her head, sucking in air. "No, no, she's fine."

"She's fine?" Ruthie frowned. The terror she'd felt disappeared in an instant. "Are you sure?"

Patty bent over, hands on her knees. Her breath sawed out of her as she spoke. "Yes, she's doing good. She's with Tom."

Relief flooded Ruthie's whole body. She smiled; her head dizzy with the rush of peace she felt. Daisy was good. She was with Tom. Then a thought pricked her like a tiny needle. "Why is she with Tom?"

Patty stood upright. Her eyes filled with tears that spilled down her cheeks. The peace Ruthie had felt melted away. Patty took Ruthie's hand in hers and held it tight. Ruthie wanted to pull away. Patty must have felt it because she tightened her grip. She forced Ruthie to look at her.

"There was a push yesterday. Biggest one we've had in a while. And... I'm so sorry, Ruthie. There was nothing we could do. When he came in, he was already gone."

"Who are you talking about?" But as the words left her lips, she already knew. "Ronnie?"

Patty bit her lip and nodded.

Ruthie jerked her hand away from Patty and she crossed her arms over her stomach. "You're wrong! That's insane. Ronnie's with his platoon. Why are you saying that? Why are you being so cruel?"

Patty pulled Ruthie into a hug. Ruthie fought to get away, but Patty held on, forcing Ruthie to be held. Ruthie sobbed into Patty's shoulder. Tears and snot filled her throat until she choked on them. *This can't be right. It has to be wrong.* But deep down, she knew Patty wouldn't lie about something like this, and she broke down again. When she could cry no longer, she pulled back, and Patty finally released her.

"What happened?"

Patty touched her arm. "I really don't know. You know they don't tell us much. There were so many bodies. It was like Hamburger Hill all over again."

Ruthie swallowed, feeling it stick in her throat. She needed to see him. It wouldn't be true until she saw him with her own eyes. "I need to see him," she said and wondered if maybe they'd already processed Ronnie's body and sent it to Grave Registration.

"I knew you would. We left him so you could say good-bye," Patty said so quietly Ruthie almost didn't hear her.

Good-bye—that one word made Ruthie's legs go weak, and she thought she might lose it again. But Patty took Ruthie by the arm and led her to the hospital. When they entered, Darryl looked up from a patient he was tending to. "I'm so sorry, Ruthie." His words made her shudder. She thought about running away, finding Daisy, and getting away from here. But how could she? Where would they go?

She let Patty guide her toward the back where the curtain hung to hide the dead and dying. The thought of Ronnie being behind the curtain made her want to vomit.

Behind the curtain, all the beds were empty and made ready for their next use except for one. Ruthie's heart pounded between her ears. She couldn't take her eyes off the covered form lying on the bed closest to the curtain. She walked closer as if in a trance, her body feeling a pull toward the form, but her mind sending warning signals to her heart—go, run away, don't look. When she stood over the bed, Patty didn't ask Ruthie if she was ready. Like pulling off a Band-Aid, Patty drew the blanket down so Ruthie could see for herself.

Ruthie stared down at the metal framed hospital bed. Her eyes burned from lack of sleep. She wanted to cry, she wanted to scream, but she stood there silently. Her life would never be the same. Her family's lives would never be the same. This war took and strangely it gave. Unfocused, dead eyes stared up at her, and in them, she saw the reflection of her dreams disintegrate into nothingness. *He's gone.* The weight of that thought sent her to her knees.

Her knees banged on the floor, but she didn't care. She reached for Ronnie's hand. It felt cold and already stiff; all life had been gone for a while. His body had been cleaned and cleared of any blood and dirt. Tiny red cuts dotted his face above and below his right eye, but other than that, she couldn't tell by looking at him what had happened. She didn't dare pull the blanket lower. She decided she didn't want to know what had happened because she couldn't handle knowing how he suffered. Now she could force her mind to consider that he laid down and never woke up, passing peacefully.

"Thank you for cleaning him," she whispered.

"Of course," Patty said. "Darryl helped too. Ruthie, can I get you something?"

Ruthie shook her head. "No, I need to stay with him a little longer," her voice broke. She swallowed. "Then, I guess, I need to write a letter to his parents." The thought of telling Ronnie's parents their only child had passed made her body sag forward, but it would be better for them to hear words of kindness from her than a heartless telegram or visit from some stoic officers.

Patty laid a hand on her shoulder. "You could tell them how brave he was and how he was a good friend to us all."

Patty brought Ruthie a chair and helped her up from the floor. Ruthie stayed behind the curtain, holding Ronnie's hand. Even though he was gone, and he couldn't hear her, she spoke to him. She whispered all of her special memories about him—a star on the football field, a kind prom date, a best friend to her brother-in-law, a hunky high school crush, a hilarious jokester. She spoke about their brief love and their secret kisses in the dark. In her words and memories, Ronnie felt alive, and she knew this would be how he'd want her to remember him.

Chapter 57

RUTHIE

Ruthie and Daisy sat in the mess hall. Daisy picked up eggs with her fingers and pushed them into her mouth. Ruthie watched her in a daze. Every time she thought of Ronnie, her heart broke again. She wished time would stop so she could wallow in her grief. But time didn't stop, it cruelly marched on. She wanted to scream. She wanted to cry. But she looked down. Daisy smiled at her; egg stuck to her cheek. Ruthie breathed in and cleaned her little girl's face.

The door of the mess hall opened, and Tom entered, wearing a green poncho. Rain poured down in sheets behind him and she sighed. She and Daisy would be drenched by the time they made it back to the hootch. Ruthie had never in her life wished for January. In Waldron, January was a miserable month, but in Pleiku, January meant no more rain. To Ruthie, it couldn't come soon enough. Tom shook mud off his boots then pushed back the hood of the poncho, causing rain to splatter against the floor. He scanned the area and found her.

"There you two are," he said, walking toward her and Daisy.

Daisy looked up and waved a fist full of egg at him. Tom chuckled, but Ruthie's heart picked up its pace. "Have you heard something from the lawyer already?" she asked.

He shook his head. "No, I think it will be several months until we hear anything."

Ruthie's tight muscles went limp.

"But I wanted to let you know I just got word you have a scheduled MARS call tonight."

Ruthie pointed to herself. "Me? Are you sure?" Thoughts of talking to Hazel or her father sent a burst of energy through her system that faded quickly when she realized she'd need to tell them about Ronnie.

"Yes, your call is at seven tonight."

Ruthie quickly did the math in her head—that would be around seven o'clock in the morning for Hazel and her dad. She looked down at Daisy, who ate without a care in the world. Maybe it was time to finally tell them about her. She could even have Daisy say the few words she knew in the receiver, and they could hear her voice, know that she was real. Ruthie's leg jiggled.

"Wait!" she said too loudly, making Daisy flinch. "Did you say seven? I'm supposed to relieve Patty at six."

Tom smiled. "I'll step in for you at ICU while you take the call."

Ruthie watched Tom head for the door to leave. The insides of her stomach fluttered, and she couldn't eat another bite. Tonight, she'd have a chance to hear her dad or Hazel's voice. It had been almost eight months since she'd heard their voices. She leaned over and gave Daisy a squeeze and tickle, making her laugh. "They're going to love you," she said, bopping her on the nose gently with a finger. "I just know it."

❧❧❧❧❧ ❧❧❧❧❧

Ruthie and Daisy left their hootch early. Ruthie felt a lightness in her step. She held Daisy close as they walked through green canvas tents and sandbags. When they arrived at the communications hootch, Ruthie stood outside the metal door. She needed to keep herself in check. She closed her eyes. She had terrible news to give, but she also had good news. Daisy touched her cheek. Ruthie kissed her hand. They'd get through this together.

Inside the communications hootch, since it was her first time using the MARS, the officers gave her a quick rundown on how it worked, what the operator did, and how when you were finished speaking you had to end with "over", so the operator knew to transfer the call to the other person. It didn't seem too hard. She placed Daisy on the floor near her with some of the handmade toys the nurses and patients had made for her—a wooden duck, a little car, and a cloth doll. Daisy picked up the doll and squeezed it to her chest.

"Okay, here you go," a soldier told her, handing her the telephone receiver and directing her to speak into a long cylinder microphone propped on a circular stand.

She took the receiver and pressed it to her ear, feeling the cold, hardness of it. *How long has it been since I've used a telephone?* She waited. Would it be Hazel? Her father? Her heart pounded against her chest, and she hoped she didn't pass out before she could figure it out. Then she heard it, and tears stung her eyes.

"Hello Ruthie. Are you there? Over."

"Daddy!" Tears spilled down her cheeks. Daisy looked up. Her mouth pulled tight. Ruthie caressed her head, smoothing down her dark hair, and smiled, not wanting her to worry. A solider near her, motioned to the microphone and mouthed, "Over." Ruthie nodded, remembering. "I miss you. Over," she said.

"I miss you too, peanut. Your sister, Sandra, Milton, Ms. Faye, we all miss you. How are you doing? Do you need anything? I've sure loved those cassettes you've been sending. Over."

Ruthie felt thousands of words bubbling inside her throat, but all she could manage was, "I'm doing good, and I don't need anything right now. Thank you though. Over." She looked at Daisy, who ran her handmade car around the floor in circles.

A beat of silence passed before her father spoke again. "I hate to do this, peanut, but I called because I've got some news for you."

Ruthie smiled at Daisy. She had some news for him too.

"It's about Joel. Over."

Ruthie's smile faded. The blood in her veins went cold. She tightened the grip on the receiver and stared down at the microphone in front of her until her eyes blurred. "What happened? Is he okay? Over."

Her father paused and it sent chills down her spine. She focused on the tiny hum in the receiver.

"He's not okay, peanut. He's been hurt. Hurt bad. He's made it to the hospital in Japan, but Hazel received a second telegram. They said he probably wouldn't make it. A good portion of his body has been burned, and he lost his left arm. We don't really know much more than that right now. Your sister is a basket case." She heard him swallow. "Well honestly we all are right now."

It felt like Ruthie's chest had caved in, her brain began to immediately deduce what could cause such injuries—a toe popper, a grenade, a mortar attack—her body began to shake. She decided to keep the news about Ronnie to herself. It would only worry her father more, and he'd find out soon enough on his own when they sent word to Ronnie's family. The news would spread quickly through Waldron.

Her father continued, "I've heard about a lot of nurses re-upping. But, peanut, please don't do that. Please come home as soon as you can. I don't know if it's possible, but could you try to come home early? Hazel needs you. I need you. If Joel does come home, he'll need you too. We can't care for him like you can. We need you, Ruthie. Come home, please. Over."

Ruthie looked down at Daisy, who stared back up at her with dark, brown eyes. "Come home," her father's words echoed in her ears. "Come home."

Ruthie's throat constricted and she thought she might pass out from lack of air. Her family needed her. They needed her now. She stared into Daisy's eyes. Daisy smiled, oblivious to the turmoil raging inside of Ruthie. She held up her wooden duck for Ruthie to see. Ruthie turned to the microphone. The saliva in her throat so thick she thought she might choke on it. She didn't want to disappoint her father. He'd never wanted her to go to Vietnam, but he wasn't the kind of father who made her feel bad for a decision he didn't agree with. He'd supported her. She swallowed, feeling a lump stick in the back of her throat. She hoped he'd support her now.

She steeled herself. "Daddy, I can't come home. Not until I'm finished here." And then she told him everything. She told him about Daisy and the day she carried her from her burning village, hurt and alone. The words spilled out of Ruthie like a gushing waterfall—Daisy's family all dead, the information from the attorney, guardianship. When she couldn't think of anything else to say, her voice shook as she said, "over," giving the line to her father.

Her heart thumped in her head. Would he demand her to come home and stop her foolishness? That's what Patty's father would do. Would he tell her she was a stupid girl—an unmarried woman thinking she could raise a child on her own? So many people wouldn't understand helping a Vietnamese girl. Even though Daisy wasn't the enemy, some wouldn't understand. Others would think it was a sin for her to be an unwed mother. Even though Ruthie didn't give birth to Daisy, bringing her home and raising her alone would be nothing less than scandalous in some people's minds.

She strained to hear any sound her father might make on the other end. She heard him cough to clear his throat, then, to her surprise, he let out a faint chuckle. "I should have known you'd chose the most difficult path home. You know that, right? You know it won't be easy? Over."

She acknowledged to him that she knew.

"Well, then is my soon-to-be granddaughter with you? I want to hear her voice. Over."

Ruthie felt weightless as she laid down the receiver and grabbed Daisy. She lifted her above her head to make her giggle. She sat back down with Daisy on her lap. Ruthie picked up the receiver. "She's here. Over." Then she pressed it to Daisy's ear, letting her little hands take hold of it. Ruthie watched Daisy's eyes light up when she heard her papa's voice for the first time. While Daisy babbled into the microphone, Ruthie thought about Joel and prayed he would make it. The whole world had been scorched and damaged by the war, and every person seared in some way—either physical or internally. It had changed them all. But Ruthie couldn't help

368

but remember something Milton said before she left to come to Vietnam. He'd let her listen as he practiced one of his sermons for church.

"When a forest burns, all we can see is the destruction, the ugliness, the charred, blackened ground and ash. But out of the scorched ground, something new begins to form. Out of the ash, new life springs forth. It doesn't make sense to us because all we see is death, all we see is the pain, but out of the ashes comes lush, green, vibrant life. It's not the same as it was before, it's something new. Let God make something new out of your pain. Out of your sorrow. Out of your suffering. Let Him turn your destruction into His glory."

Ruthie prayed for something to come from this ugliness. She prayed for her family's future.

Epilogue

HAZEL, MAY 1970

Hazel and her father arrived at the Atlanta Municipal Airport an hour early. Although the sky had begun to turn a dark navy, crowds of people still darted here and there throughout the airport terminal. Hazel's eyes took in everything. She wondered where all these people had traveled from to get to Atlanta. Her father wasted no time. He approached an employee and asked for help. The employee wore an airline uniform and looked a lot like Santa Claus. His cheeks were tinted red and sat like small apples above his white beard. He wore a blue collared shirt and matching wide legged pants with a belt. The airport's circular logo sat on the left side above his chest.

"You must be so excited to have your daughter back," the man said, motioning them to follow him past the ticket booths. "This place is a maze, lots of winding paths. Let me take you to the observation deck so you can watch when her plane arrives." He looked at his watch, stretched tightly around his wrist. "You've got plenty of time."

They followed him. Hazel thought about the winding roads she and her father had driven many times to the Brooke Army Medical Center in San Antonio to visit Joel. She remembered the first time she saw him;

she received a telegraph in the mail telling her it was now okay for her to make an appointment to see him. She'd picked up the telephone and immediately made an appointment then went out to buy herself a new chevron knit dress to wear.

When she'd arrived at the hospital, to prepare her for what she'd see, a nurse told her about the series of skin grafts and surgical procedures Joel had been through. It sounded like torture to Hazel, and her heart ached knowing Joel had gone through it alone. She'd closed her eyes and lifted her shoulders; she was here for him now, she told herself.

She'd followed the nurse into the burn room like they followed the airline worker today. Except the burn ward had been a long, cold room filled with hospital beds and men. Their raw, burnt skin and agony on display.

She had told herself not to flinch or make any faces when she first saw Joel, no matter what she saw. He didn't need that, and it didn't matter what he looked like—he was alive, and she'd love him until the day they die. But that first glimpse of him sitting upright in bed took everything out of her, and she had to force herself not to burst into tears. His once-handsome face was gone. Now half was covered with puckered red scars that looked raw and painful. His hair hung sparce and bare, and his red scalp showed through in many places. The nurse had said when he got home, it would be better if he shaved his head because his burnt skin was too damaged to grow hair like it used to do. She saw the stump where his left arm should have been. Her stomach clenched, but when his eyes met hers, she pushed everything away and hurried to his side, bringing his right hand to her lips and peppering it with kisses.

When he spoke, his voice sounded harsh and raspy, not like his own. "Don't. Please don't. I know how I look. Just turn around and walk out of here. Start over. Have a good life."

Hazel said nothing. She laid his hand down and walked around his bed toward his burned side. His eyes followed her. She bent over close to him and he flinched away slightly. She moved closer and pressed soft kisses against his red scars. A single tear escaped from the corner of his eye. "I have no life without you," she whispered.

"You look beautiful," he said, low and raspy.

Her cheeks heated and she kissed his burnt face again. She whispered. "Well, at least I don't have to fret about whether I'll be the ugly one when we get old."

He gave her a half-grin and that was all she needed. Her husband was alive, and she'd get to take him home soon. She'd had to wait another month before he came home. She didn't know what she expected when he got home, but things weren't going like she'd hoped. Joel was in pain every minute of the day, which made him irritable and short with her and Aaron. He'd started taking long walks, and she had no idea where he'd go. She'd tried to get him to talk about things, but he'd get angry. Talking was the last thing he wanted to do.

Hazel followed her father and the airline worker past chairs filled with people conversing and waiting for their luggage to arrive at the baggage claim area. She looked at them, wishing Joel would talk to her again. She knew he'd experienced so much, and when she'd gotten a tape cassette from Ruthie letting her and their father know she'd be returning home soon, Hazel had been overjoyed. Yes, she wanted her sister back, but she selfishly hoped Ruthie could help her with Joel. Maybe she'd know what Hazel could do to pry Joel from the lonely shell he'd built around himself.

Hazel and her father followed the Santa Claus in bell bottoms up a large set of stairs. They exited through a set of double doors at the far end of the airport. A gust of air hit Hazel, making her hair blow around her face. They walked outside onto a long cement walkway lined with a wire fence on both sides. The roar of the wind mixed with the squeal of engine noises made it hard to hear.

"Here you are," the airport worker yelled over the noise. He laid a hand on his side and sucked in a few deep breaths, then moved to the right side of the walkway and pointed. He bellowed, "Her plane should be landing right there."

Hazel followed his finger to the wide, gray tarmac. Different colored lines marked paths for the airplanes to park. The bright lights scattered in various places around the runways made her squint.

"You'll be able to see her from here."

Hazel stood in the exact spot the man had pointed to.

"Well, I better be getting back, folks. I'm sure someone can't find their suitcase or something. Always things to do around here. I'm glad your daughter is back and safe now," he said, shaking her father's hand.

They thanked him for his help. Hazel watched him as he left through the doors. "Do you think her flight will be on time?" she asked loudly.

Her father stood next to her. The front of his hair wiped around his face from the wind. "I hope so. It's starting to get kind of cool out here. And we'll need to find a place to stay tonight."

They both faced the tarmac, leaning against the fence.

Her father turned to her so she could hear him. "I know you are going to have a lot on your plate with Joel and everything else. But your sister is going to need us too with her new little girl."

Hazel nodded. "I know. I'm glad they didn't make her re-up. It only took another month to finalize everything."

Her father's face twisted. "You both have a lot to deal with right now. Let's wait to tell her about your mama."

Hazel felt a lump form in her throat. Their mama had passed on two months ago. Hazel had seen her one more time before her death at Oliver's request, but by that point, the amount of pain medication she received left her incoherent and sleepy.

Hazel nodded. "Yes, let's wait." The knot in Hazel's stomach felt like it doubled in size. She'd yet to tell Joel anything about Mr. Hal or Officer McConnell. She knew he couldn't handle it, and she wondered if there would ever be a good time to tell him.

"Look," her father pointed into the air.

Small lights in the sky began to grow bigger.

"I think that might be it," he said, and she could hear the excitement in his voice.

Hazel had no idea how much time passed. Her eyes blurred from staring at the lights in the sky growing bigger each minute. When the plane landed, it did so with a roar of sound. Hazel had never seen anything like it, and the experience of seeing the wheels of the huge airplane hit the hard ground so smoothly took her breath away. *Ruthie is on that plane.* Her heart picked up its pace.

They watched as men rolled a long staircase to the door near the cockpit. Hazel's legs began to jiggle as the door flew open. Hazel wondered if someone would arrest her if she scaled the fencing and ran out on the tarmac like a mad woman to see her sister.

Her father gripped her arm. "There she is!"

Hazel stopped breathing. Between the men and women dressed in fancy suits and dresses, Hazel spotted her. Ruthie walked down the stairs in her olive-green nurse's fatigues, her blonde hair blowing wildly around her face. Pride filled Hazel's heart. Ruthie held in her arms a child with long, dark hair that whipped around her face. She turned and clung to Ruthie. Hazel put a hand to her mouth to stop herself from crying. Seeing her sister with a child, her child—Daisy, made a bubbly, joyous feeling radiate throughout her chest. Out of the corner of her eyes, she saw her father wipe away tears and Hazel laughed.

"Quit laughing, girl, I'm a basket case."

Hazel began to wave her arms wildly in the air. "Ruthie! Ruthie!" she screamed, and her father joined in.

Hazel didn't know if Ruthie could hear them, but that didn't stop them. Ruthie looked up toward the observation deck. Her eyes narrowed and eyebrows knit together. When she saw them, the relief that spread across Ruthie's face was undeniable. She grinned and turned the little girl around in her arms. Ruthie pointed at them and waved her free arm before kissing the top of Daisy's head.

Things were going to be hard. Hazel knew it. Joel was shattered right now—physically and mentally. But Hazel felt a resolve settle in her chest. She'd help Ruthie with Daisy and together they'd help Joel. They could do it. They'd been there for each other ever since they were little. In that instant, she made a promise to herself to never give up until every piece the war had broken was back in its place. She knew the cracks would always be visible and would never go away, but eventually they'd all be whole again.

Thank you!

♥ · ♥ · ♥ · ♥ · ♥

If you've enjoyed my book, please take a few minutes to leave a review on Amazon and Goodreads.

Reviews are essential for indie authors like me—they help new readers find our stories and allow us to keep creating books you'll love! Your thoughts truly make a difference, and each review means the world to me.

Thank you for reading *Our Scorched Hearts* and for supporting indie authors! You help these stories reach new hearts and homes!

Acknowledgements

Thank you, dear Lord for all your many blessings and for allowing me the ability to share my stories with others.

There would be no way I could ever share my stories without my wonderful support system. Thank you, Todd for loving me, encouraging me, and sharing all my ups and downs. The writing road is filled with bumps and potholes, and I know if it wasn't for you and your prayers, I wouldn't have the strength to carry on.

Thank you to my wonderful boys (men), Wyatt, Michael, and Joseph. You make my life whole and with you, everything is more fun!

Thank you to my dad, Eddie, and my stepmother, Becky. Thank you for your encouragement, love, and support. I truly hope I make you proud.

Mom! What can I say? I miss you every day and I love you!

To my sisters, Tiffany and Tasha, thank you for always being there for me. You helped me know what being a sister is all about. You both inspire me every day!

Thank you to my father-in-law, Gil, and mother-in-law, Pat Pat, for not only loving me like a daughter, but also for encouraging me at every turn. Pat Pat, thank you for your eagle eye. You are the proof-reading queen.

I want to say thank you to my entire family. Our close family connection is what inspires me daily.

Thank you to my magnificent editor, Julia Hinton. You are amazing! You make the editing process easy and enjoyable.

Thank you to my cover designer, Robert Allen, for creating such a beautiful cover.

Last but not least, I want to thank my dear friend, Jessica Cassidy, for being brave and willing to read my book, before the edits. Thank you for taking the time to help me and for your insights and advice.

About the Author

Born and raised in Arkansas, Tennille Marie, now calls Louisiana her home. Her favorite things include walking on sunny days, exploring new places with her family, coffee, her cats, and puppies.

Tennille is also obsessed with books, no matter the genre. She finds her heart and writing are inspired by her southern roots, her close family connections, and the kindness of others.

If you'd like to follow Tennille Marie on her author journey or get more information about upcoming books, come be a part of her heart-to-heart community! As a special gift, for joining her mailing list, you will receive a complimentary copy of *A Blackberry Kind of Love* and other country stories.

https://tennillemarie.com

You can also follow her on Instagram, Goodreads, and BookBub.

https://www.instagram.com/tennillem

https://www.goodreads.com/tennillemarie

https://www.bookbub.com/profile/tennille-marie

Also By

The Waldron Hearts Series
Our Kept Hearts
Our Scorched Hearts
Our Mending Hearts (coming soon)

www.ingramcontent.com/pod-product-compliance
Lightning Source LLC
Chambersburg PA
CBHW070631180626
6817CB00006B/2095